S0-EGO-497

Dear Reader:

Mail-order brides in the old American West have always intrigued us. What would make a woman move halfway across the country to marry a man she had never seen before? Did these women find happiness? What were the unexpected consequences? When I asked three authors to create mail-order bride stories, it turned out that the reasons they picked for their women marrying strangers were as individual as the writers themselves.

In HEARTS ARE WILD (April 1993) by Teresa Hart, deLacey Honeycutt is a clever female cardsharp who is down on her luck. Desperate to get enough train fare to once again gamble with gentlemen in their private cars, she signs up with a mail-order bride agency only to get a free train ticket. Unfortunately, she runs across the very man she was expected to marry—with unforeseen consequences.

SWEPT AWAY (August 1993) by Jean Anne Caldwell is a delightful story about a girl who can't quite make up her mind whether she wants to go through with a marriage to a stranger . . . so she pretends to be the maid who is hired through the mail, not the bride. Of course she is soon unmasked.

SCOUNDREL (January 1994) by Pamela Litton is the story of a dreamy woman from Boston who has always longed for adventure. She travels west after corresponding with a man who writes proper and respectful letters. But when she arrives, she finds a different, much more compelling man waiting for her. How she turns the town, and her life, upside down will charm you.

All three of these stories start in St. Louis, where the women meet for the first time. Though strangers, the women know that the choices they've made have bonded them as sisters of the heart. I hope you enjoy these romantic stories.

Best wishes,

Carrie Feron

Carrie Feron
Jove Books

P.S.—Turn to the back of this book for a special sneak preview of *Scoundrel*, the next romantic adventure in the ''Brides of the West'' series.

Books in the BRIDES OF THE WEST series

HEARTS ARE WILD
SWEPT AWAY

Coming in January 1994
SCOUNDREL

SWEPT AWAY

JEAN ANNE CALDWELL

JOVE BOOKS, NEW YORK

BRIDES OF THE WEST: SWEPT AWAY

A Jove Book / published by arrangement with
the author

PRINTING HISTORY
Jove edition / August 1993

All rights reserved.
Copyright © 1993 by Jove Publications, Inc.
This book may not be reproduced in whole or in part,
by mimeograph or any other means, without permission.
For information address: The Berkley Publishing Group,
200 Madison Avenue, New York, New York 10016.

ISBN: 0-515-11161-9

Jove Books are published by The Berkley Publishing Group,
200 Madison Avenue, New York, New York 10016.
The name "JOVE" and the "J" logo
are trademarks belonging to Jove Publications, Inc.

PRINTED IN THE UNITED STATES OF AMERICA

10 9 8 7 6 5 4 3 2 1

PROLOGUE

Jennifer Fairchild stepped down from the train and handed the porter a silver dollar for his untiring assistance with her mound of bags and boxes. It was difficult to imagine that after all the months of planning, she was finally on the brink of realizing her dream. St. Louis. Gateway to the West. The ride from Philadelphia had appeared to take forever. Yet she would reach Kansas City by evening. The true West.

"Paper, miss?"

Jenny looked down into the face of the small boy standing in front of her. From the hopeful smile on his lips, she knew he must have seen the tip she gave the porter. Unfortunately, the train she would be transferring her belongings to would be arriving soon, so she had no need for a copy of the St. Louis paper he was brandishing about. Even so, the boy looked in need of a sale, Jenny told herself as she rummaged through her reticule for a coin.

Finding a nice new shiny quarter, she held it out to the lad. As he reached out to take it from her fingers, a man rudely pushed him aside and grabbed Jenny's bag.

"Stop, thief," she screamed, but he was around the

1

corner and out of sight before anyone could stop him. She stared down at her empty hand. Gone. Everything was gone. Her money. Her ticket to Kansas City. For a few moments she stood there, overwhelmed. All she had left was her luggage and the newspaper the lad had left at her feet. The pages flapped in the faint breeze and an ad in the bottom corner drew her eye, mocking her with its words. *Gentlemen seeking respectable women as mail-order brides. Apply at Miss Emily's Positions For Young Ladies* . . .

The next morning, Jenny found herself back in the railroad station sitting on a bench that was next to her baggage with two other young ladies. It was a shame they would be parting company after having just met. Jenny would have welcomed their continued companionship on the next portion of her journey.

Jenny leaned back and listened to the one named Lucy tell about the husband-to-be waiting for her in Starlight, New Mexico. Apparently they had been corresponding and Lucy thought his letters romantic. She wished she could be as enthusiastic about her own future. She was taking a risk. She had cheated the mail-order bride company of two train tickets and her new plan could backfire somehow. She was going to have to be very careful.

"All aboard for Denver, Colorado," came the monotone call of the stationmaster.

"Oh, that's my train." Jenny got up to try to gather her baggage. Her newfound companions stood to help her with her things, and while their attention was turned away, the thief from earlier in the day struck again! He only took a small bag, but again no one could catch him. Thank goodness the money that she had from the sale of her second train ticket was sewn into her jacket. Jenny had known that running away from home would be a lonely venture, but she hadn't quite envisioned all this danger. And with her destination changed and her future now tied to a stranger in Colorado, who knew what fate would befall her?

CHAPTER 1

Though Jennifer Fairchild knew that leaving Philadelphia was the right choice, her legs did not share in the courage of her decision. Her wobbly knees threatened to give way as she clutched the letters of introduction to her breast and stepped down from the train. Within minutes, she would be meeting her new employer for the first time. She hoped Mr. Morgan wouldn't be too terribly upset when he learned that she had applied for both the position of housekeeper and his mail-order bride.

She also hoped he would not discover this fact for a long time.

With wide brown eyes she took in the weathered buildings and the dirt road that passed in front of the station house. Gold Shoe, Colorado, was even smaller than she had envisioned, but perhaps that was a blessing. Her father was sure to send someone to try to fetch her home. The smaller the town, the less likely it would be that whoever her father hired would think to look for her there.

It would be difficult enough to explain why she had availed herself of Mr. Morgan's money and convince him

3

she was not a common thief without her father there to spew out his hateful lies. Jenny could easily imagine his anger when he returned to find her gone, but with his unreasonable accusations, he made it impossible for her to stay.

Jenny searched the nearly empty platform, uneasiness settling heavily in her stomach. Where was Mr. Morgan? Surely the employment agency hadn't forgotten to notify him to meet her. Miss Emily's Positions For Young Ladies had appeared to be an efficient agency. Jenny frowned. Yet how efficient could they be if they had unknowingly hired *her* to fill *both* of Mr. Morgan's advertised positions?

Her father would have said the situation she found herself in was no more than she deserved for running away from home—right after he called her those awful names and locked her in the attic. Well, no more. Her father would be wasting his money if he tried to send someone to fetch her home. Nothing short of marauding Indians would make her return to Philadelphia. She had taken too many risks getting as far as she had.

This was 1888 and a woman of eighteen should be able to make her own decisions without fear of retribution. If the stories in the *Philadelphia Times* were to be believed, most women of the West her age had already made names for themselves. While Jenny's own skills were limited, her young heart warmed to the romantic notion that with time and training she could be anything she wanted to be—a rancher, a miner, or even a stagecoach driver.

Somewhere in the dark recesses of her mind, neither the prospect of being Mr. Morgan's mail-order bride nor his housekeeper quite fit her dreams of independence, but she firmly shoved her doubts aside. Even though she needed the money if she ever hoped to get her sister, Izzy, away from Philadelphia, she had no intention of becoming anyone's bride, mail-order or otherwise. As for being Mr. Morgan's housekeeper, it would suit her needs for the time being.

With a gloved hand, Jenny readjusted the ribbons on her

new silk bonnet, then straightened the front of her yellow and black dress. The gesture teased a reluctant smile from her lips. Jenny was well aware that the brightly striped gown was a bit much for a housekeeper, but a willful streak of vanity had prompted her to dress the part of a mail-order bride. Gently she tugged at the corner of the matching jacket, being especially careful not to disturb the money she had sewn into the lining.

While she continued to check the road for Mr. Morgan, Jenny tried her best to ignore the grumblings of the men unloading her luggage. They kept muttering something about train schedules and other such nonsense. She could see no reason for them to turn so nasty merely because she had a few more bags than most of their passengers. It wasn't as if she could send back to Philadelphia after the rest of her things. It was bad enough that she had had to leave Izzy behind until she was settled.

Jenny walked the entire length of the wooden platform and back before again checking the watch pinned to the bosom of her yellow jacket. The sun was nearly down. Where was Mr. Morgan? She stopped beside the pile of luggage and unfolded one of the letters from the agency. She carefully reread the instructions. Her memory hadn't failed her. It clearly stated Mr. Morgan or someone from his ranch would be at the station to meet her.

A large lump slowly made its way up to her throat. What if Mr. Morgan had already discovered her deception and intended to leave her stranded here without a chance to explain? It wasn't as if she had deliberately set out to cheat him, she reassured herself. She had had more than enough money to meet her needs when she had left Philadelphia, and she certainly hadn't counted on being robbed by that dirty little man the moment she stepped off the train in St. Louis.

If she hadn't been stranded without coin or connection, she would never have considered the notion of answering anyone's advertisement to become a mail-order bride. Luckily she had read somewhere that a lady could have her passage west paid just to apply. Even so, if the interview did not go well, a young lady was not obligated to marry the man.

When Jenny had gone to the agency, she had only thought to check the possibility out. She hadn't expected the clerk from the agency to all but force her to take the position. It had seemed so simple at the time. They would give her a train ticket to Colorado and all she was obligated to do was talk with Mr. Morgan.

It wasn't until she had signed the agreement that she discovered Mr. Morgan was also seeking a housekeeper. Jenny let a reproachful sigh escape her lips. Why hadn't she merely told the clerk that she had changed her mind? But no, she had let greed overcome good sense. The money she could get from cashing in the other ticket would help recoup her stolen funds.

It still amazed her that not a twinge of conscience asserted itself when she decided to apply for the other position as well. She had merely taken the small, jeweled comb her mother had left her and pulled her long thick black hair back into a tight knot. Then perching a thick pair of discarded spectacles on her nose, she returned to the agency to claim the housekeeper's position as well.

She had to admit that finding those cracked glasses on the bench outside the general store had been a godsend. While she could barely see to walk, the lenses lent Jenny's brown eyes a distorted look that kept the overworked clerk behind the desk from noticing that both her last two customers sported the same blue traveling gown.

After seeing to her luggage and disposing of the extra ticket, Jenny was able to pay for a room at the hotel. Her train for Denver was to leave late the next morning.

After the second theft of another one of her bags, the journey from St. Louis had gone off without a hitch. The ruse may have gotten her to Colorado, but if Mr. Morgan refused to hire her after all this what good had it done? What would she do if he had changed his mind? She might have enough money to return to Denver, but what was to become of her after that?

For the hundredth time since leaving St. Louis, Jenny's fingers traced the square outline of folding money sewn into her jacket. Thank goodness, she had it. If Mr. Morgan didn't come soon, she would be forced to look for lodgings. She cast a wary eye down the long line of buildings. Only one of the wooden shingles swinging in the evening breeze proclaimed the presence of a hotel.

She had heard that most merchants close to the stations catered to people who flocked to the mining areas hoping to strike it rich. The privilege of room and board was said to run high. If the rumors were correct, Jenny couldn't afford to part with what little money she had left to meet their prices. A modest boardinghouse might be all her funds would allow.

Resigned to the fact that she would need directions, Jenny stepped into the station. Except for the stationmaster behind the glass partition, the room was empty. He looked up from a stack of invoices as she approached. Although he continued to thumb through the papers, his watery blue eyes followed her progress across the wooden floor. His unwavering gaze set the small hairs on the back of Jenny's neck to prickling. She wanted to turn and run, but Jenny was stubborn and wasn't about to let the man's rudeness scare her. It was something she had come to learn when dealing with her father.

"The gentleman that was supposed to meet me is late and I was wondering if perhaps there was a boardinghouse you could recommend?"

Carl Turner licked his dry lips at the sight before him. He'd been watching the little lady pace the narrow platform for the last hour and wondered when she'd finally be forced to come to him. And here she was, prettier than a mountain flower, asking him where she should go. He couldn't believe his luck. It wasn't often a woman was stranded in Gold Shoe and he was already going over what he would do with the money for selling this one.

Having found the invoice he needed, Carl shoved the rest of them into a drawer and again focused his attention on the young woman. She wore no ring on her finger but Carl had learned to be cautious.

"You married?" he asked.

Jenny did not care for the look of greed that suddenly flared in his eyes. Although the question seemed innocent enough, his manner hinted at more than common curiosity.

"Does the quality of the room depend on the existence of a husband, sir?" Jenny asked stiffly, determined to humble the man by remaining a lady.

He grinned. "It might."

Jenny started to give him her views on such a statement when his eyes suddenly narrowed, bringing a lump to her throat. Evil seemed to seep from his pale blue orbs. Instinctively, Jenny stepped back.

Carl savored her unease. This was going to be easier than he thought. "You one of Em's girls?" he demanded.

Jenny let out the breath she was holding. If this despicable little toad thought just because she had been reduced to seeking employment through Miss Emily's Positions For Young Ladies that she was no longer to be treated with respect, she would soon set him straight. She lifted a delicate brow. "You know Miss Emily?"

The question appeared to humor him for the obnoxious man tossed back his head in laughter. "Miss Emily," he crowed. "Now don't that beat all. Is that what she calls herself back East?"

Apprehension washed over Jenny. What had she gotten herself into? "If you would please tell me of a boarding-house, I will let you get back to your work."

Carl leaned across the counter. "Won't you be wanting to stay at Em's place?"

The agency had not mentioned having a hotel in Gold Shoe, but then why should they? After all, Mr. Morgan should have been there to meet her. Perhaps they would know what had detained him. The mocking smile on the stationmaster's face was beginning to irritate her.

"Yes, of course," she said with more conviction than she felt. "Now if you would kindly show me the way."

Carl didn't bother to hide his disappointment. Em had sure bagged herself a pretty one this time. A shame she had found this little black-haired dove on her own. With her combination of fire and innocence, she would have fetched him a pretty penny at one of the more exclusive brothels in Denver.

Well, no matter. He should have known. Only the other day Em had told him she was expecting a couple of new girls. He gave his fingers a quick lick, then ran them through the greasy strands of his lank, brown hair.

"Name's Carl, miss. Carl Turner. Em's place is a mite hard to find for a stranger. I get off in an hour," he offered, displaying a mouthful of yellowing teeth. "I'd be more than happy to take you there."

The foul odor of his stale breath curled the inside of Jenny's stomach and she stepped back. "You need not bother, Mr. Turner," she said through clenched teeth.

"No trouble. No trouble at all. Em told me to expect you. I always watch out for her girls."

"Thank you, but Miss Emily said there would be someone to meet me."

Carl couldn't hold back the loud snort. "Said that, did she?" He gave her a broad wink. "Em has her good intentions, but I'd not be countin' on them if I were you. More than likely some miner with a bag of gold and an ache in his pocket distracted her."

His words set a warning ringing in Jenny's head. What if there were no Mr. Morgan? What if . . .

No! Jenny decided. She refused to allow herself to draw such a conclusion until she talked with Miss Emily. There was no sense borrowing trouble.

She had no more than shored up her confidence when the stationmaster suddenly straightened his shoulders and looked past her to the door.

''Wasn't there to be two of you?'' he demanded.

Jenny could feel her newly formed conviction crumble with the trembling of her limbs.

''Where's the other one?'' he insisted.

Jenny took a deep breath. She was a fool to think she would get away with her deception unscathed. Even so, she wasn't about to make her excuses to this man. ''She missed the train from Denver,'' she lied.

''Em won't be pleased. No, ma'am. Not pleased at all.''

The sly grin on his lips belied any real concern on his part. But Jenny could care less about what Miss Emily thought of the absence of Mr. Morgan's bride. It was more important to settle her position as his housekeeper. All she wanted to do now was get somewhere where she could buy a cup of strong tea and think things through.

''If you don't mind, I think the matter best discussed with Miss Emily. Now if you would please show me the way.''

Carl sobered at her curt dismissal. His blue eyes narrowed. If Em didn't give him a break on the price of the pretties upstairs, he'd send this dark-haired beauty to the far end of town and let her spend the night with the coyotes. But he had other plans for this high-and-mighty miss. She thought she was too good for the likes of him. Well, she'd soon learn you didn't mess with Carl Turner. He had connections. Em would have this little lady spreading her legs for him before the night was out. It had been a long time since he had roughed up one of Em's girls, but it would be worth incurring Em's wrath to have this one beg for mercy.

He pointed to the window. "You'll be wantin' to take Eighth Street to Parker. Em's place is down on your right."

Jenny left in a swirl of petticoats. After his appalling manners, she didn't feel the need to thank him. Once outside, she hurried across the street.

The sun perched precariously on the distant mountain ridge, cast long shadows across her path, quickening Jenny's pace. It wouldn't be wise to tarry. Already the walkway lay in darkness.

Now that she was approaching her destination, she couldn't seem to justify her duplicity quite as easily as she had managed to do so far. Even her footsteps seemed to echo her guilt with each step.

The housekeeper . . . the bride . . . the housekeeper . . . the bride.

The walkway appeared to grow in length, the censorious words keeping ominous time with her slow progress.

Perhaps it was better that Mr. Morgan had been late for suddenly her rehearsed explanations did not seem adequate. While Jenny was not above bending the truth when the occasion demanded, she much preferred to cleverly weave her harmless white lies into a seemingly solid fabric of truth. She had learned when dealing with her father that it was the smartest way. Over the years, it had become the only method Jenny found effective to save both herself and her sister from his unforgiving wrath.

The sound of shattering glass stopped her. She looked around. Somewhere along the way, night had fallen and the brightly painted shop windows now lay cloaked in darkness.

Surely the boardinghouse was not much farther, she told herself as she hurried down the deserted street. The sun had taken its warmth with it and Jenny shivered in the cool night air. Despite her brave assurances, it wasn't until Parker crossed Eighth Street that she began to relax.

An abundance of lights poured from the windows up and down Parker. Jenny found herself drawn to the music and laughter that drifted from the many storefronts.

An elegant coach lumbered past and she watched it weave its way between the wagons that lined the narrow street, coming to a stop in front of a large house. Before the driver had time to climb down, several young men rushed forward to assist a beautiful red-haired woman from the coach. While the revealing cut of the woman's green gown brought a warm blush to Jenny's cheeks, she was nonetheless fascinated by the woman's striking beauty.

The men seemed quite taken with the lady as well, for they appeared to hang on her every word. Jenny smiled to herself. She had made the right choice. It was obvious in Colorado a man respected what a woman had to say.

So intent was Jenny on her study that when the door suddenly burst open beside her, she gasped. Before she could step back, a man lay sprawled at her feet. She lifted the hem of her gown and tried to step around him without attracting his notice, but it was too late. He was already crawling to his feet.

"What have we here?" he asked, his words baptizing her with a fine spray of cheap whiskey.

A cold finger of fear traced an icy path up Jenny's spine when he reached for her. His hand grasped the corner of her jacket, the fabric ripping. Jenny watched in horror as the last of her money fluttered to the ground. A gust of wind picked up the bills and threatened to carry them away.

She reached for them when another man came charging out of the saloon. The light from the doorway outlined the huge, ugly man in a dark silhouette. Jenny's wide brown eyes were drawn to the table leg he clutched in his massive hands. She watched as he lifted it over his head. A loud angry roar rolled from deep down inside him and all thoughts of retrieving her money fled.

Jenny couldn't move. Her feet were frozen to the boards. With a wide arc, the big man swung.

Dark blond hair hung nearly to his shoulders. That combined with a deep tan and startling blue eyes gave people who first met him the impression that here was the epitome of what every gentleman should be. Rugged good looks, a smile that could melt a woman's heart, and shoulders that could fill a suit coat to perfection.

It took only a frown and an arrogant toss of his head for Cade Morgan to quickly dispel any such theory. He was a man who shared few of his feelings but counted many his friend. With no conscious effort on his part, he demanded respect and got it. There were not many who crossed him and did not suffer the brunt of his swift revenge.

"The fool," he silently cursed as he ducked his six-foot four-inch frame through the doorway of the train station. It was bad enough he was late, then to have the stationmaster send his bride to Em's place was beyond belief.

But then Cade had never liked Carl Turner and had often wondered how he had managed to keep his job as stationmaster. Did the man think every woman traveling alone was a prostitute? If Miss Fairchild came to any harm, Cade would personally see to it that the railroad learned of the man's incompetence.

Cade started to climb back onto his buckboard, then thought better of it. As narrow as the street was in front of Em's place, he'd have a hard time making his way between the drunks that wandered from saloon to saloon. He'd make better time walking.

As Cade hurried along the darkening street, the furrow that lined his tanned forehead deepened. Em would not let him forget that he had had to fetch his new wife from her after all. Every since he had placed the order for a bride and housekeeper from that confounded agency in St. Louis, Em had done nothing but tease him about not giving the bride's position to one of her girls. He had certainly bedded enough of them. But then, that was Em's bone of contention. He had yet to pay for their favors. Even so, he and Em remained good friends.

He wondered what his older brother, Frank, would think if he knew his betrayal was the glue that had bonded the ten-year friendship between Cade and Em, Frank's lover. Cade's lip curled. Mutual pain had a way of doing that. Frank may have raised him when their parents had died, but he was no longer part of Cade's life and Cade liked it that way.

Seeing his brother last month had brought back all the old memories. Letitia. The betrayal. The flight across Texas. Him, Sam, and Albert driving Cade's share of the cattle up to Colorado. Not long after, Em had followed.

Cade couldn't shake the feeling that even after all this time, the betrayal was not all over. He had seen the greed in Frank's eyes when he realized what Cade had made of his life. It was evident that taking Letitia from Cade was only a sample of what Frank now wanted. Frank wanted every-thing. Cade doubted even the will leaving everything to Em would stop him.

Even though his lawyer had assured him the will was binding, he preferred the governor's solution. A wife. A wife had more of a claim over an estate than a brother.

As with everything else in his life, he had thought through his decision thoroughly. Besides helping him with the social affairs that constantly plagued him, a wife would put an end to the never-ending matchmaking efforts of his married friends' wives. A grin tilted the corners of his lips. Him finding a bride on his own would surely frost their petunias.

According to Carl, his new bride was quite a looker. While this had not been one of the qualifications he had given the agency, he was pleased. The agency assured him they would send him only their best. A mature, soft-spoken lady of quality—and a widow. After Letitia, he'd had his fill of virgins.

Always in control of his life, Cade couldn't believe the qualms of doubt he had suffered when he had first received the telegram telling him of Miss Fairchild's arrival. Now he was actually looking forward to meeting her. He was beginning to think it would be the only bright spot in a day that had tried his patience at every turn.

A late spring thaw had caught Cade by surprise and he had spent most of the morning rescuing a calf that had gotten separated from its mother when one of the valleys flooded. The ungrateful critter had shown his appreciation by branding Cade's thigh with his flailing hooves. It hadn't put Cade in the best of moods to arrive back at the ranch house cold and wet only to discover the cook and his butler, Albert, feuding over some chicken one had grown fond of and the other planned to cook for supper.

He had no time for these petty quarrels. Running a ranch as big as Trinity Ranch and trying to keep abreast of his many investments took up all his time. But at least a wife would relieve him of the domestic squabbles.

It wasn't until Cade reached Parker Street that he realized he hadn't overtaken Miss Fairchild. He stepped up his pace as he searched both sides of the street.

If not for the yellow and black striped dress, Cade might have missed her. A drunk had Miss Fairchild corralled outside Mac's Saloon and she did not appear at all pleased. No lady should have to deal with such ruffians, especially not his bride-to-be.

Cade shouted but no one paid him any heed. The idiots were treating her as if she were one of Em's girls. With powerful strides, he broke into a run. Before he could reach her, another man burst through the doors of the saloon.

It had been months since Cade had last seen Bear, but it wasn't difficult to recognize the huge miner. There weren't too many men who could match Bear for size. Even from this distance, Cade could see the anger that twisted his friend's scarred face.

When Bear drew back his club and swung, his assailant ducked and ran.

"No, Bear!" Cade shouted.

Bear checked his swing, but not soon enough. The table leg caught the young woman's brow. She fell like a shoring log cut too long for the shaft. Bear dropped his club.

"Cade?" he asked, confused that a woman lay where that no-good claim jumper, Elmer, should have been. "Did I kill her?"

Cade found himself staring. With hair as black as a raven's wing and skin an alabaster-white, Miss Fairchild was everything he had hoped for. Breathtakingly beautiful and a figure that made a man impatient with society's polite rules that said he should marry her first. It wouldn't do to let himself dwell on the fact that she didn't look old enough to be a widow, he told himself. A lot of women married young.

Cade knelt beside her and examined her rapidly purpling eye. "She's not dead, Bear," he told his friend, "but she'll have quite a shiner when she wakes."

Unconvinced, Bear dropped to his knees. It wouldn't be the first time he had killed someone in anger. Leaning over, he peered into the young woman's face.

"Are you sure she's not dead, Cade?"

Cade nudged her shoulder. "Miss Fairchild," he urged.

Getting no response, he shook her again. "Wake up, Miss Fairchild."

Jenny winced at the demanding voice that echoed in her head. She tried to open her eyes, but only one seemed to want to obey. Forcing it open, she blinked at the huge, ugly man bending over her.

It was him. The man who had hit her. She lay perfectly still. He no longer wore a fierce scowl on his scarred face, but with that unruly mane of wild red hair, he looked every bit as frightening as when he'd come rushing out the door.

"Who are y-you?" she finally managed to choke out.

"I'm Mr. Morgan," Cade answered.

Jenny blinked her good eye again. Odd how the words came out but the man's lips never moved. She closed her eye against the pain. It was no wonder, her mind was playing tricks on her. Her head felt like someone was using it for a church bell. A thousand iron clappers each vied for a chance to strike their own tune.

"Are you Miss Fairchild?"

Oh, Lord. This was going to be more difficult than she had imagined. Such a cultured voice for such a primitive face. Surely there had to be some mistake. No one could ever bring themselves to marry such a man.

Jenny struggled to find the right words, but try as she might she couldn't seem to formulate a single coherent sentence. Guilty conscience or not, now was not the time to try to conduct a clever interview. She certainly didn't want to offend a man who was capable of breaking her in two without any great effort on his part.

Jenny gently rubbed her swollen brow. "I'm Jenny, your housekeeper," she managed to say before a black curtain descended again.

Cade stood. His housekeeper! The agency had sent a beautiful, young woman like this to be his housekeeper? They must have been out of their minds. She wouldn't be with him a week. Once word got out, every miner for miles around would be on his doorstep asking for her hand. Even so, he couldn't just leave her lying here. The wind was beginning to pick up. At this time of year, it could be harboring either spring or winter. Cade knelt down and gathered her up in his arms.

"Can you help me get her home, Bear? I'll have Albert make up a bed and you can spend the night."

A smile creased the big man's face as he fell into step beside Cade. "Albert will be right upset if I do."

"It's been over eight years now. Don't you think it's about time he dropped this ridiculous feud?"

They walked on for several blocks in silence, Bear turning it over in his mind. "Wish I knew what I done to make him so all-fired mad," he suddenly said.

"You mean you don't know what started it?"

"Never could figure it out. One day we was friends; the next, enemies."

Cade didn't know what to say. The few times he had tried to bring up the subject, Albert had refused to discuss it. The little man would probably carry it to his grave.

Cade stepped along the board walkway. He could see Carl standing in the window of the train station watching them. By tomorrow, the whole town would know what had happened—at least Carl's version.

"What brings you to Gold Shoe, Bear?" he asked calmly as he kept a watchful eye on Carl. "The last I heard, you filed a claim up north."

"Decided to sell out to one of the mining companies back East. Thought I'd try my luck up around these parts."

"You can always come to work for me," Cade offered. "I could use another good man."

"Might do that," Bear answered.

Cade started to say more when he felt Jenny stir in his arms. All he needed was her to raise a fuss to add more color to the story Carl was bound to be cooking up.

"Lie still," he warned. "We haven't far to go."

Jenny opened her eye and stared. The scarred face had been replaced by the handsomely rugged features of a bronzed warrior. Pale blond hair shone like silver in the light of a crescent moon. Handsome enough to make one's heart skip a beat, she told herself. Even so, Jenny was not one to be easily drawn to such things. She had learned from experience that it was best to remember handsome is as handsome does. Many a deceiving smile hid a determinedly squared jaw of an unforgiving nature.

Jenny pushed against his broad chest. "Who are you?" she asked.

"Didn't I tell you to lie still?"

At the sharp command, Jenny immediately ceased her struggles.

"That's better," he said as he stepped off the boardwalk. "It sure would wound my pride if the stationmaster were to see me drop you."

Jenny tried to turn in his arms. "He's watching us?"

"Every move." Cade smiled at her frown. "With your torn jacket and that black eye, you're quite an attraction."

Her money! Jenny grabbed the hem of her jacket. "It's all gone," she wailed.

Cade stopped. "What's all gone?"

"My money!" Jenny shrieked. "Let me down. I've got to go back and get my money. It fell when my jacket was ripped."

Cade kept a tight hold on her. "And get yourself beaten up again?" he asked. "You can't need it that much. Besides, with that wind building, your money's halfway to Mexico by now."

Jenny fought to get down. "You don't understand. The money wasn't mine. I . . . I borrowed it."

"I'm sure whoever you borrowed it from will understand."

The thought of having to explain anything to the man who had hit her sent an unaccustomed fear trembling through Jenny's body. "You explain it to him."

"Oh, no, you don't," Cade said as he plopped her down on the seat of his buckboard. "You'll not put that on my shoulders. I'll have a hard enough time explaining to all my friends that I didn't hit my new housekeeper."

Jenny froze. "Your housekeeper? I'm your housekeeper? Then who . . . ?"

Cade nodded to the big miner behind him. "Meet Charlie Wise. We call him Bear."

"Oh!" was all she managed.

Having dispensed with the introductions, Cade turned his attention to the pile of luggage stacked on the train platform. It was no wonder Carl was working late. Someone had left him a mountain of bags to look after.

"Which bag is yours?"

"Th-the ones on the platform," she answered, still trying to sort out her mistake.

Cade's eyes traveled over the varied assortment of boxes and luggage, to the large wooden trunk placed at the edge of the dock. His brow wrinkled in a frown. None looked like the serviceable bags of a housekeeper.

"Which ones?" he asked again, hoping they wouldn't be required to dig to the bottom of that mess.

With a long finger, Jenny pointed to the pile of bags and boxes. "The ones sitting there."

"All of them?" he asked incredulously.

Jenny flinched at the harsh words. Perhaps this was not the time to mention the others the hotel in St. Louis was still holding for her. "I suppose I did bring a lot," she mumbled.

"A lot! It looks like you were planning on opening a general store."

A betraying warmth spread over her face. Were servants known to travel light? Odd, but as many as she had hired, she had never noticed. Better to brazen it out than to sit here wondering.

"Don't be ridiculous, Mr. Morgan," she said with as much authority as she could manage under the circumstances. "I couldn't very well leave my belongings behind."

The look of resignation that passed between the two men was not lost on Jenny. Thanks heavens they didn't argue; they merely bent to the task of loading the buckboard. She didn't know what she would have done had they refused. It had taken her and the servants an entire week of her father's absence to pack and she'd be switched if she was going to leave one single box behind.

Watching them haul her possessions to the buckboard, Jenny almost wished she had admitted to being the bride. Mr. Morgan surely wouldn't have begrudged his bride her things.

With a grunt, Bear heaved her trunk onto the back of the wagon. The buckboard bounced crazily under the sudden weight and Jenny was forced to grab the iron rail beside her to keep from falling. She wasn't surprised the men took no notice. But then again, perhaps that was to her advantage for they didn't appear to be in the best of humor.

Next came her boxes. They were soon stacked in a neat row behind the trunk. Jenny tried not to look at the large pile that still remained on the platform. Mr. Morgan's tight frown when he deposited his heavy jacket on the seat beside her did not speak well of her need for so many cases. But she had to give him credit. He continued to load the boxes without complaint.

As they worked, Jenny found her attention drawn more and more to the taut muscles that worked beneath the snug fit of Mr. Morgan's white linen shirt. The light from the station revealed more than just a fine set of shoulders. While lacking the massive girth of Bear's barrel chest, Mr. Morgan was every bit as intimidating. Jenny couldn't remember when she'd met someone quite so tall before. With eyes bluer than the skies over Colorado, he was most pleasant to look at. A girl could easily find herself drawn to him. Much more so than the man her father wished her to marry. A shame she wasn't in the market for a husband. Otherwise, she might have been tempted to marry the tall, handsome rancher just to show her father that she could make her own decisions.

Jenny gave herself a brisk shake. What in heaven's name was she thinking? She was to be the housekeeper, not the bride. This job was to be the beginning of a new life for her.

One of independence. One she had only dreamed about until a week ago. If she was going to succeed, she couldn't be slipping back into the ways of her father's upbringing. She had secured this position on her own and she was determined to prove to everyone that a woman didn't need a man. If a woman wanted, she could . . .

The thought lodged in her throat when Mr. Morgan pinned his brilliant blue eyes on her. It was almost as if he had guessed that she was to have been his bride and was awaiting an explanation. She had meant to explain, but not here. Not now.

"Ready?" he asked.

Jenny let out the breath she was holding. He sounded irritated, not mad. He didn't suspect. But she would still have to explain. As for the money she owed him, well that would have to wait. After all, she had tried to go back after it. It wasn't her fault he had refused to let her. Perhaps there would be ample opportunity on the ride to his ranch to bring the subject up.

Her conscience very much relieved, Jenny smiled brightly at Mr. Morgan as he lifted his jacket from the seat and climbed up beside her. After slipping into his coat, he nodded at Bear. To Jenny's dismay, Bear stepped up on the other side and calmly waited for her to move over. How was she to have the privacy she needed to apologize to Mr. Morgan?

"There's not room enough for the three of us," Jenny protested.

Cade, who had lost his patience somewhere around the tenth bag, glared down at her. "Bear would ride in the back but your luggage took up all the room. It's either the three of us on this seat or you can walk."

At his uncompromising words, Jenny slid over to make room for Bear. Mr. Morgan might be handsome, she decided, but he was certainly no gentleman. She was all but wedged between the two men on the narrow seat.

Jenny scrunched her shoulders forward, trying to make room. "I c-can't b-br-reathe," she protested.

"Stand up!" Cade snapped.

"What?"

"I said, stand up."

"I can't r-ride like that."

"Stand!"

Jenny shot up off the seat.

After a shuffling of feet, Cade pulled her down on his lap. She opened her mouth to protest, but he quickly cut her short.

"One word and you stay," he growled.

CHAPTER 2

Jenny fumed silently as the buckboard made its way through the dark streets. She had seen enough. The high-and-mighty Mr. Morgan didn't merit an explanation for his missing bride. The man was nothing more than a—a—a jack donkey!

Obviously, he had never read the articles she had in the *Philadelphia Times* or he would know the true worth of a good woman and treat her accordingly. She hoped he never found a bride. A man like Mr. Morgan didn't deserve a wife to help him carve out an empire in this wild land. Jenny lifted her chin defiantly. In fact, if he ever hoped to marry, he'd best be changing his ways.

Cade frowned when she stiffened in his arms. He knew he should apologize. He had allowed his frustrations over a bad day to color his temper. She hadn't deserved his rudeness. Not after the black eye.

Jenny had spunk. He would give her that. But if she continued to sit on his lap like a starched shirt, more than her eye would be black and blue by morning.

But her as his housekeeper? It'd never work out, especially if his bride didn't arrive soon. Nights could grow mighty lonely when you faced an empty bed. With someone as beautiful as Jenny down the hall, it'd be hard as hell to keep his hands off her.

His only salvation would be to find her a home with someone. The Carvers down in Denver might be a possibility. They were expecting their twelfth child soon and had been asking about a maid. He had to go to Denver tomorrow to wire Miss Emily's. He'd drop by and talk with Mrs. Carver about taking Jenny off his hands.

His brow furrowed in thought. The solution didn't please him as much as it should have. He'd seen the way Mr. Carver ogled the women the minute his wife's head was turned. For all his wealth and fine clothes, the man was worse than the miners that came into Gold Shoe when bad weather forced them to curtail their work. A woman and whiskey were all they wanted. No, he'd not send Jenny to him.

But then what else was he to do? She was too young to be out on her own or shut away in some miner's cabin to spend the rest of her days swatting flies and sweeping dirt floors waiting for her husband to strike it rich. Hell, she'd be safer taking her chances with him.

Cade studied her for a moment. "How old are you?" he finally asked.

Jenny eyed him thoughtfully. "Twenty-five," she boldly stated.

His brow dipped in a frown. "Twenty-five," he growled at her lie. Hell, with that exaggeration, she must be even younger than he thought.

"Why twenty-five?" he asked sarcastically. "Why not thirty or forty? Or closer to the truth—seventeen."

"Seventeen!" she shouted. "Why I turned eight—"

Jenny snapped her mouth shut in embarrassment at the devilish grin her declaration had brought to his lips. Would she never learn to control that wayward tongue of hers?

"Well, which is it?" he asked, grinning down at her. "*Eight*y or *eight*een?"

Jenny fastened her eyes on the road ahead. "You may take it for whichever you wish, Mr. Morgan. I am here merely to do my job. Age should not matter."

Cade winked at Bear over her head. "I don't know," he said, deliberately baiting her, "an eighty-year-old house-keeper wasn't what I had in mind."

Jenny turned back to face him. She didn't know which irritated her more. The sounds of Bear trying to suppress his amusement or Mr. Morgan's attempts to embarrass her. Had they not long since passed the outskirts of town, she would have been tempted to request he turn the buckboard around and take her to the nearest hotel.

"Eighty or eighteen, you'll get your money's worth, Mr. Morgan."

"Well, Miss . . ." He lifted a questioning brow. "I'm not sure I remember your last name."

"I didn't give it," she answered. "But plain Jenny will get my attention."

"Well, Plain Jenny, I'm pleased to know you are willing to do whatever is asked of you."

A suspicion was beginning to form in Jenny's head. If he thought to work her hands to the bone, he'd best think again. He was not going to make a slave out of her. "I am prepared to fulfill my duties as housekeeper, Mr. Morgan. Anything else you require will have to be taken up with the rest of your staff."

Cade winked at Bear again. "That would be fine if I had a staff, but I don't. You're it."

"But that would mean . . ."

"Exactly. You will have to do all the cooking and cleaning," he stated solemnly. She had gone rigid on his lap again. Lord, he loved the way she tilted her stubborn little chin defiantly. He was really beginning to enjoy this, but that black eye of hers had a way of putting a damper on things.

He pulled the buckboard to a stop. "Kindly stand, Plain Jenny."

"Will you please not call me that!" she snapped as she scooted off his lap.

Choosing to ignore her comment, Cade handed Bear the reins and jumped down. "I'll be right back," he said.

Jenny looked out across the dark landscape. There was nothing to be seen but tall pines and boulders. She turned to the big man beside her and whispered, "Where's he going?"

Bear suspected Cade was answering nature's call, but he couldn't bring himself to tell a lady that. Frantically he searched the trees for the answer she would accept. Finding no help there, he ignored the question and made a great show of removing a knife from his pocket, along with a small leather pouch. Loosening the strings, he dumped out a dark square of tobacco, sliced himself off a hunk and tucked it into his cheek. Seeing as how the woman was waiting patiently for his answer and was not going to give up until she had it, Bear finally mumbled, "Reckon he went to look up a prairie rabbit, Miss Jenny."

"That's silly. Who would go looking for a rabbit in the dark?"

From his uneasy shifting in the seat, Jenny could have sworn the question had somehow embarrassed the big man. She searched the side of the narrow path where Mr. Morgan had disappeared but he was nowhere to be seen.

She turned back to Bear, her good eye narrowing in suspicion. "He doesn't plan on me cooking this rabbit for supper, does he?"

Bear almost choked on his tobacco. By the time he finished coughing, he could see Cade making his way back through the trees.

"You're safe there, Miss Jenny," he said. "Cade won't want nobody cookin' his rabbit."

Cade. So that was Mr. Morgan's Christian name. "Cade." She let it roll across her tongue. Yes, she liked it. The name was strong—masculine. It somehow fit the tall, fair-haired rancher.

Jenny opened her mouth to pose another question when she heard a twig snap behind her. She swung around. Other than something Mr. Morgan was wrapping in his handkerchief, Jenny could see that he had been unsuccessful in his search for game. "Well, it appears I need not worry about having to cook," she mumbled to Bear.

"I'd not be mentioning the rabbit if I were you, Miss Jenny," he cautioned her.

Jenny nodded in agreement. She was mature enough to know you did not draw attention to a man's failures. She made a mental note that Mr. Morgan must be sensitive where his hunting skills were concerned. She gave him a big smile as he climbed back onto the wagon.

Once he had her settled again in his lap, Cade shoved his handkerchief into her hand. "Here. Put this on your eye."

Jenny took the white lump. It was cold and damp. "What is it?"

"Snow," he said, flicking the reins once more.

"Snow?" She stared down at the sodden cloth. "In May?"

"It takes a while for the days to warm up enough to melt snow in the sheltered areas."

Gingerly, Jenny touched the handkerchief to her swollen eye.

"Oh!" she gasped as the snow set her eye to throbbing. She shoved the handkerchief back at him. "If you don't mind, Mr. Morgan, I think I'll do without."

Cade ignored the hankie. "Put it back and leave it there!"

Jenny found herself automatically obeying the man and that upset her almost as much as the high-handed way in which he had issued the order. But what did she expect? Old habits die hard. Her father had always demanded immediate obedience. But it dismayed her to believe she'd traveled so far to be rid of her father only to discover that Colorado had its own share of bullies. Well, at least she wasn't married to the beast.

As the miles passed, the creak of the buckboard's wheels was joined by Bear's snores. Lulled by the gentle sway of the wagon, Jenny too began to nod.

Cade looked down when her head fell against his chest. She was sound asleep, her hat cocked over her swollen brow. Lashes the color of dark, stormy nights lay in a whisper of shadow on her ivory cheeks. Shifting the reins to one hand, he used his other to keep her from falling.

As the night grew colder, low gray clouds covered the moon. Lord, he hoped it didn't snow. Pulling the edges of his coat from between them, Cade wrapped them both in its warmth. Jenny snuggled against him and he knew he'd made a mistake. For all her young years, Jenny was still a woman.

Cade's chest tightened. A beautiful woman. One that smelled of rose petals and warm summer nights. He closed his eyes and took a deep breath. He could almost picture Jenny in his bed, her long dark curls a sensuous fan across his pillow, his fingers outlining the fullness of her lips as she lay beside him.

Cade's blue eyes suddenly snapped open. Never in the entire thirty-one years of his life had he ever given over to daydreaming. He had always been a logical, level-headed man. He hadn't spared a moment on emotions since the night he discovered Letitia in bed with his brother. They had laughed at his bewilderment and anger, saying, "Some things were meant to be shared."

Cade, who had thought himself in love, did not share in

their philosophy. Sickened, he had packed his things and left. He had been on his own ever since.

One thing was clear. He couldn't keep Jenny in his household. If she stayed, he knew she would end up in his bed. Even a fool knew it was never wise to have your mistress and your wife under the same roof.

The lusty crowing of a rooster brought Jenny awake with a start. Somber brown drapes cloaked the room in darkness and Jenny could feel the scream building within her. It took her a moment to realize she was in the housekeeper's room at Mr. Morgan's ranch, not in the attic.

The sound of voices drifted up from the rooms below. Jenny eased up on one elbow. Who in their right mind got up before dawn?

Servants?

It had to be. She had had enough of her own to recognize the sounds. Her lips twisted in annoyance. That explained the smile on Mr. Morgan's face when he told her there was no staff. Why he felt the need to tease about such a thing was beyond her, but she didn't intend to waste her time dwelling on her new employer's idiosyncrasies. She should be up and about her duties.

With a weary sigh, Jenny flung the quilt aside and slid her feet over the edge of the featherbed.

"Ouch!" she cried when her toe struck something hard.

Pulling her knees under her, she perched on the edge of the bed and carefully reached behind the kerosene lamp on her nightstand to open the drapes. A bright morning sun greeted her, washing the tiny room in light.

Her belongings were everywhere. She vaguely recalled insisting that all her things be carried up to her room last night. Given the immense proportions of the house silhouetted in the moonlight, she hadn't expected the housekeeper's quarters would be so small. The room certainly hadn't appeared this crowded when she had made her way to bed last evening. She would have to talk to Mr. Morgan about getting a larger room.

It took a bit of rearranging but Jenny finally managed to get to the bags that held her gowns. Fortunately her maid had taken great care in packing them properly. Slipping the top one out of its tissue, Jenny shook the wrinkles from the dark blue dress. The Venetian lace that trimmed the gown's snug bodice might be a bit beyond a housekeeper's budget, but she hoped Mr. Morgan was not up on women's fashions enough to notice the flaws in her wardrobe.

After clearing another space among the bags and boxes, Jenny changed out of her nightdress. Now if only she could do something about her hair. She had been too tired to brush it out before she fell into bed last night and she knew without looking it had to be a mass of unruly curls.

There was a small mirror over her washstand—if only she could get to it. Standing on her tiptoes, Jenny stretched across the pile of boxes. If she leaned to the right just a mite, she could catch a small portion of her face in the bottom corner of the silvered glass.

The swelling of her brow may have gone down, but her hair was worse than she had thought and she had no idea where the case was that held her brushes. Drats! she silently cursed as she tried to run her fingers through the curls. It took only one attempt to discover it wasn't going to work. She heaved a frustrated sigh. Might as well pin the mess up and be done with it.

Crawling back into bed, Jenny searched the blankets for the wooden hairpins she had lost during the night. After several minutes, she came up with only three. Well, three would have to do. It was getting late and she needed to go over her duties with Mr. Morgan.

Pulling her hair to the back of her head, Jenny rammed the pins into the lump of curls. There, that should do it—at least until she found the case that held her brushes and other toiletries. She straightened from the mirror.

Satisfied, Jenny made her way down the long hall to a broad oak stairway. By the time she reached the dining room below, Jenny was surprisingly pleased with her new home. Other than her own small bedroom, the rooms she could see all appeared quite large. A little dusty perhaps, but nothing she couldn't remedy.

Cade was just finishing breakfast when Jenny slid into the empty chair at the end of the long table. Her casual assumption that she would take her meals with him piqued Cade's curiosity. He didn't know what experience Jenny had listed when she applied at Miss Emily's agency, but a housekeeper was surely not among them. From her confident manner, he strongly suspected Jenny was more accustomed to giving orders than taking them.

Despite his decision that he'd be better off avoiding Jenny until he knew what to do with her, Cade found his attention straying to the pins sticking out of the clump of hair behind her left ear. Even though she looked like a squirrel skewered for a roasting fire, Cade had to admit she was damned attractive. Too damned attractive.

"Good morning, Plain Jenny," he teased.

She ignored the salutation. "Good morning, Mr. Morgan," she returned. Bestowing a stiff smile, she nodded to the short, thin man pouring Cade's coffee. "I see you have a staff after all."

He grinned. "If you consider Albert here and Cook a staff, then with you I have three."

It irritated Jenny that there was not one ounce of remorse in his smile. She unfolded her napkin and placed it across her lap. She would let his bad manners pass for now.

"I would like some coffee also, Albert. Then you may tell Cook that I'll have whatever Mr. Morgan is having."

"Mr. Morgan's had his breakfast," the servant grumbled, then left the room.

Jenny lifted a questioning brow to Cade. "Did I say something wrong?"

"Albert has a burr under his saddle this morning."

Jenny wanted to question the meaning of his statement but she couldn't shake the feeling that Mr. Morgan had already found cause to laugh at her. "Was it something I've done?" Jenny persisted.

The honest concern in her voice surprised Cade and he took a moment to answer. "He's upset with me, not you."

"Oh!"

"Well, don't look as if I beat him or something. His nose is out of joint because I brought Bear home last night, but he'll get over it."

A dirty plate sat at an empty chair close to Mr. Morgan. "Did Bear leave because of Albert?" she asked.

"Don't worry about Bear. If he'd had the time, he'd have stayed just to aggravate Albert. But Bear needed to fetch some things from his mine and wanted to get an early start."

Jenny's eyes widened in interest. "Bear has a gold mine?"

"Actually this is Bear's third mine. He was among the first to arrive after gold was discovered. He's done quite well for himself."

Resting her elbow on the table, Jenny tucked her fist under her chin and glanced around the room. The furniture looked to be of good quality, but it lacked the outward trappings of wealth so prevalent in her father's home.

"Too bad you couldn't have found any gold yourself," she said with a note of regret. "You could have been rich."

The corner of Cade's lips lifted in amusement. "I've done all right for myself. I have this ranch, a bank in Denver, a lumb—"

"Those are all fine," she said, dismissing his holdings with a wave of her hand. "My fa—my previous employer had all that." She gave a long sigh. "But a gold mine. That's rich!"

If she'd been sitting closer, Cade would have been tempted to wring her pretty little neck for blithely casting his wealth aside. "My dear Plain Jenny, if you choose to stay in Colorado, you will soon learn that the ones who get rich off the mines are the ones who supply the miners' needs, not the miners.

"The man who built this house was a miner. He struck it rich and built this house for his wife. Her people were quite wealthy and he wanted to give her something she could be proud of."

"It does seem quite large," she said as she studied the oil painting over the oak buffet that covered one wall.

He lifted a smug brow. "Mine or no mine, you can see who owns it now."

Jenny's eyes met his. "Are you trying to tell me you are wealthy, Mr. Morgan?"

It was hard to imagine he was sitting here defending himself to his housekeeper. He had never given much thought to his wealth before, but her skepticism goaded him beyond belief. Cade leaned back in his chair. "Quite wealthy."

Seeing the unmistakable arrogance in his eyes, Jenny knew she should drop the subject then and there, but tact had never been numbered among her accomplishments. She gave him her most indulgent smile. "Then tell me, Mr. Morgan. Why is it—if you're so rich—that your housekeeper is forced to make do with a room no bigger than a cook's pantry?"

Cade's dark brows shot together. "I didn't expect my housekeeper to pack all of St. Louis and bring it with her," he growled.

"Then you agree I need a larger room," she said, refusing to back down.

"I agree to nothing," he said. "When my bride arrives, you may take it up with her."

Jenny lowered her gaze to her napkin. "That would be Miss Fairchild?"

"Yes." A frown creased his forehead. "I'll be going into Denver today to wire the agency to see what delayed her." He had no intention of sending a wire from Gold Shoe. The little mining communities had big ears and bigger mouths. Inside of an hour, the entire area would know his bride hadn't arrived. "She might even come today."

Jenny had all but unraveled the hem on the corner of her napkin. "Perhaps she changed her mind," Jenny offered innocently.

Cade picked up his cup of coffee and drained it. His arrangement with his bride was merely another business deal as far as he was concerned but Jenny's words gnawed at him. "If she had changed her mind, the agency would have notified me."

"Perhaps something happened to detain her," she suggested. "In the meantime, I shall be needing a larger room."

"Don't you think it would be wiser to wait? Miss Fairchild may have other arrangements."

Jenny's lips curved in a cautious smile. Heaven forbid he should make her wait for a bride who would never show. "I'll take my chances, Mr. Morgan."

"Then do as you wish for now. Until Miss Fairchild arrives, the running of the house will be your responsibility."

"You will not be disappointed, Mr. Morgan."

She would have said more but Albert returned with a plate piled high with a fluffy mound of scrambled eggs, four strips of crisp bacon, and two huge biscuits. Jenny's mouth watered. At least the cook had not been upset by Bear's visit.

Cade pushed back his chair. "I will leave you to your breakfast."

It took all her efforts to drag her eyes away from her

plate. The tea and jelly bread she had had in Denver had long since gone to her toes. "You need not worry. Everything will be in order by the time you return for supper."

He paused by the doorway. "Just see that the rooms are aired and the blue bedchamber is cleaned in case Miss Fairchild should arrive today."

Jenny breathed a sigh of relief that he left without waiting for her answer. She'd have a hard time explaining that she could clean all of Colorado before *his* Miss Fairchild made an appearance. Perhaps after she had shown him how well she could manage his household, she would not be so squeamish about owning up to what she had done. But for now she wasn't going to let the problem ruin the nice breakfast Cook had prepared for her.

Not sparing another thought to her deception, Jenny broke open one of the golden brown biscuits and spread it with a mixture of honey and butter. After a generous bite, she closed her eyes. The biscuit was wonderful. The best she'd ever tasted.

She took another bite and sat back to watch Albert clear the dirty plates from the table. Although the frown was gone from his face, he was very careful to avoid meeting her gaze.

"How long have you worked for Mr. Morgan?" she asked.

"Long enough for him to know I don't like having those no-account miners wiping their muddy feet on my clean floors."

"Bear is one of Mr. Morgan's guests," she ventured to point out.

Albert perched his fists on his skinny hips and glared at her. "Bear ain't no guest. He only shows up to wolf down Millie's grub; then he's gone."

The strong resentment Albert had for Bear surprised Jenny. Deciding it would be best to leave things she knew nothing about alone, she let Albert return to his work and ate the rest of her breakfast in silence.

Once she finished, Jenny picked up her plate and made her way to the kitchen.

"A man like Bear gets your attention," said a tall, rawboned woman who stood at the counter, her hands buried in a huge lump of dough.

Albert's loud snort didn't wipe the faraway look from the tall woman's eyes.

"He's so . . . so . . ."

"Ugly!" Albert shouted before he stomped out of the kitchen.

It didn't take much for Jenny to see the frustration in Albert's gray eyes stemmed from jealousy. She felt sorry for the little man.

"You must be the cook."

"That's me," the woman said, bending her dark head over her task. "I cook; they eat."

"You cook very well."

A broad grin creased the tall woman's brown face. "I do, don't I? Not bad for an Indian."

"An Indian?" Jenny breathed. "You're an Indian?"

"My ma was. She died when I was born." Millie gave the bread dough another punch. "Now my pa, he was a big Swede. A regular army man till Ma up and died. First chance Pa got, he took off. Guess he didn't like havin' a half-breed hangin' on his coattails."

"I'm sorry."

"No need to be. He wasn't around long enough for me to care what he thought."

She wiped her hand on her apron, then extended it to Jenny. "Name's Millie. I heard you was the new house-keeper."

Although not pretty, Millie had a quality about her that made you look past her rough features. Jenny immediately warmed to the woman.

"Call me Jenny. Wherever did you learn to cook biscuits like that?" she asked.

Millie dipped her hand in a large jar. Scooping out a handful of flour, she gave the dough a generous dusting before she answered.

"After Pa left, the colonel's wife decided it was her Christian duty to see that I got a proper upbringing. When she finally realized I wasn't going to take to no book learning, she felt God had released her from the task of saving my savage Indian soul. I stayed out of her way after that. The kitchen seemed the best place. That's where I learned I had a real talent for—"

Millie suddenly stopped kneading the bread and studied Jenny a moment. "What's wrong with you, child? You're as fidgety as fat on a fire."

Jenny looked to see if Albert was still busy in the dining room. "To be honest," she whispered, "I've been looking for the water closet, but I can't seem to find it."

"A water closet!" Millie cackled. "The colonel's wife was always a-naggin' him for one of them fancy rooms but we don't have much need for such things here."

Jenny blushed to think Albert might have heard. Keeping her voice low, she leaned toward the cook. "What do you use then?"

"That depends," Millie answered as if the problem weighed heavily on her mind. "I see nothing wrong with looking up a prairie rabbit, but you'll probably be wantin' to visit the little house out back."

Jenny felt her face grow warm. "Looking up a prairie rabbit? What does that mean?" she asked with the suspicion she already knew the answer.

Millie flipped the dough onto a freshly floured spot, then resumed her relentless punching. "Why, you take to the woods, child," she finally said. "Everyone knows that."

Jenny winced. How would she ever be able to face Bear again? "Just show me the way to the little house out back."

"Albert!" Millie hollered.

He appeared at the door before Jenny could hush her.

"Miss Jenny needs to use the little house. Show her where it is."

Jenny eased toward the back door, her face a bright crimson. "That's all right, Albert. You can return to your duties. I'll find it myself."

If a person could die of embarrassment, Jenny knew they would be nailing the lid on her coffin soon. Never had she thought there would come a day when she would be forced to air her private business in front of a man. Thank goodness the privy wasn't difficult to find. Constant usage had worn a path through the prairie grasses.

Once she'd paid her visit, Jenny was reluctant to return to the kitchen where she was likely to run into Albert. Instead, she walked around to the front door.

Tall pines framed the house as if guarding a special treasure in a vast expanse of raw, untamed wilderness. With its tall mullioned windows and iron-railed balconies, the large wooden structure looked more like it belonged in a city such as Denver rather than a tree-studded meadow up in the mountains.

Jenny stepped up to the wide, covered veranda that ran the entire length and rounded the far corner of the two-story home. Intricate wooden curlicues trimmed the eaves and the roofline of the porch.

Jenny stood a moment admiring the craftsmanship. She liked this house. To her, it felt like home.

She slowly climbed the front steps and entered the cool foyer. She'd start her tour upstairs. If she were to stay, she'd need a different room.

It didn't take Jenny long to determine that the large sunny room at the end of the hall would best suit her needs. Not only were there two chiffoniers to hold her clothes, but it had a small room attached that would do quite nicely for the rest of her things. She checked the chiffonier next to the large bed. It was empty. Good, no one was using the room.

Once she got rid of those musty old books on cattle ranching that cluttered the room, she'd set out her lace doilies and perhaps a bowl of crushed rose petals.

Having made her choice, she rang for Albert. In no time at all, he appeared. "I'd like you to clear out everything in here but the furniture. When you are finished, you may fetch my things." She looked around with pride. "This will be my new room."

Albert studied the room as if he were seeing it for the first time. "Mr. Morgan say you could do this?"

It was evident Jenny would have to take a firm hand with Albert or he would continue to question her authority. "Mr. Morgan put me in charge before he left. If I say this is to be my room, then it is to be my room."

"But this here is—"

"I'll hear no more about it, Albert. Please do as I ask."

"Mr. Morgan. He won't like this," Albert added as he picked up Cade's pipe off the nightstand beside the bed.

"That's silly, Albert. This house has so many bedrooms I doubt he'll even notice."

Having said her piece, she left him to his work and went in search of fresh papers to line the drawers.

"He'll notice, Miss Jenny," Albert muttered to himself. "You take a man's bed and he'll notice."

CHAPTER 3

Cade flicked the reins over the broad backs of his horses, urging them to pick up their pace along the moonlit path that led to his ranch. He didn't know why that murder of the old lady and her grandson had him so concerned. Garo was a long way from the ranch and besides the *Rocky Mountain News* clearly stated the bodies had lain in that deserted barn for over a month before they were discovered. He kept telling himself that whoever had committed the atrocity would be long gone by now, but he still couldn't shake the feeling that there was more to the incident than he had put together from the details gleaned from the newspaper. Ever since reading the story, Cade kept visualizing the man coming to the door and Jenny inviting him in.

It wasn't like him to be so spooked. With all the bar fights and claim jumping that went on in these parts, foul play had almost become a way of life for some. Even so, he was relieved to pull the wagon to a halt in front of the stables.

Cade searched the darkened windows of his house. Everything seemed peaceful enough. Slowly Cade released a long sigh, letting the rigid layers of tension peel off his shoulders like wet newspapers drying in the wind.

The sound of footsteps in the dry grass brought Cade's hand to the rifle that lay beside him on the seat. He relaxed when Sam, one of his hired hands, stepped out of the shadows.

"Got them horses mighty lathered, Mr. Morgan," the man said as he reached for the lead horse.

"Thought I heard a mountain lion on the trail, Sam," Cade lied. There was no sense upsetting his men. They'd hear about the killings soon enough.

"Think we should get a few of the men and go after the critter?" Sam asked.

"Not this time, Sam. Could have been I was mistaken. No sense sending the men out until I know for sure."

"I'll leave that up to you, Mr. Morgan." Sam suddenly pursed his lips, aimed for the manure pile beside the stables, and spit. "Dadburnit!" he cursed at the brown tobacco juice that had missed its mark. "You'd think I could hit something that big. Some buzzard must have moved the pile on me."

Cade didn't answer. Sam hadn't hit a thing he had aimed at in the thirty odd years Cade had known him. It would only rile the man to point that fact out.

After tossing the reins down, Cade picked up his rifle and the rumpled copy of the *Rocky Mountain News* and climbed down from the buckboard.

"Anything been going on I need to know about?"

Sam scratched his head for a moment. "Don't rightly know of anything. That new housekeeper of yours near beat them parlor rugs to death, but other than that things have been pretty quiet around here."

He started to unhitch the horses, then stopped and looked back. "I almost forgot. Bear's been here three times today lookin' for you."

"Did he say what was on his mind?"

''Nope. Jus' said he'd be back.''

He hoped Bear had decided to work for him. He could use all the good workers he could get. ''Thanks, Sam.''

Cade tucked the newspaper under his arm and headed for the house. Sam's lively whistling followed him across the yard and Cade smiled at the bawdy tune. The old man always had a way of cheering him up.

Sam had been with Cade when he'd driven his first herd of cattle up from Texas. It seemed like a lifetime ago that they had made their way up the pass to check on the mines and discovered the lush green valley of prairie grasses. The best cattle feed Cade had seen in a long time.

Even though Jenny's comment about rich miners still wrangled, he was content with his lot. Let the miners have their gold. Those graceless brown-eyed beasts of his grazing out there would bring him in more money than he could use in a lifetime.

Hell, Ross had built the house Cade lived in with his gold. Craftsmen had come from as far away as St. Louis to do the intricate woodwork that trimmed the balconies. Two months after the house was completed, Ross had lost his mine to a crooked faro game and his wife to a handsome drifter. Cade had picked up the ranch and surrounding lands for a song.

The house was a bit large for Cade, but a man had to think of the future. Now that he had decided to marry, it was easy to picture the big house filled with the sounds of children.

Cade stepped up onto the porch and reached for the door.

''Gettin' home mighty late aren't you, Cade?''

Crouching, Cade dropped the paper. With a quick flick of his wrist, he balanced the butt of his rifle against his hip and turned.

Bear stepped out of the shadows, his empty hands clearly visible. ''Whoa there. I didn't mean to spook you.''

Cade straightened and lowered his rifle. ''What in hell are you doing hiding out here in the dark like some thief?''

Bear's ugly face twisted into a grin. "Didn't think Albert would let me in. Besides I'd rather sit out here."

Cade motioned for him to take a seat on one of the rockers by the front door, then joined him. "I take it you've heard about the killings?"

"Saw Em in town. She told me."

"With all her customers there isn't much slips by her," he said.

Bear gave Cade a toothy grin and sat down. "She didn't know your bride had gone and jilted you."

"And you enlightened her. Is that it?" Cade growled.

"Now you can't blame a fella for what rolls off the end of his tongue after he's tossed down a couple of that smooth-tastin' whiskey Em serves."

Cade's blue eyes narrowed. "I could cut off his tongue."

Bear had known Cade too long to be put off by the threat. "Said she warned you about ordering a wife sight unseen."

"It's a damn site better than her suggestion."

Bear chuckled. "She wants to sell you one of her girls in the worst way."

"I know Em better than to take her up on an offer like that. She'd charge me an arm and a leg, then have the girl working for her every time my back was turned. I can have that kind of arrangement without paying Em."

Bear laughed. "She knows it too. You should have seen the look in her eyes when I told her your bride didn't show."

"Thanks for the help, Bear. You know what she did when I lost out on that cattle deal."

Bear's grin broadened. "I thought about that. So the way I see it, if she sends you that new redhead to your bed this time, you can just point her my way."

"Go ahead and have your fun," Cade said. Leaning back, he stretched his long legs out in front of him. "I had one hell of a time sneaking the last one out of the house without one of the hired hands seeing her."

Bear was well aware of Cade's obsession for not being made to look the fool, but he chanced Cade's wrath anyway. Cade didn't need to take everything so seriously.

"Afraid the whole town would hear about it?" he asked.

Cade glared across at Bear. "No!" he snapped. "I was afraid it would be days before I got any work out of the men. Blast it all, Bear, the only thing the woman had on between her and her maker was a string tie and chaps."

Bear let out a soft whistle. "Didn't hear about that part." A sudden thought curved his lips in a broad smile. "Bet it turned up Albert's toes seeing her prance right into the house like that."

"I don't know that Albert even saw her. But let me tell you, finding her in my bed like that sure curled mine," Cade admitted. "But you didn't come here to discuss Em's sense of humor."

Bear's grin faded. "I came by to see if you or your men spotted Elmer today."

"Can't say if they did. I've been in Denver most of the day." Cade lifted a thick brow. "You still looking to beat the twaddle out of him?"

"He's sure aching for it."

"What did he do this time?"

"He filed on that old abandoned claim next to mine," the big man said.

Cade recrossed his long legs. "Don't see anything wrong in that. Didn't the old man that owned it die?"

"Fell and broke his neck one night," Bear solemnly replied.

"The man hadn't any relatives to leave the claim to?" Cade pressed on. He didn't want his friend to be courting trouble if it could be avoided. "Someone might as well have the opportunity to make something off it. At least, if Elmer has his own claim, he won't be always trying to move in on someone else's territory."

"I'd think the same thing if I hadn't caught him trespassing on my mine.'' Bear hunched forward, his hands clasped together. ''I'd been to town trying to finalize the papers on my sale. When I got back, I found that polecat goin' through our last diggings.''

Cade's brow dipped into a frown. He hoped it wasn't as bad as it sounded. Up to now, Elmer had merely been a thorn in most everyone's hide. How he had managed to keep from having a slug put through his heart was a mystery to most, but Cade didn't want Bear to be the man who put it there.

''Maybe he heard you were selling and thought to take a look.''

''I would have thought so too, but once he saw me, he hightailed it out of there,'' Bear answered before standing. ''I don't know what he was up to, but I better not catch him snooping around again. You might want to pass that on if you happen to see him.''

Bear was off the porch and out of sight before Cade could point out that the possibility of seeing Elmer would be slim.

Cade stood and stretched. He sure wouldn't want to be standing in Elmer's boots when Bear caught up with him. His big friend could easily kill a man with those massive hands of his if he took the notion.

But Cade couldn't take on everyone else's problems. He had some of his own to sort out. The answer to his telegram pretty much spelled out the fact that he'd been had. Miss Fairchild had been given the train ticket for Colorado. Beyond that, they could tell him nothing. They made it clear it was not their responsibility to see that she contacted him.

It was ironic. For years he had fought off the persistent advances of marriage-hungry women and now that he had decided to wed, the first woman to apply for the position had run out on him. He couldn't bring himself to blame the agency. Only a fool would have been unaware of the risks of having someone select his bride for him. But they were the ones who expected to find love. Love was not for Cade. His brother had taught him that love was an illusion—

nothing more than the elusive pot of gold at the end of a rainbow that disappeared in the mists if you got too close. No, Cade would settle for respect. In the long run, it was all that mattered—or survived.

He leaned down to pick up the newspaper he had dropped, then went inside. Except for the soft moonlight washing the wood floor, the foyer was dark. Striking a match, Cade lifted the glass chimney of the lamp Albert left in readiness on the front table and lit the wick.

His lips thinned into a bitter line as he crossed the foyer and mounted the stairs. Love or no love, it would have been pleasant to have a wife waiting to greet him.

Dusty and tired, Cade let his disappointment wash over him. It wasn't often he gave in to his feelings and the depth of the sudden loneliness surprised him. Up until now he had enjoyed the solitary life of a bachelor. Odd, how finally making the decision to marry had changed everything.

Wearily he pushed open his bedroom door. Instead of the familiar smell of pipe tobacco and old leather, the sweet scent of summer roses filled his nostrils. He took a deep breath. The housekeeper had done a good job airing the room.

Cade placed the lamp and the newspaper on the night table, then began to undress.

The heady fragrance nagged at him. It reminded him of something—or someone, but for the devil of him he couldn't remember who.

He closed his eyes and continued to unbutton his linen shirt. Taking another deep breath, Cade tried to recall what it was that taunted him about the scent. Then there she was—standing at the swirling edge of a remembered dream. Hair as black as night . . . skin like polished ivory . . .

''Damn!'' he silently cursed, his eyes snapping open. Jenny again. He remembered now. She had haunted his dreams last night. That was probably why she seemed to dog his thoughts all day.

He dropped his shirt onto the chair, then reached for the rumpled quilt on his bed. A soft moan brought him up short. His blue eyes narrowed as he watched the quilt shift in the dim lamplight.

Cade arched a dark brow. Another of Em's little jokes? It would be just like her to send one of her girls tonight. Anyone else would have more sense than to risk his anger. Well, he'd soon send Em's little prank on her way.

As his fingers touched the quilted cloth, he changed his mind. After the day he'd had, he could use a woman to warm his bed. And there was no question about it, Em's girls knew how to please a man. If nothing else, they could help him banish the lecherous thoughts he'd been having of Jenny all day. Hell, he'd even pay Em for the romp.

Cade reached for the lamp and turned the wick down, throwing the room in darkness. That was fine. He didn't even care who Em had sent. He knew most of them and there wasn't a one in the bunch he'd mind bedding. Besides, it might be more enjoyable trying to guess her identity once she lay in his arms.

Warming to the thought, Cade carefully pulled back the quilt and slid into the bed. It took all his willpower to refrain from taking the woman into his arms. But his body was cold and would only wake her. The game would be over before it even began. For now, he would enjoy the anonymity of his lover.

While he waited, he lay and listened to her gentle breathing, his body hardening from the nearness of her. Unable to resist, he leaned closer, thinking to identify her by the perfume that lingered in her hair, but all he could smell were roses.

Again the image of Jenny intruded. What was wrong with him? Was every woman to now remind him of his young housekeeper? Had it been that long since he'd had a woman? Well, he'd soon remedy that.

Cade reached out for the one beside him. True to her

profession, she made no protest. Instead, she nestled against him, her thin cotton gown the only thing that separated them.

"Damn her hide!" he cursed when he realized Em had dressed his companion as a shy bride. Despite his aggravation, he smiled wryly. He had to give Em credit. When she set out to get his goat, she did a thorough job. All he could hope for now was that Em had not instructed the girl to act the part of a shy bride. He was in no mood to deal with that particular charade tonight. He wanted a woman and he meant to have her.

With a surprising eagerness, Cade buried his face in her hair. He took a deep breath as he slid his hand down her slim back. Em hadn't sent Charlotte this time. This girl was much shorter.

His hand moved to her hip, tracing it up to a slim waist—much slimmer than most of Em's girls. With detached efficiency, he gently tugged at the gown that separated them. Hem in hand, he retraced his route back up her body, taking the gown with him.

Overcome by the strange new sensations that threatened to invade her dreams, Jenny offered no protest when her gown was drawn over her head for the familiar feel of the soft cotton material was quickly replaced with a seductive warmth of flesh touching flesh. Although determined never to marry, Jenny had always treasured her childhood dreams of castles and fairy tales. The gentle touch of a handsome prince was more than enough incentive to slip easily back into them.

The feel of her warm body next to his stirred an ache deep within Cade. This was going to be more pleasurable than he had at first thought. Odd, how darkness could heighten one's imagination.

Becoming bolder in his game, Cade cupped a firm, full breast. "Ah!" he groaned with both pleasure and frustration. These favorable attributes should have given him her identity. He must be a lot sleepier than he thought. Even a blind man would have remembered.

Delighted with what he'd found, Cade gently rubbed his thumb over the already taut nipple. She arched against him. There was no doubt she wanted more. Even in sleep, this little rosebud was quick to respond to a man's touch. Encouraged, he lowered his head to suckle the flower's sweet breast.

Although pleased to hear a soft moan escape her parted lips, Cade wasn't ready to give up this delightful game. He drew back, afraid he would wake her. Resting his hand on her hip, he waited for her to settle back into sleep. It took only a few moments until she gave a contented sigh and rolled away.

The innocent move tore a ragged breath from Cade's chest when she settled on her back, leaving his hand resting on the naked mound of her womanhood. No longer hampered by her gown, he trailed his fingers up, then down her slim body, taking note of each detail. But from the slender column of her neck to the silkiness of her thigh, she remained a mystery. Yet he could hardly blame his efforts. It was difficult to think about clues when his fingertips brushed her warm body.

He knew she was on the edge of sleep, but her instinctive response to his touch threatened to unleash his fragile restraint. Even now, an urgent need washed over him, warming him beyond belief. He had been without a woman too long. Despite his efforts to take it slow, desire flared, hot and demanding.

Her identity no longer mattered. She had been sent for his pleasure and game or no game, he meant to have her.

Balancing above her, he used his knee to ease her long legs apart. He was surprised, yet pleased she didn't waken when he settled between them. Normally he was not an indifferent lover and prided himself in helping his partner find pleasure in the coupling, but he had not invited the woman to his bed.

Telling himself Em's girls were used to almost anything did not ease aside the irritating twinge of conscience. Even though the woman would get paid for her compliance, he couldn't play the heartless cad.

His decision made, he covered her mouth with his. He had only meant to smother her surprise when he woke her, but the taste of her soft lips conjured up another image of Jenny.

Disgusted with himself, Cade purposely deepened the kiss. Let this little rose earn her price. He sure as hell needed something to take his mind off his young housekeeper.

Jenny fought to hold on to her dream even though something deep within her warned her she should waken. But how was she to relinquish the expert touch of her imaginary lover's hands as they wiped away the loneliness of the last few days. The languid warmth spreading through her legs seemed so real; the kiss, so seductive.

Jenny willingly returned it, her head filling with the primitive scent of horses and leather that bathed her lover's hard body. Never had her dreams of love and being loved been so vivid; the raw ache that gnawed at her, so demanding. Almost afraid she would wake, Jenny slowly eased her arms around his neck.

Suddenly he shifted his weight. "Hold on tight," he whispered before reclaiming her lips in a kiss.

Cold fear at the demanding pressure between her legs shattered Jenny's dream. She woke with a start. She was not alone. This was no dream. It was a nightmare. Desperately she struggled to breathe, screaming into the mouth that covered hers. She pushed against his naked chest, but her efforts only seemed to spur him on.

"Hush," he whispered against her swollen lips. "You'll wake everyone."

It was all the advantage she needed. With her last ounce of strength, Jenny bit down on his lip.

"What the—"

Cade raised up on his elbow and glared down at her. "Why did you do that?"

"Let me go, you—you wretched beast!" Jenny cursed as she struggled to get out from beneath him.

"Jenny?" he asked, confused that she was no longer the elusive image that had haunted him all day but a solid one in his bed.

Jenny pounded on his chest. "Who did you think it was?" she screamed up at him.

"You wouldn't care to know."

Careful not to take the quilt with him, Cade rolled over and sat up on the edge of the bed. He didn't say a word as he struck a match and tried to bring his emotions under control.

The glass chimney of the lamp was still hot and Cade welcomed the pain. It should have helped cool his ardor. The surprise of finding Jenny in his bed certainly hadn't.

He turned back to her. Her brown eyes, though wide with fright, stared accusingly up at him as if this were all his fault somehow.

"What are you doing in my bed?" he growled.

"Your bed?" she gasped, quickly averting her gaze from his bare arms and chest. Even though he no longer held her, the strange aching power of her dream still lingered. The taut nipples of her naked breast rubbed against the quilt.

Jenny swallowed the suffocating lump forming in her throat. Mr. Morgan was not the only one without clothes. When had she removed her nightdress? She studied Cade's cold blue eyes for an answer. Surely he hadn't . . . ?

Refusing to explore the possibility further, Jenny clutched the quilt to her as if it were a suit of armor. "This can't be your b—"

"It most definitely is my bed," he reiterated, glaring

down at her. The disbelief in her eyes brought a smile to his lips. "At least it was when I left this morning."

Still clutching the quilt, Jenny inched away from him. "No one was using this room. I checked the chiffonier and it was empty."

Cade smiled at the righteous indignation in her dark brown eyes. The urge to pull her into his arms was almost painful in its intensity.

"Had you bothered to check both chests, you would have found my things," he said.

Embarrassment painted Jenny's face with a soft pink that flowed with slow deliberation down the slender column of her neck to her bare shoulders. Cade found himself following the path, his memory supplying what his eyes could not see. A soft gasp at his boldness brought Cade's eyes back to hers. Anger—and fear—had darkened them to the color of bitter chocolate, but he could still taste the sweetness of her lips.

He would have apologized for the fear he saw in her eyes had he not also caught a glimpse of desire threaded within their dark brown depths. With a swift reach of his arms, Cade scooped her up, quilt and all, and pulled her to him.

"I thought to reserve the larger chiffonier—and my bed—for my wife," he said, his voice husky with renewed desire. "But if you've a mind to release those fiery passions of yours, I might consider sharing my room—and my bed—with you."

Jenny twisted wildly in his arms. "I don't want either. You can have the both of them. Just let me go you—you—"

Jenny suddenly stiffened. Her struggles had shifted the quilt and exposed her breasts to the dark blond hairs of his broad chest. She lay naked against him, tingling in the shocked realization that she ached for more.

Jenny's gaze flew to his. It was evident from the dark blue pools that he knew of her predicament. If she drew back now, could she trust him to look the other way?

A beguiling grin spread slowly across his full lips. "You didn't have to go to all this fuss, you know."

"Wh—"

He placed a kiss on the hollow of her neck. "If you were entertaining the notion of being my mail-order bride instead of my housekeeper, all you had to do was ask. It would be quite a pleasure to have you warm my bed."

She fought against the emotions that threatened to smother her. "Your bride?" she choked. "Warm your . . ." Had he discovered her deception so soon?

His lips moved to her ear. The soft whisper of passion made it difficult to keep in mind that his answer was so important. All she could think about were the seductive shivers that were racing through her body.

His hand boldly outlined her breast. "You have more than enough requirements to fill the position," he offered. "Besides, you wouldn't be the first woman whose head was turned by my money."

Outraged, Jenny kicked out of his grasp, but before she could reach the end of the bed, he caught her and pinned her body beneath his.

Jenny wished she could cut her heart out for its betraying response to his nearness. "You can warm your own bed," she said scathingly. "I'll be no man's bride, wealthy or not. I'd rather work the tar pits of hell than live under a man's thumb again!"

Cade propped himself up on one elbow and studied the naked bundle of anger beneath him. "Ah, then you're someone else's bride, Plain Jenny."

Plain! After all he had seen of her, he still thought her plain? The low-down, no-good . . . Jenny gritted her teeth. He made it so easy for her to slip back into her lies.

She shoved her face close to his. "Yes," she hissed, "and I slit his throat for touching me."

Jenny could have bit her tongue out when she saw the grin on his face.

"I take it that means you're no longer married," he teased.

"Married or not, it doesn't matter. If you don't get off me, you'll be the next to feel my knife's blade."

Despite her brave words, Cade could see the fear behind them. With a sigh of regret, he removed his hands from her shoulders and rolled away.

Jenny quickly scrambled off the bed and scooped up her cotton nightdress from the floor. Pulling it over her head, the gown drifted down over her like a cold icy cloud. She gasped as it settled around her warm body.

"Let me know when you have the knife," he said. "I'd like the chance to defend myself."

Jenny jumped at the solemn words. Mr. Morgan lay facing the ceiling, his intense blue eyes closed, giving her the privacy she needed to dress. As she stood watching, a hauntingly familiar aura skittered across the sharp angles of Morgan's tanned face. It came and went so quickly that had not she and her sister lived with their own brand of loneliness for so many years, she would have discounted it as being her imagination. Under other circumstances, Jenny would have felt sorry for the tall, handsome rancher, but not now. All she wanted to do was get away. "You'll have to wait a moment," she said as she skirted the big bed.

"Just my luck," he mumbled. "With all the bags you brought, it'll take you two days to find where you packed the silly thing."

"Please see that all my things get to Denver."

Cade opened his eyes and sat up. "What do you think you're doing?"

"I'm leaving."

"You can't leave now. It's the middle of the night."

"Watch me!"

Cade was at her side before she reached the door. "I know you're upset with me and I'm sorry." His eyes met hers. "Please believe me when I said I didn't know it was you in my bed."

"Let me pass," she said through clenched teeth.

Cade shook her. "It's too dangerous to be out alone on the road by yourself."

Jenny kept her gaze fixed determinedly on his. She'd be switched if she let a pair of broad shoulders, naked or not, set her heart to fluttering again.

"What's going to get me, Mr. Morgan? A mountain lion? Or merely a rancher who thinks I would do anything for his money?"

"I'm sorry," Cade repeated, ignoring the skepticism etched in the stubborn line of her slim jaw. "I promise you it won't happen again."

"You're right, Mr. Morgan. It won't. I'm leaving."

Cade pulled her over to the bed. "Sit!" he demanded.

Jenny's dark eyes narrowed. Obviously the bed did not dredge up any memories for him. "No!" she shouted back.

Cade wasn't sure which he wanted to do more, spank her or kiss her. "Don't be a child," he said instead. "I'm not going to ravish you. I merely want you to listen."

The sincerity of his words restirred her dream's caldron of emotions with a vengeance. Jenny took a shuddering breath at the tightness forming in her chest. "My ears work just as efficiently standing as sitting, Mr. Morgan."

Cade picked up the newspaper off the bedside table and shoved it at her. "Here. I hope it's true of your eyes as well."

He scooped up his clothes and walked to the door. Opening it, he turned back to her. "You may keep the room for now. I'll sleep in one of the others."

Before Jenny could gather her thoughts, he was out the door. She let her gaze drop to the newspaper.

Seventy-year-old Grandmother and Grandson Found Axed to Death on Farm Near Garo. Assailant Still at Large.

CHAPTER 4

The sound of voices from outside brought Jenny up out of the chair where she had spent most of the night reviewing her predicament. Stiff and sore, she walked to the window and pulled back the drapes. Mr. Morgan stood beside the buckboard, the early morning sun playing across the wavy strands of his thick blond hair.

She fought to cool the flush that quickly rose to her cheeks. Memories of what he had done to her were still too vivid. It was a shame cutting his throat was not an option after all. But she mustn't think of such things. Not now that common sense had raised its ugly head.

Jenny wished she could hear what Mr. Morgan was saying to the old man standing at the horses' heads. From the elegant cut of Cade's tailored coat to the small leather portmanteau he carried, it was evident he was planning on making a day of it.

Jenny breathed a sigh of relief. She would not be forced to face him this morning and tell him she had changed her mind about staying. Her temper boiled at the memory of what his skillful hands had done to her body, but she forced herself to bring it under control. Jenny might be mad as a hornet about his cavalier treatment of her, but she was no fool. Even if she didn't have Izzy to think about, with a maniac loose out there somewhere, this was not a good time to be striking out on your own.

If only she had allowed Albert to have his say when he had tried to tell her the room couldn't be hers, none of this would have happened. Even telling herself that the misunderstanding of the bedrooms was all her own doing did not alleviate the embarrassment that warred with her need for this position. Being stranded in a strange town without funds was not an experience she cared to repeat.

Jenny straightened her shoulders as Mr. Morgan tossed his bag onto the seat of the buckboard. Let the man and his skillful hands be hanged. Embarrassment was the least of her worries. She hadn't a cent to her name and there was a murderer out there somewhere. She had no intention of budging from a well-paying position until the fiend was caught. Her stubborn determination had gotten her this far. It would have to see her through with her plans. She couldn't disappoint Izzy.

In the meantime, she would continue to put Mr. Morgan's household in order as if last night had never happened. If her conscience still bothered her about cashing in the other train ticket by the time she was ready to leave, she would have him deduct the amount from her pay. She saw no reason to complicate matters further by confessing to him now.

Jenny went to the chiffonier and selected one of her more serviceable gowns. After quickly dressing, she left the room. Until she had actually begun cleaning yesterday, she hadn't realized how much was needed. For a man, Albert had done well. Unfortunately unless he thought something was absolutely necessary, he had tucked it away in one of the many unused rooms. Anything out of Albert's sight received little or no attention. It was soon evident that each closed door signified a haven of neglect.

She could well understand Mr. Morgan's need for a housekeeper. The condition of the front parlor alone justified the money he had paid for her services. It had taken all of yesterday afternoon just to move the furniture and beat the dust from the floral carpets. To allow such beautiful things to fall to rack and ruin was a waste she wouldn't tolerate. Mr. Morgan needed more than a housekeeper. He needed an entire cleaning staff. If he was so wealthy, why didn't he already have one? The fact that he might not want to spend his money on such things brought a smug grin to her lips. She would see that he got a staff worthy of his so-called wealth. Her smile broadened as she left the bedchamber. It would be one way she could repay him for the embarrassment he had caused her.

"Where was Mr. Morgan off to?" she asked Albert as she slid into her chair at the table.

Albert kept his eyes on the cup of coffee he was pouring. He had tried to stay awake last night, but had fallen asleep before Cade returned. Although he would give anything to learn what had happened once Cade discovered Miss Jenny in his bed, he couldn't dredge up the courage to ask.

He placed the coffee beside Jenny before answering. "Mr. Morgan. He left for Denver to check on his bride."

Jenny would need some time to carry out her scheme. "Denver, you say? Did he say when to expect him back?"

"Didn't rightly say, Miss Jenny, but Mr. Morgan's a busy man. Most times it's near two weeks before he gets back."

It was difficult for Jenny to contain her pleasure at the announcement. In two weeks she could easily hire an entire staff. If he had so much money, let him spend some. Perhaps she might even find another position for herself.

"Albert, could you please fetch me some paper and a pen and ink from Mr. Morgan's study? I want to print up a notice for you to take in to Gold Shoe for me. Then tell Cook I'll have a couple of her biscuits for breakfast this morning."

While he hurried off to get the items, Jenny reviewed what the notice should say. From what she had seen of Gold Shoe, it wasn't very large, but if she made the positions sound appealing enough, perhaps she could entice one or two good workers. Jenny might want to get even with Mr. Morgan, but she wasn't about to be totally heartless in obtaining her small token of revenge. After all, he would be getting his house put in order.

By the time Albert returned, she had settled on a few brief words. *Position open at Trinity Ranch for hardworking young woman* she wrote on the first piece of paper. She studied it a moment, then changed *hardworking young woman* to *aggressive and imaginative young woman*.

Satisfaction carved a smile on her face as she studied the changes. She was pleased with the cleverness of her wording. The woman would need to be aggressive to take on the monumental task of neglect. The applicant's imaginative qualities would provide the woman's touch that was essential to do the work without pointing out the over-whelming amount of work required.

As quickly as her smile had formed, it suddenly turned down in a frown. The handbill needed something else. Unmindful of the ink, she tapped the pen impatiently against the page. She needed something to provide that little extra incentive to entice the applicant. Something to . . .

"Ah, that's it!" she said aloud. With confidence, she added, *Possibility of bonus to someone willing to put in the late hours to please a fair employer. Apply at 10 A.M. sharp Monday morning.*

Finally satisfied with the notice, Jenny copied out five more. It wasn't until she finished that she noticed the odd-looking biscuits Albert had brought. Under the thin layer of sticky icing, the dough appeared to have been fried a golden brown. Using a tine of her fork, Jenny broke off a piece and sampled the treat. Ah . . . Millie had certainly outdone herself this time. The spicy cinnamon and moist chunks of apple in the sweet dough provided just the right touch. Mr. Morgan had found a real treasure in his cook. Jenny certainly hoped he was more cognizant of the fact than her father would have been. If he wasn't, Jenny would make every effort to take Millie with her when she left.

Having finished, Jenny stacked her empty plate and cup on the tray next to the coffee urn while she quickly went over her morning duties. She was relieved that changing rooms was not necessary for a few days. It wouldn't take much imagination on Albert's part to guess Mr. Morgan had returned and found her in his bed. The embarrassment of it all would have been even harder to bear than swallowing her pride and admitting her error to Albert. Even the thought set Jenny's cheeks to burning.

Fate was certainly not looking kindly on her efforts of late. She would just have to work harder to change her luck. Distributing the handbills would be her first step.

Picking up the tray of dirty dishes, Jenny turned and eased open the kitchen door with her shoulder. Millie stood at the far counter, setting out her supper bread to rise when Albert reached for one of the pieces of fried bread.

"No!" Millie admonished with a sweep of her hand. Flour flew everywhere.

"Now see what you've made me do," she scolded.

"I'm sorry, Millie." He turned pleading eyes on the tall woman. "Just one more?"

"All right. One more, but that's all. You keep this up and you'll be as fat as that old banty rooster you keep hiding from my pot."

Albert stiffened. "Clarence is a pet. He's like one of the family."

"He's no family of mine," Millie said, her face darkening. "And the next time that overstuffed little runt of a rooster keeps me from collecting my eggs, he'll be roastin' atop my fire."

"I told you, I'd collect the eggs."

"I like to do my own work, Albert Miller," she said solemnly. "You just keep him out of my way."

"Clarence doesn't mean no harm, Millie, and you know it. His missus is sittin' on a batch of eggs back in that hay. He was protectin' his own," he added with a note of pride.

"Ha!" Millie snorted. "That dumb rooster hasn't fathered a chick yet. It'll be just like all the other times. He struts around like he's the top stud on this ranch and every last one of those chicks when they get their feathers will be as white as the snow." She paused to catch her breath. "I tell you none of those hens will have a thing to do with that prissy little pet of yours."

Jenny watched Albert's prideful stance deflate. For a moment she thought the little man was going to cry.

"It sounds as if Clarence makes an excellent protector for the chickens, Albert," Jenny offered.

"Tell that to the butcher here," he huffed before stomping out of the kitchen.

Millie took the tray from Jenny and sat it on the counter next to the wash pan. "Don't pay him no mind, Miss Jenny."

"But he looked so upset when you said you'd be cooking his pet."

Millie smiled. "That old bird wouldn't be worth the effort it would take to pluck it."

"Then why did you say you would kill it?"

Millie gave Jenny a broad wink. "It's the only way I can get a spark of passion out of that old man." Millie placed her hands on her hips. "I've been trying to get him to take notice of me for nigh on nine years now, but the only thing he seems to care about is that confounded chicken."

Jenny had seen the looks Albert gave Millie. "I think Albert likes you a great deal. He's just a bit shy."

"Well, he'd best be getting over that," she scoffed. "I'll be thirty soon and a woman can't wait around forever."

You're wrong, Jenny thought. A woman can wait forever.

* * *

The wind, racing down the hillside in wild abandonment, expelled an icy breath of crisp mountain air. Even though the handbills Jenny had carefully penned were tucked safely inside Albert's shirt, Albert was glad to have finally arrived in Gold Shoe. He didn't know why Miss Jenny had insisted he come all the way to Gold Shoe to tack up the notices. Fairplay would have been a whole lot closer, but after the little speech she'd given him the last time he'd tried to correct her, he wasn't about to point that out.

He dismounted, tied his horse to the hitching post, then pulled one of the handbills from his shirt. He had no more than nailed the notice to the post in front of the station when the wind whipped it away.

"What's this you're putting up?"

Albert looked up to find the stationmaster approaching, the wayward paper clasped firmly in his hands. Albert reached for it. "Thanks," he offered begrudgingly. Albert didn't care much for the man.

Carl stood over his shoulder reading while Albert renailed the handbill.

"Well, well, Cade lookin' to hire some woman, is he?"

Albert turned and glared at the stationmaster. "This is the new housekeeper's doin', not Mr. Morgan's."

"Would that be that pretty little lady that arrived night before last?"

Albert didn't like the sneer that crossed the man's face when he mentioned Miss Jenny. After all, Miss Jenny was a lady—and she had defended Clarence. "That was her and right nice she is too. Knows what's important. She'll do a fine job puttin' the place in order."

"I bet she will," Carl said, chuckling. Seeing his chance to discredit the wealthy rancher, he suddenly sobered. "A shame Mr. Morgan was so rough on her the night she arrived. After the beating he gave her, he and Bear had to hold her on to the carriage seat. Poor little thing couldn't sit up on her own.''

Albert could feel the hate ooze from the man. ''Never known Mr. Morgan to hurt anyone lessen they deserved it,'' he said, tempering the words that had first come to mind. He didn't want to call the man a liar for he had noticed the black eye himself and wondered what had happened to cause it. He would have asked Cade himself if he hadn't already been so upset with him for bringing Bear home.

Carl smiled at the doubt he saw in Albert's face. Cade's men were known for their loyalties and it tickled his fancy to put a crease in it. ''Don't feel bad, Albert. Up until now, I believed Cade was a gentleman too. Guess all those rumors about him must be true.''

Albert's gray eyes narrowed suspiciously. ''All what rumors?'' he asked.

''Heard tell the new housekeeper wasn't the first. Word up at Em's place is he's real rough on the ladies. Near beat one to death only last week.''

Albert had often wondered at Cade's friendship with Em. Cade was a man who didn't have to pay for a woman, yet he knew Em and Cade were best of friends.

''I'd best be goin'. Got a lot more notices to put up.''

He pushed past Carl, untied his horse, and walked away. If Cade's friendship with Em was causing all these rumors, it was high time the man was married. It was a pure shame Cade's mail-order bride failed to show. A good woman would soon put an end to the friendship.

Before Albert knew it, he found himself outside Em's place. He tied his horse at the empty hitching post. Then in a rare display of courage, he stomped up the steps to the front door. He'd ask Em about the rumors. His knuckles had almost touched wood when the front door opened. Albert swallowed the hard, dry lump in his throat.

''Mornin', Miss Em,'' he offered politely, not quite sure what was the proper address for a madam.

Em smiled at his manners. "Most men that come to my door only want one thing. To hell with the manners. Lord, it's good to lay my eyes on a gentleman."

"I . . ." Albert blushed beet-red when she placed her fingers on the front of his shirt. "I came . . ." he tried again.

Em heard papers crinkle inside his shirt. Darn paper money. She much preferred gold. "Land's sakes, man, spit it out. Heaven only knows this time of morning there aren't too many of my girls to choose from."

Albert choked on his surprise. "I didn't mean . . . I mean . . . no I don't," he stumbled over the words.

"None of them do, love. Now which one do you have a longing for. Not the new redhead. You couldn't afford her price. And you can't have Lulabell. Doc says she's to lay off the trade until her ribs heal, but then everyone knows about that." Em lowered her voice and mumbled. "That big—"

Albert's heart fell as he waited for the words that would condemn Cade for a woman beater. He was so caught up in his expectations that it took him a moment to realize that Em was unbuttoning his shirt. He quickly stepped back.

"Well, hand it over," she demanded. "I can't be standing out in this cold wind all day. If you can't decide which girl you'll be wantin', I'll have Mitzy take care of you. She's one of my most experienced."

Albert grabbed for the notices she had pulled from his shirt, but Em managed to hold them just out of his reach.

Albert could see things were quickly getting out of his control. "I didn't come for no . . ." he shouted, then lowered his voice to a whisper, "you know . . . no . . ."

"Know what, Albert?" she insisted.

"I didn't come to be bedded," he whispered, frantically searching the street to see who might be listening.

Em tossed a thick chestnut curl back off her shoulder as she scanned the neatly penned notice. "Then what did you come for?"

The collar on Albert's shirt threatened to choke him. The little amount of courage he had quickly fled under Em's scrutiny.

"I shouldn't have bothered you, Miss Em. I only thought to tack up one of the notices outside your place," he lied.

Em thoughtfully perused the handbill. "Cade thinking of hiring one of my girls away?" she asked.

"Oh, no, Miss Em," Albert quickly answered. He knew his soul was hovering on hell's abyss, but he couldn't for the life of him whip up the courage to tell her he'd come to find out if Cade was beating her girls. "We'll be lookin' for some help at the ranch and I thought you might know of someone who would be needin' the work."

Em grinned at his embarrassment. "You saying Cade wants me to find a girl to be cleaning that big fancy house of his?"

If the suspicious light growing in Miss Em's eye was any clue, Albert was in real trouble. "No, ma'am," he hurried to say. "I just thought I'd stop by and see if you knew of anyone." Albert took a moment to wipe the beads of sweat forming on his brow. "No need to mention to Cade I was here, Miss Em."

"No reason at all," she assured him.

Contrary to what she might say, Albert could tell by the grin on her face, she was hatching a plan. If Cade ever found out, Albert's life wouldn't be worth turkey spit. He still had the rest of the handbills to tack up. He could almost picture the gleam in Miss Em's eyes when she saw them. If Albert knew what was good for him, he'd tear up the other three and toss the pieces to the wind. But Albert had always prided himself in being an honest man and knew he couldn't face Miss Jenny if he did. With a heavy heart, he went back down the steps and climbed onto his horse.

No, he'd post one up in front of the stables, then take the last two handbills and tack them up in Fairplay. Jenny might be a little put out with him, but at least they would be posted. Besides, she had a better chance of getting someone from Fairplay.

Jenny looked along the long line of occupied chairs Albert had set up in the foyer for the prospective maids. She checked the watch pinned to the front of her blouse. It was twenty minutes before ten and already there were over twelve women who had answered her handbills.

If this kept up, she would be interviewing all day. To make matters worse, Albert appeared to have developed a nervous twitch about his left eye with the arrival of the applicants. She had to admit the steady stream of carriages had unnerved her also. She hadn't realized so many women would apply. Jenny frowned. It was obvious from the richness of most of the women's clothing, they had suddenly fallen on hard times. The West was proving to be a strange place. In all the years she had managed her father's household, never had the servants applied wearing such finery.

"I suppose I should go ahead and start the interviews," she whispered aside to Albert.

The little man had grown suddenly pale. "No sense in you doin' all the work, Miss Jenny. Let me take a few for you."

"Nonsense. I've always interviewed my own staff. Now bring the first one into the study."

Albert seemed to wilt before her very eyes. She hadn't meant to hurt his feelings. Perhaps she was changing things too quickly. "I promise not to hire any of them until I've talked with you, Albert."

That seemed to brighten him up a bit and he sent in the first applicant. She was tall and thin—actually somewhat pretty in a rather pale sort of way. Unfortunately, she looked more in need of a cleaning than Mr. Morgan's house.

Jenny offered the woman one of the brown leather chairs

before taking her own behind the desk. "Tell me," she began, "what experience have you had, Mrs. . . ."

"Miss Thomas, ma'am," she said as she raised one bosom to give her rib a healthy scratch, then let it drop. She gave a weary sigh before continuing, "Never did get married. Never seemed to be enough time. Bore thirteen young uns for the good reverend down by Manitou, I did. None of them lived though. Buried the last of them a week after their father. Heard they was hirin' able bodies up this way and thought I'd give it a try."

She paused for another scratch, then gave Jenny a broad wink. "Don't reckon there are any more able bodies than mine."

Jenny stared in fascination. "I'm sorry for your loss," she finally managed to say. "It must have been very painful for you. But while I can see you're more than qualified for having children, I need someone who can clean."

Miss Thomas drew her shoulders back in indignation. "Clean!" she shouted. "I didn't come to clean no messes."

Jenny arched a dark brow. "Then why did you come?"

"I heard Mr. Morgan was trying to buy himself a wife."

"B-buy himself a w-wife," Jenny choked out. Was it common knowledge that Cade was seeking a mail-order bride? The woman made it sound so crass, yet wasn't that what it all boiled down to? She had almost sold herself to the man.

"Yeah, ain't it something. Imagine that. Me, one of them mail-order brides." Miss Thomas smiled smugly. "Thought it over and decided I'd just come on along and save Mr. Morgan the trouble of shippin' one from back East."

Jenny stood. She could feel her cheeks growing warm. "I can see there's been some mistake," she replied evenly despite the knot forming in her stomach. "Mr. Morgan handles his own interviews. You will have to make your appointment with him."

Miss Thomas took her time rising from the chair. "Don't

you think you should ask Mr. Morgan. He won't be pleased to hear you turned away a good breeder like me,'' she said as she bestowed Jenny with a tight smile. "The good reverend, God rest his soul, would be the first to tell you I know how to please my men.'' She punctuated her words with another scratch.

Embarrassment quickly turned to anger at the woman's bold assumption that Mr. Morgan was available for the indiscriminate plucking by anyone who came along.

"Miss Thomas,'' Jenny began, "after conceiving thirteen of your own, I don't doubt one bit your capabilities of pleasing *your men,* but I think I can speak with confidence when I say Mr. Morgan is looking for a wife who will give him a fine brood of healthy children without a crop of lice.''

Having finished, she walked to the door and held it open. "Good day, Miss Thomas.''

"Well, I never . . .''

Jenny's brown eyes darkened. "Obviously a lie, Miss Thomas. You yourself have admitted to at least thirteen occasions. Now if you'll excuse me, I have several more people to interview.''

After the woman left, Jenny remained standing in the doorway, baffled by her unusual display of unprofessional behavior. Her anger had been inappropriate and she knew it. It wasn't the woman's fault Mr. Morgan had decided to obtain a bride with no more thought than ordering a pattern from a dress catalog. The man certainly deserved to get anything that came along.

Jenny motioned to Albert who was standing patiently beside the next applicant. "Have the two chairs Miss Thomas sat in removed and taken out back,'' she whispered when he was close. "I'm afraid she left us several unwelcome reminders of her visit. Have the chairs washed down thoroughly with kerosene.''

Albert nodded, then stepped past her to get the one out of

the study. ''Drown them if you have to,'' she added before turning back to the old woman who was next.

''Come along,'' Jenny said, pleased that Albert had thought to use the other door of the study that led to the back hall. Mr. Morgan may not suffer any qualms about airing personal matters to all of Colorado, but she would not be responsible for adding any additional unpleasant rumors to an already overproductive grapevine.

Although Jenny had not planned to hire someone quite so old, the woman seemed more than qualified—and clean. After Miss Thomas, she was quickly hired and asked to wait outside until Jenny had spoken with the others.

A tall, willowy woman was next. Jenny tried to be polite and not stare, but the woman's beauty made it very difficult. She had ebony hair and dark-lashed blue eyes. If it hadn't been for the two rosy spots on her cheeks and lips painted a bright red, her white face would have appeared to have been carved from marble. But it was the dress Jenny found hard to ignore. A shimmering indigo-blue, it clung with a provocative grace to each curve of the woman's slim body.

She must not let the woman's manner of dress influence her decision, yet she couldn't help but think that having a maid this attractive would be a mistake. There was always Cade to think about.

CHAPTER 5

Cade gazed out the train window and lazily watched the early morning workers scurry about the platform as the train pulled out of Denver. He had spent the entire last five days trying to concentrate on his work. Even with all the things that demanded his attention, he could think of nothing but Jenny.

She would be gone by now. Finding her in his bed had been unfortunate. Joining her had been a mistake. But letting her leave—that was criminal.

Every time he closed his eyes his thoughts drifted back to that night. The whisper of breath against his chest. The silken feel of her warm body under his exploring hands. While he wasn't in the habit of seducing those in his employ, the fact that he had not tried to get Jenny to stay would haunt him for days to come.

"You're certainly losing your touch, old man," he said to himself, continuing to let the memory of heated passions wash over him. So strong was the vision materializing within his mind he could almost catch the spicy scent of roses woven through the silken strands of her black hair.

Cade was not one to dwell on fantasies of past liaisons, but Jenny seemed to constantly linger at the edge of his thoughts.

The train rushed up the mountainside and Cade settled back in his seat. Perhaps that was where the problem lie. Jenny had not been his lover. She had merely kindled the fires, then left them to burn without quenching his primitive thirst.

Damn Em and her jokes. If not for her, Cade would not have crawled into bed with his housekeeper. His mouth would not have tasted Jenny's lips only to hunger for more. His fingers would not know the silken touch of her smooth thigh, nor the feel of her firm, full breasts.

Unable to handle the bitter emptiness suddenly growing inside him, Cade shoved the memory aside. Despite the empty hole it left inside him, Cade soon found himself smiling. It was ironic. Em always tried so hard to get his goat and now, without lifting a finger, she had managed to pull off her best joke ever and she didn't even know it. He could almost see the look on her face if she ever found out.

Thank goodness he and Jenny were the only ones to know of his blunder. From her embarrassment, he was fairly certain Jenny wouldn't tell anyone and he sure as hell wasn't going to mention it himself. Keeping his pride intact was too important to him. Letitia had shattered it once. He wouldn't give a woman the opportunity to do it again.

He had worked hard to earn not only the wealth he had accumulated but the respect of his neighbors and business associates. Em was one of his few friends who knew what had happened. Although she was constantly telling him that holding on to the hate would only blacken his heart, Em never betrayed his secret. What she didn't know was that it was too late. The edges of his heart had turned to stone ages ago. It no longer had the capacity to hurt—or to heal.

The only thing that mattered to him now was his ranch and his investments. Making sure they were successful was a challenge he was willing to meet. Em might nag at him for being so serious about everything, but at least he was in control of his life. This way no one else had the power to hurt or humiliate him. It was one of the reasons he had elected to select his bride the way he had. When respect meant more than love, Cade didn't need to waste his valuable time playing the games men needed to play to woo a woman. Like with most of his business ventures, he elected to hire to have the work done and Miss Emily's Positions For Young Ladies had assured him they would have no trouble finding a woman to fit his qualifications.

Someone tapped him on the shoulder. "You going to be getting off here, Mr. Morgan?"

Cade looked out the window in surprise. Gold Shoe. He couldn't believe they'd come over Kenosha Pass and he hadn't noticed. He grabbed his satchel of papers and left the train. His bag of clothes was waiting for him when he stepped down. He leaned down to pick it up when a man placed his polished leather boot on the bag. Cade looked up to find Carl smiling at him.

Cade opened his mouth to tell the man to remove his damn foot when Carl shoved a paper at him.

"You want me to toss this notice now that Monday is here?"

Cade reached for the paper but Carl pulled it away. "Albert posted them last week," Carl said, watching the puzzlement grow in Cade's eyes. He had guessed right. This was the first Cade knew of the handbills. "Em got one too," he added with feigned innocence. "Want me to collect it for you?"

Carl's attitude was beginning to irritate him, but Cade kept his own features carefully schooled. Why would Albert post a notice, much less one at Em's place.

Even without reading the words, Cade knew he wasn't going to like what was written on the paper. The sly smile on Carl's thin lips said as much.

"It would appear to me that if Albert hung the notices, you should be asking him, not me."

Carl wiped his watery blue eyes on a soiled handkerchief. "Thought about that, but he said that housekeeper of yours has been keeping him mighty busy."

His housekeeper? Hadn't Jenny left? Cade plucked the paper from Carl's fingers. "Thanks for looking after it," he said as he folded the paper without reading it. Once he had the notice tucked safely in his breast pocket, Cade pulled his bag from beneath the stationmaster's boot, tipped his hat, and left the station.

It was hard not to smile when Carl's grin faded in disappointment that Cade had left without reading the notice. Cade had known for a long time that the man harbored a heart full of hate where he was concerned. Damned if he knew why.

At one point in his life, he would have cared. Odd how his brother had taken that from him. Cade stopped dead. Would he someday become like his brother? Never caring how what he did affected others? It was a sobering thought.

Cade started walking again. When had he become so absorbed in his own affairs that he overlooked the needs of others? Even his cavalier treatment of Jenny had been uncalled for. He certainly owed her an apology for his ungentlemanlylike behavior. Having made the decision to do just that when he got back to the ranch, Cade pulled the notice from his pocket and read it.

It was plain from the advertisement, Jenny had changed her mind about staying, but why the vague advertisement about a maid? What did the fool woman think she was doing? It sounded more like Trinity Ranch was seeking a mistress than a maid. Cade's blue eyes narrowed.

If Carl was right and Em did have a copy of this notice . . .

Puzzlement quickly turned to anger when he realized what everyone would make of this. Cade would be a laughingstock for miles around and that's the one thing Cade wouldn't tolerate. To hell with apologies. Jenny would have to go.

By the time he reached the stables to retrieve his horses and buggy, Cade was barely civil to those who nodded a hello. From the smirks on their faces, it was evident everyone knew about the handbill. It must have made a good story in the telling, he bitterly surmised.

Jenny had said she would get even. Well, she had succeeded. He stepped up his pace. He couldn't wait to get his hands around her pretty little neck.

Normally the old man who ran the stables chatted with Cade as he hitched up the horses to Cade's buggy, but today Jake was unusually quiet. Cade knew the old man to be fond of gossip. If anyone knew how folks were interpreting the handbills, it would be Jake. His uncustomary silence was unsettling to Cade's already taut nerves.

"You might as well spit it out, Jake. That frown of yours is liable to crack your jaw if you hold on to it much longer."

Jake spun around on the heels of his boots. "Mr. Morgan," he said, his frown deepening, "always thought you were a gentleman. I'm real disappointed in you. Real disappointed. I've seen a lot of things in my lifetime, but what you're a tryin' to do beats everything."

It took all Cade's efforts to remain calm. "What is it you think I've done, Jake?" he asked, his voice deadly calm.

Jake threw back his shoulders. "I heared what you done to that nice little lady that came all this way to be your bride."

"Miss Fairchild?" he asked. Had she come to Gold Shoe after all?

"Can't say as I heared her name," Jake mumbled half to himself as he opened the stall for Cade's horses.

"Where is she?"

Jake stared at him as if he were some monster destined

for hell. "Don't you remember where you put her after you beat her plumb silly?"

"Beat her? What are you talking about?"

Jake paused in his harnessing of the horses and cocked his head warily at Cade. "Word is she changed her mind about marrying you. Decided Em's place was more to her liking." Jake fixed a critical eye on Cade. "Folks say you beat her bad when you fetched her back."

"Fetched her back? Why I've yet to see her. Miss Fairchild never arrived."

"Carl said she did. Right pretty she was too. Said she—"

"Carl said I beat Miss Fairchild?" They meant Jenny, of course. He didn't know why he had not anticipated the error. Within hours of sending the telegram to place the order for his bride, the entire town had known. No one remembered that he had ordered a housekeeper as well. He supposed it was easier to picture Jenny as a bride. He himself had made the same mistake. "She wasn't my bride, Jake. She was my new housekeeper."

"You beat your housekeeper?"

"No, I didn't beat anyone. Let's just say she happened to be standing in the wrong place when someone swung a club at a claim jumper."

Jake straightened from hitching the horses to the buggy. The furrow in his brow deepened. "Then why is she trying to hire someone to take her place in your bed?"

"Wh-hat?" Cade nearly choked in his surprise.

"Yup. Put up notices everywhere. Even posted one outside Em's place. Offered a bonus to anyone who could satisfy you."

It was even worse than he imagined. "Is that what everyone thinks?"

Jake waved his hand. "You can read it for yourself. One's out front. Albert put it there last week."

Cade strode to the door and tore the handbill from its nail. He could feel Jake's eyes on him as he read the paper. It was the same notice all right, but he had hoped everyone wouldn't interpret it this way. But then he knew the truth. No one else did. Colored as it had been with Carl's story of Jenny's black eye and torn jacket, why wouldn't they expect the worst?

Cade climbed into the buggy and picked up the reins. "You can tell anyone who's interested that I'm hiring a maid and nothing else. If they want the job, they're more than welcome to apply."

A quick flick of the reins started the horses for home. Cade didn't look back. He'd said his piece. Everyone would soon learn the truth.

As soon as he reached the ranch, he'd send Jenny packing. If this was how the agency screened their applicants, he could do as well running an ad in the papers back East himself. He'd insist on a photograph. A mature woman was what was needed for the position, not some delectable little . . .

Cade shoved the image aside. "No more of that," he said between clenched teeth. "You're acting like some schoolboy still wet behind the ears."

It wasn't often someone got the best of him and it didn't set well with Cade. Bent on telling Jenny a thing or two before he put her on the train back to St. Louis, he let his anger build all the way home.

The row of fancy carriages in front of his house only confirmed his fears. Em had sent her girls. There must have been ten hired hands holding the heads of the horses. Ignoring their broad grins, Cade tossed the reins of his horses to Sam and stomped up to the house.

He opened the door and stepped into the foyer. His worst fears were realized. At least seven of Em's girls were seated around the room.

Seeing Cade, they sat up straight and waved.

"Hello-o, Cade," one of them cooed.

"Where is she?" he shouted across the crowded room at

Albert. Some part of him wondered at his unusual lack of self-control, but the part that wanted to wring her pretty little neck had too powerful a grip on him. "Where is she?" he shouted again when Albert didn't answer.

Albert lifted a pale, shaky hand and pointed to Cade's study.

While her applicant's manner of dress seemed inappropriate, Jenny rather liked the tall attractive woman. Lil Hayden seemed most willing to work. If Albert agreed, Jenny would hire her.

"The work is hard, Miss Hayden," Jenny warned for the third time. "I must have someone who will obey without question. Mr. Morgan is a very demanding em-employer," Jenny said, stumbling over the memory of kisses, hot and enticing.

The annoying pink flush that came readily to her face blanched white when the study door burst open. Cade's broad shoulders filled the doorway, anger etched in every line of his tall frame. Jenny opened her mouth but couldn't seem to form the words past the lump in her throat.

Miss Hayden appeared to have no such difficulty for she immediately stood and extended her gloved hand to Mr. Morgan. "Good morning, Cade."

While Jenny watched in awe the woman stepped closer and laid her silk-clad body next to his. Throwing her head back, the woman glanced up at him and pursed her red lips in a seductive pout.

"Cade knows I'm very good at what I do."

Jenny felt her insides twist in brittle knots when the woman ran a polished nail down the front of Mr. Morgan's tailored jacket.

"The more demanding Cade is, the better I like it," the woman added, batting her long dark lashes up at him. "Isn't that right, Cade?"

He didn't answer Miss Hayden, but Jenny could see a fire flicker in his blue eyes.

Jenny wasn't sure if he blushed under his dark tan or not. She didn't care. All she could see was the woman crawling into Cade's bed, her white sensuous body lying next to his. His fingers trailing down—

The knots inside Jenny tightened. Her brown eyes darkened. She'd have none of that nonsense going on in her house!

In a few short steps, Jenny was beside the woman. With a quickness that surprised even her, Jenny took Miss Hayden firmly by her arm and pulled her through the study door.

"I'll send Albert after you if I find we need your services, Miss Hayden."

Lil looked back at Cade. "You know where to find me," she said. "I'll be expecting you."

Jenny didn't wait for Mr. Morgan's reply but gave Lil's arm another tug. At the giggles from the others in the foyer, Jenny stopped. Her eyes quickly scanned the filled seats. Other than the old lady already interviewed tucked in the corner at the far end, all the women were dressed in much the same manner as that of Miss Hayden.

Well, if that didn't beat all. Every last one of them were looking past her to the study, coy smiles wreathing their red mouths. A quick glance at Mr. Morgan's uneasiness told her he knew them also. His evident embarrassment was almost enough to hire them all. Almost, but Miss Hayden's boldness spoke volumes on the stupidity of such a foolhardy decision.

Jenny let Miss Hayden's arm drop. "Thank you all for coming," she said sweetly, "but the position has been filled."

"Filled? By whom?" they asked in unison.

Lil plucked at the silk flower on her shoulder. "By me," she announced. "Isn't that right, Cade?"

Cade, whose anger had quickly cooled upon seeing the unexpected jealousy flare in Jenny's eyes, coated his words with ice. "The decision is up to my housekeeper. After all, the maid will be working solely with her."

"With her!" Lil shrieked. "The notice said I was to satisfy you, not some . . . some . . ." Lil stiffened. "I'll have you know I'm not that kind of woman."

After all the trouble Jenny had caused him with her handbill, Cade was sorely tempted to leave it at that, but he was afraid the gossip it would cause would only come back to haunt him.

"Lil," he said, keeping an eye on Jenny, "I doubt you would enjoy the dusting and cleaning that is required of a maid."

"D-dusting? And c-cleaning?" Lil sputtered. "Em said you wanted someone to warm your bed, not haul out your coals."

Cade could see the confusion in Jenny's brown eyes beginning to clear. He hoped the blush painting her cheeks would keep her mouth shut until he got rid of Lil and the others. "Em was wrong," he stated flatly.

"Well, who in hell wants to dust and clean?"

"The maid, Lil," he pointed out. "The one advertised for in the handbill."

"You wanted that kind of maid? An honest-to-goodness working maid?"

"That was the reason for the notice."

"But the notice said—" Lil paused, her blue eyes suddenly narrowing to angry slits. "You did this on purpose, Cade Morgan, didn't you? You lured us all out here making us think we had a chance at pleasing you— maybe even marrying you. Well, you may be good in bed—one of the best I've had—but I don't do housewifely things for any man. Not even you."

Lil turned to the other women. "Let's go, girls. There's

easier money to be made at Em's and you don't have to get off your backside to do it.''

Everyone filed out the front door, but the old woman in the corner. Cade waited for Jenny to speak. When she finally lifted her eyes to him, he wasn't prepared for the shock in them.

"They thought . . .'' Jenny paused, unable to put into words the horror she felt.

"They certainly did.'' Cade tried to keep a stern face but was unsuccessful. "What did you expect they would think when you worded the notice the way you did?''

"Do not laugh at me,'' she said. "I meant it as an incentive for being a good maid, not a good—''

"Whore?'' he asked, the dimple on his cheek deepening.

At his vile word, Jenny could feel a blush warm her face. "Fallen woman!'' Jenny corrected him.

The corner of Cade's lips twitched in amusement. "I admire your spiritual generosity,'' he said. "To most women, a whore is a whore. To hell with the circumstances.''

"When you come to know me better, Mr. Morgan, you will find that I am not like most women.''

"I've already discovered that, Plain Jenny, and I was most pleasantly surprised.''

"I wish you wouldn't call me that,'' she chose to say. It was best to ignore his attempt to embarrass her over finding her in his bed.

"You're right of course.'' He reached out and touched her cheek. "You're anything but plain.''

Jenny stepped back as if his touch had burned her. "Mr. Morgan!''

"Cade.''

"I cannot call you Cade.''

"Why not?''

Jenny's fingers combed through the gathers of her skirt. She needed this job and she wasn't going to allow him to frighten her. "Even if you were not my employer, Mr. Morgan, it would be unseemly to be so familiar. After all, I hardly know you."

"You forget, Jenny. You know me more intimately then most."

"Most of whom?" she asked, her words clipped and cold. "Those women that were just here, vying for a position in your bed? I know nothing of you, Mr. Morgan, and I prefer to keep it that way."

Cade stepped closer. "Ah, but surely you haven't forgotten."

Jenny leaned back and boldly looked up into his ice-blue eyes. "I remember nothing," she stated.

Cade loved the way she stood up to him. It had been a long time since anyone had. His wealth and cold looks intimidated most people. If the bittersweet darkness of Jenny's brown eyes was any indication, neither had any effect on her.

"I remember everything," he countered.

The huskiness of his voice sent an odd tingle curling its way up her back. Jenny took a deep breath. She'd not let him upset her.

"That is your problem, Mr. Morgan, not mine," she said. "I, myself, have no difficulty in putting unpleasant memories behind me."

"Perhaps mine were not as unpleasant as yours."

Although he didn't touch her, the silkiness of his words stroked her body more powerfully than if he had.

Jenny acknowledged her lie—to herself, if not to him. She may have thought at the time he was a part of her dream, but she remembered everything he had painted with his touch. The ache—and the fire. Even the kiss that had finally woken her was burned forever in her mind, tattooed next to her heart. A reminder that some emotions were not to be trusted. She was a woman determined to have a life of her own. She'd not let the lure of a handsome set of broad shoulders sway her goals.

"Mr. Morgan—"

"Do you intend to stay, Plain Jenny?"

His words were cold, clipped. "I asked you not to call me that," she said, matching her tone with his.

"I'll call you that as long as you call me Mr. Morgan," he stated matter-of-factly. "But you haven't answered my question. Do you intend to stay on as my housekeeper?"

Jenny straightened her shoulders defiantly. "I accepted this position, Mr. Morgan. I need the money, therefore I intend to see it out."

"Then, as an employee, you should honor your employer's requests."

Jenny's brown eyes narrowed. "I'm aware of the duties of my position Mr. Morgan. You'll have no reason to complain."

Cade wasn't sure why he wanted her to call him Cade. He really didn't care one way or the other, he told himself. It was only because she stubbornly fought him on it every step of the way that he was making an issue of it. He merely wanted to hear it on her lips.

"I'll make a deal with you, *Jenny*," he said. "You call me Cade and I'll pay you an extra dollar a month wages. That should be more than enough to soothe your sensibilities."

Soothe her sensibilities indeed! She wasn't even sure if he had bothered to hide his sarcasm, she would have believed him. There weren't many men she trusted. They always had such a way of dumping anything ladylike in a box and labeling it silly. She would have liked to be able to tell him she'd take a dollar less if he stayed out of her way, but money was money and she'd need all she could get her hands on if she was ever to earn enough to send for Izzy.

Jenny studied him for a moment longer. Perhaps there was another way to fetch Izzy sooner. She had gotten away with so much up to now. Dare she risk her luck once more?

"I'll accept your offer on one condition," she finally said, crossing her fingers.

"And what would that be?

Jenny took a quick breath. She had gone this far, she might as well cross the next hurdle.

"There was an excellent maid at my last place of employment. She is seeking a new position. I would like your permission to send for her."

"And where was your last position?"

Having already decided she would give the name of the family butler should Mr. Morgan ask for references, she answered without hesitation. "A banker in St. Louis."

"Which bank?"

Jenny hadn't expected the question and was momentarily lost for an answer. She couldn't very well tell him it was First Savings. It wouldn't take much to learn the name of the president was Henry Fairchild and then her goose would be cooked. He'd know she was his missing bride.

"The name of the bank is not important, Mr. Morgan. Let's—"

"Have you forgotten our agreement so quickly, Jenny? If you can't call me Cade, our deal is off. No dollar a month extra and I'll hire the maids myself."

Jenny quickly bowed her head. He mustn't see the chagrin certain to be written on her face. If she conceded on this minor point, he was going to let her send for Izzy. "I'll do my best, C-Cade."

The familiar use of his name brought the memory of waking in his bed rushing back. Jenny caught her bottom lip between her teeth and slowly raised her eyes to his. From the teasing smile on his full lips, she knew he had guessed her thoughts.

"Jenny . . ." he whispered.

The painful huskiness of her name sent a molten fire spreading across Jenny's body like hot wax spilling over the side of a candle. She tried closing her eyes, but it only served to sharpen the images of her dream. She knew it would take no effort at all to relive the moment she had awakened to the feel of his warm, naked body atop hers, his lips claiming hers with a passion so strong it left her weak and trembling.

Cade wondered at the brief glimpse of emotions he saw playing across Jenny's flushed face. He ached to reach for her—to pull her wantonly into his arms and carry her off to his bed.

She had hinted that she had been married at one time. But slit the man's throat? He doubted it. She more than likely had run away from her husband. The thought that she might be in need of someone herself crossed his mind. The taste of passion he had sampled that night was a thirst he ached to have quenched, but he'd take no man's wife.

Some things are meant to be shared.

His brother's words mocked him. The realization that he might be no better than Frank was a sobering thought. Never had he imagined he would want a woman enough to compromise his principles.

"Send for whomever you want," he stated coldly, then walked from the room.

"Does that mean you'll not be wantin' my services?" the old woman in the corner ventured to ask.

Jenny spun around. She had forgotten about the old lady. "How are you at cleaning?"

The woman grinned. "A damn sight better than you are at handling that man." She walked across the room and extended her hand. "Name's Sarah."

"Well, Sarah, I haven't changed my mind. If you can start now, you're hired."

CHAPTER 6

Jenny left the new maid in Albert's care. He was upset with her for not asking his opinion on who she hired, but getting her sister here was more important. She couldn't believe the ease with which she had gotten Cade to agree.

She swept back into the study and closed the door. First, she'd have to send a letter to Pritch, her father's house-keeper. After Jenny's escape, her father would be checking Izzy's mail. Jenny wished she could see Pritch's face when she learned the contents of the note. The old housekeeper would not be pleased that Jenny had sent for Izzy so soon. Pritch had never supported the idea of Izzy traveling alone. Even if she didn't approve of Jenny's plans, she would see that Izzy got the letter.

Once finding the pen and paper, it didn't take long to word the note. As Jenny sealed it, a smile eased across her lips and she allowed herself a moment of triumph. Another note to the hotel in St. Louis notifying them that her sister would be picking up the rest of her boxes and she would be finished.

Izzy would certainly be surprised to find that Jenny had

found a position so quickly. With both her sister and herself working, they could get their own place sooner. Perhaps they could even afford one of those nice little homes at the edge of Gold Shoe until Jenny came into an inheritance her grandmother had left her.

In the meantime, she planned on working her fingers to the bone for Mr. Morgan—Cade. She must remember to call him Cade. She needed that raise.

After sending Albert to post her letters, Jenny gathered her cleaning cloths and mounted the stairs. She had discovered the door leading to a closed wing of bedrooms a few days ago and meant to investigate her find. Now that Cade was back she didn't feel safe remaining in his room.

Jenny turned the knob and pushed at the large oak door. With a loud protest, it finally opened. Other than a narrow cherry table along one wall, the hallway was empty. Jenny stepped inside.

Sunlight from the various bedchambers shone ineffectually through the multipaned transoms over each door. Jenny sneezed repeatedly in the air thick with dust. It was obvious the rooms had been closed for some time.

After setting her bucket of water on the floor, Jenny tucked the hem of her skirt into her waistband. Even without the cumbersome cloth, each step she took set little clouds of dust to churning on the bare floors.

A quick glance into the closed rooms told her that once the rooms were cleared they would do nicely for both Izzy and herself. The wing had been attached to the back of the house forming a short T. Not only would they have their privacy, but there was more than enough room to store all the extra things she had brought with her from Philadelphia.

After checking each room thoroughly, Jenny settled on the one at the end of the hall. It was spacious. Almost as large as Cade's. With one wall of windows facing the broad valley and mountains and the other the pine-studded yard, the room was ideal.

Careful of stirring up more dust, Jenny stripped the covers from the furniture and began cleaning. Dampening one of her cloths, Jenny tied it securely to the straw wisps of her broom, then slid it slowly over the floors. The dust quickly formed into long damp clumps that Jenny easily plucked from her broom.

With a single-minded determination, Jenny worked late into the afternoon without stopping. Once she finished her cleaning, Albert helped move her things. Thank goodness Cade remained locked in his study while they worked. Even so, Jenny was forced to endure the questioning glances Albert threw her way. She didn't want to appear rude but she wasn't about to explain that Cade's presence was disturbing enough without sleeping in the man's bed.

By the time she cleaned two of the other rooms and put fresh linens on her bed, Jenny was exhausted and took her supper in her new room. She was about to fall asleep in the chair when a knock sounded at the door. Jenny opened it to find Albert carrying a large copper tub. A tall, thin man followed him with two steaming buckets of water.

Albert handed her a note. ''Cade said you might be wanting to wash some of the dust off.''

Jenny had assumed Cade had left again. It was quite a surprise to learn he not only was at the ranch but that he knew what she'd been doing. ''Please thank him for me,'' she said as she reached up to push a stray curl back in place. ''I could sure use it.''

''Sam and I'll be back in a few minutes with more water.''

Jenny tossed the note on her bed, then grabbed up her ivory-handled brush. Her hair was a mess and she'd have to hurry if she was to get it brushed before they brought the rest of the water for her bath.

Unpinning the prim coil at the back of her head, she leaned forward and slightly to one side. With a toss of her head, Jenny sent the black curtain of curls tumbling down the front of her dress. Her hair needed a washing as much as she did. With relentless determination, she worked the brush through the stubborn tangles.

The sinking sun made its way through the window beside her, painting Jenny with a warm pallet of iridescent colors. She closed her eyes and expelled a contented sigh. Despite the weariness that marked her every movement, Jenny was pleased with what she had accomplished. With the liberal applications of soap and beeswax, the room smelled fresh.

Jenny ran the brush once more through her hair. By this time tomorrow, she would have Izzy's room ready. She hadn't realized how much she missed her sister until now. It had hurt her deeply to leave Izzy behind, but they had both decided that the adventure would be uncertain enough for one woman, let alone two. Besides, this was Jenny's dream, not Izzy's.

Having finished brushing her hair, Jenny retrieved a fresh washcloth and towel along with a bar of soap. While she waited for Albert and Sam to bring up the water, the room grew dark and Jenny lit the lamp on her bedside table. As the sun set over the distant mountain peaks, she traced the etched rose on her small glass bottle of bath oil and paced the floor.

When the last of the water buckets were emptied into the tub, Jenny poured a few drops of the precious oil into the steaming water. It immediately formed a moist cloud of rose-scented vapors, filling the room with its sweet fragrance. Jenny took a deep breath and began to undress.

Cade stepped out onto the balcony of his bedroom when a light in the opposite window caught his eye. He could see Jenny pace the floor of her room, her dark hair flowing around her. His muscles tensed at the sensual images she had a way of evoking.

He had purposely stayed away from her the rest of the day and he was certain she had done the same. Yet why didn't it seem to lessen his disgust with himself for his behavior?

He didn't know what came over him every time he was in her company. It was obvious that she needed the job and he was only making it more difficult for her to stay. The note he had sent with the bath had been a mistake. He tried to justify his actions by telling himself he only meant to save her from herself. It wasn't safe for her to stay here. Not with the emotions she stirred in him. She was so very young— and so very serious.

But he should understand that. He was serious himself. Too serious according to his friends. So why did he feel the need to bait Jenny for the same fault? It was almost as if he regretted the way he had let his own ambitions take over his life and didn't wish to see her walk the same lonely path he had for the last ten years.

If he was honest with himself, he would admit that the mixup with the bedrooms could have happened to anyone. Seeing the look on her face today convinced him more than anything that the handbills had been another mistake. Despite how much he had thought otherwise, she had not set out to deliberately embarrass him.

He would like to think she did these things on purpose so he could dismiss her, but Cade was nothing if not fair. Her apparent naive innocence was a fact not easily discounted. Things just seemed to happen with Jenny about. It was best not to dwell on her.

It was so easy to tell himself that. But much as he tried to keep his mind on his accounts, Cade found himself watching her progress through his study window. She'd worked steadily all day. Dusting and cleaning. She deserved the bath he ordered for her, he told himself again—but not the note. He had only meant to tease, but it wasn't a good idea to encourage these lustful thoughts running through his head of assisting with her bath.

As he stood in the darkening room and watched Albert

and Sam make their third trip to fill the tub, he wondered if she even realized the new bedchamber she had chosen for herself could easily be seen from his room.

The agony of seeing her prepare for bed each night and not being able to have her sent Cade hurrying back to his desk. Although most men wouldn't mind, he had a real problem with robbing the cradle. Grabbing up pen and paper, Cade scribbled off a note to the newspaper in St. Louis. The agency hadn't been of much help. He should have handled this himself from the very beginning. A photograph and a list of qualifications should help him narrow the possibilities.

"There," he said to himself when he finished. "A wife should curb those lustful appetites of yours, old man."

Jenny undressed, then stepped into the tub. Slowly she eased herself down into the warm water. "Ah-h-h," she sighed, leaning back against the bathing sheet that protected her from the hot copper sides. She must remember to thank Cade for the bath.

Eyes closed to mere slits, Jenny lazily surveyed her new room through dark lashes. The pale pink roses of the wallpaper were a stark contrast to the rich dark mahogany woodwork that trimmed the windows, doors, and floor. Chairs of the same wood stood on each side of a large marble fireplace. A fainting couch had been placed opposite the dressing table along the long row of windows that overlooked the side yard.

Jenny sponged warm water over her bare shoulders. After the day she had had, the large four-poster bed interested her the most. Her gaze strayed to the elaborately carved headboard, tracing its intricate pattern down to the crocheted counterpane she had found closeted away in a large blanket chest. The folded note she had tossed on the bed earlier caught her attention. She had been in such a hurry to prepare for her bath she had forgotten all about Cade's note.

Odd that he had sent one. Why hadn't he merely given the message to Albert? She wanted to stay in her bath longer but curiosity finally got the best of her. She quickly washed her hair and stepped from the tub. The room had grown cold and she wished she'd taken the time to light a fire in the fireplace. By the time she was dressed in her cotton nightdress and had combed the tangles out of her hair again, Jenny was shivering. She grabbed up the note and crawled into bed. Once under the blankets, she opened it.

Since you no longer wish to share my bed, I thought you might at least share my tub.

Jenny tossed the paper from her as if it were some vile insect. She had bathed in his tub!

Vivid memories of his hard body lying next to hers brought a warmth soaring through her that had nothing to do with the amount of blankets on her bed. Drat that man! He was doing this deliberately. He knew that dreadful newspaper story had kept her from leaving before. Now he thought he could do or say anything he pleased because she was too afraid to leave. Well, she didn't care about ax murderers anymore, she told herself. If she hadn't sent the letter for Izzy, she'd leave in the morning.

Jenny stormed into the dining room and marched up to Cade. She slapped the note down beside his breakfast plate. "You are the most . . . the most . . ."

"Thoughtful person you have ever known," he finished for her.

"Thoughtful would be the last word I would use. Diabolical would be more accurate."

Cade lifted a questioning brow. "How could sharing my tub with you be diabolical?" he asked. A slow grin made its way across his lips. "Unless, of course, your memory of sharing my bed has improved."

"My memory has nothing to do with this, Mr. Morgan,"

she shouted, knowing the warmth that flooded her face branded her a liar.

"What of our agreement, Plain Jenny?"

The extra dollar a month was cause enough to pause. Heaven only knew, she could use the money. But what of the unwanted familiarity that seemed to go along with it?

"You can keep your dollar. Our agreement is off!"

Cade casually leaned back in his chair, his gaze finding and holding hers. "Mr. Morgan seems a bit formal after all we've shared," he said with a soft chuckle. "Or didn't you enjoy your bath?"

Jenny could barely contain her anger. "I did until I learned it was your tub I was using," she said between clenched teeth. "And it will be the last thing I share with you, Mr. Morgan."

"Ah, then I have done the right thing."

Jenny couldn't seem to breathe. Had he found someone else to replace her? If so, how was she ever to stop Izzy before she left Philadelphia? A telegram was the only thing that would reach her in time and Jenny had no money to send one. "What are you saying, Mr. Morgan?" she somehow managed to get out.

"I have composed an advertisement for a bride in the St. Louis paper."

"A bride?" she asked.

Cade grinned at her apparent confusion. "Yes, a bride. You do remember that I am looking for a wife?"

"Yes, but I thought . . ."

"I had thought so also but you have this aversion to sharing," he said, his voice a husky whisper. "Any wife of mine will not only share my bed and my tub, but her . . . her many attributes, shall we say, as well."

Jenny stiffened at the tingle his words sent racing up her spine. "It is not my sharing or not sharing that is an issue," she said, letting anger speak for her. "It is your assumption that the positions of housekeeper and mail-order bride are interchangeable that has you confused. I may have applied for b—"

Cade frowned at the sudden fear on her face. A fear so strong Cade could almost reach out and touch it.

"You may have what?" he demanded. A strange hope rose within him. "You may have considered it?"

Jenny clamped her mouth shut against the hysterical laughter that threatened to bubble to the surface. Too little sleep was beginning to wear her down. She had almost revealed what she had done. Grasping a tenuous hold on her emotions, Jenny straightened her shoulders. "I have not considered it, Mr. Morgan. Nor will I. Now, if you will please excuse me, I will take my breakfast in the kitchen."

With an indignant swish of her skirts, Jenny was gone, leaving Cade to study the closed door. He carefully reviewed their conversation. What was it she was going to say that had frightened her so? He didn't know why it seemed so important that he find out, but as long as it did, he'd make it his business to find out and he'd start with her references with Miss Emily's Positions For Young Ladies.

Jenny stepped into the kitchen to find Millie, Albert, and Bear standing in the middle of the kitchen, their attention focused on the door. When they saw her, Millie hurried to the stove, Albert grabbed up a pot of coffee, and Bear took a chair at the table and set to work on finishing a stack of pancakes. She knew without asking they'd heard her arguing with Cade.

"Millie, you missed your calling," Bear said, breaking the silence that hung like a thick fog in the kitchen. "You should take a lesson from them whiskey peddlers and run a wagon up to the mines."

"What for? I ain't got no whiskey."

"Not whiskey, Millie. Food. Any miner I know would gladly hand over half his poke for a stack of these here pancakes."

Albert slammed the coffeepot down on the table next to Bear. Its dark contents soaked into the clean checkered cloth that covered the table. "I haven't seen you plunk down no gold dust."

A wide grin softened the harsh lines of Bear's hard jaw. "I would if Millie asked me to," he taunted.

"He don't have to pay for my pancakes, Albert," Millie said. "He's company."

Jenny plucked a pie apple from the basket on the counter. She knew this entire conversation had come about to help cover her embarrassment. After all, why would a miner pay so much for a stack of pancakes?

It was sweet of Bear to think of her feelings. "Millie's right, Albert. Bear is company and is welcome anytime."

Ignoring Albert's scowl, Jenny put her apple in her pocket to eat later and started gathering up her cleaning things.

"Are you ready to start now?" Albert asked.

Jenny could plainly see Albert was reluctant to leave Bear alone in the kitchen with Millie and took pity on him. "Sarah and I will start on the rooms upstairs. Why don't you stay down here and help Millie clear up the breakfast things? I should be ready for some warm water by then."

Sarah peeked her head around the pantry door after Jenny had gone. "What that woman needs is a man."

Bear's gaze met Sarah's. He thought a moment, then nodded his agreement. "And what Cade needs is that woman."

"What would you know about it," Albert asked. "Cade can pick his own woman without any help from you. He's done wrote an advertisement for another one of them mail-order brides. Sent Sam off with the letter this morning."

Bear solemnly shook his head. "He's wasting his time."

"How would you know?"

"Loved me a woman once," Bear answered. "I know."

"I got me someone I care about too," Albert blurted out in defense. He ventured a quick glance at Millie, but she seemed not to have heard. "It doesn't mean I can read Cade's mind," he added.

Bear pointed his fork at Albert. "You don't have to read his mind. Listen to the way he talks to her. Watch the way he looks at her when he thinks no one sees." Bear paused to spear another forkful of the hotcakes. "When was the last time you heard Cade tease a woman?"

Millie refilled Bear's coffee cup. "Not since I've been here and that's a fact. Besides, Albert wouldn't know true love if it jumped up and bit him."

"And Bear does?"

"If you'd stop and think about it, it would make sense to you too. Every since Miss Jenny came there's been this smile in Cade's eyes and that's a fact."

"A smile in his eyes," Albert snorted. "Whoever heard of anyone having a smile in their eyes?"

Bear shoved back his chair and stood. "I have," he said, winking at Millie. "You would too if you didn't wear those horse blinkers everywhere you go," he tossed back at Albert.

"You would too if you were in love," Albert mimicked.

Millie pointed her pancake turner at Albert. "Don't you make fun of us, Albert Miller, or you'll be taking your meals in the bunkhouse with the rest of the cowhands, eating Sam's stew for breakfast."

Although Albert knew Millie often baked extra for the hired hands, he wasn't about to try his luck and end up sleeping with the smelly old cowhands. Besides, it would leave the coast clear for Bear to pay court to his love.

"What do you expect me to do about it, Millie," he whined.

"You and Sam could quit doing such a good job around here." She raised her hand when he started to protest. "Don't think I haven't noticed how you and Sam always try to solve all the problems with running this ranch. That's why this house is in such a mess. You're too busy making Cade's decisions for him."

"We don't do too much. Besides they're just little decisions. And Cade—he's in Denver most of the time."

"That's my point. How are we going to get Cade and Miss Jenny together if Cade's always in Denver? Love has to be coaxed along and how are we going to be able to do that if you and Sam keep making it easy for Cade to run off to Denver."

"We? What do you mean we?"

"You and Bear. And Sam if he's a mind to."

"Me and Bear?" he asked. "How can Bear help? He's off playing at his mine most of the time."

Bear grinned at Albert. "I've decided to take Cade up on his job offer. I'll be here for whatever Millie needs me to do."

With hands on his hips, Albert glared at Bear. "And just what is it I'm supposed to do?"

"Do you want to tell him, Millie, or shall I?"

Millie stepped between the two men. "Land's sake, Albert, don't you know nothing about courting? If we're ever going to get them two together, we've got to keep Cade here on the ranch or at least close—not running off to Denver every time the wind blows."

"And how am I supposed to do that? Hog-tie him to one of the hay wagons?"

"No. All you have to do is make sure the ranch isn't running as smoothly as it normally does. Then Cade will have to stick around to solve the problems."

Albert looked over Millie's shoulder at the big miner. "And what is he supposed to be doing while Sam and I make sure the ranch goes to pot?"

Bear took Millie by the arm and moved her aside so he was facing the angry little man. "I have my own ways of keeping Cade on this mountain."

"Are you planning on sharing them with the rest of us?"

"No."

"I'm not surprised you don't have any plan. I never knew a miner who could see past his fat poke," Albert mumbled to himself.

Bear ignored the snide remark and continued. "You'll know when I'm ready for you to know."

"But what about the bride Cade is advertising for? Won't he want to marry her instead of Miss Jenny?"

Millie placed her hands on her hips. "Don't you worry about no mail-order bride, Albert. Cade's already picked his woman. He just don't know it yet."

"And you do?"

Millie chuckled. "The way I see it, those two hate each other just enough to be in love."

CHAPTER 7

Em stood in the foyer at Trinity Ranch and slowly pulled at first one fingertip, then the next of her soft leather gloves while she watched the slim dark-haired girl walk down the broad oak staircase toward her. So this was Jenny. Although Em was only thirty-one, the aura of innocence about the girl brought forth memories of her own lost youth.

When the girl reached her, Em shifted her gloves to her left hand and extended her other.

"You're everything my girls said. Young. Beautiful." She paused and nodded to an old woman polishing the stairs. "And a woman who expects work out of those she hires."

Jenny liked the woman's warm smile and returned it. "It's either them or me and I'm too tired to work for the both of us."

"You're a smart girl," Em answered. "It's exactly what I would tell my girls."

"And you are?"

"Em. I own the local brothel. Well, I will once I make my last payment to Cade. But that's not why I'm here," she said as she breezed by Jenny and entered the parlor. Once inside, she crossed the room to the sofa by the fireplace and sat down. She knew from experience that the farther you got from the front door, the harder it was to toss you out on your ear.

"I came to see who it was who was trying to hire my girls away."

Jenny followed in her wake. "I—I wasn't," she protested. "I mean I was trying to hire someone. I just didn't know it was your girls who would apply," Jenny managed to get out. "I merely wanted someone to clean."

Em studied Jenny's flushed face a moment. "You know you really should have stated your notice in those words. You set my girls at each other's throats, trying to get that position." Em smiled brightly. "There ain't a one of them wouldn't like to have had that place in his bed you offered."

"But I didn't—"

"Maybe not intentionally, but that handbill sure sent a person's imagination soaring and my girls—well, let's just say their job requires a vivid imagination at times and I only hire the best."

Jenny looked to the closed windows, then back at her guest. The room had grown exceedingly warm in the few short minutes they had been there. "What was it I can do for you?" she asked, hoping to change the subject.

Em patted the horsehair cushion beside her. "Please make yourself comfortable. I have a lot of questions I need to ask you."

Normally Jenny would have asked someone so pushy to leave, but she wanted some answers herself. Such as why Em would be making payments for her place to Cade. She pulled the bell cord for Albert and then joined Em on the sofa.

"What did you want to know?"

Em was extremely pleased Jenny was going to be reasonable. Everything she had heard about the young girl had told her she might be the one for Cade. Somehow in the last ten years, she had come to feel responsible for Cade. It was ludicrous, of course. Cade was a grown man. And it certainly wasn't her fault that Cade's brother had done what he did. She had been hurt by Frank almost as much as Cade. But she had gotten over her loss. She wondered if Cade would ever get over his.

"I want to know about this ad Cade is running for a mail-order bride."

Jenny was relieved when Albert stepped into the room. It would give her a moment to think about whether she should answer.

"Yes, Miss Jenny," Albert said, his eyes as big as dessert plates on seeing their guest.

"Albert, would you please bring us some coffee and ask Millie if she has any of those fancy breads left from breakfast."

He hurried from the room and Jenny turned back to Em. "You will have to ask Mr. Morgan your questions. I had nothing to do with placing this advertisement."

Em laid her gloves on her lap. She took her finger and slowly outlined the seams. The girl was going to be stubborn after all. Maybe even stubborn enough to toss her out before she'd had her say. She could feel it in her bones, but then Em was not one to be easily dissuaded. She looked up from her gloves and met Jenny's gaze head-on.

"Wouldn't you like to have something to do with it?"

Jenny lifted her chin. "What Ca—Mr. Morgan does is none of my concern."

"Oh, but it is, Jenny."

Jenny could feel her stomach tighten. Had Em heard about the error in bedchambers? "There has to be some mistake," she finally said. "I am only Mr. Morgan's housekeeper. Why should I care who he marries?"

Em let out a sigh. "Do you honestly think if Cade

marries, his wife is going to allow him to keep such an attractive housekeeper?''

Cade might be forced to dismiss her? Then what would she and her sister do to earn the money they needed for their own house? The possibility hadn't even occurred to Jenny. No, that wasn't quite true. Ever since Cade had told her about the advertisement, her stomach had felt like a rock had somehow tumbled into it. Now it all made sense. Fear for her position had caused it.

''Even if I wanted to, there is nothing I can do to stop Mr. Morgan from marrying whomever he wants.''

Em let out another dramatic sigh. ''Use your head, girl. It may be too late to destroy the letter to the newspaper, but you can make sure he doesn't get any answers.''

Jenny thought for a moment. ''Won't he be suspicious if he doesn't receive any replies?''

Em tucked her fist under her chin. ''You may be right. Let me think on this a moment.''

Albert returning with the coffee gave Em the chance she needed. By the time he left, she had her answer.

''Open the letters!'' she exclaimed.

Jenny paused in pouring the coffee. ''Wouldn't he notice that?''

''No. Most of the mail I receive arrives half open. It shouldn't take much more to ease the envelope the rest of the way and take a peek at the correspondence, then put it back the way you found it.''

Jenny picked up a white linen napkin from the tray. She carefully placed it under Em's cup of coffee and handed them both to the chestnut-haired woman.

''And if he finds out?''

''Don't looked so scared. He won't eat you, you know.''

''He could fire me.''

''There are only two things Cade Morgan would not forgive you for. If you lie to him or if you fall in love with him. Anything else and all you'll have to do is bat those big brown eyes of yours and he won't care.''

''I can't do it.''

''Suit yourself,'' Em stated sourly. It would be just like this girl to take the respectable route and Cade would end up with some straight-laced lady of *quiet background* who would make sure that Cade was able to maintain the wall he had erected against any emotional involvements. ''Just remember when you lose your position here that I did warn you.''

Jenny handed her a plate of Millie's special fried bread. ''Why do you care what happens to me?''

''I don't, but I do care what happens to Cade. He's been hurt too much and this advertising for a wife will do him no good. His idea of the perfect marriage is based on how comfortable he might find it, not on love.'' Em plucked a large fritter from the plate. ''I'm asking your help to see that he doesn't marry until he finds the right woman.''

Jenny wanted to tell her that any man who would tease a woman unmercifully over such a small thing as sleeping in his bed didn't deserve the love of a good woman.

Having placed the plate of fritters on the small table beside her, Jenny calmly folded her hands in her lap. ''Rest assured, Em, I will do all I can to warn off any woman I feel unsuited for Mr. Morgan. I too would like to see Mr. Morgan get what he deserves.''

Em couldn't quite put her finger on what it was about Jenny's answer that bothered her. Usually she was pretty astute about such things, but this time was different.

Picking up her napkin, Em dabbed at the sugar on her lips. Yes, there was definitely something she had missed. She was sure of it. Well, until she figured it out, she might as well get back to work.

Em stood. ''I want to thank you for the coffee and fritter.'' When she got to the door, she stopped and turned back to Jenny. "If you're smart, you'll at least think over what I've said."

Jenny remained seated for several minutes after Em left. She was inclined to agree with the older woman. Cade's marriage might very well prove an end to her position here, but she didn't think it wise to destroy all the letters. He would surely find out. No, Cade needed to get those from the ones he would never accept. She just hoped she could tell the difference.

A full moon washed the valley floor in a hauntingly silver hue. The lone rider sat astride his horse atop the hill and watched Morgan and his men round up the last of the cattle. He had heard how something had spooked them, scattering them halfway across South Park.

Last week it had been the corral fence and Morgan's horses. Normally Morgan having a string of bad luck such as this would have pleased him, but he had been counting on the rancher's absence to have a little private . . . talk with the new housekeeper. One that would ease this ache in his loins.

He'd had Elmer watching the ranch for over a week now but he couldn't spare him much longer. There were other things Elmer needed to attend to. Like that new claim they had to file on.

He'd watch Morgan himself, but his job kept him busy until late at night. A calculating grin made its way across his thin lips. There was always the possibility of taking off a few days like he had when he'd disposed of the old woman and the boy. Not that he minded doing what had to be done. Actually he'd welcomed it, but a second long absence from work would be difficult to explain.

If he thought Morgan would stay with the men to drive the cattle instead of returning to the ranch, he might have risked paying a visit on the little lady now, but it was almost light and he had to get back to town. No, he'd wait until he heard Morgan had left on one of his many trips.

Sweat ran in tiny rivulets down his tanned face. Cade removed his hat and ran the back of his sleeve across his forehead. The sun sure was warm today and chasing down these contrary critters hadn't helped any. For the life of him, he couldn't understand what had spooked them. But then, everything that had happened over the last two weeks would be difficult to explain. The skunk under the back porch. The horses breaking down the corral fence. The squirrel that had gotten caught in the chimney in Jenny's room.

Cade smiled. He'd rather enjoyed that little incident. She'd woken the entire household with her screams, but the best part was when she stood trembling in his arms, her thin cotton gown hiding none of the generous curves that still haunted his dreams.

He stuffed his hat back on his head. Hell, he didn't need to be dreaming to have her haunt him. All he needed to do was recall the feel of the taut nipples of her full breasts against his chest and he started aching with his need for her.

Cade spurred his horse forward and caught up with Sam. It wouldn't do to let his imagination take wing now. It was a long way back to the ranch and spending the day in a saddle was uncomfortable enough as it was.

"How far you figure we are from Fairplay, Sam?"

Sam turned his head and aimed for the scrub oak beside the path before answering. The tobacco juice landed with a disappointing thud just short of the tree. With a sigh, Sam scanned the distant hill. "Reckon we're still a few hours away, boss."

"That's the way I figure it too," he said before pulling ahead of the old man.

"Where you headed?" Sam hollered after him.

"To find a wet drink and a willing woman."

* * *

By the time Cade reached Fairplay, he was more than ready for a quick tumble among Sadie's well-worn sheets. He pulled his horse to a stop before the saloon and dismounted. Walking to the door, he pulled his hat from his head and stepped into the cool interior of the tavern.

Even this early in the day, the room was filled with smoke, drunken miners, and the smell of cheap whiskey. A good brisk wind coming down off the mountains would take care of that. Cade stepped up to the bar. "How's it going, Tom?"

"Seen better, Mr. Morgan." He gave the bar a quick wipe. "What can I get you?"

"How about telling Sadie I'm here?"

Tom went back to wiping down the counter. "Sadie's with a customer," he mumbled. He hoped Cade didn't question him further. Sadie was in one of her moods and had taken off when she'd seen Cade ride up.

"Give me a whiskey then," Cade said. He might as well wet his whistle while he waited.

Tom pulled a bottle from under the counter and uncorked it. "Better take the whole thing. Sadie will be a while."

Cade carried the bottle and a clean glass to a table at the back of the room. Once settled, he poured himself a generous drink. After tossing it down, he poured himself another and sat back to wait. The fire spread quickly through him.

He needed that. The last two weeks had taken their toll on his patience. He couldn't remember when so many things had gone wrong. He'd had to cancel most of his appointments. Thank goodness his partner had been able to meet with the others. While Ned had quite a head on his shoulders for finances, he hated the social aspects of the partnership. Cade had understood this and tried to take on those duties himself. If this kept up, Ned would either be forced to become adept at handling the clients or throw up his hands and leave. Cade hated like hell to lose the man. Good partners were hard to find.

It didn't take much to let his thoughts drift back to his housekeeper. Despite what he had first thought, Jenny was proving to be worth every cent he paid her. Not only was the house positively gleaming under her supervision, but she had proved invaluable at handling the household accounts as well. If it hadn't been for all the misfortunes that had befallen the ranch of late, he would have felt comfortable with spending more time taking care of his investments in Denver.

It wasn't until he noticed his whiskey bottle was empty that he realized how long he had been waiting. It had turned dark outside and plenty of miners had climbed the wooden stairs to the bedrooms above and returned, but Sadie still hadn't come down. While Cade didn't visit as regularly as she would have liked, Sadie always managed to make time for him.

Cade eyed the stairs for some time before he decided to take matters into his own hands. Cade never asked for any special treatment, but Sadie had spoiled him with her favors. He swallowed the last of his drink and made his way up the stairs. Right now he needed Sadie's special talents to help rid himself of Jenny.

As he made his way down the hall, he tried to ignore the moans and grunts coming from behind the curtained doorways he passed on the way to Sadie's room, but the liquor had only heightened his need. By the time he reached the end of the hall, the ache was so bad he found himself pounding on her door.

"Who is it?" Sadie called from the other side.

"It's me, Cade. Let me in."

"Go away, Cade. I don't feel well."

In all the time Cade had known her, Sadie had never been sick. For the first time since he had started visiting the establishment, he wished she had only a curtain covering her door like the other girls. He tried the door again. It was still locked.

"What's wrong, Sadie?"

"Nothing. Just go away."

Cade could hear the tears in her voice. He'd be damned if he was going to leave without seeing what he could do. Backing up, he sized up the door. It looked mighty solid. Thank goodness the framework didn't look as stable. Hunkering his shoulder to take the blow, he ran toward the door. "Get away from the door," he yelled moments before impact.

The door broke lose from the hinges and slammed to the floor. Sadie stood red-eyed and weeping next to her bed. Her blond hair lay like a soft golden curtain around her thinly clad body.

"Are you all right?" she asked between sobs.

Cade rubbed the hurt from his shoulder. "I'd have been a hell of a sight better if you would have unlocked the door."

"Oh, Cade," she said, running into his arms. "Where have you been? I've missed you so."

Cade caught his hand in her long blond hair and forced her to look up at him. "I know," he said bitterly. "I could tell by the way you dropped everything when you heard I was here."

Tears flowed anew. "Don't scold me, Cade. I've been heartsick ever since you told me you were going to get married."

"Well, I'm here now." He dropped his hand to her buttocks and ground her womanhood against his evident need.

"Why don't you dry those tears and take advantage of what I have for you."

Sadie smiled up at him. "I hoped it would be this way." She reached up and placed a kiss on his lips. "She can't satisfy you the way I can, can she?"

How could Cade explain to Sadie that he suspected Jenny could more than satisfy his needs, but she wouldn't?

"I'm not married yet if that's what you're asking."

Sadie grabbed his hand and pulled him over to her bed. Over the years she had fancied herself in love with over a dozen of her lovers, but Cade was by far the best. It wasn't often that a whore had a client who could bring that rare combination of pain and sweet ecstasy to their lovemaking. So rare in fact that she had never asked him for the exorbitant fee she charged her other clients. Even so, Cade had always been more than generous in other ways.

Once she had him up against her bed, she laid her body seductively against his, letting him feel the heat that was already building in her. Slipping her hand between them, she carefully unbuttoned his shirt and pushed it from his shoulders. Once free of it, she ran her fingers lovingly down the hard chiseled planes of his broad chest to the top of his leather chaps. They'd have to go of course. Bringing her other hand down, she clumsily fumbled with the fastenings.

Cade suddenly grabbed her by the shoulders and shoved her from him. "Don't!" he commanded.

He could see the surprise, then hurt, that crossed her face, but for some unknown reason he couldn't go through with it. How could he tell her he no longer wanted her?

"I shouldn't have come," he said, reaching down for his shirt.

"Don't say that," Sadie cried. "You need me. You know you do." She ran her finger along the top of his chaps. "It takes a woman like me to handle a man like you."

Cade pulled his shirt on. She was right, but now that he had decided to marry, his taste for prostitutes had waned.

"I don't need anyone," he stated, but he knew it was a lie. He still needed Jenny. If she weren't so young, he'd take her as his mistress. Without another word, Cade tossed a gold coin on the bed. It was the first and last time he'd pay for a woman.

* * *

"Why did you let him get away like that?" Albert shouted as he rode up to the herd. Millie had been on him every minute since Cade had left two days ago. She had told him to keep Cade on the ranch. How was he to know those fool cows would wander so far after they'd stampeded them out of that canyon.

Sam took out his knife and cut a fresh plug of tobacco. "I didn't let him get away. He just up and took off for Fairplay without giving me a chance to come up with a reason to stay."

"Millie was hoppin' mad when I left this morning. If she finds out Cade went to visit one of his women, she'll have my hide."

"Don't be for telling her," he said before tucking the tobacco in his cheek.

"Don't be for telling who what?"

Albert spun around in his saddle to find Bear grinning at him. "What are you doing here?" he demanded. All he needed now was for Bear to tell Millie what happened.

"Millie sent me out after Cade. She was beginning to worry that he and the men were never coming back. Said they took off after some cattle pert near three days ago."

"Well, they're back now," Albert said, trying to steady his horse. "So you can be getting back to your mine. I'll take it from here."

Bear puckered up his lips and aimed for a pile of rocks. When he cut loose with a brown stream of tobacco, a snake that had been sunning itself arched its back, then took off in the grass. Sam watched in awe.

"You aimin' for that snake, were you, Bear?" he asked.

Bear cocked a bushy brow. "He a friend of yours, Sam?"

"No, no. Just wanted to know if you were aimin' for him—or maybe that bush just south of him," he added hopefully.

"If I was aimin' for the bush, I would have hit it. Now where's Cade?"

"He took off for that woman of his in Fairplay late this morning," Sam answered, his eyes still on the rock.

Albert groaned. "You didn't need to tell him that."

Bear pulled his own mount up beside Albert's. "Now why's that? You afraid I'll tell Millie your idea backfired?"

"You'd just love to do that, wouldn't you?" Albert snarled. "Well, ride on back and tell her. At least I *had* an idea. I haven't heard you come up with one yet."

"With you keeping him so busy, there hasn't been a need for my ideas."

Albert raised on his toes and looked Bear in the eye. "I guess that's as good an excuse as any."

"I wouldn't be so proud of your accomplishments if I were you. Putting a skunk under the back porch isn't my idea of using your head." Bear chuckled. "Millie said it took you two days of scrubbing before you could sleep in the house again."

"It kept Cade from leaving for Denver that day, didn't it?" Albert said defensively. "Besides, Miss Jenny must have come out twenty times to check on our progress. Every time Cade was takin' a turn at scrubbing, Miss Jenny was right there a helpin' carry that water to him."

"Sounds like your idea worked right well."

Albert eyed the miner suspiciously. "You sayin' you approve."

"I wouldn't say that exactly. I think I'd a picked something a little less smelly than a polecat. But it seemed to work and that's what counts. A shame you let Cade go into Fairplay though. It'll set things back some."

Albert glared at Sam. "It weren't me that let Cade get away."

"Don't look at me that way," Sam bellowed. "When Cade's got an itch, there ain't no one can stop him."

Bear leaned forward, resting his arm across the neck of his mount. "It appears I'm going to have to stay around to see that Cade's in the right place next time he gets this itch."

CHAPTER 8

It was dark by the time Cade rode in. He turned over his horse to Sam and headed for the house. He couldn't believe he'd rode out of Fairplay without taking care of his need for a woman. Three days in the saddle had not put him in the best of moods, but he shouldn't have taken it out on Sadie.

Even Sam seemed to be upset with him. Sam was probably tired himself. Cade should have told him to stay home. After all, it had been a lot of years since Sam and he had herded cattle and Sam wasn't exactly a spring chicken anymore.

The sound of humming brought Cade up short. Except for a light in Jenny's window, the side of the house was dark. He searched along the balcony until he found what he was looking for. Jenny stood in the shadow of a tall pine, her hair a dark curtain around her. Cade could just make out the ivory brush that gleamed in the moonlight as she pulled it through the thick strands. As he stood there watching, he could almost feel the silky softness of the curls in his fingers.

A gust of wind suddenly swept across the yard and the

pine growing next to the balcony bent in its wake. Cade sucked in his breath as the pale moon sent elusive shadows of seduction dancing sensuously across her young body—stroking, caressing. With wild abandonment, they sought out and touched each alluring curve.

Jenny stepped out of the shadows. As if in response to a time-old mating ritual, Jenny closed her eyes and tossed back her head, letting the luxuriant strands of her hair fall free. With sensual innocence, she arched her body into the wind.

Cade's mouth grew dry. The light coming from the room behind Jenny outlined her as clearly as if he were once more running his hand down the delectable lines of her young body. A groan escaped his lips at the enticing way the soft cotton of her nightdress molded against her. He didn't have to be standing next to her to imagine the firm twin buds that strained against the thin material.

The urges he had failed to satisfy earlier returned stronger than ever. How could something so beautiful cause so much pain?

Suddenly Cade's desire turned to anger. Was she deliberately parading across the balcony in hopes of gaining the attention of one of the hands? With swift strides, he made his way around to the front door. His anger mounted with each step he took. By the time he reached Jenny's room, he didn't even bother knocking. He paused only to turn down the lamp on the desk before stepping through the door onto the balcony.

Jenny stood at the rail, bathed in moonlight, apparently unaware of his presence. In a few strides he was beside her. She gasped as he grabbed her by the arm and pulled her back into the room.

"What do you think you're doing?" Jenny shrieked after him.

Once he had her in the room, Cade turned back to face

her. "I haven't decided whether I'm protecting you from yourself or my men from you."

She dug at the fingers biting into her arm. "And who is supposed to protect me from you?"

He leaned toward her, his words a whispered threat. "You need no protection from me, Jenny. My tastes don't run to married women."

"But I . . ."

A bitter laugh escaped his lips at her confusion. "You don't think I believed that little story of yours, do you? You may have run away from your husband, but I don't think you killed him."

It took Jenny a moment to remember. He thought she was married? That was why he left her alone?

Her silence taunted him. Did she think she could fill her hours of boredom by flaunting herself before everyone? Perhaps a taste of the danger she was flirting with would teach her a lesson. Determined to punish her, Cade ran the back of his hand down the side of her face. "What happened, Jenny? Did he grow tired of your games?"

"Games?"

He pulled her up against his chest. "The ones you play with me and my men. Or are you going to tell me that you had no idea we could see you parading half naked on your balcony?"

Shocked, Jenny struggled. "I—I didn't . . ."

Wrapping her tightly in his arms, he slid his hand down her back until it came to rest on her firm buttocks. "Oh, but you did, my dear," he whispered as his fingers began a slow massage. "Do you have any idea what it does to a man to see such a delectable morsel flaunted before him?"

He leaned down and nudged her hair aside. Exposing her ear, he gently tugged at the delicate lobe with his teeth. "Do you have any idea what it does to me?"

His warm breath sent tantalizing shivers cascading through Jenny's body. For the life of her, she couldn't pull away. She felt like a fly caught in a giant web. Already he had woven her into his warm cocoon.

Mesmerized by his spell, Jenny arched her neck, inviting him to suck the very life out of her. She almost welcomed her fate as she waited for him to feast.

Her calm acceptance sent a warning coursing through him. She was a married woman—a married woman who apparently cared nothing for her wedding vows. Was this the way it had been with Letitia and Frank? Had Letitia cared so little about him that she had flaunted her charms before his older brother until he had succumbed.

No. The night he had found them together Frank did not look the victim. He had appeared generally oblivious to the pain they had caused Cade.

"Answer me," he said against the hollow of her slim neck. "Don't you care what you're doing to me? Don't you care that you're hurting someone?"

"I'm hurting you?" she asked.

Her voice was a breathless whisper and Cade could feel his resolve to remain detached begin to weaken. It would be so easy to pick her up and carry her over to the bed. After all, it wasn't as if she would fight him on this. He could tell she wanted him every bit as much as he wanted her. If only she weren't married. Cade bit back a groan of regret. Hell, if she weren't married, he'd see that she was his bride before the sun set on another day. Never had he wanted a woman so bad.

"Did you find the dynamite?" Millie whispered, her eye still on the window of Jenny's room.

"I got it. It was right where you said." Albert carefully laid the package on the table next to the porch window. "All these years and I never knew old man Ross left it here."

"Good. Now we'll get Cade out of there."

"But I don't understand," Albert whispered. "I thought

you wanted them together. Well, we finally did it and now you're trying to get Cade out of her bedroom.''

Millie glared at him. ''I want them together, but not this way, you oaf. Don't you know if a woman gives herself to a man without his ring on her finger, he has no reason to marry her.''

''I would,'' Albert said quietly.

Millie gave him a warm smile. She knew he hadn't meant for her to hear. Albert was different from most men. She had to make him understand.

''You saw that advertisement he sent to the papers. Cade says he wants a woman of quality. Well, I lived most of my life in a house of a *woman of quality* and let me tell you, Cade doesn't need that. What Cade needs is a woman of fire and Jenny has that fire. The only way we're going to get Cade to see that is if he wants her so bad it hurts.''

Albert could understand that. His heart had ached many a night as he lay awake and thought of Millie.

Albert unwrapped the soiled rags from the sticks. Darn. What was wrong with the blasted things. If he didn't know better, he'd swear the things were sweating. He hoped they were still good.

''Here's the dynamite,'' he said.

Millie eyed the bundle skeptically. ''Isn't that a bit much? We want to get Cade out of her room, not blow up the house.''

Albert wasn't about to admit he knew nothing about using dynamite. He'd assured her he could do the job. If she knew he'd not so much as wired a fuse before, Millie would have sent for Bear for sure.

''The way I see it,'' he said, ''you blow up those there trees and the flying limbs will make them think the house is falling down around their ears.''

Albert juggled the damp bundle as he rechecked the fuse and the blasting cap. ''We'll be needin' one for each tree,'' he said, trying to impress Millie with his knowledge. "Then—"

Millie snatched the sticks from his hands. "Have you gone mad? Even I know better than that. You use that much dynamite and you'll be picking up pieces clear all the way to Fairplay and back. One stick should be more than enough."

With a red face, Albert sought to redeem his blunder. "I brought the extra ones along in case one was bad," he said as he pulled another stick from her fingers and stomped off.

When his hand found her breast, Jenny couldn't deny the tremors that ran through her. Was this how it felt? Other than Izzy, Jenny had never known what it meant to be loved. Her only memory of her mother was one of sadness. She had run away after Izzy was born and her father was too full of his own anger and busy with his work to notice that his daughters needed him. Like everything else, he paid someone to supply them with what he could not give.

But this was different. This was the touch of a man who needed her. Jenny laid her head on Cade's broad chest and let the masculine scent of him fill her. Despite the turmoil of emotions running through her, she felt as if someone had wrapped her in a glowing blanket of adoration. If this was what love was all about, Jenny could spend the rest of her life in its exciting grip.

His lips touched hers and Jenny knew what it was like to surrender her soul. The pain, the ecstasy, were nearly overwhelming as she returned his kiss. Never had she felt the fires of such passion. Not even in the throes of her most vivid dreams.

Somewhere along the way, he had undressed her. She vaguely remembered the sound of ripping, but it did not matter. All that mattered was that he love her. She did not protest when he carried her to the bed and laid her on it.

He stood over her, a towering giant, and unbuttoned his

shirt, his piercing blue eyes holding her captive. Her heart seemed to stop when he let the shirt fall from his broad shoulders. Dark golden hairs covered his tanned chest. She stared in fascination as he finished undressing, then joined her on the bed.

With all the authority of a man who gets what he wants, he leaned over her. His intense gaze sent warning shivers skittering up her spine, but heaven help her. It was too late.

His hands were like magic, bringing life to those secret desires she kept carefully buried within her. She now knew what it was like to be caught with no chance of escape. She couldn't even manage a whisper of protest when he cupped her buttocks and lifted her against him. Slowly he lowered her until her hips rested against his.

A soft gasp of surprise escaped her lips. His body was like a hot branding iron thrust against hers. A warning screamed in her head. This was not the kind of love she sought.

Jenny tried to move away but he rolled with her, his knee finding a hold between her legs. She opened her mouth to let the screams ringing in her head escape.

Without a proper light, Albert was having a hard time wiring the fuse. Although he had seen it done a few times, he still didn't have enough confidence that he knew what he was doing. It looked right.

Crouching down, he backed away from the tree, unrolling the fuse as he went. When he had gone a safe distance, he laid it on the ground and lit the end. Albert watched the thin stream of smoke as the fuse took.

The explosion was everything he had hoped for. The tree splintered in two, sending branches soaring like arrows into the night sky. Hot points of light greedily licked at the branches still dry from their winter's sleep. Like all hungry things of nature, they grew quickly on the nourishing diet.

He wouldn't have to use the other stick after all, but

Millie need not know. Planning on retrieving it in the morning, he tossed it over his shoulder. The second explosion sent Albert sprawling on the ground. When he lifted his head, he knew it was too late to wish that he'd gone after Bear to set the charge. He'd blown up the outhouse. Albert just bowed his head and tried not to think of what the chunks might be that were raining down on his head. He hoped Millie was happy.

A loud explosion sounded from outside her door, followed by a bright light. The bed shook.

Jenny could hear Cade cursing over the fire and brimstone that seemed to be raining on the rooftop.

She was surprised to see Cade standing at the edge of the bed pulling on his heavy denim trousers. She hadn't felt him leave her.

When he finished, he scooped up his shirt from the floor. Light flickered and danced across the patterned wallpaper as he crossed the room to the door. When he reached it, he paused and turned back to her.

"I'll be back," he said. "Don't forget where we were."

Jenny stared at the open doorway. God had come to punish her. She was sure of it. Didn't the Bible say it was a sin to lie in the arms of a man you weren't married to?

Oh, why hadn't she paid more attention in church? With all her little white lies, Jenny had always considered herself somewhat of a sinner, but God had certainly been swift to point out that she had gone too far this time. She had sampled forbidden pleasures. She had taken a bite out of Satan's apple. This was it. She might as well get up and take her punishment.

Dragging in a ragged breath, Jenny climbed out of the bed and grabbed her clothes. A bright glow writhed outside her window. Hell's fires had come to claim her. Tears wet her cheeks as she dressed. Did hell require that she brush her hair as well?

Taking a deep breath to bolster her courage, Jenny squared her shoulders and stepped out into the glowing orange landscape. Another explosion lit the sky, knocking Jenny back into the room. The last thing she remembered was the awful smell that filled the air.

The next hour was a state of pandemonium as everyone rushed around trying to contain the small fires behind the outhouse. Albert jumped in and did his part, carefully avoiding Bear's questioning glances.

"Who in the hell blows up a man's outhouse," Cade demanded once the fire was under control. "First the horses. Then the cattle. Now this. What's it going to be next? The house?"

"You sure have been having a lot of bad luck lately, Cade," Bear stated innocently.

Cade frowned at him. "Luck is what you make it and I'd have to say someone's been awful busy lately making mine. It's almost like someone is trying to run me off my land. Well, if that's their game, I got news for them. No one gets what's mine.

"First thing in the morning, I'll be sending a note down to my partner in Denver. He'll have to handle things until I catch who's behind this."

"Sounds like the best thing to me," Bear offered. "Me and Albert will help if you need us."

"You and him patch things up?"

"I'm not saying he's forgiven me for whatever it was I did, but at least he's talking."

Cade slapped him on the shoulder. "That's a start, Bear. And thanks for your offer of help. If you get any wind whatsoever of who might be behind all this, let me know. No one's going to run me off my own land."

After Cade left, Bear stood and watched the fire burn low before he went in search of Albert. This stunt had all the earmarks of an amateur and he couldn't think of anyone who fit the bill more than his little friend.

When Cade got back to Jenny's room, he found Millie sitting in one of the chairs outside her door calmly peeling apples.

"Where's Jenny?" he asked.

"That last explosion knocked her clean off her pins. Being the genteel *lady of quality* Miss Jenny is, she naturally took to her bed."

What the hell was she talking about? Genteel? Jenny? Not the little bundle that had returned his kisses this evening with a passion matched only by his own. There was nothing genteel about his Jenny. She was hot fires and sweet honey, a smoldering caldron of untapped emotions, and he intended to be the one to bring them to a boil.

"If she's still up, I'd like to speak with her."

Millie gave him one of her brightest smiles and continued to peel her apples. "I gave her a nice hot cup of coffee laced with some of that brandy of yours. Last time I looked in, she was fast asleep."

Cade tried to hide his annoyance, but Millie had known him for too many years. Besides, she'd have to be blind not to have seen the torn nightdress on the floor.

"Thought I'd just stay here tonight," she said, knowing she was dashing any hopes he might have had of finishing what he had started. The dynamite might have been a drastic measure on her part, but from what she had seen it had served its purpose. "A *lady of quality* like Miss Jenny ain't used to brandy and such and I'm afraid I gave her a bit too much. She might be a little tipsy when she wakes."

Lady of quality? Why did Millie keep saying that? Was Millie trying to tell him Jenny was not to be seduced? He could swear she was scolding him for trying.

It almost sounded as if she had decided to set herself up

as Jenny's protector? He wouldn't put it past her to have given Jenny the extra brandy on purpose.

He walked past Millie and into Jenny's bedroom. He didn't even glance at the bed as he strode across the room to the door that led outside. He could hear Millie's footsteps as she followed. Once out on the balcony, Cade looked to the house. Just as he thought. Jenny's bedroom was in full view of the small back porch where Millie relaxed of an evening.

Cade spun around to face the tall woman. She didn't cringe, but met his gaze defiantly. She had seen everything. Her disapproval was evident, but just how strong was it?

Get a grip on yourself, old man. She may not condone your behavior, but no one blows up an outhouse to keep two grown people apart.

"Finish your apples, Millie," he said before turning to walk away. "I'll see you in the morning."

By the time Jenny woke, Cade was already closeted in his study. After a quick breakfast, she set Albert to take care of the upstairs rooms, while she concentrated on the ones downstairs. Jenny was pleased with how the house was coming along. She hadn't even made her way to the attic and already she had found many wonderful things tucked away in every odd corner and unused bedroom.

She had unpacked a few of her things yesterday and wanted to see how they would look with the furnishings. Cade never mentioned her efforts, but then he was a busy man and if anyone should understand how inattentive busy men were, it would be her.

But Jenny was determined not to let that bother her. Cade had taken her in his arms last night and made her feel loved. Jenny found herself humming. It was wonderful—this feeling of being loved. Of course, after what had happened last night, he might be asking her to marry him. If so, she'd have to enlighten him quickly on that point. She was never going to marry. She had too many dreams to give up.

Jenny rearranged the doily on the foyer table for the third time and let her eyes stray to the closed study door. He had been in there an awful long time. He was going over her accounts. She was sure of it. She had been spending a lot of money, but what did he expect? The house had been neglected for far too long.

He wouldn't be upset because she had brought up someone from Denver to wallpaper the front parlor, would he? She would have done it herself, but she was no good at things like that. While her taste for decorating was unerring, she couldn't even crochet a proper doily. Besides, the man had told her she was getting the wallpaper for practically nothing. And Cade had to admit, the colors did help bring out the elegance of the petite point chairs and love seat.

She had never had the full responsibility of decorating before and she found she rather enjoyed it. Her father had frowned at her efforts to make their house into a home where one could feel welcome. Well, he should be pleased now for she had brought all her things with her.

She was about to listen once more at the study door when a great roar from within sent her scurrying past. Cade burst from the room.

"Who in the hell does she think she is?" he growled. Cade went to the stairs and looked up. "Albert, get down here. I need you to go to the telegraph office at once."

Jenny pretended to straighten the porcelain vase on the hall table and watched out of the corner of her eye. Who had upset him so? If the devil had had blond hair, Cade could have posed as his brother for fire and brimstone seemed to dance at his side as he paced the floor and waited for Albert. She had never seen him so angry.

Suddenly his eyes met hers. Jenny froze as he strode toward her.

"I just received the bill from Miss Emily's," he said.

Jenny swallowed hard. "Yes?"

"I'm not going to pay it," he stated bluntly.

Jenny could feel the floor begin to spin. He had found out. "I can ex-plain," she choked out.

Cade's dark brows shot together. "Explain? How can you explain? The woman's not only trying to cheat me, she as much as called me a liar."

"A liar?"

"She said she checked at the depot and Miss Fairchild boarded the train for Denver."

"Perhaps she changed her mind and got off there."

"She checked. Miss Fairchild took the train on to Gold Shoe." Cade fixed her with a reproachful eye. "Are you sure she wasn't on the train with you?"

Jenny thought a moment. No, she had not looked in her mirror the entire time on the train. "I do not recall seeing your Miss Fairchild," she said with a clear conscience. She was about to add that she was the only woman to board the train to Gold Shoe, but Albert appeared and Cade took him off to the study.

Albert had saved her. If Miss Emily had gone so far as to check that Miss Fairchild had boarded the train, she might also be privy to the fact that Miss Fairchild was the only woman on the train.

Jenny had to get a hold of some money. If the bill was not paid, it was obvious Miss Emily would continue to check. Eventually she would discover that Jenny was the missing Miss Fairchild. Perhaps Cade would give her an advance on her wages.

She dusted and redusted the tables in the hall and in the foyer until she saw Albert leave, then she went to the door and knocked.

"Come in."

Jenny opened the door slowly. Cade looked up from a letter he was holding and motioned for her to enter. One look told her his mood had not lightened. He wore a deep scowl on his face. "May I speak with you a moment?"

He stood and waved the letter angrily at Jenny. "I was

going through my correspondence and what do you think I found?''

Wary, she stepped back. ''Should I come back later?'' she asked.

He gave her a half smile and returned to his seat. ''No, come on in. I'm sorry if I upset you. I just received a letter addressed to *Miss Fairchild*.''

The announcement hit Jenny in the chest like a sledge-hammer. She stepped closer to get a better look at the letter. It had to be from Izzy. No one else knew where she was. How could she have neglected to tell her sister she was not using the name Fairchild?

''W-what did it say?'' she finally managed to say.

''I didn't open it.'' He studied the letter again. ''Do you think I should?''

Relief swept over Jenny. Leaning across the desk, she plucked the letter from his fingers. ''I'll try to catch Albert,'' she said. ''If we send it to the agency with a note saying Miss Fairchild is not here, perhaps she will believe you then.''

She hurried out, shutting the door behind her before Cade could offer an objection. With the letter clutched to her bosom, Jenny sped up the stairs and along the hall to her bedroom at the back of the house. Once inside the room she closed the door and shoved the lock home.

With trembling fingers she tore open the letter. It *was* from Izzy. They would be there on Friday. They? Surely Izzy wouldn't be bringing Father with her?

CHAPTER 9

With shoulders thrown back and head held high, Jenny walked into the train station to await her sister's arrival. It was difficult to ignore the stationmaster's stares as she crossed the small room to take a seat, but Jenny did her best. The letter had said they would be on the noon train. If the stationmaster had been anyone but Carl, she would have inquired to see if the trains were running on schedule.

The last few days had been a nightmare as she wondered if her father was coming with Izzy. Even if she was able to convince him she would never be returning to Philadelphia, her charade would be up. Cade would know she had lied to him. If Em was to be believed, it was one of the things Cade would never tolerate in a woman.

Thank goodness he hadn't asked her about the letter she was to have given back to Albert and for that she was grateful. None of the explanations she had come up with sounded viable.

Fortunately Cade had been tied up with another problem concerning his cattle and Sam had driven her into Gold Shoe and was out and about on his own errands. She couldn't have dealt with Cade's company today. Ever since the night on her balcony, he seemed to be watching her every move. It was a bit nerve-racking to find him always underfoot, his intense blue eyes a constant reminder of what had almost happened between them.

"May I bring you a cup of coffee?"

The words startled Jenny and she jumped. "No, thanks," she answered.

"Are you sure?" Carl asked again. "It wouldn't be no trouble at all."

If truth be known, he didn't care if she drank it or wore it. He only meant to impress the railroad inspector who had been dogging his footsteps for the last two days.

"No, really I'm fine."

"You certainly look better than the last time I saw you."

"Pardon?"

"The night you arrived. Mr. Morgan came carrying you back here." He paused, then raised his voice for everyone to hear. "It looked like someone had beaten you."

Jenny glared up at him. "If someone hadn't sent me on a wild goose chase, it would never have happened."

Carl's face flushed, but he quickly recovered. "I apologized to Mr. Morgan about not having you wait here," he said humbly. "But he really should learn to control that temper of his. The townsfolk around here don't cotton to a woman being treated like that."

Jenny started to correct him, but the arrival of the noon train sent every other thought flying from her mind. She hurried out onto the platform and waited for the passengers to disembark. Izzy was the first to step down.

Tears coursed down Jenny's cheeks as she hugged her little sister. "Where's Father?" she asked, looking over Izzy's shoulder.

Izzy stepped back and studied her sister a moment. "Why would you think I would bring Father? Don't you think I can be trusted to escape without him?"

"You said there would be someone with you. I thought it was Father."

"It was me," a loud voice boomed out.

Jenny spun around. "Pritch!"

"You seem surprised to see your old housekeeper. Did you really think I would allow Izzy to travel by herself. You may choose to put your life in danger, but I refuse to allow you to do the same to Izzy."

Jenny ran into her arms, burying her face against Pritch's ample bosom. "I'm so glad you came. I missed you both so." Jenny suddenly pulled away. "But Father. What will he say when he sees you both gone?"

"I turned in my notice the moment we got your letter. So when Izzy went to stay with a friend for a few days, no one noticed that I was packing Izzy's things along with mine." Pritch studied Jenny for a moment as they walked toward the buckboard. Despite the dark circles under Jenny's eyes, she looked happy.

"What about you, girl?" she asked. "How did you end up being some man's housekeeper?"

"It's a long story, Pritch, but wait until you see the house. It's as big as ours back in Philadelphia. There's even an extra wing in back that I've been staying in."

"Is there enough room for the three of us?"

"More than . . ." Sam was coming back. She'd have to hurry. Jenny glanced over her shoulder. No one was near. "Listen carefully," she whispered. "When Cade asks, you're both from St. Louis. You know me only as Jenny and you worked with me at my previous place of employment."

Pritch lifted a stern brow. "Cade? Who is Cade?"

Jenny rolled her eyes. She had forgotten how strict Pritch could be on some things. "Cade owns the ranch. He's our employer. I'll explain it all later."

"And who was it that we used to work for, if I may ask."

"A banker in St. Louis."

"Does this banker have a name?" Pritch stubbornly asked.

"None that I've given," she whispered in return before stepping around them.

"Ah, there you are, Sam. The bags are being unloaded now. I'm afraid we have quite a few. Put what you can in the carriage and then have someone come back after the others."

"Yes, Miss Jenny," he said, punctuating his agreement with a spit of tobacco.

Pritch pulled Izzy back from the path of the dark brown liquid.

"Sorry, ma'am. I was aimin' for that spider. Darn if I didn't miss him, but you-all just wait right here. I'll go talk to the stationmaster about keeping an eye on your bags."

Jenny touched his arm. "Sam, I need to stop by the post office and pick up our mail. You can pick us up there." She had Izzy by the arm and down the walkway before he could answer.

Clutching a handkerchief to her breast, Pritch hurried to catch up with the two young girls. "If that is what your West is like, I think we'd best be taking the next train back to Philadelphia."

Izzy giggled. "You didn't warn us that people treated your paradise like the bottom of a spittoon."

"Quiet now," Jenny pleaded. "I admit things are a bit rough around the edges here, but it's worth it. No one tells you who you can talk to and who you can't." Jenny lifted her skirt and stepped off the sidewalk onto the dusty street.

"Why I even had a lady of ill repute come to visit a couple of weeks ago," she added.

"L-lady of what!" Pritch squealed, stopping dead in the middle of the street.

Jenny took her by the arm and pulled her to the other side. "Don't split a seam, Pritch. She's a friend of Ca—Mr. Morgan's."

Pritch was beside herself. "Your employer has fallen women traipsing through his house in front of a young girl like you?"

"I'm not a young girl, Pritch. I'm a grown woman and Em happens to be a very old friend of Cade's. She's not his lover."

"And what would you be knowing about such things?"

"I asked her and she told me."

"She said that to you?"

Pritch's voice had taken on a frantic high-pitched squeal and people were beginning to stop what they were doing and stare. Jenny shoved her into the general store. "I'll explain everything once we get to the ranch," she whispered. "Now is not the time."

Izzy was disappointed that they did not continue for the topic of meeting such a woman interested her immensely. Always the baby of the family, she had never been allowed to sit in on adult conversations. She smiled to herself. It was a little difficult to be sent to your room out here in the middle of nowhere. She followed Jenny to the back of the store. Already she was beginning to like Colorado.

"Do you have any mail for the Trinity Ranch?" Jenny asked the woman behind the cage.

"Land's sakes, do I ever," she said as she handed a large bundle through the opening. "You folks must be pretty busy out your way. Cade hasn't sent anyone in for over a week now."

Jenny waited until the woman's attention was occupied with another customer before she looked through the mail. There were three letters from St. Louis. One was clearly marked Miss Emily's Positions For Young Ladies. Why were they writing? Jenny thought with a frown. She had made good her debt that she had incurred by cheating them by scraping together every cent she had earned—and then some. This letter spelled trouble. She was sure of it. There was no way she could let Cade see the letter.

Jenny took a quick glance around the store. Izzy and Pritch were looking at bolts of cloth and the only other customer was catching up on all the gossip while she got her mail.

Jenny stepped behind a stack of wooden kegs. She considered tearing the letter up in little pieces and letting the wind carry the evidence of her crime away, but she knew he would only receive others until the problem was resolved.

With trembling fingers, Jenny tore open the letter and read it. Instinct had served her well. The agency had done some further checking and discovered that the housekeeper's ticket had not been used but instead had been redeemed for cash.

It went on to explain that a careful questioning of the clerk led them to believe the housekeeper and his mail-order bride were possibly one and the same. They enclosed a bank draft in refund of their services, apologizing for any trouble they might have caused him and recommending he dismiss the housekeeper at once. They awaited further word from him as to whether they should continue to look for a bride on his behalf.

After tearing off the return address, Jenny stuck the letter in the pocket of her skirt. She purchased a piece of writing paper and an envelope. Using the small writing desk in the corner she composed a letter thanking the agency for their efforts on Cade's behalf and declining their offer to find him a bride.

Thankful that the problem could finally be put to rest, Jenny sealed the envelope and mailed it off. Having finished, she rounded up Izzy and Pritch from the pattern books and went out to wait for Sam.

Pritch and Albert took an instant dislike to each other. Pritch, who had been head of the Fairchild household for the last twenty years, resented Albert treating her with no more respect than he would have for a new maid, and Albert resented Pritch's tendency to take charge. By the time Cade returned home, Jenny had given up trying to placate the two of them. She sent Izzy off to mend the linens and concentrated her own efforts on bringing the house account books up-to-date.

Setting up her things in the small back parlor, it took her the rest of the afternoon for her thoughts kept returning to the other two letters from St. Louis. They had to be answers to Cade's advertisement. One of them could very well be the one Cade would marry. The one he would take to his bed. The one whose lips would burn with his kiss.

A heavy stone seemed to have settled in her heart. Who Cade married was none of her concern, she told herself. What would happen to Izzy and her if Cade's bride took a dislike to them was the only thing that mattered. Em's idea of somehow opening the letters was sounding better all the time. After all, men were such fools when it came to women. Cade could very well be taken in by a pretty face. She would be doing everyone a favor if she took a peek at the letters herself.

Jenny didn't have to search Cade's desk. The letters were lying on top. She was too late. Cade had already opened them and from the paper lying beside them, he was in the process of answering the top one when he had been interrupted.

Jenny picked up the photograph from the first letter. A lump formed in her throat as she gazed at the soft curls framing a beautiful face. It was no wonder Cade was in such a hurry to answer the woman. The old bitterness roiled within her. She doubted Cade even took the time to take note of the tight lines surrounding the pretty mouth.

She was about to toss the photograph down and leave when she noticed the corner of the second letter peeking out from beneath the first. Curiosity prompted her to examine it also. Unlike the first photograph, the woman who wrote the second letter was plain to the point of ugly.

Jenny immediately took a liking to the woman. It was a shame the woman would not be given a fair chance. Cade was like every man. He would pick the beautiful one. Jenny started to replace the photograph when an idea suddenly occurred to her.

Her lips curved in a smile. It just might work but she would have to hurry. If she wasn't mistaken, that was Cade she heard in the foyer now. Being careful to replace everything like she had found it, Jenny switched the pictures.

"There," she whispered to herself when she finished. "That should do it."

Returning her account books to their place on the shelf, she met Cade at the door. "Good evening, Mr. Morgan," she said as she swept by him.

"Good evening, Pla . . ."

She was gone and he felt that old emptiness come over him. He knew it was his fault she was avoiding him of late. She was his housekeeper and he had tried to seduce her. It was a wonder she hadn't turned in her notice. There had to be plenty of openings for good housekeepers in Denver.

He sat down at his desk. He couldn't shake the feeling that she was hiding from someone. It had to be the husband she mentioned. It was the only thing that made any sense. She needn't worry. He would protect her. But first he needed a wife to protect him from her.

He dipped his pen in the crystal inkwell. He had been fortunate. One of the women to apply appeared to meet all the qualifications. Miss Truman had assured him in her letter that she was not only an experienced hostess, but well versed in the ways of handling children since she had assisted her mother in raising two younger sisters. She was beautiful too.

Cade slid the photograph out of the envelope to take

another look. His dark brows shot together in a frown. This wasn't the woman he planned on asking to be his bride.

Confused, he checked the signature on the letter. *Miss Sarah Truman.* He quickly checked the other photograph. Yes, this was the one. He wrote a quick note inviting Wilma Cox to come to the ranch, then slipped it into an envelope.

Damn. The seal didn't hold. That was the fourth one out of his last order that he'd had to glue. After digging out an old glue pot from the bottom drawer, Cade sealed the letter.

It didn't take him long to finish the last of his correspondence, then he replaced the paper, glue pot, and envelopes in the desk and rang for Albert.

"Yes, Mr. Morgan."

Cade reached out to hand Albert the correspondence. "I'd like for you to mail these letters for me."

They both stared at the flap on one of his letters curled up like a fat sausage.

"What the . . ." Cade began. "Looks like I'll be needing a fresh glue pot as well."

"Millie has something in the kitchen that ought to work," Albert offered.

"Use it. I want the letter out as soon as possible."

"Will do."

Cade straightened the last of the papers on the top of his desk, then followed. At least he'd had the foresight to recheck the letter before he answered it. He sure didn't want to send for the wrong woman.

The sun had set by the time Pritch came up from the kitchen with a supper tray for Jenny and her sister. She plopped the tray down on the table.

"I met your Mr. Morgan."

"I'm sorry I didn't think to introduce you," Jenny said as she moved the covered dishes onto the table, "but Izzy and I have been working on the linens. The repairs are all done now so we can start on the new drapes for the front parlor tomorrow.''

"Forget about the drapes," Pritch growled. "I want to know why Mr. Morgan would be surprised that you didn't take supper with him tonight."

Jenny's hand hovered over the cups. "I imagine it was because I generally dine with him when he's home."

"Since when does a housekeeper eat at the family's table, young lady?"

Jenny cringed. Even Izzy was looking at her as if she'd lost her mind. "Never having been a housekeeper before, I guess I didn't think much about it."

"Didn't think much about it!" Pritch screeched. "When have I ever taken my meals at the dining table?"

"Pritch, you're beginning to sound just like Father."

Izzy gasped. Pritch pursed her lips together and stomped out of the room.

"Oh, Jenny, don't ever say anything like that about Pritch. She could never be as strict as Father."

Guilt tugged at Jenny's heart. She could have cut her tongue out. Pritch had always stood by them. When Jenny had had to lie to save someone from her father's wrath, Pritch was always there to lend credence to the story.

Jenny ran after the old housekeeper and threw her arms around her. "I'm sorry, Pritch. Please forgive me."

Pritch stood unbending in her arms. "You had no call to say that, missy," she said with tears in her eyes. "Not after all I've done for you and your sister. You would have starved to death if I hadn't risked my job to sneak that food in to you every time that man locked you in the attic."

Jenny smiled to herself. "Having to live on bread and water for a few days is hardly starving," she pointed out.

"I'll remember that next time you get locked in an attic."

"No man will ever do that to me again," Jenny exclaimed.

Pritch winced at the bitterness Jenny still carried within

her. Mr. Fairchild was a hard father. There was no denying it. But not all men were like him and she hoped one day Jenny would be able to put the pain behind her and discover that for herself. She gathered Jenny in her arms.

"Your supper's getting cold. How about you eat first. We'll discuss your arrangement with Mr. Morgan later."

Jenny wasn't sure herself what the arrangement might be. How could she explain to Pritch that there must be a huge sign on her chest that said "Take me in your arms. I want to be loved." And Cade always seemed willing to oblige.

Cade leaned against the door of the station and watched the passengers disembark. After his last experience waiting for a prospective bride, he hadn't told anyone his reason for going to town.

"Mr. Morgan?"

Cade's blue eyes narrowed at the woman stepping from the train. Did he know her? With the severe cut of her black traveling dress and the bitter twist of her thin lips, she reminded Cade of a troublesome crow. Even so, she did look vaguely familiar.

"Yes?" he asked politely.

She extended her hand to him. "I'm Miss Cox. Wilma Cox."

Cade could only stare as she lowered her eyes modestly, then bestowed him with a toothy grin. Good grief, she was trying to flirt with him. Cade had heard the term "snaggle-toothed old biddy" but up until now he had never met anyone who fit the description so aptly. He thought he was going to be sick.

He glanced down at the photograph. There had to be some mistake. This tall, thin woman bore no resemblance to the one in the picture. While he rarely judged a person by their looks, he knew he would never have considered this woman for his bride. Then he remembered. She was the other one who had answered his ad. He must have gotten the photographs switched somehow.

All he wanted to do was send her back on the next train before anyone saw her, but that wasn't due for some time. In the meantime he couldn't just leave her standing here on the platform.

He held out his arm for her to take. "There's a real nice hotel down the way. Let me buy you a cup of coffee and we can discuss this."

She quickly stepped forward and slid her arm under his. Good grief, she was simpering.

Carl watched the rancher and the woman crossing the street. Every time he saw the tall, handsome rancher hate festered anew. Good fortune came easily to Cade. Not so with him. He worked twice as hard as the rancher and didn't reap half the rewards.

He wished it'd been Cade's head he'd split with that ax instead of the old woman. It would have done his soul good to have seen Cade beg like she had. But like everything else he wanted, he knew he'd be denied the pleasure. Besides, you couldn't hack up a man like Cade Morgan without people raising a stink. They didn't shrug their shoulders and forget like they had with the old woman and the boy.

But he'd get his chance, and when he did, he'd make sure everyone thought it was an accident. And the beauty of it was no one would ever suspect it was him.

By the time Cade put Miss Cox on a train back to St. Louis, he was ready to drop the whole idea of a mail-order bride. Despite his reservations, he had tried to give the woman a fair interview, but Miss Cox had proved to be more prickly than a pinecone. She hadn't taken the explanation of his mistake well. After an hour in her company, Cade was prepared to remain a bachelor the rest of his days.

The stack of letters that rested on his desk at the ranch could damn well remain there. At least until he recovered from his encounter with Miss Cox.

Cade walked to his carriage when he heard someone shout at him.

"Morgan!"

Cade pasted on a smile as he waited for the rancher to catch up with him. Just his luck. A few more minutes and he'd have escaped. "Good afternoon, Hiram."

"Afternoon." The man fastidiously wiped the dust from his brow. "Did Albert give you my message?"

"He said something about you going down to Denver for another meeting with the governor."

Quick to take offense at the slightest criticism, Hiram puffed out his rounded chest. "I'm going to keep going until that man realizes I mean what I say," he growled. "Wouldn't hurt for you to talk with him too, Morgan. Us ranchers need to protect our interests."

Cade knew what he really meant. Hiram was a stingy, tight-fisted old man who didn't care about anyone other than himself. His only concern for the ranchers standing together was that he felt it gave him a stronger position. Hiram was only interested in looking after Hiram's interests.

"What did the governor have to say?" Cade asked for politeness only. He had already received a note from the governor begging him to do what he could to keep Hiram away from the capitol.

"Said we should get together and elect a representative to send to Denver."

"Sounds like a good idea to me. What about Toliver? He has a good head on his shoulders."

Hiram shook his head. "Don't know much about him. Only met the man a time or two."

"Well, you can remedy that easily enough. Call a meeting of the ranchers. Sit down and discuss your concerns. See what Toliver has to say."

Hiram fixed his gaze on a nondescript point over Cade's shoulder. ''That's a fine idea, Morgan, but my wife. You know how it is. She's been feeling poorly of late. I'd hate to put this on her.''

Cade knew how it was all right. ''Feeling poorly'' was putting it mildly. Word was that Hiram's wife dipped liberally into the whiskey jugs Hiram took home after his visits to Em's place. It was the only time Hiram was unstintingly generous. Cade couldn't remember the last time he had seen the woman sober.

''Notify the others,'' he said. ''You can all meet at my ranch next Friday night. About eight o'clock? And I'll make sure Toliver is there.''

''That's mighty nice of you, Morgan. The little woman has been nagging at me to see the inside of that house ever since Ross built the place. She'll be pleased to know she'll finally be getting her wish.''

Cade could have kicked himself. He should have known Hiram would turn this into a social gathering now that the expense wouldn't be coming out of his own pocket. It was times like this when he knew the governor was right. Cade needed a wife.

Jenny moved the stack of letters for the third time in as many minutes. They were obviously answers to Cade's advertisement so why wasn't he opening them? She shifted the pile again. She didn't know how Cade had worded his ad, but judging from the response wealth must have been listed among the benefits.

She wouldn't put it past him to leave the letters there knowing she would see them. It would be just like him to want to flaunt them before her since she hadn't expressed an interest in marrying him herself. What he didn't realize was that no matter how tempting the offer, Jenny would never submit to a man's rule again.

Cade might set her heart to fluttering at times, but she was no fool. Once he put that ring on her finger, things would change. Those tender looks would be gone—replaced by the cold unyielding demands of a man who had complete control over you, body and soul. She had watched her mother wither under such a marriage. Her friends could say what they wanted to about marriages being made in heaven. Jenny knew they were conceived in hell.

Jenny ran her finger along the edge of the desk. Perhaps she should open the letters and go through them. When she was a child, she had caught her father opening her mother's correspondence, then resealing it. As most children would be, she was fascinated with the process and had boasted of her knowledge in her father's hearing. It was the first time her father had locked her in the dark attic. Jenny never forgot.

"I'll not be doing it for myself," she whispered to the deaf study walls.

"One never knows. There might be some poor innocent creature among these who believes all those sugar-coated lies."

Jenny picked up the letters and carried them to the back room where she had put the sheets to soaking in a tub of lye water earlier. Thank goodness the water was still hot.

"I might very well be saving the woman from a fate worse than death," she mumbled to reassure herself.

Cade might be covering up a mean streak as uncontrollable as her father's. Heaven only knew, her father was a master at hiding it from everyone—everyone but his family. Now that she and Izzy were gone, she wondered who was the victim of his tempers now.

As luck would have it, the water was still warm and it didn't take much to heat it to boiling. Once the cloud of steam was rolling off the churning water, Jenny swung the pot away from the hot coals. Mindful of the heat, Jenny used the iron tongs she used to stir and lift the sheets to hold the first letter over the steam.

As soon as the seal on the envelope began to lift away, she opened the letter. She didn't have much time to check the photograph and read the letter. The glue mustn't be allowed to dry or it was the devil to reseal the envelope.

With each letter she had to reheat the water. It was a slow process, but it worked much more effectively if the water was boiling. By the time she got to the twelfth one, the room was filled with the strong lye vapors, burning her eyes.

So far her efforts had been a waste of time. She couldn't conceive of Cade answering any of them favorably. From the little she had gleaned from the letters most of them were widows hoping to remarry. She hadn't realized there were so many ugly women looking for husbands.

The next letter gave easily after only a few minutes over the lye pot. When Jenny slipped it out of the envelope, a photograph fell to the floor. The woman was beautiful. One of the most beautiful Jenny had ever seen. Giant butterflies beat helplessly against the walls of Jenny's stomach as she read the exquisite handwriting. Everything in the letter bespoke of elegance and grace. With a heavy heart, Jenny stuffed the contents back into the envelope and smoothed the flap back in place. She knew with a certainty this would be the one Cade answered.

Tears of frustration coursed down her cheeks. Darn! The seal wouldn't close. What was she to do now? She couldn't return it with the others. Cade was sure to notice.

She mustn't panic, she told herself as she thoughtfully tapped the envelope against her chin. Perhaps Cade would be better off if she didn't return this one to the stack. After all, why would someone who looked like this woman have to answer an advertisement in order to get a husband? For all Jenny knew, the woman could be one of those who married lonely men for their money.

Putting it that way made it so much easier to toss the letter into the fire. The thirteenth one she put in the pile to return to Cade's study. The next three went into the fire.

Odd, how easy it was after the first. She didn't even bother reading the letters anymore. The photographs were enough to make a decision. Even so, Jenny fretted over the last one. The woman wasn't very pretty, but then she wasn't ugly either. Oh, well, the fire was getting low. She tossed it in beside the ashes of the others and left.

When Jenny placed the letters back on the desk, she noticed that most of the envelopes had not held their seal. One or two, she could have ignored, but with this many Cade was sure to become suspicious. She searched the desk drawers until she found a glue pot. She smeared a generous portion on the flaps. She hadn't much time. Steaming open the letters had taken longer than she had anticipated and Cade was due back at any moment.

Jenny had just finished the last one when she heard footsteps outside the door. She quickly dropped the jar back into the desk and shoved the drawer shut. The door opened as she moved away from the desk.

When Cade saw who was in his study, he closed the door. Jenny had been trying to avoid him ever since the night someone dynamited the outhouse. She was up to something. He could feel it in his bones.

He had thought about showing up at her room again, but the arrival of the two new maids made that rather awkward. He had tried sending for her, but the old one kept showing up to see what he wanted. He had pointed out that he wanted to see Jenny, but it had gotten him nowhere. There always seemed to be a convenient excuse for her not to be available or someone came with her. It was as if everyone in the house was conspiring to keep him from having a private conversation with her. He would have pressed the issue, but it was evident she would fight him on it. It wasn't worth creating a potentially embarrassing situation. He had her now. That was what mattered.

He stepped closer. "Anything I can do for you?" he asked, reaching out to outline the fullness of her lips.

"I was—I was just leaving," Jenny stammered. A heat warmer than the steam from the boiling pots soared through her, leaving her legs weak—her hands trembling.

Cade leaned down. He could see the fear leap into her dark brown eyes. He paused a moment, his lips hovering close to hers. Her entire body began to tremble. Good, he thought. Let her want me like she's made me want her.

He nibbled at the corner of her mouth. She can damn well burn with the passions that have kept him awake, tossing and turning, for the past few weeks. He moved the flat of his hand boldly up her arms.

With a gasp, Jenny turned and fled the room.

CHAPTER 10

Cade stood looking at the door for a long while before walking around the desk and sitting down. Damn! He should have held her there until she talked to him.

He had believed that she was married. Now he wasn't so sure. Pritch always called her *Miss* Jenny; the younger one, more often than not, referred to her as just Jenny. He'd lay his money by what the older one thought. She was such a stickler for what was considered correct in a servant—and an employer.

He reached up and pulled the bell cord behind his desk. Just as he expected, Pritch was the one to answer his summons.

"Yes, Mr. Morgan," she said, offering him that unreadable expression he was becoming to know.

"Have a seat. I wish to ask you a few questions about Miss Jenny."

He could see her puff up like a bullfrog as she sat stiffly in the chair across the desk from him.

"I don't know whether it would be proper of me

answering them,'' she said in that even tone she used in all her dealings with him. ''Her being over me and all.''

''You'll not lose your position if that's what's worrying you.''

She didn't say anything so he proceeded, ''Do you know what Jenny's last name is?''

''Yes.''

Cade patiently waited for more. None was forthcoming.

''Would you mind sharing it with me?'' he finally asked.

Pritch shifted uncomfortably in her chair. ''I don't know that I can.''

''Let me make it easier for you, Pritch.'' He leaned forward, resting his elbows on the desk. ''What name did she go by where you worked before?''

He could swear he saw relief cross her normally schooled features.

''Oh, I can answer that,'' she said, a suspicious twinkle in her eyes. ''She was called Miss Jenny.''

''Then she's not married?''

The twinkle died as suddenly as it had appeared. ''I . . . well, I—''

Cade was fast losing his patience. ''Surely you know if she is married or not.''

Pritch was at a loss. Jenny had said nothing about any marriage. The girl was going to have to learn to share her lies or live by the truth. That's all there was to it.

''No, Miss Jenny is not married. Now,'' she added hoping to cover whatever Jenny had said to him.

''That will be all, Pritch.''

He relished the maid's bewildered frown as she left the room. He wondered if she'd run to Jenny with the tale.

Cade smiled. Let her try to get out of this one. He had no doubt but what she would come up with some story.

So the little vixen was no longer married. She had foolishly thought to tame him with the threat of a nonexistent husband. She had no idea how effective the lie had been, but no more. Jenny would soon be his.

The sound of rustling papers pulled him from his lecherous thoughts. His attention focused on a stack of letters on the corner of his desk. The pile tipped precariously as the letters rose on curled flaps, then tumbled onto the desk.

What the . . . ? He picked one up and checked it more closely. It looked exactly like the letter he had tried to seal a while back.

Cade's eyes suddenly narrowed in suspicion. Everyone's glue couldn't have turned bad. He checked the drawer where he had set the glue pot. It was gone. He quickly searched the other three drawers. Nothing.

The center drawer caught his eye. No. It would never fit in there. Nonetheless, he looked. Halfway open, the drawer refused to budge. Cade ran his hand along the bottom. There was something stuck in back. After several attempts to reposition the jar, he finally managed to free it. It was the glue pot. He knew without a doubt someone had been using it. He picked up one of the envelopes. Why would someone need to reseal the letters?

There was only one answer. The person must have also opened them. But who?

Jenny?

She had looked frightened enough when he had caught her in his office. Had curiosity prompted her to open his personal correspondence? The letters had certainly been sitting there long enough.

He quickly shuffled through the other pile of correspondence to see if she'd found the letter that had been returned from St. Louis. If so, she'd know he had been checking out her references. The letter was intact. It wasn't as if he didn't have a right to. He just didn't want to confront her on it yet.

Next time he'd know better than to leave the answers to his ad lying around, but how could he explain that he had no enthusiasm for the task of going through them? The prospect of picking a bride in such a cold manner no longer appealed to him. But he would have gotten to them eventually.

One by one, he opened and read each one, discarding those he didn't wish to consider. It wasn't until he finished that he realized he had discarded each and every one.

He laid out all the photographs and studied them one more time. There wasn't an applicant among them he cared to meet. He had told himself that looks did not matter to him, yet he found himself searching each picture for that special something that would tell him this was the one.

Cade restacked the letters, then leaned back and studied them a moment. He could have sworn that there were at least five or six more. If so what would Jenny have done with the others and why? It wasn't as if he would marry any of them. All of them were wrong for some reason or another.

Cade frowned. Perhaps not. If Jenny had thrown some of them out, then he had no way of knowing what the others were like.

He yanked the cord behind his desk, then paced the floor until Pritch arrived.

"Tell Jenny I want to see her and I want to see her now!"

"But she's—"

Cade strode over to the old woman. "I don't care if she's up a tree tying ribbons in the branches. I want her here. Now!"

With her lips set in an angry line, Pritch turned and left the room. She's no more upset than I am, he thought as he continued to pace the room.

Whatever had possessed Jenny to think she had the right to go through his mail, much less decide which letters he was to see? One of them could have been everything Cade was looking for in a bride.

Cade suddenly stopped pacing. Jealousy? No, it couldn't be that, he told himself as one insane idea after another formed in his mind. Jenny wouldn't have disposed of all the promising applicants because she didn't want Cade to marry, would she? He had to admit the prospect was flattering.

By the time Jenny arrived, Cade's anger was dissipating. He greeted her with a smile that quickly turned to a frown when he noticed Pritch hovering in the doorway behind her.

"You may return to your work, Pritch."

Her lips were still pursed in a rigid line and for a moment Cade thought she was going to argue with him. Instead she glanced at Jenny, then left.

Cade went around to the front of the desk and casually leaned against its edge. "Thank you for being so prompt, Jenny. Please sit down."

Jenny eyed him suspiciously as she took her seat. From what Pritch had said, Jenny was sure Cade had discovered what she had done. The man grinning down at her was not the Cade she had expected to confront. This one was positively beaming from ear to ear. At least he wasn't sporting that false smile men tended to wear.

Jenny ventured a peek at the letters. Her eyes widened at the untidy pile. She had been so careful to leave them all in a nice neat stack. What happened? Then she saw the flaps. Every one of them she had repaired with the glue had curled up. There was no doubt about it. He knew someone had tampered with his mail.

Jenny lifted her eyes defiantly to his. The amusement reflected in their bright blue depths caused her a moment's uneasiness. He should be livid yet here he was smiling as if he'd just caught her with her hand in his bank till.

"Is there something I can do for you, Mr. Morgan?"

Cade reached around and picked up the letters. With a diabolical grin, he waved them in her face.

"You didn't need to do this, you know. I would have let you see the letters if you had asked."

Jenny stiffened. "Why would I be interested in your mail?"

Cade arched a dark brow. "Why indeed?" Cade set the letters back on the desk, then leaned forward and placed his hands on the arms of her chair. "Why didn't you ask me who had opened them? Or why the flaps on most of the envelopes are curled now?"

Jenny eased back in her chair. He moved with her. He was so close she could feel the warmth of his breath bathing her lips. Despite her attempt to look elsewhere, his dark blue eyes held hers.

"You must have forgotten you opened them," she offered lamely.

"Try again, Jenny. They weren't opened when I left earlier this morning."

His voice was deceptively soft—almost seductive. It reminded her of her father's when he knew without a doubt she was guilty. His words had always been as sweet as fresh nectar dripping from a honeysuckle vine. It wasn't until you ended up in the attic that you recognized the vinegar hidden between the petals.

"Just what are you trying to say, Mr. Morgan? That one of the staff opened them after you left?"

"Not one of the staff, Jenny. You."

Jenny dropped her gaze. "Why would I—"

He took her chin in his hand and forced her to look at him. "That's what I want *you* to tell me."

As he waited, he could almost see the excuses she dredged up, examined, then discarded one by one. "You might try the truth," he suggested as he continued to hold her chin in his fingers.

How could she tell him the truth when she wasn't even sure she knew what it was herself? How could she explain the knot in her stomach when she had held the photographs? What had started out as a way to check out someone who might become the mistress of the house had turned into a challenge to insure that he didn't marry any of them.

"Perhaps I can help," he offered sweetly. Too sweetly. The sticky honey seeped into her heart, leading the way for the hurt that was sure to follow. Jenny struggled to swallow the dry lump forming in her throat.

Just when she was about to regain control of herself, he moved his thumb to trace the outline of her lips. The butterflies immediately returned to wreck havoc in the pit of her stomach. The false smiles of her father were nothing compared to the seductive intimidation of Cade.

"I can speak for myself," she blurted out.

"Can you now?" He might as well jump in with his suspicions. Even if he was wrong, it should make her angry enough to tell him the truth. "Can you tell me why you destroyed the other letters?"

"Wh-what other letters?"

"The one from Miss Longfellow, the one from Ruby Crandall, and at least a half-dozen others," he rattled off the names as if he had known them for years. One look at the surprise on her face and he knew his bluff had worked. She had destroyed the letters. There was only one possible explanation. She didn't want him to marry. He could understand that. After all, hadn't he been relieved to discover that she wasn't married.

He leaned down and kissed the corner of her mouth. "Given your reasons, I'm prepared to forgive you."

Jenny tried to push him away. "Forgive me!" she exclaimed. "For what?"

First he kissed her cheek, then her ear. "For trying to keep me all to yourself," he whispered against the slender column of her neck. "I was pleased to hear you were no longer married."

It took all of Jenny's efforts not to give in to the mysteriously exciting tremors that shot up her spine, leaving her helpless. She'd die before she admitted anything. "Have you lost your mind?" she asked breathlessly.

He lifted his head and gazed into her eyes. The beginnings of a smoldering passion had darkened them. Oh, how he was looking forward to fanning those flames.

He took her hands and pulled her to her feet. Their bodies touched and a fire, hotter than he had ever known, raged through him.

"I'll leave the light burning in the hall tonight," he said, holding her to him. "After everyone is asleep, come to me."

Jenny gasped. "What are you saying?"

He grasped her hips and moved her boldly across the front of him. "I'm saying I want a sample of the merchandise before I purchase the whole bolt of cloth."

"Sample the merchandise! Why you—you—" Jenny drew back her hand and hit him across the face. The sound seemed to fill the room.

He grabbed her hand. "Why did you do that?"

She shoved her face close to his. "You're nothing but a conniving self-centered jack donkey, Mr. Morgan, and I pity the woman who marries you. As for me, don't worry about not getting a sample first. I wouldn't let you purchase so much as a thread let alone the entire bolt of cloth as you so cleverly put it."

She walked out and slammed the door behind her. He didn't try to stop her.

"You'll learn soon enough, Plain Jenny," he whispered to the empty room. "I always get what I want. And right now, I want you."

Jenny spent the remainder of the afternoon avoiding Pritch. She didn't want to face the fact that she may have cost them all their positions. What would they do if Cade dismissed her because she wouldn't share his bed?

Thank goodness news that a wild herd of mustangs had returned sent Cade and most of the cowhands out after them.

Jenny was just counting herself lucky when Izzy came to tell her she had company waiting in the parlor.

"An attractive woman with beautiful chestnut hair. And a frightfully sinful dress," Izzy added in a whisper.

Em!

Jenny ordered tea to be sent to the parlor, then went to join her guest. "What can I do for you?" she asked as she swept into the room.

Em took a seat. "My, my, aren't we in an awful hurry?"

"I'm sorry, Em. Mr. Morgan is expecting a lot of guests this Friday night and I have a lot of things to do."

"That's why I'm here. I came to warn you."

Jenny joined her on the settee. "Warn me? About what?"

"Word's out that a few of the women guests are intending to use this opportunity to attract Cade's fancy. Word has it that several have traveled down to Denver for new gowns."

"Why should that interest me?" Despite what she said, Jenny could feel the lump rising in her throat, threatening to choke her. "The quicker he finds a bride, the happier I will be."

Em's red lips lifted in a smile. "Cade finally made his move, did he?"

Jenny was relieved to see Izzy arrive with the tea. She had no intention of confiding in Em. Cade's ungentlemanly behavior was humiliating enough without sharing the details of her disgrace.

Jenny poured the tea and handed the cup to Em. "Would you like one of Millie's special tea cakes? They're quite good."

"Everything Millie cooks is good. There isn't a rancher around that wouldn't give his eye teeth to hire her."

"Bear says the same about the miners," Jenny said, happy that the topic of conversation was away from Cade.

Em bit into the frosted cake. "Mm-m-m," she said. "There's no doubt about it, Cade has a gold mine in her. He could give up ranching tomorrow and still make a fortune selling these cakes.''

Perhaps things weren't so bleak after all. If Millie could teach her to cook like this, she wouldn't need to be Cade's housekeeper. She could set up a bakery in Gold Shoe and sell her wares to the miners. She could become rich, then she wouldn't have to put up with Cade's mysterious hold over her emotions. She would be independent.

Jenny stood abruptly. ''I'm sorry, Em, but I have to get back to my duties. I appreciate your coming by. I'll keep in mind what you've said, but there are still a hundred things to do before Friday and I must get back to them.''

Amusement curled Em's lips as she took her last sip of tea. Bear was right. Cade was showing a decided interest in Jenny and if she didn't miss her guess, he had let Jenny know of the attraction. Em set her cup down. She had done all she could for now. It was only a matter of time and the two would be sharing more than a passing interest.

Jenny tucked the pillow under her chin, then reached for the fresh pillowcase. It had been two days since Cade and the others had left to catch the wild mustangs but the pillow still carried the faint scent of its owner. Jenny closed her eyes and breathed deeply. With the masculine smell came the pain. A pain so piercing it brought tears to her eyes.

When had this happened? She couldn't explain it. The man certainly wasn't worth it. Hadn't he proved that over and over again?

Cade was willing to order up a perfect stranger to be his bride, but with her he required a demonstration of her skills as if she were some unbroken mare he would have to train to the saddle. She must have proven a great disappointment the few times he had kissed her. A tear slipped down her cheek. So if the man was such a bastard, why couldn't she get him out of her head?

Jenny hugged the pillow to her. It wasn't fair. Of all her

friends, she had always been the one most adamant she would never marry and now she lay awake nights wondering what it would be like. The few hours of sleep she got weren't much better than none at all. Sleeping meant dreaming and in her dreams, she was in his bed again, his hard-muscled chest crushed against her naked breasts. His lips teasing her body until she thought she would die of the agony, then . . .

That's when she woke up. Not in his arms as she had the first time, but in a cold, lonely bed. A sad smile touched Jenny's lips. Pritch would be the one locking her in the attic if she knew the direction Jenny's thoughts had taken lately.

Jenny slipped the pillowcase on the pillow and finished making up the bed. The room had grown warm and she opened the window. The sound of hoofbeats told her the men were returning. She was about to withdraw from the window when she saw Cade. He sat astride a tall white horse. Even from this distance she could see that the other horses gave Cade's a wide berth. Animal and rider were magnificent.

Jenny was quite a horsewoman herself and she could appreciate the strength of command it took to keep such a mount under control. She had no doubt but what Cade was such a man.

She took a deep breath, closed her eyes, and allowed her mind to trace the dark blond hairs that covered his tanned chest. It didn't take much to envision his strong arms around her, his powerful leg thrown across hers while his bold hands had their way with her body.

If only her surrender did not bring back the memories of her father's domination—or the dark attic that was her punishment for her need to fight back. How was she to know all men were not like her father? Cade appeared different, but hadn't her father been the perfect gentleman in front of others?

Cade was a powerful man. He had to be to run a ranch the

size of this one. Was there some part deep within her that wanted to be controlled? Why else was she so attracted to Cade?

She wished there was someone she could ask about what was happening to her. It would be nice to know if these feelings were like an illness that would go away with time, or was she to be cursed with them the rest of her days?

Jenny pinned the last curl in place, then checked her reflection in the mirror. The pale peach dress did nothing for her. She was tired of always picking her most unflattering gowns. Tonight was special and she didn't want the other women who might attend to outshine her.

But there was no hope for the situation. Even though Cade had asked that she act as hostess for the affair, Jenny would not allow herself to hope he might want more. He had carefully explained that the men had business to discuss and someone was needed to keep the women occupied.

Occupied! He made it sound like they were a herd of mules that night get into the garden patch if they were not properly distracted. She wondered what he'd do if she set up the tables in the front parlor for a rousing game of poker. Bear had been teaching her the rudiments of the game and she found she had quite a liking for it. It would certainly show old Mister ''I want to try the merchandise before I purchase the whole bolt of cloth.''

Jenny suddenly realized she was being the worst kind of fool. She had spent the last week moping around because some bullheaded man had offered her the opportunity of earning a place between his bed sheets and she had refused. Of course, she had refused. The offer was an insult.

What had happened to her pride? Surely she hadn't traveled all this way to gain her independence only to have the first handsome man who crossed her path rob her of it. She was a fighter and she would darn well continue to be one. Cade Morgan wanted a hostess tonight. Well, he would have one. Jenny! The real Jenny. The one she had been forced to hide for too long.

Happy with herself for the first time in days, Jenny rummaged through her dresses until she found the black lace creation she sought. Next she got out her sewing shears and snipped the threads that held the extra row of lace her father insisted the bodice of her gown needed.

She had to admit the gown suited her dark hair and eyes. Without the lace she had discarded, it was low enough to entice Cade's interest without actually exposing her bosom. Perfect. Now the necklace.

The diamond chains that hung from the emerald collar sparkled against her throat as they dipped provocatively into the bodice of her black gown. Jenny clipped on the earrings that matched and turned in front of the mirror.

There! Let Cade explain to his guests how his house-keeper came to afford such jewels.

Jenny ignored Pritch's gasp as she walked into the parlor where Cade's guests had already begun to assemble. Although she had made up her mind to avoid Cade, her eyes sought him out.

He stood next to the fireplace, a tall, bronzed god. Except for his white shirt and diamond stickpin at his throat, he was dressed all in black. All he needed was her black hair to make them a matched set.

Jenny stood firm as his bold blue eyes traveled from the diamond necklace at her throat to the tips of her black satin slippers, then back. So intense was his gaze that she ran her hand across the snug waist of her gown to assure herself that she had indeed dressed before leaving her room.

His eyes locked with hers and everyone else seemed to disappear. That familiar haunting tingle was back, making its way up her back. Goose bumps rose along the heated flesh of her body. She knew without a doubt that had they been alone, he would have strode across the room and ravished her on the parlor floor. Somehow the knowledge gave her a feeling of power.

Pasting a saucy smile on her lips, she made her way to his side. It felt good to have every eye follow her progress across the room, but her only interest was in Cade.

"Good evening, Cade," she purred.

"Are you trying to embarrass me?"

"I don't know what you mean."

Cade reached out and lifted one of the diamond strands at her throat. The blue eyes that held hers were like two chips of ice.

"From an old lover perhaps?" he asked disdainfully as he let it fall. "Or is everyone supposed to think it's from me?"

Despite the coldness of his glance, the huskiness of his voice caressed her like soft velvet. She tilted her head to one side and offered him one of her most provocative smiles.

"Would it surprise you to know that some men are willing to gild the cloth without sampling the fit?" she whispered.

"From all I've seen, those men are fools."

Hiram slapped Cade on the back. "What men are fools, Cade?" he said, stepping boldly up to Jenny. "I don't know what this man has been telling you, miss, but some of us are quite likable."

"And you are?"

"Mr. Holcombe, ma'am, but you can call me Hiram." he waved his thin arms. "I put this here party together."

Jenny immediately took exception to someone claiming the credit for all the work she and her staff had done. "I had not realized you were the owner of Trinity Ranch, Mr. Holcombe," she said coldly.

Hiram coughed to hide his embarrassment. "I don't exactly . . . what I mean to say is Cade here owns this ranch, but him being a bachelor and all, I handled all the arrangements for him."

Only Cade recognized the fire building in Jenny's eyes. It was past time he stepped in.

"Perhaps I should introduce you, my dear."

The room fell silent as everyone strained to hear who the mysterious beauty was.

"Hiram, I'd like to present Jenny, my housekeeper."

"Your housekeeper!"

A chorus of whispers echoed the words. Cade ignored them.

"Why should you find that a surprise, Hiram? After all, I don't have a lovely wife like you and the other ranchers. So I make due with what I have. I think it most generous of Jenny to graciously consent to be my hostess for the evening."

There! The smiles had returned to the old biddies' sour faces. He turned and offered Jenny his arm.

"Come, my dear," he said. "I believe Millie was waiting for you before she served up supper."

Jenny tucked her arm in his and let him lead her to the dining room.

When they were safely ahead of the others, he leaned down to her. "When will you learn, Jenny, that revenge is often a two-edged sword?"

Keeping to the trees as much as possible, Carl quietly crept toward the lighted windows. Jealousy, then anger filled him as he watched the ranchers gather in Cade's parlor. It should not matter that he had not been invited, he told himself. One of these days he would be richer than all of them put together and the governor would be begging him for an invitation. Until then, he would watch Cade and lay his plans.

Something across the room had captured Cade's attention. The tall rancher excused himself and started to the door, then changed his mind. He picked up a drink and returned to stand in front of the fireplace.

''What's this?'' Carl mumbled to himself as he stretched his neck to get a closer view of what had upset the normally calm rancher.

Then he saw her. A vision in black lace walking up to Cade. Soft black ringlets framed one side of her face, trailing down to the ivory column of her slim neck. Her throat . . .

A thousand lights danced off the necklace as the candles from the fireplace caught the tiny prisms. The short man stepped out from his hiding place. He couldn't take his eyes off the diamonds. All this time he had been dreaming of getting his hands on the gold in the stream that ran through Morgan's pasture and here was a fortune right under his nose. If he played his cards right, he might end up with them both.

For the life of her, Jenny couldn't have said how she made it through the meal. Although she sat at one end of the long table and Cade sat at the other, Jenny never felt she was free of his scathing glance. It was a relief to retire to the parlor with the other women.

''How long have you worked for Cade?'' one of the older ladies asked.

''Almost two months.''

''I wouldn't mind working for a man like Cade,'' a young girl exclaimed.

Mrs. Holcombe grabbed her daughter's arm and sat her down on the sofa. ''Now, Beatrice, you musn't talk like that.''

''Why not, Mama,'' she whined. ''Just look at all the beautiful things in this room. I'd get down on my hands and knees and lick his boots clean if he'd offer to make me mistress of this house.''

A striking blonde ran her finger down the side of the silver coffee urn. ''I'd rather lick that gorgeous body of his.''

"Tammy Sue! You should be ashamed of yourself, young lady. What would your mother say if she heard you talking like that?"

"Once she saw this house, she'd say do whatever it takes, girl."

Mrs. Holcombe pulled her handkerchief from her dress sleeve and dabbed at the sweat beading up on her forehead.

"You'll have to forgive the girls, Jenny," she said. "Ever since we heard Cade was looking for a wife there's been no controlling them. A man as handsome as Cade Morgan is bound to turn a few heads."

From all she had heard tonight, Cade's fortune was the main attraction, not him, but Jenny graciously accepted the apology. If she had known all Cade's money she had spent beautifying his home would serve as bait for these money-hungry little vultures, she would have hid the treasures before they arrived.

"Have one of Millie's cakes," she said.

What Mrs. Holcombe really wanted was a drink, but she took the cake instead. "Cade's real lucky to have Millie." She leaned forward as if she thought the walls had ears.

"Heard tell a miner came all the way down Mosquito Pass to buy a sack of those fancy breads she makes. Offered her half his mine if she'd come cook for him."

"She's a fine cook," Jenny answered automatically, the wheels of her mind spinning beyond control. The answer to their problem was right here all along and it was Millie. If everything worked out as she hoped, they'd be in their own home before the year was out.

CHAPTER 11

"The governor had hoped to make it here himself, but something came up at the last minute," John said as he sank down in the leather chair in Cade's study. "He told me you can talk all you want, but it's not going to change the fact that you're the man the governor wants."

Cade poured them both a whiskey before joining the governor's assistant by the fire. "I didn't want you saying that in front of the other ranchers. Toliver's a good man and I want them to remember that when they pick their representative."

"The governor's got nothing against the man, but he'd hoped to get you." John took a sip of the whiskey. "Nice stuff," he said appreciatively.

"I had it shipped here over seven years ago. It's a special recipe that comes all the way from Kentucky."

"No wonder your partner wants you back in Denver. With whiskey as smooth as this, I'd want you close too."

"The whiskey has nothing to do with it. I think Ned's a little overwhelmed having to make all the decisions. He can be such a worrywart at times. I've had more important things to take care of.''

John smiled. ''And such a fetching little thing too. The governor will be pleased you took his suggestion to marry.''

''It would be nice if that were the case. Unfortunately, there's more to it than just proposing. The lady insists marriage is not for her.''

''The Cade I know wouldn't let that stop him.''

''Normally it wouldn't, but with all the things that have been going on around here lately, it hasn't left me much time to convince my housekeeper some things are more enjoyable than her independence.''

He went on to tell John what had been happening—his prize cattle, two of his men disappearing, the cut fences, and the explosion.

''Sounds as if someone's taken a powerful dislike to you, Cade.''

Cade set his glass down. ''I thought it best if I stay close until we find out who that might be.''

John nodded his agreement. ''A man needs to put his own house in order first. Just be happy that crazy lunatic with the ax hasn't paid a visit to you.''

''He's killed again?''

''There have been three more murders since the first.''

''I hadn't heard anything.''

''They've been pretty spread out. The last one was a miner up near Tarryall. He'd just sold his mine that day and was planning on going back East with his gold.''

''Right smart of him, I'd say. Most miners never get to enjoy their finds. It's a shame when one of them finally plays it safe and then he doesn't live long enough to spend his earnings.''

John frowned. ''All they found when they searched his shack were the two double eagles he got for his mine.''

Cade arched a questioning brow. ''Not much for a claim

in that area. Does the sheriff think the man didn't know the worth of what he had or that he was robbed?''

"It's hard to say. Most of those miners are pretty closemouthed about what they find. His poke could have been taken, but then why did his murderer leave the coins?''

"It's no stranger than the first murder.'' Cade got up and refilled their drinks. "What could anyone have wanted from that old lady and the boy?''

John leaned forward. "That brings me to the next thing the governor wanted me to discuss with you. A lot of mines have been changing hands lately.''

"That happens, John. It doesn't take long for a man to realize working a mine is a wagonload of hard work for a fistful of dreams.''

"If they were those types of mines, I wouldn't be worried, but I'm talking about ones that assayed high—the real finds.''

"No miner is going to sell that for a lousy two double eagles.''

"That's what has the governor so concerned, and what makes it worse is that the same man seems to be buying them up. W. E. Smith.''

"I've never heard of him.''

"Neither have I. The whole thing doesn't set right with me.''

"You think there's some connection to the murders?''

"It wouldn't surprise me. Gold changes men. I'd appoint a man to investigate, but I know how touchy miners get about sharing information. They're afraid if someone knows what their claim is really worth they won't live long enough to work it. That brings me to the favor we have to ask of you.''

Cade took a sip of the whiskey. "I'm listening.''

"You've known Bear a long time now.''

"A little over ten years.''

John stared down into his glass. "Bear's a miner himself

so the other miners won't suspect anything if he were to check around discreetly and find out what's going on with the others. Do you think he'd do it?''

"That's something you'd have to ask him."

"We were hoping you'd do that for us."

"Why me?''

"Because, for now, he'd rather no one else but the three of us know what we suspect and you're the only one I know who can ask Bear to do this with no questions asked. So, if you'd just agree, we could get back to the party."

"John, it's no wonder the governor makes such a good politician. He's the only man I know who would send his assistant to attend a party to help his voters only to go away with a solution to one of his own problems."

"You'll do it then?"

"First thing in the morning. But only because it might have something to do with the murders." He held the door for John. "Now let's get back to this meeting before Hiram elects himself as our representative."

Jenny checked her reflection in the mirror as she tied the ribbons of her straw bonnet under her chin. She had taken great pains with her toilette. She hoped Em's advice was valid. If a woman's beauty opened a man's purse, she was sure enough going to do everything she could to get her fair share of the contents.

She couldn't believe the ease with which she had talked Millie into making up a batch of her sweet rolls. Then to have caught Bear coming out of Cade's study was more than even she could have hoped for. Bear had agreed to escort her to some of the mines close by. Her luck thus far was certainly running high.

Despite her qualms at what she was about to do, Jenny couldn't suppress the grin that curved her lips when she left her room. He hadn't even asked what she was going to be doing. She wished dealing with Pritch had been half as easy.

Pritch had wanted to know every detail of her scheme before she'd help. Only the threat of never including her again had brought Pritch over to her side.

By the time she returned to the kitchen, Millie had already wrapped the warm sweet rolls and put them in baskets. Bear helped her load them in the buckboard and they were off.

Four dozen rolls. She didn't even know how much to charge, but the two hours it took for them to get to the mining camp gave her plenty of time to decide that she would try for one dollar each. If Em was right about Millie's cooking, the miners would gladly pay the exorbitant price.

Giving one of the baskets to Bear and carrying the other one herself, Jenny walked along the path toward the working men. They set down their tools and stared when she approached.

"Good afternoon, gentlemen."

They mumbled a gruff welcome. Jenny refused to be put off by their cold response to her greeting. Em had told her how lonely the miners were. If only she could gain their sympathy for her predicament, perhaps they wouldn't mind so much paying a dollar for the rolls.

Jenny batted her eyes and explained how she worked as housekeeper for Cade Morgan and she and her sister were trying to raise enough money for a small place of their own near Gold Shoe and she wondered if they would like to purchase a sweet roll. "I know the price seems a bit steep, but it costs a lot of money to set up housekeeping."

"I'll help you out, little lady," one of the miners said.

Once Jenny set the baskets on a rock and uncovered the sweet rolls, the tantalizing smell brought the other miners scurrying close to get one.

"Here's my gold," the first one said. "Take two dollars' worth out. I'll be wanting one for my partner too. He's back up at the cabin. Been feelin' poorly."

Jenny stared at Bear. ''Do you know how much two dollars is?''

Bear picked up the miner's poke and poured a generous portion from the small canvas bag. He winked at the fat miner. ''This here ought to be enough. Right, Wallace?''

''I'd feel a damn sight more generous about it if you were to bring some of that there whiskey Morgan hoards in his cellar.''

Jenny's eyes lit with interest as the other miners echoed his suggestion. ''How much are you willing to pay for the whiskey?'' she asked.

''Miss Jenny!'' Bear whispered. ''Cade won't take kindly to you selling his whiskey.''

When she ignored him, he grabbed her by the arm and pulled her aside. ''You had better stick with selling the rolls.''

''Nonsense, Bear. I was in the cellar only a few days ago. Cade has more bottles than he can count.''

''But Cade ordered that whiskey special.''

''Every one of those bottles is covered with dust. So they can't be too important or he would drink it.''

Before Bear could warn her that Cade was aging the whiskey, the miner shoved him aside.

''I'll pay you twenty dollars for a bottle of Morgan's whiskey if you can throw in an apple pie and a few of these here rolls,'' he offered. He dug in his pocket and pulled out the gold. ''I'll even pay you in advance.''

Jenny snatched the double eagle from his hand. ''It's a deal,'' she said. ''I'll be back in two days with the merchandise.''

Bear followed her back to the wagon. ''Cade's not going to like this, Miss Jenny. That whiskey came all the way from Kentucky.''

''You're wasting your time, Bear. I promised the man I would bring him a bottle next trip, and I plan on doing just that. With the profit I'll make, I could buy Cade all the whiskey he could ever want. But of course I won't. I would never make a profit doing that. But tell you what I will do. If it will make you feel any better, I'll split the profit on the whiskey with Cade.''

He doubted she even knew how expensive good Kentucky whiskey was.

''Fifty-seven dollars and sixty cents! Can you believe that? That's not even counting the twenty dollars I got toward my next order.''

Izzy ran her fingers through the golden flakes one more time. ''Are you sure it's worth that much?''

''I had Bear stop by the assayer's office in Gold Shoe on the way back. Just think, Izzy, I made more money off four dozen rolls than we make in a week working here.''

''I don't know,'' Izzy said doubtfully. ''It seems like you're stealing their money.''

Pritch stomped into the room. ''She is stealing their money! She's overcharging them and one of these days she'll get them riled enough, they're going to hang her.''

Jenny rolled her eyes heavenward. ''I told you they were pleased to get the fresh rolls. I even have orders for my next visit.''

''You're not planning on going again tomorrow, are you?''

''Heavens no. Do you think I'm stupid? Cade's bound to notice if I disappear two days in a row. I'm going day after tomorrow.''

''That's too soon. I won't let you go.''

''I've already given the orders to Millie. Besides, I promised the miners I'd be there then.''

Bear ran his fingers through his red hair and left it standing on end. ''She promised them the whiskey when we return in two days. What am I going to do?''

''Let me think a moment,'' Millie said as she stirred the

pot of stew she had cooking for supper. "I hadn't counted on her wantin' to sell Cade's whiskey."

Albert took down the plates to set the table. "I say you refuse to make any more things for her to sell and then we mind our own business."

Millie shook her wooden spoon at him. "You don't have a romantic bone in your body, Albert Miller."

"At least the ones I have aren't broken and that's only because Cade doesn't know what all you've talked me into doing. If he ever finds out we let Jenny sell his whiskey, we're as good as dead."

Millie paused in her stirring. "It would surely make him sit up and take notice."

"I'd rather he didn't notice me," Albert grumbled.

Bear nodded. "I agree with Albert. Cade's going to be mad as a hornet when he finds out."

"Cade will try to wring her neck and that's a fact, but once he's got his hands on her throat . . ." Millie's black eyes sparkled. "Yes, that should work."

"You want him to choke her?" Albert cried.

"You sound like he's going to kill her," Millie admonished.

"Isn't that what happens when you choke someone?"

"Sometimes, Albert, you have no imagination at all." Millie stood over her stew and sighed. "Once Cade's close enough to have his hands on her throat, he won't be wasting his time choking her. He'll kiss her."

"Kiss her? Hell, he'll kill her," Albert mumbled to himself.

Carl's mouth watered in anticipation. He'd kill her, but first he'd make her beg for mercy, then beg for more. He wasn't the best of lovers, but with her it was bound to be different. Her sweet innocence ignited a raging fire in his loins. Why should Morgan have all the fun?

He read Elmer's note one more time. It said she had to

have found the gold the same place the old lady had. Even if Elmer did work part-time at the assay office sweeping up, you couldn't always trust his information. But where else would she have gotten it? Well, she'd soon find out she couldn't file on the claim. He'd tried that himself but discovered Morgan owned the land.

Now he'd have to kill Jenny and Cade. Just like he'd killed the old lady and the boy.

After carefully stuffing the mail into her apron pocket, Jenny stepped up onto the bottom rail of the corral fence. The new mustangs shied away. Albert said Cade was looking over the horses, but she couldn't see him. She was about to step down when she spied Albert's pet rooster strutting across the corral.

"Get out of there, you stupid chicken."

Clarence ignored her screams and continued on his way across the dusty arena.

Jenny climbed to the next rail while the horses nervously circled the enclosed area. Tucking her shirt up, she swung her feet over the fence and dropped down.

"If you don't get away from those horses, you dumb bird, there won't even be enough of you left to make a good stew."

A roan mare took exception to the colorful chicken marching arrogantly up to her colt and reared over Clarence. A lump lodged in Jenny's throat as she pictured Albert's pet rooster being trampled beneath the powerful hooves.

Unmindful of her own danger, Jenny ran between the mustangs to rescue him. All the mares scattered—but one. The roan reared above Jenny.

"Get out of there!"

Jenny heard the shout, but she couldn't seem to get her legs to move as the horse came down, barely missing her. Clarence, seemingly bored with the whole thing, puffed up his feathers, shook himself off, and strutted away.

The mare squealed her anger. Up she went again. Like in a dream gone bad, Jenny could feel the vise of fear squeezing her chest at the hooves that hovered over her. She couldn't move—couldn't breathe. Somewhere there were footsteps. Someone was coming, but it was too late.

The breath she was holding burst from her lungs. Bright lights exploded. Screams echoed the fireworks in her head, then darkness.

Cade shoved the mare aside and scooped up the lifeless form. He buried his face in her dark hair. "Jenny," he whispered, his voice a tortured sigh of relief.

Luckily the mare's hoof had only grazed her head. She'd have a bruise, but he shuddered to think what might have happened had he not pushed her aside at the last moment.

One of the hired hands held the gate as he carried her through. "Get the buggy," Cade shouted at another one of his men.

With Sam's help, Cade soon got her on the seat. "I'm going to take her to see Doc Woods," he told Pritch when she came carrying a quilt from the house.

Cade wasn't going to take any chances. Not with his woman. He wrapped the quilt around her, gently tucking in the edges.

Lowering himself onto the seat beside her, Cade picked up the reins. Suddenly he stared down at his hands. They were shaking. Always calm in a crisis, the depth of his concern now caught him by surprise. Could he really care that much for this little brown-eyed vixen?

"Lie still or I'll tie you to the bed," Cade threatened.

Jenny sat up on the doctor's guest bed. Defiantly, she tossed back the black curls that framed her face. "The doctor said I was fine. I can't spend all my time in bed. I want to go home. I have things to do and I'm going to get up and do them."

With a stubborn grin, Cade pushed her back down on the

pillow. "Doc said you were to rest. The sooner you start following his directions, the sooner you'll get better."

Jenny struggled against his hold. "Maybe I don't want to get better," she screamed up at him.

"Oh, you're going to get better, Jenny. I'm going to personally see to it."

Jenny didn't care for the devilish grin that swept across his face at the statement. "You've done nothing but scold me for the last hour. Why should you care if I get better or not?"

He took her chin in his hand and forced her to look at him. "The sooner you get better," he whispered, "the sooner I can tan your hide for pulling such a foolish stunt."

An odd thrill coursed through Jenny. Despite what he said, she knew there was no malice behind his words. She should know. She was an expert on threats. A small smile made its way from her heart.

"You'd do that?" she asked, her eyes searching his.

The smile was his undoing. He took her in his arms and pulled her to him. This was the woman he had been searching for. The one he wanted to marry. He placed a kiss on her forehead.

"Oh, my Jenny, who but you would risk her life for a chicken?"

His voice was low, rich as the scent of pines on a warm day. Resigned to her fate, Jenny lay her head on his broad chest. "It wasn't just any chicken. It was Clarence."

"I should have let Millie cook that damned bird ages ago."

Jenny snuggled closer. She smiled when she realized the thundering of his heart matched hers. It all felt so right.

"Don't let it bother you, Cade. Millie would never have done it anyway. She knows how much Clarence means to Albert."

Cade held her from him. Her eyes. Would he never tire of

looking at them? They were big and beautiful—trusting, like a gentle fawn.

"My wife will mean even more to me, Jenny," he said.

Jenny's heart fell like a stone. The moment was gone. Him and his bride! Could he think of nothing else?

With trembling hands, she reached into her apron pocket and took out the letters. "I almost forgot. These are for you."

Cade reluctantly took them. He knew without looking they were from St. Louis. He could see the hurt in her face. Cade smiled down at her. "You're actually going to let me see them first?" he teased.

Jenny pounded on his chest. "Why would I care who you marry?"

He tipped her chin. "Because you're in love with me."

"I'm in love with no man, Cade Morgan, and I'll thank you to remember th—"

Cade's lips covered hers with a kiss. A kiss so moving—so complete—Jenny could feel the reasons behind her argument slipping away. Was he right? Could she be in love with him?

She relaxed in his arms and let the strange concept curl its way into her heart. Heaven help her if it found a place to nestle and grow. Loving a man was not in her plans.

Before she knew what was happening, he parted her lips and thrust his tongue into her mouth. Jenny was lost. With a shyness only love can overcome, she gave in to the passion that sent one trembling quake after another careening through her young body. She clung to him, never wanting the kiss to end.

Jenny's response pleased him, but the doctor's bedroom was not the place to seduce your lover. Cade pulled away. Seeing Jenny's disappointment, he gave her a playful peck on the lips.

"Now will you admit that you love me?"

"Never!" she cried at the smugness of his smile. Had he

no shame? The man was advertising for a bride, yet he was insisting on laying her heart bare. "I'll never love anyone," she cried.

"My but you're a stubborn woman. I've half a mind to lock you in the attic and feed you bread and water until you admit what's in your heart."

She stiffened in his arms. Damn, what had he said? Her face was as white as the pillow behind her.

"What's the matter, Jenny? Are you all right?"

She looked him in the eyes and the icy coldness he saw there sliced through him.

"Take me home, Cade," was all she would say.

CHAPTER 12

The next two weeks were hell as Cade tried to piece together what had upset Jenny so. Something told him if he didn't come up with an answer soon, she would be gone.

He wanted to talk with her, but she always made sure they were never alone. Ever since Jenny had rescued that misfit of a chicken, Albert followed her around like a damn puppy. He had half a mind to kill the bird himself and put an end to this nonsense, but he knew it wouldn't do any good. When Jenny wasn't with Albert, she managed to be either in the kitchen with Millie or off on some jaunt with Bear.

He tried questioning Bear, but that did no good. The big ugly miner got downright upset when Cade casually asked about the trips they took every day or two. If he didn't know better, he'd swear the entire household had taken Jenny's side and Cade didn't even know what the war was about. Well, he wasn't about to sit around and do nothing. Next time they rode out of here, he'd follow.

Jenny's thoughts, as always of late, were on Cade as she helped wrap the last of the baked goods and packed them into the baskets. At least Pritch was pleased with Jenny for going out of her way to avoid the tall, handsome rancher. She had this notion that Jenny was overly attracted to the man. If Pritch only knew. Cade thought no more of her than her father had. Locking her in the attic! Was that how men handled everything? Well, not with her. Never again would she be forced to face the darkness. Not anymore. A couple more months and she would have made enough money for them to leave.

Albert helped her pack the baskets in the wagon. The sales should be brisk today. Millie had included six fresh cherry pies. Perhaps it would help make up for the fact there would be no whiskey this trip.

The shelves in the cellar were becoming noticeably empty. Cade's supply of the Kentucky whiskey was almost gone. Before she sold any more, she would have to purchase replacements for the bottles she had already taken. With the gold she had stashed away, she should have more than enough.

After leaving the money and instructions for Albert, Jenny set out with Bear to the mines. Word had spread about Millie's pies, cakes, and fried rolls and the number of miners increased with each trip. Jenny felt a mite guilty about soliciting Bear's help each time, but he seemed not to care and spent his time talking with the miners while Jenny conducted her sales.

Finished, Bear and Jenny shared a cup of black coffee with the others, then headed home. The hot sun beat down on them and Jenny was glad for the parasol she had remembered to bring.

"We'll be going back a different way," Bear informed her. "There's a few miners just north of the ranch I want you to meet."

"But I don't have anything left to sell."

Bear couldn't hide his proud grin. Helping Jenny with her little money-making scheme had worked out well for him.

Within a few weeks, he had gathered more information than he had thought possible when Cade had first solicited his help.

Cade had been right to be concerned. Too many miners were meeting their maker ahead of schedule. Other than the one who was axed in his cabin, there wasn't anything anyone could put their finger on. But there was definitely a skunk in the woodpile somewhere. He only had to check out some of the rumors, then he would report to Cade.

"You can always take orders, Miss Jenny, and we can deliver them the next trip."

"I suppose you're right, but I just didn't want to overwork Millie."

"Don't you worry about Millie. She's right happy to help you out." Right happy, indeed.

Millie had the crazy notion this whole pitiful scheme would open Cade's eyes. He wasn't as certain that hate and love bedded down all that well. But if the frown he saw on Cade's face when they left was any indication, he would soon find out.

Albert stared at the small pouch of gold in his hand. How did Jenny expect him to replace Cade's four cases of good Kentucky whiskey in a town the size of Gold Shoe? He doubted there was that much in all of Colorado, but he'd do what he could. After all, Jenny had saved Clarence's life.

He stepped up to the high white house and knocked on the door. If anyone would have some, it would be Em. She was one of the few madams in town who didn't water down her drinks.

"What do you want at this ungodly hour of the morning?" someone screeched from the other side of the door.

"I need to speak with Em."

"Come back later. We open at five."

Albert pounded until the window rattled. "Tell her I'm from Cade Morgan's ranch," he hollered at the closed door.

The key scraped against the lock and the door flew open. "Why didn't you say so?" an old woman scolded. "You wait in the parlor and I'll fetch her for you."

The parlor was red—red walls, red carpet, red furniture. Albert clutched his hat to his chest and stared at the portraits over the various settees. Red walls and naked women. This had to be the hell the preachers warned everyone about.

"You have a message for me?" Em asked.

Albert spun around. It took him a moment to recall the purpose of his visit. "Whiskey, ma'am. I came to buy whiskey."

Em bit her lip to keep from smiling. "You want whiskey?" she finally said.

"Good whiskey, ma'am. I need four cases of the best you have."

"Is this for yourself?" she asked.

He couldn't very well tell her it was for Cade. She might say something to him. "Yes, ma'am," he lied. "It's for me and my friends."

"How much did you want to spend?"

"Not much, ma'am," he said, shoving the gold at her. "If you could give me a bargain, I sure would be appreciating it."

Em's smile softened. She had dealt with enough drinkers to know Albert was no connoisseur. But then the whiskey she had in mind was no prize either. Even so, she wasn't one to cheat a man. She'd give it to him for cost and they'd both be happy. He'd be getting his whiskey at a good price and she'd be getting rid of a bad batch.

"Tell you what, Albert. I had a shipment come in last week that I can give you a pretty good deal on. It's not the best, but I think you'll like the price and best of all I can let you have four cases."

Albert couldn't believe his luck. Four cases and at a good price too. "I'll take it," he said.

* * *

Richard Fairchild checked the hall, then closed the study door before taking his chair behind the large oak desk.

"What did you find out?" he asked the pale man seated across from him.

Mortimer Krebs paused to take out his reading glasses before answering. It wasn't often he had a client who paid as well as Mr. Fairchild and he wanted to savor the moment. With a great show of importance, he opened his notebook.

"The oldest Miss Fairchild purchased a ticket to St. Louis. According to the authorities, she reported her reticule stolen. I–"

"Why are you wasting my time with all this. I told you she tried to withdraw funds from her account from St. Louis. Tell me something I didn't know."

Mortimer puffed out his thin chest. "Did you know she applied at Miss Emily's Positions For Young Ladies to be a Colorado rancher's mail-order bride?"

The announcement brought Mr. Fairchild to his feet. "Are you saying my daughter married some unwashed rancher from God knows where in Colorado?"

"Not exactly," he said. He ran his finger beneath a collar that had suddenly grown tight. "One of the clerks there said she took the ticket and just disappeared. I checked all over St. Louis but no one remembers having seen a Miss Fairchild. So I went back and talked with Miss Emily herself. She seemed quite upset over the entire affair. Seems she didn't believe the rancher when he first wired her to find out what had become of his bride. Thought he was trying to get out of paying her the fee. She did some checking on her own and believes that your daughter actually applied for two positions."

"And the other position?"

Mortimer consulted his notes again. "That of a house-keeper."

Richard slammed his fist down on the oak desk. "A

housekeeper! What in the hell would a rancher need with a housekeeper? Last I heard, cattle were raised to be eaten, not dusted.''

Mortimer was pleased that he had thought to ask that very question. ''Cade Morgan is a very wealthy man. He not only owns a considerable amount of land, but several other large investments as well.''

Mr. Fairchild stood silently staring past the detective. Mortimer cleared his throat and asked, ''Would you like to know about your other daughter?''

''Mr. Krebs, you have been searching for Jennifer for almost two months now. Haven't you learned anything about her in all that time?''

Mortimer swallowed hard. ''She's a right smart lass,'' he ventured to offer.

''Mr. Krebs, let me tell you where my younger daughter can be found. Isabel is with Jennifer.'' He tossed a bank draft across the desk. ''Now leave your report on my desk and get out. Your services are no longer required.''

Mortimer, untouched by Fairchild's anger, let a smile crease his lips. He had long ago learned it was always wise to withhold a few pieces of information.

''Did you also know that she was traveling with a Miss Pritchard?''

''Pritch? But—''

''Exactly. Told everyone she was going to live with a cousin, didn't she? Well, it was a smart move all right. Gets her out of the house a day or two before Isabel disappears. Who's to suspect they would be in this together?''

He paused to savor Fairchild's reaction to his next bit of information. ''That rancher your daughter is working for . . .''

''Yes.''

''It's said he beat her, then took her to his bed.''

''You're sure of that?''

''The whole town was talking about it.'' Actually the

stationmaster was the only one to mention it, but that wasn't important. What was important was what Mr. Fairchild did with the gossip.

Richard looked at him with cold contempt. "Those two men you recommended from Colorado, Mr. Krebs, they'll do what I say—no questions asked?"

Mortimer beamed. "The best in the business, Mr. Fairchild. They'll do anything if the price is right and they know how to keep their mouths shut afterward."

"Perfect," he said, a vengeful smile curving his lips. "See that you're ready to leave for Colorado in the morning. I'll be coming with you."

Jenny folded up the paper she had used to scribble her new orders on, then tucked it into the basket with the others. Millie would need some help filling all these. She'd do it herself but she had never been any good at cooking the few times she'd tried. She'd have to ask Pritch.

After setting the basket back in the wagon, Jenny grabbed up her parasol. It looked as if Bear would be a while. She might as well see a little of the claims and how they were worked. It didn't take her long to realize that miners sacrificed a lot of personal comforts to scratch a future out of the creek beds. Their homes were nothing more than wooden shacks with an opening cut for a window and a door.

One miner had rigged up a series of sluice boxes and was shoveling in piles of dirt and rock. Another knelt beside the rushing water, sloshing dirty water around in a pan. Once the water and most of the dirt had floated away, he dug around with the tip of his knife in what was left. Sometimes he found what he wanted in the sludge at the bottom and sometimes he merely frowned and tried again.

Jenny stood and watched him pan for the tiny bits of gold. The whole process didn't look all that difficult. All you needed was a pan. She spotted an old beat-up one lying next to some bushes. Obviously no one wanted it anymore, but she wondered how she could retrieve it without anyone noticing when one of the miners let out a shout.

"Hallelujah! Would you just look at that." The old miner held his prize up for everyone to see. "Ain't seen one that size for more than a month of Sundays."

Jenny snatched up the pan by the bush and tossed it out of sight before she went to admire the miner's find. She held the small stone in the palm of her hand and a million dreams floated through her head. The miners had been paying her in gold for weeks, but this nugget was different. This nugget had been lying on the ground waiting for someone to come along and pick it up. And best of all, where one could be found so could others. After handing the miner back his gold, Jenny went to retrieve her pan.

She glanced back down the stream at the other miners. Bear was talking with a small group at the far end and the others were back at work. No one paid her any attention when she made her way over the rocks and down the stream. Once out of sight of the others, she began looking for a place that suited her fancy.

She moved farther and farther down the way, trying her hand at several spots, but no luck. Gold was harder to find than she thought. She knew she should head back. Bear would be wondering what had happened to her but the lure of a discovery drove her on.

She laid her parasol aside, rolled up her sleeves, tucked the bottom of her skirt into the waistband, then stooped down beside the stream. Using the edge of her pan, she stubbornly continued digging. After filling her pan with water she swished the contents around like she had seen the miners do. When most of the dirt had sloshed over the edge, Jenny searched the gravel at the bottom.

She blinked at the dull yellow stone in the bottom of her pan. Could it be?

"Find something?"

Jenny turned to find Bear looking down at her. She held the nugget out. "Did I strike it rich?"

"Well, let me take a look at that, missy." He lay the tiny stone across the palm of his hand. "It's gold all right."

Jenny spun around, her arms hugging her chest. "I'm rich, Bear. I'm rich!"

"Well, I'd hardly call one itzy little nugget rich," Bear pointed out. "It's smaller than Joe's back there." He didn't have the heart to tell her the gold wasn't hers. In her wanderings, she had crossed over onto Cade's ranch.

Although Cade often let some of the old miners work the creek, he hadn't given Jenny the same privilege. But unless Cade said otherwise, it was Cade's land and Cade's gold.

"Don't get your heart set on striking it rich, Miss Jenny. There's more than likely a reason no one's working this here claim."

"They gave up. I just know it. They walked away not knowing what was here. Well, I'm not that easily discouraged."

Jenny stuck the nugget in the pocket of her dress and went back to her digging. "This is just a start, Bear. Why, there's bound to be more just lying here waiting for me to find it."

"I hate to rush you, Miss Jenny, but shouldn't we be getting back?"

"But what about the gold?"

"This land more than likely belongs to someone, Miss Jenny."

Jenny looked down at the beaten pan. "Do you really think so?"

The sadness that settled around her cut Bear to the quick. "I might be wrong, Miss Jenny," he said, not wanting to be the one to disappoint her. Bear held out his hand to help her up. "Why don't we go for now."

Jenny took his hand. "Maybe we can check with those

miners you were talking with," she suggested. "They might know if anyone owns this land."

"One of these days we'll do that."

At the sight of her hiked skirt, Bear looked the other way. Embarrassed, he cleared his throat. "Miss Jenny, it might be a good idea for you to lower your skirt before we return to the wagon."

Cade rather enjoyed the provocative view he had of her bare legs and nicely turned ankles and was disappointed Bear had brought them to her attention. Carefully moving backward among the scrub oaks, Cade was trying to decide whether he was amused or annoyed at today's revelations. Jenny had hardly spoken two words in his presence since he had accused her of being in love with him and now this.

He had suspected for quite some time that having no money and nowhere else to go was the only thing keeping Jenny at the ranch. From what he had seen today it wouldn't be long before she sold enough baked goods and was off on her own.

His heart was strangely heavy as he mounted his horse and rode for home. He could always put a stop to what she was doing, he told himself, but that wouldn't change the fact that she wanted to leave. Somehow he had to bridge the gap that had sprung up between them and show her he cared. A smile lit his eyes as he mounted his horse. He knew just how to do it.

"Come on in," he said, stepping aside for Jenny to enter his bedroom. "I see you brought help."

Jenny shoved a reluctant Izzy in ahead of her. "She needs the training," she mumbled. The mockery in his dark blue eyes was evident and Jenny couldn't stop the wild beating of her heart.

"For what I have in mind, we'll only need the two of us."

The huskiness of his voice left no doubts. He meant to play havoc with her emotions again. Darn him anyway! Why was he doing this to her?

"That's quite all right, Mr. Morgan. Izzy will merely observe."

His eyes traveled slowly over the young girl. Her hair might not be as dark as Jenny's, but those dark brown eyes gave her away. "Where was it you worked before, Izzy?"

Jenny stepped between them. "What is it you want, Mr. Morgan? We have a lot planned for today."

He wanted Jenny alone and if Izzy was a relative like he suspected, he knew just how to go about it. "I want to know where Izzy worked before," he answered. "Surely that is not too difficult a question."

Jenny stared at him defiantly. "This is Izzy's first position."

"Then step away from her and allow her to tell me so." He waited a moment. "Well, Izzy."

With head lowered, Izzy came around Jenny. "This is my first position," she mumbled.

"How is it you came to know Jenny then? And I want to hear your answer, not hers."

Izzy looked up at her sister. She had never been as clever as Jenny at improvising her answers. "I—I—"

"Izzy lived next door to the family I worked for," Jenny announced. "But that isn't what you really wanted, was it? This time you win, Morgan. The next is my turn." She took Izzy by the shoulders and guided her to the door. "Run along now. Millie will be needing you to clean the breakfast things."

She waited until Izzy reached the stairs, then she slowly turned back to Cade. "If you've brought me here thinking we can continue our last conversation, you're wrong. I will nev—"

"I brought you here to ask your advice," he said with an

innocent grin. "You have redone all the rooms but this one."

Jenny didn't know how to answer. After waking in his bed, she had a difficult time coming into the room without thinking of the things his skilled hands had done to her body. "This is your room and—and I—"

He stepped closer and the words froze in her throat.

"Yes?"

Jenny swallowed. "I thought perhaps . . . your bride . . ."

"My bride?"

"Yes, your bride. Wouldn't she want to redo this room herself?"

Another step and he was standing over her. "Pretend that you are to be my bride." He ran the back of his hand down the side of her cheek. "Pretend that this was to be our room. Our windows. Our walls. Our bed."

The velvet huskiness of his words washed over her, leaving her insides trembling like a leaf in the wind. "I . . . can't," she murmured.

"It isn't so difficult, Jenny," he said as he took her by the hand and led her over to the bed. "Imagine that this is where you and I will be lying naked next to each other, burning with the passions God meant for a man and his wife to experience." He looked down at her. "Would you have the sheets made of soft white linen or would you rather the coolness of silk caressed our warm bodies?"

Jenny's throat went dry and her heart raced beneath her breast. "Linen is more practical," she forced herself to answer.

"Practical!" he mocked. Turning her so she was forced to face him, Cade backed her up to the bed. "Since when is the joining of two people—drawn to each other with a mutual need—put on the same level as having to wear your hat in the sun?"

Cade trailed his hand down her back. "Ah, Jenny, you

disappoint me.'' When he reached her firm buttocks, he pulled her gently against him. Her large brown eyes widened.

"Passion is never practical, Jenny. It's never dictated by a convenient time or place. Passion is a texture that claims your heart and your soul. Be it practical or impractical— linen or silk—this room will be for our passions. Dress it carefully for this is where we will explore the wondrous secrets of our love—and of our mating.''

He turned and left. Jenny sank down on the bed, her knees trembling. She wished he'd locked her in the attic instead.

Her first visit to Denver, Jenny couldn't believe it had been over two months since she had arrived at the ranch. She twirled in front of the mirror, taking one last look at her bright pink day dress, then hurried to catch up with the others. She, Pritch, and Izzy were going to shop for the things necessary to redecorate Cade's room. She was surprised he was still letting her go after all the questions he had put to her. Imagine wanting to know about all the large purchases for flour and sugar when he knew she had a train to catch.

Jenny reached the foyer to find it empty. Drats! Where was everyone? If Cade had made her late, she'd be furious. She grabbed up her parasol from its holder by the front door and ran out. Sam stood beside the carriage at the bottom of the steps. Well at least they hadn't left without her.

She had no more than settled herself on the leather cushions when Cade came marching out the front door and down the steps. "Looks like it's me and you, Jenny," he said as he climbed in beside her.

"What about Pritch and Izzy?"

"You were so late, I had Albert take them in the wagon." Cade picked up the reins and snapped them across the backs of his horses. "Get along, boys, we don't want to miss the next train."

Jenny grabbed the side to keep from falling. "If you hadn't detained me, I could have ridden with the others," she shouted over the sound of pounding hooves.

Cade tossed her a crooked smile as he reined in the horses to a sedate walk. "Don't try laying this at my door, young lady. If you hadn't taken so long coming up with that cockamamy answer for where all the supplies were going, you wouldn't have been late."

"Cockamamy?" Jenny sat with her shoulders rigidly squared. "Well, Mr. Morgan, if you don't feel what I have to say is worth hearing, then I won't waste any more of your valuable time with my trivial conversation."

"I guess that's as good a way as any to avoid having to answer my questions," he muttered.

Jenny wholeheartedly agreed and opted to keep her mouth tightly closed the rest of the trip. But Cade, who seemed to have a new story to relate with each change of scenery, did not make it easy for her.

"You sure do make it difficult for a gentleman to entertain you, Plain Jenny," he finally said.

"I am your housekeeper, Mr. Morgan. Nothing more. Therefore you should not feel the need to entertain me."

Cade let his gaze drop from the fire in her eyes to the embroidered jacket of her pink day dress. "No one ever said you couldn't be more," he said, lifting his eyes once more to hers.

Jenny stiffened. "Your mistress, for example?"

He stepped up the pace of the horses. "That would do for starters."

"Oh, yes, I almost forgot. You have an aversion to purchasing goods you haven't tried."

The corner of Cade's lips twitched. "That's the long and the short of it. Whiskey and women. There's some good, but there's more bad. A smart man samples the batch before he buys the bottle.''

A hard lump formed in Jenny's stomach. Had Cade really sampled the dusty bottles of whiskey in his cellar? Whiskey all smelled the same to her. Awful! Didn't it all taste the same? Surely, smelling so bad, whiskey couldn't be judged like a fine wine. Why, her father had never even served it at his table. What little he did have was kept in the study with the brandy in case a guest preferred a glass of the stronger spirits. It was something she needed to find out before Cade opened one of the bottles Albert had purchased.

''Do you always sample your whiskey before you buy it, Mr. Morgan?''

''It isn't necessary. I only buy Kentucky whiskey and old man Martin has been making the best whiskey Kentucky has to offer for the last forty years.''

She'd have to remember to check the bottles Albert put in the cellar. ''Since your mail-order bride will more than likely not come with the same recommendations as 'old man Martin's' whiskey, are you going to tell her you require a sample of her wares before you'll give her your name?''

Lord, he loved the saucy tilt of her head. ''If her lips are as sweet as yours, perhaps not.''

Jenny's fingers curled around the handle of her parasol. She was so mad she could spit. ''Don't give me that line of spoiled sausage, Cade Morgan,'' she said between clenched teeth. ''Remember I'm the one who knows the casing won't hold water.''

''Ah, I see you're still upset because I didn't offer the position to you on the merit of your kisses alone.''

Too late he realized what she held in her hand. With a loud thump she got off one good whack before he managed to wrestle it from her hand and toss it to the floor of the carriage.

''Glory be, lady,'' he yelled as he turned his attention back to the horses that had taken exception to the sudden outcries from the carriage and now flew across the prairie grasses in an attempt to escape the fracas. "You sure make it difficult for a man to propose to you."

"Propose! You call this a proposal?"

The horses once more under control again, he turned to her with a sheepish grin. "I was working up to one," he said, then quickly raised his hand to halt any objections she was about to voice. "Hear me out first. I know I've not treated you the way I should, but dammit that's your fault."

"My fault!"

"Yes, your fault. There's something about you that brings out the devil in me."

"And here all this time I've been under the impression he was merely a close relative of yours. Now you're telling me he's you."

Cade's grin broadened. "Be nice, Plain Jenny. You wouldn't want to stir up the devil in me again, would you?"

"Will you stop calling me Plain Jenny?"

With his finger, he tilted her chin toward him. "I think I can manage that. After all, I've seen more of you than most and I can definitely vouch for the fact that you're anything but plain."

Jenny pulled her head away. "When are you ever going to let me forget about that mistake?"

His eyes searched hers. "When I can forget it."

The intensity of his gaze sent a warm tingle through her. It would be so easy to try to close the door on all that her father had done to her and lean on this man, but she couldn't let herself weaken. Jenny looked away, breaking the spell. A lifetime of fighting the darkness was not easy to let go.

CHAPTER 13

Cade spent the rest of the trip pointing out various bits of scenery along the way. He had deliberately not come out and said the words that would ask her to marry him. He would rather she had some time to think about the idea first. A day spent shopping, a nice dinner at the hotel in Denver, then he would ask her.

He pulled the carriage to a stop in front of the livery, then climbed down.

"Looks like we made it just in time," he said as he grabbed her by the waist to lift her down. "I think that's the train coming now."

Cade held his arm out and Jenny took it. As always, his touch set her heart to racing. But today was worse. How was she to concentrate on fabrics, furniture, and wallpaper when Cade had all but asked her to marry him? Darn him anyway. Didn't he know how what he had said would affect her? He probably knew, but didn't think it important enough to care. She hated the feeling that with him she was never in control.

To make matters worse, she had to lean closer than she

cared to in order to hear Cade over the whistle of the train. "What did you say?" she shouted.

"Wait right here," he said. "Millie had a letter she wanted us to drop off at the post office. With the train already here, I'll have to see if Jake can have someone do that for us."

Jenny found herself dwelling on the snug fit of his tailored jacket and pants as he walked away. Flushed with the embarrassing turn of her thoughts, Jenny spun around. Opening her parasol, she forced herself to concentrate on the activity on Main Street, instead of the tantalizing swing of some man's backside.

Her attention was immediately captured by the familiar face of a miner stepping out of one of the stores and heading her way. She wasn't very good at remembering names, but orders she remembered. He was one of her best apple pie customers.

Drats! She couldn't pretend she didn't know him, but she'd sure as shootin' have to get rid of him before Cade returned.

He stopped and removed his hat when he reached her. "Mornin', Miss Jenny," he said. "Don't reckon you got in that new shipment of whiskey, did you?"

Jenny took a quick glance over her shoulder. The door to the livery was empty. She had thought not to sell any more of the whiskey, but she hated to disappoint a good customer.

"As a matter of fact," she said, "I'll have some on my next trip. Would you like me to save a bottle for you?" she asked.

"That'd be mighty nice of you, Miss Jenny. I'll take two and add an extra pie on my order, if it won't be too much trouble."

The additional profits were already ticking off in Jenny's head. "I'll have it for you, day after to-mor . . ."

The word dried in Jenny's mouth when an ominous shadow fell across the miner. She spun around. Cade! His eyes were the color of a summer storm. There was no doubt about it, he had heard.

"You'll have what the day after tomorrow, Jenny?" he asked evenly. "More baked goods?"

He knew! That's why all the questions about the missing flour and sugar. He had known all along. Jenny opened her mouth to speak, but her ready answers failed her.

"Morgan," the miner said. "You know this little lady too?"

"You could say that."

His cold blue eyes never left her. Was it too much to hope for that the earth would open up and swallow her? For the first time in her life, Jenny wished for a dark closet to hide in. Any place to escape having to see the set of that rigid jaw and the smoldering anger in those powerful blue eyes.

Somewhere in the corner of her mind, she heard the miner telling Cade about the whiskey. She strained to concentrate.

". . . need to order some yourself, Morgan."

Jenny tried to look away, but Cade's eyes held hers prisoner as effectively as if he had chained her gaze to his. For the life of her, she couldn't think of what she might say that would send the miner on his way. Every word the man spoke only added another foot to her already deep grave.

"Good whiskey, huh?" Cade asked, never once looking at the miner. "There's nothing I like better than to relax with friends over a good shot of whiskey. Ordered mine over seven years ago. Came all the way from Kentucky."

He ran his hand slowly up Jenny's arm. Guilt was written all over her face. "That's the thing about whiskey. It's better as it ages."

Jenny wanted to die.

"Don't know about your whiskey, Morgan," the old miner said, "but this here stuff was the smoothest I ever did taste. You might want to order more 'an one bottle. So's you don't run out."

With his finger, Cade traced the outline of Jenny's lips.

"Jenny will let me have all that I want. Won't you, Jenny?"

She flinched at the desire that flared in Cade's eyes. Instead of diluting his anger, it appeared to strengthen his want until it burned with a savage relentlessness that threatened to choke her. At first Jenny thought the shrieks of the train whistle were screams of denial echoing inside her head, but it was only the train leaving the station.

It took her a moment to realize the miner had left and Cade had a firm grip on her arm.

"Let's go, Jenny. There's a lot of things we need to discuss."

Jenny stumbled along beside him. She no longer needed to look into his eyes to know what was hidden there. His rigid profile and the stiffness of his carriage already told her more than she cared to know.

"Where are you taking me?" she managed to ask.

He stopped short and turned to her. "We're going home."

Jenny almost fainted when he pulled her into the livery. The horses were still harnessed to the carriage. Cade tossed the man a coin, then shoved her up onto the seat.

The ride home was one long nightmare as Jenny imagined all the things he would do to her. Even though Albert had replaced the whiskey two days ago, Cade was bound to notice the nice shiny bottles next to the few remaining ones of his precious Kentucky whiskey still covered with dust.

When they reached the ranch, Cade drove the horses to the front steps and helped her down. He didn't say a word, but continued on to the stables.

Jenny flew up the steps and threw open the door.

"Millie!" she shouted frantically as she hurried to the kitchen. She must get her to dust the other bottles in the cellar before Cade checked them. Her footsteps echoed through the house as she crossed the rooms.

No one was in the kitchen or the dining room. She looked

into the parlor. It was empty. She listened for any sound that she was not alone. Silence. Where had Millie gone?

She was halfway up the stairs when she heard Cade's heavy tread as he walked across the front porch and opened the door. She took one look at the triumphant grin on his face and ran the rest of the way up the stairs and down the hall. He knew they were alone. If she could only reach her room, she could lock the door and hide there until either Cade's temper cooled or someone showed up.

She didn't know he was close until he had her by the arm. "Let me go," she shouted as he dragged her back to the stairs.

"First we'll pay a little visit to the cellar."

Jenny had to hurry to keep from falling. "Where is Millie?" she asked as they went through the kitchen. Cade stopped and she ran into his broad back.

He turned slowly. "She looked wore to a frazzle," he said, frowning down at her. "No doubt due to all the extra baking being done around here."

There was nothing Jenny could say. She had been so busy trying to get enough money to get away she hadn't stopped to think about what all the extra work was doing to Millie.

Cade could see the remorse in her eyes, but it didn't change the way he felt about what she had done. If she had sold his whiskey, she was going to pay.

With Jenny still in tow, Cade lit a lamp and started down the cellar stairs. "If you're thinking someone might show up to help you, think again. I let Millie have the day off. She went to Fairplay and won't be back until late," he said.

Jenny remained silent as he set the lamp next to the wooden cases stacked on the shelves. He lifted a dusty bottle of the Kentucky brew to the light, then one of the new bottles. Even she could see that the labels were similar.

"I can see it surprised you too," he said, "but unless I miss my guess, this bottle just recently found its home here.'' He turned it slowly as he read the label. Cade returned the dusty one to its case and picked up the lamp.

''Follow me,'' he growled.

After seeing the two bottles, Jenny was feeling much better. So why was he still mad? Albert had done a good job of replacing the whiskey. Even if she had to confess to selling his, the crime didn't seem nearly as bad.

Cade set the bottle and the lamp on the table. ''Get out two cups,'' he said. ''I'll be right back so don't think about leaving.''

''Why would I do that?'' she asked defiantly.

He paused in the doorway. ''Don't look so smug until after I've tasted it.''

Jenny set the cups beside the bottle. She didn't know why Cade was being so contrary. Whiskey sitting in a musty old cellar for seven years couldn't make all that much difference, could it? Albert said he had gotten a good deal on the new bottles.

Cade still wasn't looking any too pleased when he returned with another bottle. He poured a small portion from each bottle into its own cup, then held the cup of aged whiskey out to her.

''Drink!'' he demanded.

She stood holding the cup. ''I'm no judge of whiskey.''

''You will be after today. Now drink!''

Jenny daintily pinched her nose shut before lifting the cup to her lips.

Cade caught her hand. ''What are you doing?''

''I'm drinking like you told me to.''

''No, not that. Why are you holding your nose?''

''I can't abide the smell,'' she said. ''I tried it as a child once. The only way a person can get this foul stuff close enough to their mouth to drink is to hold their nose. Besides, it helps the taste.''

Cade grabbed the cup out of her hands. ''Give me that,''

he growled. He downed it in one gulp, then set the cup down. "Now that's good whiskey."

Jenny crossed her fingers when he picked up the other cup and drank. He had no more than taken a swallow when his face turned a bright red. With all the spit, sputtering, and coughing, she thought he was going to choke to death.

She pounded him on the back. "See what I mean. You should have held your nose."

The look on his face stopped her from expanding on her theory. "Is there something wrong?" she asked innocently.

"Where did you get that rotgut?" he finally managed to get out between coughs.

Jenny backed away. "Albert got it from Em."

"You replaced my good Kentucky whiskey with that . . . that kerosene!"

Jenny took another step backward. She didn't like the look in his eyes.

"I'll pay you back," she said. "I have gold. Lots of it."

He moved toward her. "I've no doubt but what you do, but I don't want your money," he said, a cold smile curving his lips. This little minx had tormented his dreams for too many nights. Now this. He took another step.

"But you owe me, Jenny. You owe me a lot. The baked goods. The whiskey."

A chill slid up Jenny's spine. "T-then what is it you want?"

Cade reached out and pulled her to him. "You were married once. It shouldn't take much for you to know what I expect in payment."

Jenny wanted to scream that she had never been married, but this was not the time to point out another one of her lies. Besides, married or single, she knew what he wanted. The tingling of her own traitorous body was evidence of that.

His lips touched her neck and Jenny gasped. Heavens, as many times as he had taken her in his arms, she would have thought she would have become accustomed to it by now, but instead her heart thundered in her chest. His fingers dug into the small of her back and she arched against him as bittersweet chills ran up her spine.

''Yes,'' he moaned into the soft black curls that hung behind her ear. His lips found hers and he swept her up in his arms.

Some part of her said to fight, that she mustn't let him take her like this, but she had fought the feelings he stirred in her for too long. What was so terribly wrong with wanting a man anyway? Remaining a virgin until you married sounded like all of her father's other strict rules. You didn't get locked in the attic if you obeyed them. Well, she had left her father and the dark attic behind. She was her own woman now. If she wanted a man to make love to her, then she would have it.

Jenny threw her arm around Cade's neck and returned the kiss. A moan from him was all the encouragement she needed.

Now that she had decided to toss aside all the old rules, she admitted that she wanted everything she had woken to that night in his bed. Not only his kiss, but the seductive way his hands warmed and caressed her and his naked body lying next to hers.

With her free hand, she started unbuttoning the vest that covered his white linen shirt. By the time she reached the last one, he was standing beside his bed. His lips finally released hers and with deliberate ease he let her slide down the front of him.

Cade gave her a long searching look. ''That whiskey cost me a pretty penny and I can be a very demanding lover for that kind of money. Are you sure you're up to picking up the tab?''

She stood in the circle of his arms, reveling in the power a woman might have over a man if only she played the game. He wanted her. The fire in his eyes told her that. But it was the hint of blue brimstone that sent a delicious tingle through Jenny.

He took her experience in such matters for granted and instinct told her to do nothing to correct the error. His desire for her was like a forbidden potion. Determined to drink the enticing waters, Jenny cocked her head to one side and glanced up at him through her long lashes.

"Demanding?" she asked with her most teasing grin.

He slipped out of his jacket, then cupped her buttocks and crushed her against the evidence of his desire. Jenny gasped, but he seemed not to notice her shock. With slow sensual circles, he ground his hips into hers.

"Does that tell you how demanding?" he asked, his voice a velvet thrust of desire that left Jenny weak.

Smile brightly, she told herself. *You've been wanting this ever since you awoke to find him nestled between your legs, but if you're not more careful, your inexperience is going to give you away. He doesn't want some green girl. He wants a woman and if you want him, you'll be that woman.*

"I always pay my debts," she said with a throaty whisper.

Jenny's heart hammered against her ribs as he reached up to remove the pin that held her small bonnet. There was no turning back. She was going to let him make love to her and she felt no shame. Perhaps her father was right after all. She shared a bad seed with her mother. But it was too late to wonder about it now. All that mattered was the fire burning in her soul.

He undid the small pearl buttons down the front of her dress while she tackled the ones on his shirt. They were like two starving people, determined to take it slow lest the food was some cruel mirage that would disappear with their first bite.

With a coy smile firmly pasted on her lips, Jenny slid back onto the bed. Cade stood over her like a fine animal, powerful muscles rippling across his broad chest. He was as magnificent as she remembered. In fascination, her eyes followed the swirl of dark golden hairs that circled his taut nipples and trailed down . . .

Now was the time to panic, she told herself. It wasn't too late to change her mind. She knew without asking the mating would be painful, but the ache gnawing inside her won out. The only way she would ever rid herself of the fantasies that continually plagued her was to make love to him and be done with it.

A telltale warmth colored Jenny's cheeks when she realized she had been staring. Cade chuckled at her embarrassment.

"You're not going to get shy on me now, are you?" he asked as he crawled into bed beside her.

She moved boldly into his arms and tried not to think about how mad he would be when he realized she knew nothing about pleasing a man. In order to cover her ineptness, she knew she'd have to take her cues from him. In a way, she was no better than the whiskey Albert had bought. Cade was getting rotgut when he thought he was purchasing a fine Kentucky brand. She should feel bad about shortchanging him this way, but she didn't.

Cade's lips covered hers and all other thoughts fled. Slowly he ran his hands over her body, his fingers striking all the right notes just as if she were a violin and he the bow. So intense was her pleasure Jenny forgot she had intended to duplicate his every move. It wasn't until he released her from his kiss that she remembered.

"My turn," she whispered. Gently she pushed her body against his until their positions were reversed. She lay half across him as he had her. With each touch freshly etched on her body, he had made it simple for her to follow his lead. Placing her hands on the bed just above his shoulders, she rose above him. Not yet comfortable with the intimacy of making love, Jenny felt awkward with her first attempt but she could only see approval in his blue eyes.

Pleased with her success, she lowered herself to kiss him. His eyes closed and a strangled moan tore from his lips as her breasts brushed his. The feeling that she was somehow the one wielding the sword this time gave Jenny a heady sense of power. She kissed each closed eye, deliberately rubbing her breasts along his furred chest. Compared to the fiery passion of his kiss, hers seemed tame, almost shy, but the results were more than she had hoped for. His eyes flew open. Even to her, the primitive desire she had unleashed was unmistakable. Hot and wildly savage, it nearly shook her to her toes.

She had barely time enough to catch her breath when Cade grabbed her by the waist and lifted her over him. With experienced ease he settled her atop him. With her hands still braced on each side of his head, Jenny found herself straddling his stomach as if he were a mount she was to ride. He gave her no more time to think of their intimate positions as he raised his head and caught one of her breasts in his mouth. He seized her nipple between his teeth, alternately nibbling and suckling. All the memories she had suppressed of waking in his bed came rushing back. Her need was like a knife blade of pleasure spearing her young body. Jenny threw back her head and screamed.

Cade released her breast. His determination to take their lovemaking slow was shattered at her uninhibited response. Their eyes met. Gazing into the brown liquid pools of raw desire, Cade knew he was no longer in control. She wanted him, and for now, she carried the reins. He was only meant to follow. He, who had meant to extract a just payment, was now the one to pay. Cade felt his body tremble at the unfamiliar turn of events. The knowledge only served to stoke the fire of his own need.

Wantonly he ground his stomach against her open legs. Like a woman born to ride, she clasped her knees tightly against his sides and moved with him. With eyes closed, she arched her back, provocatively offering him the fullness of her womanhood. He was lost.

With a moan that threatened to tear his heart out, Cade rolled to his side, taking her with him. She tightened her legs around him, and all the nights of wanting her overwhelmed him.

Cade dug his fingers into her smooth back. She countered by raking her nails down his and Cade thought he would die with his need for her. He rolled on top of her.

"I can't wait any longer," he breathed against her parted lips.

"Who said you had to," she brazenly answered.

Cade covered her mouth with his. He wanted nothing more than to thrust home, burying himself deep inside her, but he didn't know how long she'd been without a man. Even experienced prostitutes had difficulty accommodating him at first.

He'd all but torn Letitia when he'd taken her virginity when they'd bedded after she'd consented to marry him. It didn't matter that she was the one to lure him to her bed; she had cursed him for his clumsiness, calling him an animal. Obviously she'd had no such problems with his brother.

Well, he was no longer an inexperienced eighteen-year-old lovesick pup in a haste to sample a woman's mysterious delights. He was a man who had always learned his lessons well. One, he must always bridle his passions; two, never bed a virgin.

He released her from his kiss and carefully positioned himself above her. As if impatient with his efforts to spare her, she dug her heels into his back.

Jenny couldn't control the tremors that shook her body. "Now!" she demanded.

Cade took a deep breath and buried his face in her hair. "Jenny, we have to take this slow," he said. "I don't want to hurt you."

"I don't care," she screamed in his ear. "I need you."

Cade swore softly against the restraint he was forced to use. She was not making this any easier, yet he knew the consequences of giving in. He must first test the waters, before taking the swim.

Gently, he shoved at her door. Damn, it was going to be even tighter than he thought. He raised up on one arm and looked down into her face.

"I'm sorry, Jenny, but this is going to hurt you too much."

Jenny frantically searched his face. He wasn't changing his mind, was he? Please, no. Not now that she had come this far. Not with this terrible ache deep inside her.

Without an ounce of shame left, Jenny used her heels to dig into his back. As she had hoped, it gave her the leverage to thrust herself against him. "I told you I don't care," she said through clenched teeth. "I mean to pay my debt and be done with it."

He chuckled at her efforts. "If you're that determined, I guess I'd better do my part."

Despite all the brave words, he watched the pain flash across her face as he slowly began his descent. Angry that it had to be this way, he lowered his head to kiss away the pain when he came up against the unmistakable evidence of her virginity.

Jenny saw his eyes widen in surprise, then anger. His face blanched white and his lips pressed together in a bitter frown. Before she could ask him what she had done to displease him, he rolled off her, leaving her to deal with the unfulfilled ache that still tormented her.

Tears welled up in her. Cade had sampled her merchandise and found it wanting. She'd failed miserably. What was she to do now? She loved him. Jenny closed her eyes against the awful truth. When she opened them again, he sat slumped forward on the edge of the bed, his face buried in his hands.

With a great emptiness in her heart, she scooted around

him and off the bed. Her feet had no more than hit the floor when she felt his hand on her arm. He spun her around.

"You lied to me," he shouted. "You said you had been married."

His anger was so intense, it filled the room, nearly choking her. Jenny swallowed hard to catch her breath. She would have turned and ran but the pain of her rejection was too fresh. She wanted to hurt him as much as he'd hurt her.

"What's so wrong with being a virgin?" she shouted back. "Every woman has to be one at some point in her life." She paused a moment before sending her arrow to its mark. "Or aren't you man enough to blaze a new trail?"

His fingers bit into her arm. "Give me a woman who knows how to handle me and I'll blaze a thousand trails."

As soon as the words were out of his mouth, he wished he could take them back. Her eyes, already bright with unshed tears, reflected the pain of his rash statement.

He wrapped his arms around her. "Be fair, Jenny. Surely you know the consequences of what almost happened?"

Jenny wasn't in a mood to be fair. All she wanted to do was get away and lick her wounds. "Yes, the noble Cade Morgan almost made love to his housekeeper, but you needn't worry that it will happen again for I quit!"

CHAPTER 14

Tears coursed down her cheeks as she packed her things. How could she have been so foolish as to quit? It wasn't as if she'd have to worry that Cade would ever try to make love to her again. After today, he'd have no interest in bedding her.

She folded the last of her underthings and closed the bag. What was she to tell Pritch and Izzy when they returned? If they ever found out what had happened, they would quit for sure, and heaven only knew, they needed the positions. Her hoard of gold dust wouldn't last forever.

Jenny stopped in the middle of packing her brushes. Of course, that was it!

With a wild frenzy, she opened her latched bag and tossed out the day dresses she had just packed. Where she was going, she'd have no need for them.

Jenny stepped from behind the flannel curtain and walked to the mirrored glass in the corner. Thank goodness, there were no other customers in Neil Babcock's Mercantile Store today. While it wasn't all that unusual to see a woman dressed as a man in Colorado, Jenny still felt uncomfortable in the stiff denim jeans and cotton shirt.

Pritch would lay an egg for sure if she saw her now. The tale about Jenny staying in Gold Shoe until their house was built hadn't gone over all that well as it was. Jenny rarely lied to Pritch and deeply regretted having to do so now, but she couldn't very well tell her the truth.

She plucked one of the dark felt hats from the shelf beside the mirror and shoved it on her head. "Do I have enough left to add this hat to my order?" she called over her shoulder.

Mr. Babcock looked up from the paper where he was totaling her purchases. As soon as he caught sight of Jenny in the snug denim britches, his brows shot up in alarm. Lord Almighty! He should never have recommended the attire, not to someone who filled them out as provocatively as Cade's housekeeper did.

"I'll throw in the hat, Miss Jenny, but I think you should maybe consider the riding skirt instead of them jeans."

"Do you really think so?" she asked, turning first one way, then the other in front of the glass. "Now that I've tried them on, I rather like the way they feel."

Neil pulled at his stiff collar. "It's the way they . . . look, Miss Jenny. Fittin' as well as they do and all, some might consider them well a . . . a . . . well a bit revealing," he ended in a rush.

Jenny assessed her purchase with a new eye. Yes, they were a bit revealing, but perhaps that wasn't such a bad thing. Maybe if she turned a few heads, the high-and-mighty Cade Morgan might regret having so callously tossed her aside. "I think I'll keep what I have on, Mr. Babcock," she said. Jenny turned once more in front of the mirror. "Is my order ready yet?"

"It's all right here. I put in everything you're going to need."

Jenny eyed the pile skeptically before she collected the

assorted items he had set aside for her. It took most of her gold dust and several trips out to the hitching rail where she had tied the horse she'd borrowed from Cade. If Mr. Babcock had not assured her all the things were necessary to pan for gold, she would have abandoned half of them.

Once ready to leave, Jenny lifted the pick, stared at it a moment, then at the horse. Her gaze then dropped to the shovel and the mountain of other supplies. How was she ever to get them on the horse? She was still contemplating her dilemma when Em walked by.

"What have we got here?" the madam asked as she circled Jenny and the untidy pile.

Jenny dropped the handle of her pick into the leather scabbard behind the saddle and smiled proudly. "I've got myself a claim. I'm going to pan for gold."

"My, my, a claim and you all dressed to work it too. What does Cade think about this, you being his housekeeper and all?"

Jenny picked up one of the gunnysacks by its rope tie and hung it from the saddle horn. "Oh, he doesn't know. Bear and I found it up near Tarryall." She paused to pick up the shovel. "Besides, I quit," she added before her smile suddenly faded. "Only thing is, I don't know how I'm going to get all these supplies on my horse."

Em tucked her chin atop her hand and studied the situation for a moment. Last she heard, all the claims up near Tarryall had been filed on. She thought about mentioning it, but changed her mind. If she wasn't mistaken the girl already had Cade's prize mare. The claim was more than likely one of Cade's too. She'd like to be a little spider in the corner when Cade found out. If that didn't make the man stand up and take notice of what was right under his nose, nothing would.

"'Pears you need a mule, lass."

"Where would I get one of them?"

Em knew she should be ashamed of herself for what she

was about to do, but Bear thought the two ought to be together and she'd do just about anything for Bear. "Only available mule I know of hereabouts is eatin' his head off behind Cade's barn. You talk real nice to him and he might make you a good deal on the beast."

Talking to Cade, nice or otherwise, was the last thing Jenny wanted to do. After his humiliating rejection, she never wanted to see the man again.

"I don't have any gold dust left to pay for it," she lied. "Besides, Mr. Morgan and I aren't exactly on good speaking terms at the moment."

Em couldn't wait to hear what Bear had to say about this. "What you going to do with all these things then?"

Jenny reached into one of the boxes of supplies and plucked out the large piece of canvas Mr. Babcock had included. After spreading it out on the ground beside her horse, she began tossing the odd and end supplies from the box onto it.

"I'll just have to fit everything on this horse," she said, adding a tin plate, cup, and utensils to the pile.

Her brown eyes widened in alarm at the pistol and box of shells sitting in the bottom of the box. What was she supposed to do with these?"

"You know how to use that thing, don't you?" Em asked, nodding to the gun.

Jenny studied the chestnut-haired woman for a moment trying to decide just how much of their conversation would be repeated to Cade. "I can hit the eye off a potato at a hundred yards," she said, mimicking Bear's bragging to Sam of his spitting abilities.

Em shook her head in wonder. "If you miss, just give them a good look at that outfit of yours. Their tongues will be hanging out so far, they'll trip over them trying to get to you."

Jenny beamed at the compliment, but made a mental note

that she would have to have one of the miners show her how to load the confounded thing. The rest should be easy.

Mr. Fairchild leaned out the door of the train station. "Pick up my bags and get them over to the hotel," he growled at the two gunmen Mortimer had hired. "Then tell Mr. Krebs I want to meet with him in an hour."

The two men continued to watch the woman in the snug denim britches trying to lift the bulky canvas bundle onto the back of a golden mare.

"I'm going to have myself a little taste of that fine piece of Colorado stud bait," Will Short informed his partner as he bent to retrieve one of Fairchild's bags.

Quirt James closed one eye and let the smoke from his cigarette curl up the side of his face and didn't answer. Quirt was not one to let a woman distract him. There was plenty of time to satisfy any urges he might have after a job was complete, but the well-defined backside of this little lady could make any man forget his obligations.

Fairchild stepped out of the train station. With a cocky swing of his cane, he walked up to the two men. "I told you to take my bags to the hotel."

"On our way, Mr. Fairchild," Quirt said with a respectful touch to his hat.

The man's polite manners didn't fool Richard Fairchild. The man was a killer and his black lifeless eyes said he didn't really care who was the victim, but Richard had no complaints. It was exactly what he had paid for.

"See that you do," he said before heading for the bank.

Will waited until he was well out of earshot. "He better be paying us damn good money is all I can say."

Quirt slapped him on the shoulder. "Top dollar, Will, my boy. Enough to buy a pretty little bauble to tempt that sweet thing over there to take you to her bed. Now come along. We got a job for us to take care of, and nothing stirs a man's juices more than a good killing."

* * *

Cade stood over the big miner, his voice raised in anger. "You knew she was selling my whiskey?"

Bear hoped Albert and Millie would remember to keep their mouths shut. Cade was no fool. If he knew they were all involved, it wouldn't take him long to figure out why they had done it.

"Worked out real fine, didn't it?" Bear said innocently as he cut off a small chunk from his plug of tobacco. "Them miners were more than happy to tell me everything that had been happenin' around their diggings."

He paused a moment and looked up at Cade. He could see his tall, handsome friend still had his doubts. "Didn't find out nothing about that there Mr. Smith though, but I did learn that no-good Elmer's still sniffin' around the claims a lot. Does that help?"

Cade slumped down in the other chair. How could he be upset with Bear when he was only doing what Cade had asked him to? Besides, he had to admit, helping Jenny sell baked goods and whiskey was a perfect cover to do his investigating.

"I don't know if that's any help. We already suspected that extra gold dust Elmer's been spending so freely at Em's place came from pilfering at the claims."

"You want me to start keeping an eye on him?"

Cade smiled for the first time since Jenny had stomped out of the house. "No, I have another job for you."

"What's that?" Bear asked, although the devilish grin on Cade's face told him he might not want to hear the answer.

"Jenny quit today. I thought when she cooled off she'd change her mind, but Em just sent me a message to say that Jenny has decided to try her hand at panning for gold. I don't want her getting shot for working someone else's claim. I figure you were the one to introduce her to this little enterprise, you ought to be the one to see that she doesn't get into trouble."

Bear stuffed the hunk of tobacco in his cheek. "No need to worry about that. She's panning for gold along the stream that cuts through that piece of land you have up near Tarryall. You know the one. It shows a bit of color now and then and you let the old miners work it."

"First, she sells my supplies to the miners; now, she's mining my gold. Does everyone think anything that's mine is free for the taking?"

Bear knew Cade wasn't only thinking of Jenny. Em had told him how Cade's fiancée and brother had betrayed him. "You want me to point that out to her?"

"No. Let her go ahead and work the claim. I'll decide later what I want to do about it. It would serve her right if she worked like a dog, then I came in and took it all away."

Jenny felt like she'd been walking for days. It was getting late, her new boots hurt like everything and she doubted very much that she covered more than five miles since she'd left Gold Shoe.

She stopped the horse and readjusted the load for the twentieth time in the last hour. Jenny's lips twisted in a wry grin. At this rate, she might reach her claim in about a week. If only she had been able to sell a few more batches of Millie's rolls she might have had enough gold for a wagon.

No use crying over might have beens, she told herself. She had a whole new life ahead of her. A few months of hard work and she would have enough gold to show Cade Morgan that she didn't need him or anybody else. She'd have her own spread and build a house even better than Cade's. Then she'd hire Albert and Millie away from him.

A rumble behind her brought Jenny's daydreams to a halt. Someone driving a wagon was coming. Using the brim of her hat, Jenny shaded her eyes to get a better look. Drats! They were too far away to tell if it was Cade or one of his men.

Normally she wouldn't worry, but there was the little matter of the horse she had taken. She couldn't believe her luck when she was ready to leave to discover the mare tied in a stall in one of the barns. It was almost as if someone knew she was going to be needing a horse.

But she hadn't been stupid about it. She had made sure she left a note asking that wages due be applied to the price of her mount. She wouldn't put it past that low-down scoundrel to put the sheriff on her trail for horse stealing.

She thought about hiding in the trees until they passed, but unless she dumped her supplies along the road she didn't have a prayer of reaching them before the wagon caught up with her. Even so, she had to try. After tucking her long hair up under the brim of her hat, Jenny headed the mare away from the beaten path.

Within minutes, she knew it hadn't worked. Whoever it was pulled off the trail after her. She wanted to look behind her, but if it was the sheriff following her, she didn't want to appear guilty of anything.

"Jenny!"

She froze. The tiny hairs along the back of her neck prickled in alarm at the sound of a man's voice. Even if she let the horse go, she'd never make it to the grove of pines.

Her heart in her throat, Jenny turned to face her pursuer. Relief almost choked her when Bear pulled the wagon to a stop beside her.

"What are you doing here?" she shouted in frustration.

"I might ask you the same thing. Gold Shoe is back that way."

Her brown eyes suddenly narrowed. "Cade didn't send you, did he?"

Bear's gaze wandered to the mare. "Where did you get that horse?" he asked, purposely avoiding answering her question.

"Oh, that," she said with a casual wave of her hand. "I took her in exchange for my wages."

Bear smiled to himself. Cade would never part with that golden mare. Not after he'd taken it by rail all the way to St. Louis to have it bred. She was the first of a line Cade was starting.

"Cade know you took this particular mare?"

Jenny looked at the horse again. She was a rather good-looking mount, what with her silver mane and tail, but anyone could see her stamina wasn't the best. Even though they hadn't gone very far, she was beginning to look a mite tuckered out.

"I left him a note saying that I was taking a horse."

Ah, so Cade didn't know yet. Bear's smile deepened. Cade was going to have them both strung up when he found out what she'd taken of his this time. One thing for sure, they'd be seeing Cade soon.

"Why don't we put your supplies in the wagon and I'll take you to your claim?"

Jenny stepped back. "How do you know that's where I'm headed?"

Bear laughed as he climbed from the box. "Even if I hadn't seen the gold fever burning in your eyes the other day, that shiny new pick a-wavin' up there like some damn flag pretty much says it all. Now get it out of that scabbard before it falls and cripples your horse."

Jenny was happy for the hat that hid her blush. She was no better than the other greenhorns everyone ridiculed. To make matters worse, Bear had to help her get the pick out of the scabbard. Without the help of the boarded sidewalk, Jenny was too short. It didn't take him long to transfer her supplies to the wagon. Jenny said a prayer of thanks that he'd come along. With the sun sinking as fast as it was, it would soon be dark and Jenny had heard enough coyotes howling at the ranch to know the mountains were crawling with them.

After tying the mare to the back of the wagon, they were on their way. Jenny wished Bear would say something. At least before, with her feet aching and trying to keep the supplies atop her horse, she'd had no time to think about what had happened between her and Cade. Now her heart hurt every bit as much as her feet.

Cade had discovered she was a virgin and hated her for it. Every time a man had smiled at Jenny, her father had swore at her, saying no man wanted a tainted woman, then locked her in the attic. A lot he knew. Cade wouldn't make love to her because she had no experience at being tainted.

Jenny turned to Bear. "How does a woman become experienced if no man ever wants to make love to her?"

Bear swallowed his tobacco.

At the choking gasps coming from Bear, Jenny got on her knees beside him and administered several hard whacks to his back. "Are you going to be all right?" she asked when he finally stopped coughing.

"Give me a minute," he gasped.

Jenny turned around and sat back down. "You really should see Doc Woods about that problem of yours. This isn't the first episode you've had, you know."

"Holy Christmas, Miss Jenny, don't you know any better than to ask a man a question like that?"

"I was worried about your health. Any one of your friends would have done the same."

"No, I meant the other one."

Jenny's brow dipped in a frown. "You mean about making love?"

"That's the one."

"If I'm not to ask a man about it, then who am I supposed to ask? I can't say anything to Pritch. I doubt she's ever been with a man. And Izzy's too young."

One of the horses' attention wandered and Bear snapped the reins along its back. "How about Millie?" he asked.

"I can't ask Millie. She might tell Albert, then Albert would say something to Cade and I wouldn't have that low-down buzzard knowing I was even curious."

Bear glanced over at Jenny. "You wouldn't be in love with the buzzard, would you?"

Jenny was glad night had finally settled so Bear couldn't see the tear that slipped down her cheek. "His own mother would have a hard time loving a man like Cade Morgan."

Yep, she was in love with him all right. He couldn't wait to tell Millie.

Richard Fairchild, his anger carefully held in check, reached across the table and picked up Mortimer's notes. "You're sure this stationmaster knows what he's talking about?"

"I showed him the photograph. He says the woman Mr. Morgan beat up on is your daughter. Seems he ripped her clothes and blacked her eye."

"And now she works for him." It was more of a statement than a question. Richard was already formulating a suitable punishment for both his daughter and the man who had lured her to Colorado.

His voice lowered, the detective leaned across the table. "It seems Mr. Morgan has quite a reputation at the local brothel and suddenly discontinued his visits once Miss Fairchild arrived."

"Yes?" he asked with an outward calm.

Mortimer didn't take heed of the hate growing in Fairchild's pale gray eyes and blithely continued with his gossip. "The stationmaster thinks the arrangement with your daughter entailed more than keeping Morgan's house in order. Word is the rancher has taken her to his bed."

Richard's vision clouded with hate. He had done everything he could to curb Jennifer's willful ways, but in the end she had proved no better than her mother—a harlot. There was only one recourse. Kill her lover, then take her back and lock her up for the rest of her days.

He slid back his chair and stood. "Have your men bring

Morgan to me, but make it clear they are not to hurt him. I want to be there to watch the bastard die.''

Jenny woke up to the smell of hot coffee. Stiff, sore, and still sleepy, it took her a moment to realize she was in a wagon, wedged in among her supplies. She sat up and peeked over the wooden sides.

Bear sat hunched over a crackling fire, stirring something in a skillet. She sure hoped he was cooking enough for the both of them. She was starved. The hardtack she'd eaten last night had all but settled in her boots.

"Good morning," he called to her. "Ready to start to work?"

Jenny rummaged through her gear until she found her pan. She waved it in the air. "Ready," she proclaimed as she slipped off the end of the wagon. "Where do I start?"

"Near as I can figure, you can work the creek anywhere from that marker over there to the one at the top of that little rise."

Jenny followed the direction of his knife. "That's not a very big area. What happens if I want to go beyond that point?"

Cade stepped into the clearing. "Someone will likely shoot you," he said matter-of-factly.

Jenny spun around. There he stood, arms folded across his chest, legs slightly parted as if braced for battle. Calm, deadly anger radiated from him like heat from a fire.

Jenny took a deep, steadying breath. "What are you doing here?"

"I came for my horse," he said evenly.

Out of the corner of her eye, she saw Bear slip discreetly away. She'd get no help from that quarter. It was up to her to handle the situation. But then, it always had been.

Despite the rock that had settled in the pit of her stomach, Jenny stepped closer. "The mare is mine. I took her for the wages you owe me."

A muscle twitched along his unrelenting jaw. "Between the flour, sugar, and whiskey you got a lot more than you had coming."

Jenny lifted her chin defiantly. "I've got some gold left. I'll pay you for her."

"Lady, I have a thing about people settling their debts with me. I like it to be with money other than my own."

Mortification, hot and suffocating, swept through her. "I—I have this claim now. I . . ."

"This claim?" he sneered. "And you're sure it's yours?"

He had a way of cutting her plans out from under her that she didn't like. "Of course, the claim is mine," she shouted up at him. "Do you think I would work one that belonged to someone else?"

"Yes."

"Well, you're wrong. I found it and it's mine. In a few weeks I will have enough gold to pay you top dollar for your precious horse."

"A few weeks! Lady, you couldn't earn enough gold in twenty years to have the kind of money it would take to buy that horse and the colt she's carrying." He uncrossed his arms. "Unless, of course, you . . ."

Her mouth went dust dry when he started unbuttoning his shirt. The devilish glint in his eye told her she didn't want to know the words he'd deliberately left unsaid.

"You can take your horse and get off my claim, Cade Morgan. I don't need you or your horse. From now on, I'll be doing my business with someone who'll give me a fair bargain."

He grabbed her arms and pulled her up against him. "I offered you the best bargain you'll get from anyone."

Helplessly, she pried at his fingers. "And what was that?"

His hands dropped to her backside and he pulled her hard against him. "Marriage and this."

Jenny's mouth flew open in surprise. Before she could answer, he covered her parted lips with his. Hints of a passion, barely held in check, left her clinging to the front of his shirt. As if he sensed her vulnerability, the kiss deepened. His tongue slipped between her teeth, taking her breath away.

With the skill of a master, his hands caressed her body as his tongue raped her mouth—and her soul. Tasting, then teasing, then demanding. Jenny's heart thundered against his chest. Then just as suddenly, he released her.

"When you've had your fill of playing miner," he said, "look me up. If money and independence are so important to you, I'll show you how a real woman can earn the kind of money you want." Without looking back, he untied the mare from her tether and started to walk away.

"I know how to be a real woman," she shouted after him. "It's you that doesn't know how to be a man."

Cade turned and walked slowly back to her. Jenny wished she could take the hateful words back, but it was too late. Their eyes met and Jenny felt a knife of raw, unbridled passion slice through her. She not only loved this harsh, unyielding man, but now she knew she needed him also— needed his intimate touch—his kiss—his soul.

Jenny opened her mouth to tell him so, but the look of cold contempt that washed his features stopped her.

"Only a fool thoughtlessly takes a child's virginity," Cade said with words as cutting as a winter's wind.

"A child! I am not a child, Cade Morgan. I'm a woman."

He cupped her chin in his hand and looked deep into the bitter sweetness of her dark brown eyes. "Then marry me and prove it."

"No!" she snapped before she remembered that most men were like flies. They sometimes needed honey to coax them into the web.

Jenny placed her hands on his chest and smiled coyly up at him. "I can prove it without marriage."

"Not with me, you won't," he growled as he turned to leave.

Jenny watched him walk away. "I'll never marry you, Cade Morgan," she vowed.

He kept walking. "Then you'll be a virgin the rest of your life."

"I'll bed the first man that comes by," she threatened.

Cade stopped and looked back over his shoulder. "Then be prepared to dig his grave."

CHAPTER 15

Jenny squatted down where the water poured over the rock ledge and dug her pan into the dirt and gravel at the bottom of the creek. After filling it, she held it just below the surface of the water and began the relentless circular movement that would slosh the dirt and lighter gravel over the edge, leaving the tiny flakes of gold dust resting at the bottom of her pan.

Three days and already her fingers were cracked and bleeding from digging out all the worthless gravel to recover a few precious particles of gold. Jenny sighed. In truth, her entire body ached beyond belief and what had she to show for her labors? One small nugget and barely enough dust to cover the bottom of her leather pouch.

But she would never give up. She would show Cade Morgan that she was not a child if it was the last thing she ever did. Jenny plunged her pan into the water again and brought up another scoop of dirt. While she swirled the loose gravel in the water, she gently tapped the edge against the flat of her hand like Bear had shown her. She had to admit it helped settle the gold faster once she'd mastered the technique.

Jenny didn't know how she would have made it without Bear's help. He had set up their little makeshift camp and even cooked the meals. When he wasn't working around the camp or out hunting something up for his pot of stew, Bear sat on the bank whittling a whistle and telling her stories.

Unfortunately, most of them were about Cade. How Cade's parents had been shot down by a drunken gunman when Cade was only three and Cade had been raised by Frank, a much older brother. How Cade had grown up thinking no one was as good as Frank. She was on the point of saying she didn't want to hear any more when Bear told her how, in the end, Frank had betrayed Cade.

Jenny scooped up another pan of gravel and began the process all over again. She had often wondered why a handsome man like Cade Morgan would choose to advertise for a stranger to be his bride when there had to have been plenty of opportunities to have found someone to love and marry. Now she knew. Cade had loved once, only to find her in the arms of his own brother. It was safer to marry for convenience than it was for love.

Jenny turned her back to the sun in order to shade her pan. Ah, three more flakes. Her thoughts returned to Cade's predicament as she took the tip of her knife and lifted out the small pieces of gold she had uncovered. It was evident now convenience was behind the reasons for Cade's offer to her. Hadn't Cade said as much? He had picked her because she was already at the ranch and he happened to want her in his bed. Well, it would take a lot more than convenience and desire to get her to marry him now. It would take a loaded shotgun and someone willing to use it on the other end, and then she wasn't sure she wouldn't prefer the bullet.

She was about to toss the residue when the small piece of gravel remaining tumbled to one side. She picked it up.

Gold! The biggest nugget so far. She screamed and waved her find at Bear.

In her haste to show him what she had found, Jenny didn't watch where she was going and scraped her knee on a sharp outcrop of the ledge. Darn! If the pick wasn't up by the campfire, she'd knock the point off before she killed herself.

"Wait until you see what I found," she hollered, waving the nugget in her clenched fist.

If he was smart, he'd take his shotgun and march her off to the preacher. No, on second thought, if he was all that smart, he would have taken her up on her offer to begin with. He would have bedded her and been done with this nagging ache in his loins. Cade couldn't remember a time when a woman had caused him so much grief. It was grief when he was with her, grief when he was away.

Even though he trusted Bear to keep her safe, Cade found himself heading for the claim before daybreak each morning. He sat atop a large formation of rock and watched as Jenny worked hour after hour. He had to give her credit, she was really taking this seriously.

Cade stood and stretched his tired legs. It was getting late. The sky was already awash with the colors of a sinking sun. Cade was just about to call it a day when Jenny shouted. He watched her come running up from the creek to show Bear something she had found. Bear must have confirmed her find, for she threw her arms around him and placed an enthusiastic kiss on Bear's red cheek. Cade may have asked Bear to see after Jenny, but he couldn't help but think Bear was enjoying his assignment entirely too much.

If Cade hadn't been so damned gallant about the whole thing, it could have been him down there receiving her kiss. But now, he not only wanted Jenny, he wanted a commitment from her. Instinctively he knew she wouldn't stay without one. Jenny was like no other woman he had ever met. Most would have given anything to have what she was turning down, but for some reason she stubbornly refused to trust her future to a man.

Cade picked up his canteen and the remains of the lunch Millie had packed for him. He had some things he needed to take care of at the ranch. He'd put his offer to her again when he could return. After a week of back-breaking work, she might not be so quick to turn him down next time

Dread clutched his chest like a blacksmith's tongs when Elmer saw Jenny jumping up and down beside the creek. He was sure she'd discovered the rich gold vein that started where the water tumbled over the short ledge. His partner would not be pleased that someone else had stumbled onto their find.

He listened carefully to hear what they were saying. Thank goodness, the small cavelike niche where he lay hidden served to funnel most of the sounds up from their camp. He breathed a sigh of relief to realize it was only another gold nugget.

If they had found the vein, he didn't know what to do. But then, Carl was the one to take care of such matters.

If not for Bear, Elmer would have hit Jenny over the head and taken her to him. Elmer didn't like all the killings, but he could see where they might be necessary.

The find was one of the richest Elmer had stumbled onto. The old woman and the boy didn't really know what they had when they had brought the samples into the assayer's office. Even after killing them, it had been difficult to extract the gold. Morgan may have let the old woman and the boy pan for gold on his ranch, but he would never have allowed Elmer the same privilege.

Every bit of gold he had gotten had to be chiseled out of the ledge at night or when he was certain no one was in the area. He'd even carved out this niche at the base of a large rock where he could hide the gold until he could haul it away.

Unfortunately, his workings had deposited some fairly good-sized nuggets into the streambed. Their only salvation had been the fact that the other three old miners that had stumbled onto the place had also used the assayer's office in Gold Shoe to determine the worth of their find. The unusual high rating of the ore and the fact that they didn't attempt to register the claim told Elmer where they had gotten the gold.

It was his partner's idea to kill them so brutally. He said the nature of their deaths would point to the indiscriminate killings of a crazed, demented person, not someone set on keeping their victims' mouths shut. Elmer had to give him credit. Carl had been right. So far, no one had guessed the real reasons behind the murders.

Elmer stretched out his cramped legs. He'd give anything if he didn't have to tell his partner. Even though he knew the killings were necessary, Elmer couldn't shake the feeling that Carl got some kind of sick pleasure out of the brutal slayings.

Besides, anyone could tell that after only three days, the girl was exhausted. She would probably desert the entire project if it weren't for Bear. Bear would know the worth of what she'd found.

"Let's go into town, buy a big fat steak, and celebrate," he heard the girl say.

Elmer held his breath as he waited for Bear's answer. If they would only leave, he could see if the vein had been disturbed since he was last here.

"If you want to go, we'll go, but it's getting late," Bear said. "It might be better to spend the night in Gold Shoe."

"As tired as I am, I think I could stand a night in a bed for a change." The girl threw her arms around Bear. "Thanks for all your help," she said.

Elmer couldn't believe his luck. He'd not only have time to check the ledge, but he might even be able to chip away some more of the gold before Bear and the girl returned in the morning.

A shower of rock suddenly tumbled past the hidden entrance to his little alcove and Elmer almost wet his pants. Someone was on the rock above him and they were coming down.

Elmer ventured a peek around the bushes. His jaw dropped at what he saw. It was Morgan and judging from the things he was carrying, he must have been up there long before Elmer arrived. Besides, Elmer was sure he would have heard him climbing the rocky perch.

Lord Almighty! As much as he wanted to, he couldn't keep this from his partner. Carl knew about the girl, but not that Bear was helping her. Now Morgan knew about the gold too.

Elmer swallowed the gorge rising in his throat. Carl had bragged enough about the gory details of the other murders for Elmer to be able to envision the bloody slaughter this news would bring. He was almost tempted to get as much gold out tonight as he could and leave, but he was afraid Carl would hunt him down and murder him also.

It suddenly struck him that with the girl working the area, Carl would not know that Elmer had had a chance to extract any more of the gold. This might be Elmer's only opportunity to see that he got a fair share of the takings.

The thought had Elmer scurrying down the hill after everyone had left. He would put off telling Carl until later. In the meantime, he'd stash away as much of the ore as he could.

Elmer grabbed up Jenny's pick on his way through the deserted camp. There was no time to lose. Once he knocked the ledge loose, he'd still have to carry the ore up the hill to his hiding place.

The sun was just peeking over the distant ridge when Elmer stashed the last of the rich ore up against the back wall. It'd be close quarters for a while. He wished he'd had a chance to haul the ore away, but he'd have to settle for what he had been able to accomplish. Cleaning away all the telltale rubble he had made was a difficult task with only the pale light of the moon to assist him. As it was, he barely had enough time to walk through the dense stand of pines, then across the meadow to retie his horse and be back in his hiding place before Bear returned with the girl.

Jenny's lusty humming echoed across the valley floor. Bear was pleased to see her so happy, but if what he'd just learned from the old assayer was true, at least four other miners had brought in similar samples over the last six months. One had been the old woman who had gotten herself killed. It may be just a coincidence, but it was definitely something Cade would want to know.

Jenny's song suddenly stopped. "Do you think I should file on my claim like the assayer said?"

Why must she always throw these questions at him before he'd had time to think of a convincing answer. If she tried filing, Cade's plan would blow up in as many pieces as the outhouse. She'd learn soon enough who really owned the gold she had been panning for the last three days. Bear wouldn't like to be around when that fat hit the fire.

"No sense filing yet," he said, keeping a watchful eye on her. "It'll only send all the other miners rushing to the area to see what they can find."

Pleased that she seemed to see the wisdom of his answer, Bear smiled and leaned back confidently on the wooden seat.

"The way I see it, the only reason you need ever file is when you smell a claim jumper. If that happens, we'll drop everything and run to the nearest claims office."

"What if he beats us to it?"

"No one will file on that claim before you do, I guarantee it."

Jenny wished she was as confident as Bear. Just the times they had visited the miners, she had heard enough sad tales to make her leery. But she'd have to trust that Bear knew what he was doing. After all, he had owned several claims himself over the years.

Even so, she was relieved when they topped the hill and could see their camp below. After a good night's sleep and a clean change of clothes, Jenny was ready to get back to work.

To be honest with herself, it wasn't just the break from her labors that had inspired the urge. While she was in Gold Shoe, she had taken her earnings into the bank and opened an account. While the poke hadn't amounted to a whole lot, it had weighed out more than she had thought it would. Now that she had a good start, Jenny was anxious to see her savings grow.

She wished she could send a note to Pritch and Izzy, telling them of her progress, but she knew better than to rock Pritch's comfortable boat with the truth. Instead, she helped Bear unload the supplies they had bought, then prepared to go back to work.

Jenny picked up her pan and stepped into the stream. The water seemed even colder than she remembered or perhaps she had been so numb with fatigue that she hadn't noticed before. Without thinking, Jenny sidestepped the ledge that jutted out under the water. She turned to yell at Bear to bring the pick when she noticed the ledge no longer poised a hazard. Overnight, the sharp point had given way along with a good deal of the ledge. Jenny leaned down and peered into the water. She didn't want to be tripping over the blamed thing while she panned. When she couldn't find the stone lying at the bottom, she ran the toe of her boot along the rough gravel. Not a sign of the large hunk.

"Can you come here a minute?" she called to Bear.

He tied the horses to the back of the wagon and headed down to the stream. "Find another nugget, did you?"

Jenny watched him stop and pick something up from the grass. He seemed perplexed about his find. She was too.

What was the pick doing down here by the water anyway?

She waited until he was close. "The jagged end of the ledge is gone," she said solemnly.

Bear looked at her, then at the pick. He didn't answer but stepped into the water. He inspected the fresh marks on the ledge. "Someone's been cuttin' away at it for a fact."

"A claim jumper?" Jenny asked, almost afraid to hear the answer.

"Sure looks like it."

He could have bit his tongue off when he realized what he'd just said. Jenny didn't even give him a chance to take it back. She scrambled up the side of the hill and began to untie the horses before he'd cleared the water.

"What do you think you're doing?" he demanded when he reached the wagon.

"You saw the ledge. I'm going to file on my claim before someone else does."

From the stubborn determination he saw in her brown eyes, Bear knew it would do him no good to argue. He'd told her himself that it was what she should do. Next time he'd learn to keep his big ugly mouth shut.

Bear took the reins from her. "You get into the wagon," he said. "I'll take care of the horses."

Albert answered the knock at the door. When he opened it, two men shoved their way past him.

"Where is he?" they demanded.

Albert could only stare at the shotgun pointed at his chest. "W-where's who?" he finally managed to get out.

"Your boss, Cade Morgan," a gentleman said as he stepped into the foyer.

The man was tall and impeccably dressed, but there was a hard line around his mouth that told Albert he was every bit as dangerous as the two men with the guns. If only he could warn Cade.

As if the stranger knew what Albert was thinking, he

stepped up to him and shoved his clean-shaven face into Albert's.

"We've been watching the house so don't waste our time—or yours—trying to tell us he isn't here."

Albert took a deep breath and pointed to the stairway. "Last door on the right."

The man took a small pistol out of the pocket of his vest and nodded to the other two gunmen. "Bring him down," he ordered, "and be quick about it. I want to be out of here before his men return."

Albert was helpless to warn Cade. They couldn't have picked a better time. Other than Millie and the three maids, Albert was the only one left at the ranch. What hands weren't out on the range with the cattle had gone with Sam to take the wild mustang herd over to a neighboring ranch to begin the breaking.

Albert's heart fell with a thud when he caught a glimpse of Pritch starting out the dining-room door. The commotion overhead must have gotten her attention. Thank goodness the woman had the sense to close the door when she saw the man holding a gun on him. Albert hoped Pritch wouldn't tell Millie until after the gunmen left. The stubborn woman would probably come charging out the door with a pistol of her own.

"You could at least wait until I got my boots on," he heard Cade shout from the top of the stairs.

The taller of the two shoved his gun into Cade's back. "You won't be living long enough to miss them."

Albert nearly fainted dead away when they left. They were planning on killing Cade. He had to get help.

"Faster, Bear!" she shouted over the sound of the thundering hooves of the horses. "I want to get my hands on that no-good, low-down, conniving son of a jack donkey."

"I understand why you're upset, Miss Jenny, but I wish you'd put that gun away. It ain't going to make the horses go any faster and you waving it about makes me uneasy.''

Jenny laid the gun in her lap. "I'm going to make him sorry he did this to me."

Bear looked at the pistol. "You ain't planning on shootin' him, are you?"

"I haven't decided."

"Well, you better be knowing soon. We'll be there in a few minutes."

"As far as I'm concerned, we can't get there soon enough."

Cade was certainly going to be upset with him. He was supposed to keep Jenny from trying to file on the claim and he had failed. He looked over at Jenny.

"Maybe you should wait until you've had time to think this thing through."

Jenny glared back. "I don't need to think anything through. He made a fool of me and I'm going to have his hide for it."

"Now, Miss Jenny—"

"Don't you now, Miss Jenny, me. Didn't you see the look on the assayer's face when he told me I couldn't be filing on another man's land? The man thinks I'm a fool and didn't know any better."

"I'm sure he didn't mean it."

"Oh, he meant it all right. According to him, even the gold I've taken from the stream belongs to Cade Morgan. I worked my fingers to the bone for that gold and if Cade Morgan thinks I'm going to turn it over to him, he better think again."

"Cade has let miners pan for gold on his land ever since he bought the place. He never took the gold they found, why would he take yours?"

"Because the man is lower than knees on a mosquito when it comes to me. He could have told me that I was on his land, but no. You take my word for it. Cade plans on taking my gold because I sold his precious whiskey."

Bear didn't bother to defend Cade. Hell, if Jenny provoked Cade, that's just what he'd do. He'd never met two such stubborn people in his life. Why they didn't just admit that they loved each other and put an end to all this craziness was a mystery to him.

The ranch house was up ahead and it was Cade's problem now. Bear slowed the horses. He knew without looking that Jenny was clutching that fool pistol again. He'd worry about Cade's safety if he didn't know Cade could charm a bird out of a tree if he put his mind to it.

The horses were pretty much lathered by the time Bear pulled the team to a stop in front of the big house. Jenny didn't wait for Bear to assist her. She jumped down and hurried up the front steps. She threw open the door to find everyone gathered in the foyer—even Sam. Millie was wiping her eyes on her apron and Pritch had her arms around Izzy and Sarah.

"What's happened?" she asked.

The men were no help. Albert couldn't keep his eyes off his feet and Sam seemed to be looking for a suitable place to spit. As usual, it was Pritch who took command.

"Your father was here about an hour ago. He and two men took Cade away."

Jenny grabbed the door handle for support. "Father?"

"One of the men said they were going to kill Cade," Albert bellowed.

Kill Cade? When her father was upset, there was no reasoning with him. But murder? She didn't know whether he was capable of it or not, but she wasn't about to take that chance. Not with Cade's life at stake.

"Why are you just standing here?" she demanded. "Send someone to bring in the men and another to Gold Shoe to bring back the sheriff."

Sam gave up trying to find a spittoon and deposited his tobacco in his handkerchief. "Albert met up with me and one of the hands a couple miles down the way," he said.

"We sent him back to get the others, but it will take a while. The men had a few days coming. After we dropped the horses off, Cade said they could go on over to Fairplay for a day or two."

"What about the others?"

Albert lifted his head. "They're out with the cattle. There's no telling how long it will take for someone to round them up."

Never having been a patient person, Jenny wasn't about to sit around waiting for her father to kill Cade. "Sam, you go to the sheriff and explain what happened. Albert, Bear, and I will see if we can catch up with my father."

Pritch stepped around Izzy and the other maid. "Let the men handle this, Jenny. There's no need for you to go. Your father sees you and he may just decide to be rid of you too."

"He would never kill me, Pritch," she said bitterly. "It would be too quick and easy. He would rather I rotted away, locked in his attac, begging for my freedom."

A cold chill ran up Pritch's back. She couldn't argue with the statement. It was what would have happened to Jenny's mother had she not escaped and all because she innocently returned a man's smile. Pritch hated to think what he would do to Jenny for running away.

CHAPTER 16

Jenny sat quietly atop her mount and let Albert fill Bear in on the details of what had happened. She was relieved when Bear didn't ask her any embarrassing questions about why her father might be seeking revenge. How did you explain to a person that with her father it didn't have to make sense? Complete control and pride were the only things that mattered to him.

Hour after hour passed and still they hadn't caught up with the men who had taken Cade. Jenny didn't know what she would have done had not Bear been so good at following a trail or her father had not been so confident as to leave such a blatant one behind. It was almost as if he defied anyone to follow.

Despite all their efforts, it was nightfall before they overtook her father and his men. They had made camp in one of the few clearings going down the mountain. In the glow of the fire Jenny could see Cade with his hands tied over his head, swinging from the branch of a tall pine. One of her father's men stood in front of Cade. As they watched, he drew back his fist and hit the rancher in the stomach.

Jenny pulled her gun out of the waist of her britches. But when she started forward, Bear grabbed the bridle of her mount.

"You can't go charging in there with your gun blazing," he whispered harshly.

"Why not?"

"I know those two men. I've crossed their trail before. The first sign of trouble, they'll kill Cade and you too."

Jenny lowered her gun. "What can we do then?"

"We'll have to bide our time until we can catch them unawares. But for now, follow me."

Reluctantly, Jenny did as he asked. They secured their mounts down the stream a ways, then made their way back to the camp. Jenny's father now stood in front of Cade.

Bear dropped down on his belly and motioned the others to do likewise. Crawling through the underbrush, the three managed to get close enough to overhear what was being said.

"How many times do I have to tell you," Cade shouted. "Your daughter didn't take the train."

Jenny cringed at the words. Never had her lies come back to haunt her so vividly as they had since meeting Cade. It was almost enough to make a person swear to never tell another lie as long as she lived. Thank goodness, she was made of stronger stuff.

Jenny watched her father run the handle of his whip along Cade's chiseled jawline. "Somehow I knew you'd say that," he said with the deceivingly sweet voice Jenny had learned to dread.

Cade jerked his head away from the whip. "It's the truth. If you don't believe me, ask them at Miss Emily's Positions For Young Ladies in St. Louis. I wired her the next day telling her that Miss Fairchild hadn't made the train."

"Funny thing about that," Richard Fairchild said as he uncoiled the length of whip. With a smug grin on his face he let the rawhide snap against the side of his polished boot.

"We checked at Miss Emily's. She said, at first, you tried to avoid paying her, but later paid the bill."

Cade lunged, but the effort only caused him to spin. "I never paid a dime on that bill and if she said I did, she'd be lying."

"Now why would she do that?"

Cade finally righted himself. With legs braced wide, he shoved his face at Fairchild's. "I don't know," he said through clenched teeth. "Why don't you ask her?"

"Oh, you'd be surprised at all the people we've asked, Mr. Morgan. First, there was the conductor on the train from St. Louis. Then, the one on the train up from Denver. And last, the stationmaster in Gold Shoe. My daughter is very attractive, Mr. Morgan. They all remember her."

"She could have been on every train from here to California and I wouldn't know about it. I told you, she never made herself known to me."

Richard snapped the whip inches from Cade's feet. It aggravated him to no end that the man didn't even flinch. Morgan just stood and stared at him with those cold blue eyes. For the first time, Richard was happy for the choice of men Mortimer had hired. They weren't the type to quibble over a little hanging and if any man deserved to die it was Cade Morgan.

"How do you explain the fact that the stationmaster saw you with her? He said you'd beat her up and tore her clothes, then hauled her off to your ranch and made her your mistress. Then told everyone she was your housekeeper."

"I never beat any . . ." Cade paused and looked Fairchild in the eye. "My housekeeper, you say? Your daughter wouldn't go by the name of Jenny, would she?"

"I see your memory has improved, Mr. Morgan," Richard said, then looked over his shoulder. "Take him, men. We're going to have ourselves a hanging."

Jenny was sure her heart stopped beating. Bear and Albert cocked their rifles. She pulled back the hammer on her own pistol, but she knew they were no match for the hired gunmen. She had to put a stop to this. If she didn't, they'll end up dead.

By the time Jenny got to her feet, the two men had a rope looped over Cade's neck. "No!" she screamed as she closed her eyes and pulled the trigger.

She had expected all hell to break loose, but when she opened her eyes everyone seemed to be frozen in place. Her father and his men weren't looking at her at all, but at a long line of rifles on each side of her. Cade's men had finally caught up with them.

"Untie him," Bear growled.

Richard grudgingly signaled his men to obey. "You've led us quite a chase, Jennifer," he said coolly.

Cade rubbed his chafed wrists. "Not as much as the one she's led me on, Fairchild," he said as he strode across the clearing and took the gun from Jenny's hand. "You lied to me from the beginning, haven't you, Jenny? You came here as my bride, but never intended to marry me. Why?"

Bear and Albert looked at her with pity in their eyes. She wanted to protest that she had never wanted to hurt anyone but tears seemed to swell in her throat, closing it off.

When she didn't answer, Cade told Bear to leave him one of the horses, then clear everyone out but Jenny and her father. He didn't say anything until they were on their way, then he spoke not to her, but her father.

"Before I turn her over to you, I want an explanation."

Richard's eyes were two angry slits when he looked at his daughter. "I'm not proud to say, Jenny is an evil, willful child, Mr. Morgan. She lies. She steals."

Cade grabbed Jenny by the waist when she lunged for her father. "Tell me something I don't know, Fairchild."

"Yes, Father, tell him how you drove me to it with your constant accusations. Tell him how you locked me in the attic for days all because someone may have smiled at me."

Richard ignored Jenny. "Mr. Morgan, I apologize for my

daughter's behavior. Her mother was the same way. A bad
seed through and through."

"A bad seed, huh?"

"Don't you look at me that way, Cade Morgan. If I've
done anything wrong it was because I was forced into it."

"Who forced you into lying about being my bride, then
taking the housekeeper's pos . . ." Cade's eyes suddenly
narrowed. "That was it, wasn't it? You somehow managed
to apply for both positions, didn't you?"

"I needed the money from the other ticket," she said
defiantly. "I would have paid you back."

"Like you did for the baked goods and the whiskey?"

"This was different. A man stole my bag as soon as I
stepped off the train in St. Louis." She tossed her father a
bitter frown. "When I tried to wire the money from my
account in Philadelphia, I discovered my father had closed
it and taken all the money my grandmother had left me."

"I was your father and your guardian. I had a right to
protect your inheritance."

"My guardian!" she shouted. "What you did left me
stranded in a strange town with no money for either food or
lodgings. How was that protecting me?"

"You shouldn't have run away. And you shouldn't have
encouraged Isabel to follow." He was pleased his knowledge had silenced her for the moment.

Richard threw his arms wide in an appeal to Cade. "See
what I've had to deal with. Isabel is only sixteen years old.
It will take me years to rid her of Jennifer's unstable
influence."

Jenny would have clawed his eyes out if Cade didn't have
such a tight hold on her. "I'll kill you if you lock her up like
you did me."

Her father didn't give her so much as a glance. "With
such behavior, Mr. Morgan, you can see why I was so
anxious to find my daughters. Up until now, I had hoped to
marry Jennifer off. But after what she's done, there's no

hope of that. Even the size of her fortune will not entice a decent man to accept soiled goods. No, Jennifer will have to live out the rest of her days with me.''

"As your prisoner," Jenny spit out.

Fairchild finally looked at his daughter. "As much as I deplore the strict treatment you force me to employ, it is the only way I have of curbing your promiscuous ways.''

Fear, like bile, rose in Jenny's throat. Her father was telling Cade she was no better than one of Em's girls. Jenny tried to swallow the sour lump that threatened to choke her, but couldn't. She didn't know why but suddenly it seemed important that Cade not believe her father's lies. She stood rigid in his arms, waiting for his answer.

Cade studied the Easterner for a moment. He didn't like the cold, callous way Fairchild had of talking about Jenny. Besides, what he was telling Cade didn't make sense. The type of woman Fairchild was describing didn't reach the age of eighteen still a virgin, even if her father did lock her in the attic.

"Much as I sympathize with your situation, Fairchild, I feel that Jenny needs to pay her debts to me first.''

"I agree, Morgan. If you let me know how much she owes you, when we get back to Philadelphia, I'll wire the money to you.''

"It's not money I want from Jenny. It's her hand in marriage I require.''

Jenny struggled in Cade's arms. "I'll never marry you!'' she shouted.

"I've heard that before," he said as he tightened his hold.

"I'd rather return with Father to Philadelphia than marry you.''

Cade had to step aside to avoid her thrashing feet. "Only because you think you might have a better chance of escaping from him than you will from me.''

Richard's lips curved in a tight smile. "She's yours, Morgan," he shouted over Jenny's protests, "but I'll be seeing the vows exchanged before Isabel and I return to Philadelphia.''

"Fair enough," he said. Cade didn't fool himself that Fairchild was thinking of his daughter's reputation. The cold hard cruelty in the man's eyes told him that his cooperation came from more of a need to hurt his daughter than to help her.

Cade dragged Jenny, kicking and screaming, over to the horse and put her up on its back. "The preacher in Gold Shoe won't be leaving on his circuit until tomorrow morning," he said over his shoulder. "What say we have this taken care of before he does?"

Jenny waited until he was on the horse behind her. "You can't make me marry you," she whispered through clenched teeth.

Cade waited until Fairchild had mounted the bay, then nudged his own horse forward. "I think it would be to your advantage to at least think it over."

"Why should I care what you think?"

"If you weren't squalling like some damn magpie, I might tell you."

Jenny closed her mouth and crossed her arms. And waited.

"Well?" she finally said.

Cade dug his heels into the side of his mount. The horse immediately sprinted ahead of the bay.

"I've decided that after all the trouble you've caused me, you can wait until tomorrow to hear what I have to say."

Jenny scooted forward and dropped over the side of the horse, but Cade grabbed her before her feet reached the ground. "Are you trying to get yourself killed?" he shouted as he pulled her up against him. The horse danced nervously to one side.

"Let me go," she screamed. "I don't want to get married."

"It's too late to think about that now," Cade said as he

settled her back in front of him. "I've already told your father that I'll make an honest woman out of you. So you might as well get used to the idea." He tipped her chin. "I'll even buy you a wedding present."

Jenny frowned up at him. "Like what?"

"What would you like?"

"I want the land where I was panning for gold," Jenny stated with her fingers crossed. "And any gold I might find there." If he knew she wanted it to pan enough gold to leave him, he would never agree.

"Found a promising nugget, did you?"

Jenny didn't need the light from the full moon to see the mocking smile on his lips, she could hear it in his voice. He was making fun of her. "It's none of your business what I found."

"I don't want your gold, Jenny. I want you."

"Then you should have no qualms about deeding the land over to me."

Damn, did she think he was stupid? He knew why she wanted the gold. Gold meant freedom to Jenny. But what could he do?

"You win, Jenny. I'll sign the land over to you, but I have one condition."

She eyed him suspiciously. "And what is that?"

"There have been three more murders like the old woman and her grandson. I don't want you working the stream by yourself. You must make me a promise that either Bear or I will be with you when you pan for gold."

Jenny smiled. She didn't mind having Bear around. In fact, she rather enjoyed his company. Besides, when she got ready to leave, Bear might tell Cade, but he wouldn't stop her. Thank goodness, she didn't have to worry about Cade. He was much too busy to watch after her.

"I promise," she agreed.

Cade knew he should be happy that she wasn't going to continue to put up a fuss about marrying him, but he wasn't.

Making her marry him didn't mean she would stay. She had to want to stay and to do that, she had to love him.

The preacher said the final words that bound them forever as man and wife and Jenny felt as if her heart had turned to stone. She ventured a glance at Cade. He didn't look the least bit remorseful for what he'd done to her. In fact, if the smug grin on his face was any indication, he looked to be enjoying the whole thing much more than he should.

Jenny took a step backward, but he followed. Sweeping her up in his arms, he covered her mouth with his. Jenny knew it was part of the ceremony and politely let him seal their agreement, but he wasn't satisfied with that.

Cade deliberately deepened the kiss, demanding a response from her. She struggled in his arms. He didn't care what the preacher or her father thought. He'd get this little hellcat to return his kiss if it took all night.

With a practiced skill, he forced her lips apart and took what was now his. He could feel the first tremors of desire ripple through her body. It took a moment to realize that he had accomplished his goal. Jenny was kissing him.

He released her then. Her hooded eyes told him what he wanted to know. She still wanted him as much as he wanted her.

Cade paid the preacher, then took Jenny by the arm. "We'd best be getting back to the ranch," he said. "Say good-bye to your father."

Richard held the door for them. "We can do that later. I still have to collect Isabel from your ranch. We'll be wanting to catch the early morning train for Denver."

Cade stopped in the doorway. "Didn't I tell you, Fairchild? Isabel won't be returning to Philadelphia with you."

"She has to," Richard said smugly. "I'm her father."

Jenny gasped when Cade's hand dropped to the gun he had tucked into the top of his denim pants. Neither man was used to being crossed. She squeezed Cade's arm.

Cade was pleased with her concern for his welfare and hugged her hand close to his chest. "As Jenny's husband, Mr. Fairchild, I will be assuming responsibility for Isabel."

"You can't do that. You have no right."

After shoving Jenny behind him, Cade eased the gun out and pointed it at Fairchild. "This gives me the right." He waved the gun toward the sidewalk. "Now get out of here and don't come back. The people around here don't cotton to your way of raising children."

Richard edged by Cade. "You're the fool here, Morgan. I give you a week and you'll be sorry you ever married her. Jennifer is just like her mother. She'll run off the first chance she gets."

The words seemed to linger long after Fairchild left.

Cade stood looking out the door. "Is it true, Jenny? Will you leave me the first chance you get?"

Jenny didn't answer.

The ride home was one of silence as each laid their own plans. It was late when they finally arrived at the ranch.

Jenny may not have answered, but at least she hadn't lied to him this time. Cade knew he should be thankful for that.

Jenny stopped outside the door. "Thank you for letting Izzy stay. After all the trouble I've caused, I know I don't deserve any favors."

"You're right, you don't." He took the back of his hand and tilted her chin. "But you didn't really think I would let him take her after all he's done to you, did you?"

Jenny shrugged her shoulders. She knew he wanted more—he wanted a commitment, but she had done too much to earn the freedom she had to place her fate back into the hands of another man. How did you explain to someone that every smile—every glance—every word uttered from your lips had been twisted and used against you for too many years? Unless they had shared the hopes of your dreams—and the despair of your nightmares—they would never understand.

Cade reached behind her and opened the door. Everyone must have heard them arrive for they were gathered in the foyer.

Izzy seemed not to notice but ran over to Jenny and threw her arms around her. "Oh, Jenny, I don't want to go back with Father," she wailed.

"We don't have to."

Izzy pulled away and stared at her as if she couldn't believe her ears. Jenny looked past Izzy to Pritch. "Cade and I exchanged our vows tonight," she said solemnly. "You and Izzy will be living with us now. Father can't hurt us anymore."

With a frown on her face, Izzy studied Cade a moment. "But, Jenny, you said you were never going to marry."

"A woman is allowed to change her mind, isn't she?"

Pritch moved across the room to stand beside Izzy. Cade and she warily eyed each other. Jenny couldn't help but think she bore a strong resemblance to Albert's banty rooster when he was thinking of taking on the big old barnyard bird. "You love the girl?"

"Let's just say I love her every bit as much as she loves me."

"And you, girl?"

Everyone seemed to be holding their breath, waiting for her answer. Cade arched a dark brow. "Well?"

Jenny suspected Cade only used that "you'll never get the better of me" smile when it concerned her and it was beginning to annoy her. She wanted to say if he thought he was so damn clever with his reply why didn't he just go ahead and answer for her, but she knew Pritch would never settle for that. There was only one way to handle this man. She'd say the very last thing he expected to hear.

While everyone watched, Jenny looked lovingly up at

Cade. She wanted to laugh at the suspicious frown that was making its way across his face but she somehow managed to maintain a serious demeanor.

She clutched the handkerchief dramatically at her bosom. "I love him with all my heart," she sighed with all the passion she had kept buried for too long.

"I hate you!" she raved up at him.

Cade cupped the side of her face in his hand. "What happened to 'I love him with all my heart'? Was that all a lie?"

"Don't you mock me," she said as she swatted his hand away. "It was no more of a lie than what you led everyone to believe."

Cade picked up his pipe. "I don't lie, Jenny," he said as he knocked the cold ashes out onto a small glass bowl that rested on the corner of his desk.

"You said if I married you, you would deed over the land by the stream to me. Now you're trying to weasel out of our agreement."

He took his time dipping out the fresh tobacco from the humidor and packing it down. "I'm not trying to weasel out of anything, Jenny. Ask anyone and they will tell you the same thing. We are not truly married until we consummate our vows."

Jenny glared at him. "And what will it be after that? We're not truly married until we start a family?" She punched his chest with the point of her finger. "The answer is no, Cade Morgan. I won't let you get away with this. A promise is a promise."

The corner of Cade's lips twitched in amusement. "I especially like the one where you said 'I will love, honor, and obey.'"

"We both knew the vows we were exchanging were nothing more than lies."

''Oh, I don't know,'' he teased. ''I definitely plan on forsaking all others.''

''Don't do me any favors,'' she said as she stomped out of the study and slammed the door.

He listened to each resounding footstep as she made her way up the front stairs. A smile teased his lips when the sounds stopped at the top of the stairs. He put down his unlit pipe and followed.

She stood poised at the top of the stairs. ''Finally realized you can't return to your old bedroom, have you,'' he said more to himself than her. He could tell from the stiffness of her back that she had heard. ''It wouldn't do to have everyone know you lied about loving me, would it?'' he whispered up to her.

Jenny tossed him a triumphant smile over her shoulder, then turned down the hallway to his room. He didn't have to hear the slam of the door or the sound of the lock hitting home to know what she had in mind. His wife thought to keep him from collecting his marital rights.

Boy, did he have a surprise for her. He doubted there was a door made that could stop a determined husband.

He ran up the last few steps and down the hall. When he reached his room, he knocked on the door. ''Warm the bed for me, love. I'll be right there.''

With that, he took a step back, raised his foot, and kicked.

CHAPTER 17

The door frame splintered, then gave way. Jenny gasped as the door flew back against the wall. Cade stood in the hallway, a giant in dark shadows. Even the dim light couldn't hide the assurance with which he faced her. He meant to have her. The knowledge set Jenny's traitorous body to trembling.

He had tricked her into marrying him. Now he wanted to claim his rights as her husband. The last time she'd gone willingly into his arms he had callously tossed her aside. She couldn't see how a wedding could change all that. If she wasn't worthy then, she wasn't worthy now.

"Don't touch me," she warned.

When he took a step forward, Jenny backed away. "Get out of here."

Cade didn't say a word, but reached around and closed the door.

"I told you to get out," she snapped.

Other than seeing that Jenny didn't bolt for the door, Cade ignored her while he positioned the empty chiffonier across the broken frame. The little vixen had stolen from him, lied to him, and generally played havoc with his thoughts for weeks now. She wasn't about to escape him now. Not until he taught her what happens to young ladies who tamper with a man's emotions—and his whiskey. Cade turned to face her. "I came to collect what's mine."

Jenny took a deep breath at the desire she saw growing in his blue eyes. Reaching down, she snatched up a marble statue from the writing desk and held it threateningly over her head.

"We've been through this before," she said evenly despite the wild beating of her heart, "only this time you're the one not good enough for me. If I ever decide to give myself to a man again, it will be to one who can follow through."

"Ah, so that's it," he said, taking a step toward her. "You're still angry about the last time."

Jenny banished the statue menacingly, but still backed away from the devilish grin on his lips. "It doesn't matter if I am. You had your chance. I refuse to give you another one."

"I don't recall that having someone's permission or not ever stopped you and it's certainly not going to stop me." He took another step closer. "I plan on taking a lesson from you, Jenny. I'm going to take what I want."

"Don't come any closer, Cade Morgan, or I'll bust this over your hard head."

Cade ducked and made a dive for her. The statue missed by only inches to bounce off the front of the chiffonier. He stopped dead, then slowly he turned to note the damage. "You want me to retrieve it so you can try again?" he mocked her.

The man was more than a jack donkey. He was a bastard. Hoping to put a safe distance between them, Jenny quickly backed to the far side of the room. When he followed, she jumped up onto the bed. Her feet immediately sank down into the feather ticking. She took a few unsteady steps, then stood braced on the mattress, ready to jump either way should he make a grab for her.

Like a hound after a treed squirrel, Cade skirted the bed, his massive shoulders hunched forward, his arms outstretched. She'd not get away from him.

"Leave me alone," she shouted.

He chuckled at the sight she made as she tried to maintain her balance. Jenny was mad as a wet hen, but he didn't care. He was upset himself. He knew without a doubt Jenny would never acknowledge their marriage unless they consummated it. He dropped his hands and began unbuttoning his pants.

Jenny eyed him warily. "What are you doing?"

"Did you think mouthing the proper words in front of the preacher was all there would be to a marriage?"

"No, but then I didn't think it would turn you into some kind of . . . of . . . ."

"Animal?" he finished for her as he dropped his pants to the floor and stepped out of them. "Lady, you're not the first to call me that."

Jenny was baffled not only by his words but by the bitterness she detected in his voice. "I don't want an animal," she said, her announcement no more than a whisper. She tried not to think what was visible if she only had the nerve to let her gaze wander.

Cade's face darkened. For a brief moment she could see the indecision written there, then anger won out.

"That's all well and good, but you said you wanted a man who would follow through, damn the consequences. As near as I can figure, Jenny, that's the one you're going to get."

A disloyal tingle of excitement swept through her at his threat. He hadn't even touched her and already she could envision the bittersweet pain of their joining.

Her eyes met his. The slumberous blue depths of his half-closed ones mirrored the undeniable desire building within her. Like a fire, hot and hungry, it ate a wide path to her soul, leaving her aching for more. He lifted his hand and beckoned her. It was as if he sensed she no longer had the strength to fight him.

"I hate you," she said as she walked to the edge of the bed.

He met her there, silently taking her into his arms. With tantalizing slowness, Cade slid her body down the front of his. Her feet had barely touched the floor when he crushed her against him.

Cade was well aware of the risks he was taking. He had refused to bed another virgin after Letitia. Even after all these years, he could still see the look of disgust on her face and hear the words she had screamed up at him. He almost wished Jenny'd had other lovers before him so what he had to do wouldn't hurt so much.

Damn! He should have kept to his original decision and married a stranger, not someone he cared for as much as he did Jenny. What she thought of him mattered too much. Now here he was. Damned as a husband if he made love to her; damned as a man if he didn't.

Cade dug his fingers into the small of her back. "Your hate now is nothing compared to what it will be before this night is over," he whispered into her hair.

For all the lies she had told, Jenny had expected Cade to extract his measure of revenge, but why the bitterness and regret in his words? Where was the mockery at her defeat?

When he finally released her, Jenny searched his face, looking for the smugness of his victory. All she saw was a burning need that echoed her own.

Jenny stood still as Cade started with the buttons on her cotton shirt, his fingers fumbling with the small holes. She smiled and reached up to help him.

The process went slowly for Cade insisted on savoring each inch of her skin he uncovered—tasting—teasing— until Jenny thought she would die from the longing.

When her clothes finally rested on the floor beside his,

Cade picked her up and laid her on the bed. He stood over her then, his eyes traveling down the length of her, pausing at each intimate part where, only moments ago, his kisses had evoked a shy blush.

Cade wanted to remember her like this—her head on his pillow—her body anxiously awaiting his touch. After he made love to her, everything would change.

He turned down the wick on the lamp, then joined her on the bed. With tender care, he gathered her into the circle of his arms. Like a bear who has just discovered a hidden cache of honey, he planned to sample the sweetness before ravishing the comb.

Cade buried his face in her rose-scented hair and took a deep breath. Heaven help him. Jenny meant everything to him. She was roses and warm sunshine—cloudless skies and the sparkle of wet dew—and he would never get enough of her.

Intent on memorizing each sensual curve, Cade traced the provocative outline of her body, down her slender back, past the tiny waist to the flare of her full hips.

By the time he reached her long legs, there was no doubt in his mind. Jenny was one of those rare women who was born to love and be loved. She was like a kitten purring against him. With each stroke, she writhed in innocent pleasure, driving him to distraction.

It only confirmed his earlier assessment of her. Jenny had the insatiable lust of a prostitute bent on perfecting her craft. She took directions well and the room soon warmed to the heat of their passions. It didn't take long before his beautiful new bride discovered the immediate effects of a carefully placed touch—or a simple kiss. She used her new knowledge well. Never had Cade wanted a woman so desperately; yet, at the same time, regretted that he was to have her.

Jenny pulled at him until he half covered her, but she was not satisfied to have him merely lay atop her. She moved her hips invitingly against his. In desperation, Cade bit down on the tender lobe of her ear. She gasped not in pain, but exquisite delight. Heaven help him. Somewhere the time for changing his mind had come and gone. There was only one choice left to him now. He must have her.

"Are you ready?" he whispered against her exposed ear. "You've tortured me until I can't hold out any longer. Now all I want to do is make love to you."

"Is that so bad?"

He raised up so he could see her face. "It can be," he cautioned. "So you'd best ready yourself now while there's still some gentleness left in me."

She laughed warmly up at him. His concern only excited her all the more. "Did I say I wanted you to be gentle?" she teased, enjoying the newly discovered power she had over him.

Determined to give him no respite from the torment of their lovemaking, Jenny reached up and licked one of the nipples on his broad chest. She alternately circled, then suckled the firm brown nub. His response was immediate.

"Don't do this, Jenny," he warned.

Exhilarated by her ability to humble him, Jenny took his hand and laid it on her thigh. "Are you afraid of me?" she asked huskily.

Cade took a deep, steadying breath. "You don't understand what can happen."

"Then why don't you show me?"

The ragged moan her actions tore from his throat only intensified the primitive need deep within her. She tugged at him. "Now, Cade," she whispered.

When he settled between her legs, Jenny could sense he still hadn't abandoned his reluctance to take her. He had wanted her earlier and demanded that he was going to consummate their marriage. What had happened to that determination? she wondered. Did he no longer want her?

"Cade?"

His name on her lips was like a knife to his chest. She still didn't understand the risk he was taking. Helpless, Cade dropped his head to hers and buried his face in her long black hair. "Give me a minute," he said. "I don't want to hurt you."

Jenny arched her body against his. She'd not give him time to back out again. He'd shown her all the tricks of how to make him want her and she was willing to use them all if she had to, to get him to abandon that blasted control of his. She wrapped her legs around him. With her heels dug in, she lifted her hips to his. "Take me, Cade," she whispered against his parted lips.

"No, Jenny, please no."

Cade tried to pull away, but Jenny held firm. With her lips pressed to his, she kissed him, her tongue plundering his mouth. Her evident need only fired his own, until he could think of nothing but tasting of her pleasures. When she moved her hips demandingly against his, he knew he was lost. There was no turning back now. His need for her was too great.

"You win," he said, his voice a tortured rasp.

He tried to move slowly, but she was having none of his gallantry. Stubbornly, she dug in her heels and clawed at his back. It was as if she knew she was calling the shots and was not about to relinquish the position of authority it gave her.

Cade slanted his lips across hers and entered her. He thought his heart would burst when he swallowed her screams. He knew he had hurt her, but still she didn't pull away.

He lay quiet a moment, not moving, hoping to let the pain ease within her. A shudder seized his body. Already he ached at the unnatural restraint.

Jenny lay in shock at first, absorbing the raw pain. Then the ache of unfulfillment roused her. Why had he stopped? Surely he didn't intend it to be his revenge. All her life, she had fought her father's unfair punishments and she would do no less with this man. Even if she had proved a disappointment, he had no right to deny her this.

Despite the burning discomfort, Jenny pushed against him. No man would be master of her fate again.

When Jenny rose beneath him, Cade knew there was no more help for him. Letitia was right. He was nothing more than an animal. No matter how much he might want to save Jenny pain, the primitive need for release was greater.

"Forgive me," he whispered as he dug in.

Jenny gasped at the exquisite combination of pain and pleasure. Cade took her up to the clouds of heaven, then swept her down to the fires of hell, but Jenny hungrily rose to meet each new invasion.

At Jenny's wanton demands, Cade lost what little control he had left. He lifted her hips and ravished the tender depths of her. Jenny's passionate cries filled the room as she stubbornly accepted all he had to give. Cade knew he should stop, but he couldn't. Then she shuddered beneath him, her release coming only moments before his own.

Cade was afraid to move—afraid to ask if she hated him as much as he hated himself. If she never spoke to him again, he would deserve it. Even knowing the consequences, he had selfishly taken his pleasure with her.

He leaned down and kissed the tears from her cheeks and each tightly closed eye. "I'm so sorry, Jenny. I tried to be careful, but . . ." His voice broke and he couldn't finish.

Jenny opened her eyes. She was surprised at the raw emotion etched in his face. "Is the mighty Cade Morgan apologizing to me?" she asked.

A lump formed in Cade's throat. It didn't sound as if she hated him. Gently he cradled her in his arms and rolled to his side, taking her with him. His heart soared with his love for her.

"Don't let it go to your head," he teasingly told her. "For each one of mine, you owe me a half a dozen."

She smiled up at him. "But I'll not be as generous with mine."

Cade searched her face. "I'll settle for your love."

Jenny couldn't face him. She couldn't acknowledge the seriousness of his statement. "From all I've seen, love is a curse, Cade Morgan. You'd do better to settle for something else."

Cade put his arm around her waist and pulled her up against him. When he had her nestled into the curve of his body, he moved her hair aside and placed a kiss on the side of her neck. "Maybe I have a liking for curses."

Her low throaty moan told him that while she might not believe in love, she couldn't deny her need for him.

Jenny woke up to a knock on the door. "Go away," she groaned.

Pritch knocked again. "Your husband's here, Jenny. He's ordered you a bath."

"Then let my husband take it. I'm not moving unless I absolutely have to."

"Let me handle this," Cade whispered. He reached in front of Pritch and opened the door. Jenny lay buried under a mound of covers on the far side of the bed with a pillow held over her head. After he stood the bathing screen in front of the big oak bed, Cade motioned Albert in. "Sit the tub in front of the hearth, then you can start bringing the water up."

When a mournful groan came from behind the screen, Cade grinned. His new bride had been more than willing to return to his arms last night, but was now just as determined to play the abused wife. Cade knew better. Her lust for their lovemaking was enough to swell any man's pride.

Cade had Pritch sit the breakfast tray on the writing table, then motioned for her to leave. "It's nearly ten o'clock, Jenny," he said as he stepped behind the screen. "Time to get up."

A groan was Cade's only answer. He reached down and pulled the blankets from her bed. "If you want me to sign over that land to you, you'd best be getting up."

Jenny opened one eye. "You sound as if the offer expires at noon."

"Maybe it does."

Jenny propped herself up on one elbow. "Are you going back on your word?"

"No, I said I would give the land to my bride."

With a long mournful groan, Jenny crawled from the bed and gathered up her clothes. "So what's the problem? I married you, didn't I?"

Cade stood barring her path, his legs braced, his arms crossed over his chest. "But are you going to stay and be my wife?"

Standing in front of her tall husband with only the bundle of clothing to cover her left Jenny feeling small and vulnerable, but she wasn't about to be intimidated. "I made it clear when you forced me into marrying you that I'd be no man's wife. I married you. Now I want my land."

"That's the way I thought you'd see it." Cade let his gaze slip leisurely down her body. "I figured that little ceremony you agreed to last night wouldn't last long and my offer is only as good as long as you're my wife."

Jenny lowered her voice at the sound of footsteps. "You're not planning on reneging, are you?" she whispered, trying to ignore the tingle of anticipation his hungry scrutiny had sent winding its way up her body.

Cade waited until Albert had poured the water into the tub and left the room before he answered her. "I'm not reneging, only warning you that the offer expires the minute you consider our marriage over."

So that was the way it was going to be, was it? Well, she'd soon put a stop to that nonsense. She drew herself up to her full height. "Then you'd best be drawing up the papers now, Cade Morgan. I'll be wanting to sign them as soon as I'm dressed.''

''As your husband,'' he said evenly, deliberately letting the significance of the title settle around her like the silken strands of a spider's web, ''I think it best you relax in a nice hot bath before you dress. We'll discuss the finer points of our bargain after you've had your breakfast.''

''I already know the finer points,'' she snapped. ''I married you. Now, *as your wife,* I get the land.''

Cade reached out and pulled her up against his chest ''And, as your husband, I said you are to bathe and breakfast first. Keep in mind, my dear, a wife always bows to her husband's wishes. You told me that yourself.''

Jenny's brown eyes darkened at the amusement that lifted the corners of his sensual lips. ''You think you're clever, don't you?''

''So I've been told.''

''Well let me—''

Albert interrupted them with a knock on the open door. ''More water,'' he called from the other side of the screen.

From the sounds of footsteps, he had brought help. The buckets were soon emptied. ''Your bath's ready when you are,'' Albert said as he closed the door.

''Well, let me tell you,'' Jenny began again, ''you may think all this is amusing, but as soon as I have that paper in my hand, I'm gone and I'm never going to come back.''

Cade's hands tightened on her arms. ''Don't you think I know that?''

''So you plan on keeping me here, dancing to your tune, until you decide I've earned the land. Is that it?''

''Don't worry, Jenny. You'll get your damn piece of paper. I'm not so desperate for someone to warm my bed that I have to blackmail you into staying. Any one of Em's girls would be more than happy to take your place.''

As soon as the words were out, Cade wished he could take them back. Hurt warred with bitter fury in the eyes she turned up to him. Cade dropped his hands. "I'm sorry, Jen."

"Sorry!" she raged back at him. "You needn't be. You're no different than I expected a husband to be. Now get out of here so I can 'bow to your wishes' and take my bath."

If she hadn't mocked him, he thought, he would have left. Now a stampede of cattle couldn't get him to go. "What else did you expect from a husband?" he asked. "This?"

Jenny gasped in horror as he grabbed the bundle of clothing from her hands and tossed it to the floor. "What are you doing?"

Cade swept her up in his arms and carried her around the screen. When he stood beside the tub, he lowered her into it, then knelt beside it. "I'm going to bathe my wife," he finally answered.

Jenny struggled to get out. "You don't have to. I can do this myself."

"Ah, but it's much more enjoyable if your husband does it for you," he said.

The velvet huskiness of his voice set her body to trembling inside. With a masterful authority she was beginning to recognize, Cade reached for the washcloth and began lathering it. Jenny knew if she allowed him to do this, she was lost, yet she didn't have the strength to stop him.

He touched the cloth to her body and anticipation ripped through her. Cade's gaze met hers. She held her breath as he slid the washcloth over the curves of her body, painstakingly defining each line and molding them to do his will. She leaned back in sweet agony. Total surrender was her only option—for he was the sculptor; and she, nothing more than his clay.

With the skill of a master artist, his sensitive fingers stroked the edges of her raw need, calling forth a ragged moan from deep within her. Like a statue that Cade had brought to life, Jenny writhed against his touch, demanding he bring relief to her tormented soul.

Cade had never known such a responsive lover. She may

not want him for a husband, but it was evident she wanted him for her mate. One day she might change, but for now, he knew he would have to settle for what she was willing to give.

Cade scooped Jenny up in his arms and carried her to the bed. Eyes heavy with passion watched him undress and slide into bed beside her. Jenny came to him then—wet, wild, and wonderful. He knew she had to be sore from their night of lovemaking, but without saying a word she seemed to embrace the pain and ask for more.

Afterward, as he watched her sleep, Cade thought his heart would burst with love. Jenny was everything he could have hoped for and more, yet she stubbornly denied him the thing he wanted the most—her commitment.

He sat up on the edge of the bed and cupped his forehead in his hands. How could Jenny give so freely of her body, but not surrender her soul? He told himself he should be pleased that she hadn't turned from him in disgust, but somehow that fear no longer plagued him. Deep within him, he couldn't shake the feeling that Jenny loved him but was determined never to admit it. After all, it wasn't a secret that her need for their lovemaking was every bit as great as his own. But dared he hope for more?

His blue eyes suddenly narrowed, and Cade stood. He was a fool. By satisfying his own lust, he was giving her the only thing she wanted from him—his body; and as long as he was willing to oblige her, he wasn't giving her a chance to search her heart for the love she might have buried there.

Cade quickly dressed. As difficult as it might be, he'd not take her to his bed again—not until she told him she loved him. But he'd make sure he wasn't the only one to suffer. Before he was finished, she'd be aching for him too.

He reached down and pulled the covers off the bed. "Get up, Jenny," he said. "If you want your land, be in my study before lunch. Otherwise, the deal's off."

* * *

When Jenny came stomping into his study, Cade looked down at the hands on his pocket watch. "Thirteen minutes," he said. "Not bad time for a woman."

Once again Jenny was struck by the inappropriateness of a devil sporting Cade's blond good looks. It wasn't fair. If he wasn't going to look the part, at least he should have the decency to wear a sign warning a person to what he really was.

With a frown on her lips, Jenny focused all her attention on the dimple in the middle of his chin. "I can do without your comments, Mr. Morgan," she said bitterly. "Just sign over the land and I'll be on my way."

Cade studied her a moment before he bent to sign the documents. "I am turning over five feet of land on either side of the existing stream. That should be sufficient to pan for your gold. But you do realize, don't you, that when the cattle are grazing in the area, they have a right to drink at the stream?"

"I have nothing against four-legged creatures trespassing on my land. It's the two-legged kind I object to."

Cade looked up to find Jenny staring at him. Her flushed cheeks and the storminess of her dark brown eyes told him she was still upset, but not as upset as she was going to be when she found out he and not Bear would be watching over her.

She had the deed safely tucked away in the small portmanteau, but she didn't feel the elation she thought would come with the ownership. She dreaded saying good-bye. She just wanted to get to her land and start panning again, but when she opened the front door, everyone was waiting for her. With their stiff backs and disapproving frowns, they looked like a set of mismatched toy soldiers come to haul her away.

Izzy broke away from the others. "Don't go, Jenny."

Though she held her sister tight, it was Cade's face she watched. Why hadn't he asked her to stay? It was as if last night had meant nothing to him.

Damn him anyway. He was giving her everything she wanted, but she knew that smile touching his lips. It said it would never make her happy. Well, she would show him.

"I won't be gone long, Izzy," she said more to Cade than to her sister. "I'll work hard, then we can have a home of our own. Now dry your eyes and give me a smile."

Her lips trembled a bit but it was all Jenny needed to convince herself that what she was doing was right.

With her arm around her sister, Jenny said her good-byes to everyone. She thought Cade would at least help her up onto the wagon seat but it was Sam who stepped forward.

"Hurry back, Miss Jenny," he said. "We'll all miss—"

Clarence stepped out from under the wagon and stepped on Sam's boot, then marched across to Albert. With his head thrown back and his chest puffed out, the cocky little rooster let loose with a magnificent crow.

Millie rolled her eyes. "That dumb bird doesn't even know night from day."

Albert's mouth turned down in a pout. Clarence had let him down. He started to walk away when movement under the wagon caught his attention. "What . . . ?"

Clarence drowned them out with another crow and out came a mother hen followed by a lone chick. Even at its young age you could tell who was the proud father.

"Well, will you look at that," Bear said. "Clarence finally did it."

Albert smiled broadly. "I told you his missus was sitting."

"Must be all this damn love in the air," Millie said with a snort.

Cade looked at Jenny. "Yes," he said. "I suppose it is."

CHAPTER 18

Jenny didn't know how long she had been bending over the stream when she first heard the sound of horses. She stopped her panning and looked around for Bear. He must have left to look for meat for even the rifle he normally left sitting against his bedroll was gone.

Jenny stood and watched the band of men top the far hill. In all the time she and Bear had been at the stream, these were the first visitors they had seen. Catching her bottom lip between her teeth, she thoughtfully studied them as they guided their mounts down the rise and through the trees. Not counting the men on the wagons, there had to be at least twenty riders. Still too far away to identify, she didn't like the idea of having to greet them without Bear.

Although Jenny had never used her pistol, the fact that Cade had refused to return it to her suddenly left her feeling alone and vulnerable. Her standing in the water, clutching her pan, would be a dead giveaway as to what she had found. What would she do if the men were after her gold?

Jenny bent down and dug her pan into the gravel at the bottom of the stream. Once assured it was safely hidden, she waded out of the water. It was too late to bury her poke. Even if she managed to hide it away in her makeshift shelter, the men might see her. The only safe place was with her. Jenny turned her back to the horsemen and tucked the leather poke into the front of her cotton shirt.

Although they were out of sight behind a pile of rocks for the moment, Jenny was sure they must have seen her in the stream. She had to find something to make them think she and Bear had merely camped by the stream for the day.

Drats! How was she to fool them when she couldn't find the water bucket and Bear had long since put the tin plates and other breakfast things away. It was then Jenny spied Bear's bedroll.

Grabbing up the wool blanket, she ran back to the stream and plunged it into the water. Jenny expelled a deep sigh as the men skirted the last of the boulders. She had made it with only moments to spare.

Hoping they would pass her by, Jenny merrily sloshed the blanket up and down in the cold water and began to sing a few bars of a tune she'd picked up from one of the miners.

"Won't you be mine, my pretty little Miss Carolee?" she bellowed out with gusto. *"Won't you take a chance and marry me? Though your father is the sheriff, it is my belief to a very merry wedding he'll agree."*

She hummed the next few bars and listened for the approaching horses. *"I'll wear one of them fancy hats on my head. Change the manners you've come to dread. If you'll only be mine, Carolee."* They were definitely getting closer. But if there was a surefire way to get someone to leave her alone, Jenny knew it would be her singing. On the best of days, she couldn't carry a tune even if someone packed it in a basket for her.

"Sorry to say his smooth talk caught her," she continued. *"Soon he married the sheriff's daughter. Happiest couple that you ever saw—"*

Jenny's voice broke when she heard one of the horses

come to a stop behind her, but she took a deep breath and continued to sing at the top of her lungs. *"All too soon his dreams of life had faded. Carolee grew old and jaded . . ."* Jenny paused to catch her breath, then continued. *"And right now he wished he'd never gone a courtin' and unto that lovely maiden said, 'Won't you be my pretty little Miss—'"*

"Please spare us another chorus."

Jenny spun around at the sound of the familiar voice. Even with the sun to his back, she couldn't miss recognizing the tall blond man on the big red horse. Jenny's heart leapt in her chest. It'd take a lot longer than a week to forget what it felt like to be in his arms.

Jenny dropped the bedroll onto the rocks. "If you don't like what you hear, Mr. Morgan, you're free to move on."

Cade motioned for his men to dismount, then turned back to her. "Lady, with a voice like yours, I'm surprised you haven't used it earlier."

"What do you mean?" she asked suspiciously.

Cade leaned forward, propped his arms across the neck of his mount, and smiled down at her. "If you'd tried singing that song to me the night I carried you off to the preacher, I might never have married you."

"I'm told I have quite a nice voice," she said arrogantly, trying to give credence to her bold-faced lie.

"And who told you that? A deaf old gent with an eye for your body?"

Jenny ignored his uncouth reference to the indiscriminate taste of a possible admirer.

"Obviously, living in the wilds for so long has dulled your sensibilities, Mr. Morgan."

"Well, *Mrs. Morgan,* when something sounds like a dying calf in a hailstorm, a man of sensibility has no other choice but to take out his gun and shoot it."

"And you're a man of sensibility?"

Cade waved his arm to take in his men patiently standing next to the wagons pulled in beside her small lean-to. "Only a man of sensibility would consider the comfort of a wife that had walked out on him.''

Jenny looked from Cade to the logs piled high on the back of the wagons. "You brought me firewood?" she asked with a frown.

Cade let his gaze drift slowly over the gift. "I suppose you could burn them if you want to, but building a small cabin was more what we had in mind."

"A cabin?" she breathed. There was no use trying to disguise her pleasure. Sleeping on the cold, rough ground had not been the type of adventure Jenny had envisioned when she dreamed about striking out on her own. "When will it be finished?"

Shading his eyes, Cade looked up at the sun, then back at his men. "Can't be much past eight o'clock," he said. "You men think you can have this done by nightfall?"

Sam nodded for them. "Nightfall it is," he said confidently, then leaned over the side of the wagon to spit at a troublesome stray dog that had been following them for the last three miles. His eyes widened in surprise when he hit it.

He had done it. Sam handed the reins to one of the men and stepped down. With his shoulders thrown back, he swaggered up to Jenny. "We'll have you in your house today."

Jenny eyed the wagons. "That's an awful lot of work. Don't rush yourselves."

"Beggin' your pardon, ma'am, but we'll be finished a damn sight sooner than Albert will be a-stuffin' and a-stitchin' that feather mattress he insisted you'd be needin'."

Cade let the reins lie across the neck of his mount. "Albert was out running down some of the chickens when I left. He was a little shy of filling the flowered ticking he bought a few days ago."

"He's going to kill some poor chicken for my bed?" Jenny asked, aghast at the idea of sleeping on something she had been lovingly feeding for the last few months.

"If that were the case, I wouldn't give it another thought," Cade said as he climbed down from the bay. "As it is, you may be forced to sleep with your blanket thrown across the ropes on a bed frame for a few nights until he coaxes those contrary birds to part with a few of their tail feathers."

Sam screwed up his mouth, then turned his head and let go with a healthy spit of tobacco. Hitting his target a second time almost made him forget what he meant to say. "If Albert was so all-fired concerned with the thickness of your mattress, he'd have taken an ax to Clarence. It's plumb sinful the feathers that old rooster has and I told him so."

"Oh, no!" Jenny protested. "I could never sleep on Clarence."

Cade stepped close. "I'm glad to hear you're reserving that position for me."

An embarrassing warmth crept up Jenny's neck. It was disheartening to discover that forming an attachment for a man wasn't the only thing a woman should work to avoid. Passion was proving to have its own unique pitfalls—pitfalls that were every bit as debilitating as love and commitment.

"I would rather sleep on Clarence," she smugly informed him.

Carl lifted the small cavalryman's spyglass to his eye and cursed at what it showed him. The rumor was true. Jenny was back at the stream. It was said Morgan had signed over the property to her on their marriage. And if the men notching the logs at her campsite were doing what he thought they were, Cade's new bride wasn't planning on abandoning her wedding gift anytime soon.

The ironic thing was, if they hadn't been chipping away at the rich deposit on the ledge, Jenny couldn't have panned enough gold to fill the eye of one of her darning needles. As it was, finding the small pieces of gold they had dislodged only served to keep the woman working away.

Carl had been fortunate so far. Other than showing Jenny a few pointers when it came to panning, Bear had stayed away from the stream. But their luck wasn't going to hold out forever. One of these days, curiosity of her find would entice Bear to investigate. If the old woman's grandson had found the rich deposit so easily, a miner with Bear's experience would have no trouble at all.

But Bear was not the real problem. Even if Carl could manage to kill the big ugly miner, he knew Jenny would continue to pan. No, Jenny was the one he needed to eliminate. Without her, neither Cade nor Bear would have a reason for being here.

Somehow he would have to come up with a plan to get rid of her. If it hadn't been for Bear's continual vigilance, he'd have done it days ago. The ugly miner was beginning to try his patience. Even when the man went hunting, he never strayed far from the camp. Carl had thought about shooting both Bear and the girl, but Bear was so big, he doubted even a buffalo gun would bring the miner down. One thing was sure, Carl had no desire to come face-to-face with Bear even if he did manage to wound the man.

No, he had to get Jenny off by herself and make it look like an accident. Otherwise, Bear wouldn't be his only problem. Cade would be after the ones responsible and Cade was not a man to give up until he found them. With Cade out for someone's blood, Elmer was sure to crack under the pressure.

It was a shame an accident was the only answer, for Carl had grown fond of his fantasies of running a knife blade along the sensuous curves of her ripe, young body. He'd just have to find a way to hide what he really intended to do to Cade's woman.

Jenny shaded her gold pan from the bright afternoon sun and counted eleven tiny yellow flakes. Not too bad. The dream of a home for her and Izzy was coming closer to a reality.

With her back to the sun, Jenny took the tip of her knife and lifted each small gold particle out of the black sand, then dropped them into her leather poke. She knew she should take a break to ease her aching back but she also had to keep busy in order to take her mind off Cade. Watching him while he helped notch the logs conjured up too many memories of sharing his bed.

She ventured another peek at the workers. It was amazing to see how much they had done in so little time. After marking out a site, they'd leveled it, then started erecting the log walls. Sam and two other men had left when they had unloaded all the logs from the wagon but they were back now with a load of clay and had set to work caulking the walls.

Cade stood in the makeshift doorway, hammering the finishing slats up against the chiseled opening in the logs. The muscles of his bare arms flexed provocatively in the afternoon sunlight with each swing of the hammer and Jenny could feel the familiar knot forming next to her heart.

Even from this distance, Jenny could see the swirl of dark blond hairs that trailed down his stomach to the pants that now hung low on his slim hips. What she had once intended to claim with the harmless casualness of a lover now lured her with the force of a woman possessed.

Jenny lowered her head and closed her eyes. The sweet agony was almost more than she could bear. If only it were possible to keep the love that tore at her heart separate from the longings that tore at her body, she would willingly quench the raging fires of her desire in Cade's arms.

She took a deep breath and opened her eyes. She might as well accept the fact that it could never be. Freedom was too precious to toss aside. It was better to suffer in the light than to lock yourself in another dark attic. Jenny dumped the black sand from her pan and went back to her work.

The day seemed to drag on forever as she tried to ignore the activity going on around her, but the tantalizing smells coming from Bear's stew pot made it almost impossible. Without lunch, Jenny's stomach growled in protest. Her back ached, but she refused to stop. It would be dark soon. There would be plenty of time to rest after everyone left.

It wasn't long before the sun dropped behind the ridge and Jenny was forced to quit. She stood at the edge of the stream and watched the last of the men leave.

The cabin was finished. It was small, but she couldn't complain. Most miners' cabins were small and Jenny was a miner now. To eat at a table and sleep in a bed again would be a real luxury.

Jenny climbed the small rise to where Bear's stew bubbled on the fire. It was then she noticed that someone had taken down her lean-to. She walked to the door of the cabin and peered inside.

"Come on in and take a look," a shadowy figure seated at the log table said.

Jenny stiffened. "I thought you left with the others."

Cade struck a match and lit the lantern. "You didn't think I'd leave you here all by yourself, did you?"

"Bear is all the protection I need," she said haughtily.

Cade studied her a moment. "Bear had to leave."

"W-will he be back?"

Amusement lifted the corners of Cade's lips. "When he finishes a little job I had for him. Until then, you'll have to put up with me."

"I can look after myself," she hissed.

"I'm sure that's what the other miners said just before someone buried a blade between their shoulders."

"You think someone would do that to me?"

"No one knows why this madman picks one person and leaves another. But until he's caught, I'll be right here to see that he doesn't pick you."

Jenny wanted to tell him again that she could take care of

herself, but in truth she was happy to have anyone's company. "Where's the things that were in my lean-to?" she asked instead.

Cade lifted the lantern and swung it in a wide arc. "They've been put where they belong."

Jenny took in the items stacked neatly on the shelves behind the table. For the first time, she let her gaze wander around the cabin. A weathered stand stood beside the boxed bed that took up one end of the room. Someone had placed another one under a broken piece of silvered glass by the front door. A water bucket and wash pan rested on its scarred surface.

"A gift from the men," he told her when she looked back at him. "They also rounded up an old iron stove so you wouldn't have to cook on an open fire. They'll be bringing it by in the morning."

Jenny didn't have the courage to admit that Bear had been doing all the cooking. "I'll have to remember to thank them," she said, then nervously wiped her hands on the back of her breeches. "And you also," she added when he made no move to leave.

Jenny held her breath when he stood up from the table and hung the lamp on a wire hook suspended from the wooden rafters. Light spilled into the far corners of the room, reminding Jenny of the closeness of the bed to the table where Cade stood, a sun-bronzed statue of perfection.

Dark blond hair lay in casual disarray, enhancing the chiseled features of her husband's handsome face. The massive muscles along his naked chest and arms seemed to ripple with life in the sensual patterns of lamplight and shadow. He made it difficult for a woman not to reach out and touch them.

Jenny ran her tongue over her dry lips. No man should be blessed with so many enticing attributes, she told herself. It wasn't fair. As it was, she didn't know whether to be relieved or disappointed that he made no move toward her.

His intense blue eyes suddenly locked with hers. "I'll tell you right now," he said, his voice rough with emotion. "I expect a more tangible display of your gratitude than a mere thank you."

Jenny could feel the air being sucked from her lungs. She took a step backward. "The stew," she said, edging toward the door. "I'd best be dishing it up before the pot boils dry."

"Won't you be needing some plates?" he asked.

"Plates? Oh, yes, the plates. And those would be . . ."

"Over here on the shelf behind me," he finished for her.

Jenny didn't have to look at his face to know he found this all very amusing. She could hear it in his voice.

Keeping her head bowed, Jenny skirted the end of the table only to find that there wasn't enough room between the table and the shelf to slip in behind her husband. And he knew it.

"Would you please move?" she asked quietly.

Cade stepped closer. "I would much rather help."

"Then turn around and hand me two plates."

Cade did as he was asked. "Wouldn't you like to have some of Millie's fresh baked bread to go with the stew?" he asked sweetly.

"She sent some?"

Cade pinned her snugly against the shelf. "Sorry the cabin's so small, but I'm sure you feel that panning for your gold is more important than the inconveniences." He reached around her to get a covered basket from the far end of the shelf. "The bread's right over here," he said as he pressed his body next to hers. "Millie sent it especially for you."

Jenny pushed against his bare chest. "How nice of you to place it in such a convenient spot," she said through gritted teeth.

Cade grinned down at her. "I always try to plan ahead."

Jenny was not amused. "Then next time try to work it out

so I don't have to fight off the local riffraff before I can dish up my supper.''

''By that am I to take it that dallying with the local riffraff after supper is also out of the question?''

''How perceptive of you,'' she said evenly, though her heart pounded wildly at the prospect. ''Now if you will kindly step aside, I'll get the plates and dish up the stew.''

''Certainly,'' he said, lowering his hand to rest on her hip. ''And by the time you get back, I should have everything ready for us.''

Jenny refused to dwell on the implications of his statement. She didn't mind sharing a meal with him, but surely he knew she'd not share a bed with him again. When he stepped back, she grabbed up the two plates and headed for the door.

Night had fallen and Jenny carefully picked her way through the rocks to the campfire. She was half tempted to eat her supper by the fire before returning with his, but she knew Cade well enough to know he'd only join her. If she was going to be forced to eat with him, at least the table in the cabin would be more comfortable than the cold ground.

Jenny knelt and picked up Bear's large cooking ladle that rested on a broken piece of crockery by the fire. She started to fill the plates when she realized her mistake. If Cade wanted more, he'd have to leave the cabin to get it. It might be the only chance she had of bolting the door after him.

With a plan building in her fertile mind, Jenny quickly dumped all but a small scoopful back into the pot, then returned to the cabin. ''Here we are,'' she said as she pushed open the door.

Cade sat waiting for her. In the short time she had been gone, he had covered the table with a blue gingham cloth and placed the few utensils she had by each wooden bench. The bread was cut and a buttered slice sat beside each fork. Jenny placed the plates of stew next to them and sat down.

Cade looked down at the small portion on his plate. "Afraid I would get fat, were you?"

Jenny slid her fork through the stew. "One should never eat a lot after working in the hot sun," she said sternly. "It might make you ill."

Cade picked up a square of cloth, then headed for the door. "It may make you sick," he said over his shoulder. "It only makes me all the more hungry."

After he left, Jenny stood beside the door a few minutes. When she heard him by the fire, she slammed the door and reached for a latch. There was none. All there was, was a long board set between two wooden hooks on the back of the door. He was almost to the cabin when she spotted another hook beside the frame. She slid the board home only moments before he reached the door.

"Unlock this door, Jenny." His voice, low and threatening, was accompanied by a kick to the wooden slats.

Jenny backed from the door. "Go home, Cade," she shouted. "I don't need you here."

With her eyes focused on the door, Jenny listened for his reply. Nothing. Where had he gone? Then she heard the rip at the window. As she watched a fist tore through the oiled paper, then reached across to the door and pushed the board out of the hook.

"What's the sense of having a lock on your door if anyone can reach in the window and open it?" she shouted at the angry figure standing in the doorway.

Cade stooped to retrieve the pot of stew. "The lock is to keep the four-legged animals out of your cabin, not your husband."

"Some two-legged ones can do a lot more harm than the four-legged ones."

He gave her chin a quick squeeze. "That's why you have me, love. I'll keep the bad ones in line."

"And who's to keep you in line?"

Cade sat the blackened stew pot on the table, then

motioned for her to take her seat. "Since when have you wanted me to play the gentleman?"

He waited, but she didn't answer. "Why can't you just admit you enjoy being my wife more than you expected to?"

Afraid he would see how close he'd come to the truth, Jenny refused to look at him. "Let's eat," she said, plopping down on the wooden bench.

"You haven't answered my question."

"It was a dumb question," she said between bites of the spicy stew. "Ask me something else like how was the panning today and I might answer you."

Cade slipped onto the other bench and pulled the stew pot over next to his plate. "I'm hungry so we'll do it your way this time. How was the panning today?"

Jenny's head shot up, her brown eyes narrowing suspiciously. "Why do you ask that?"

Cade stopped filling his plate and stared at her. "You told me to."

With a warmth creeping up her neck, Jenny cut another slice of Millie's bread. "Oh, well," she said, trying to appear casual. "I was merely giving you an example. I didn't actually mean for you to ask me that particular question. Bear says a smart miner never brags of his take. It encourages unsavory characters to lift your poke."

"And you do everything Bear says."

Jenny could have sworn it sounded as if her husband was jealous of the miner, but that couldn't be. Bear had told her weeks ago that Cade had been worried about her safety and cautioned Bear to watch over her. A jealous man wouldn't have done that.

"Bear knows all there is about panning for gold. He's been a tremendous help."

Cade knew it was foolish to let the resentful feelings about Bear's closeness with Jenny eat away at him. After all, Bear was only doing what he had asked him to.

Nonetheless, Cade finished his stew in silence. Each spoonful threatened to stick in his throat, but Cade stubbornly swallowed every one. When he was finished, he took Jenny by the hand and led her over to the bed.

"Climb in," he said.

Jenny pulled her hand out of his. "I'm not going to sleep with you, Cade Morgan. If that's what you had in mind when you sent Bear away, you might as well head back to your ranch."

"Don't be such a pampered prissy," he growled. "Sleeping in the same bed doesn't mean I plan on touching you. It merely means we won't freeze tonight."

Jenny struggled to ward off the tears that threatened. He couldn't have humiliated her more if he'd slapped her.

"You take the bed," she said haughtily. "I'll keep warm enough on my own out by the fire."

Jenny was surprised and hurt when he didn't try to stop her. It was cold outside and it took her some time to pile enough wood on the fire to melt the ice that had formed around her heart. It wasn't until she was finished that she remembered Bear's wool blanket.

Jenny made her way down to the rocks by the stream. What would she do if Bear had taken it with him? She needn't have worried. There it lay in a heap just as she had left it—cold and damp, but better than nothing. She gathered it around her and returned to lie by the fire.

That was where Cade found her an hour later when he took the plates down to the stream to wash. He smiled to himself. He needn't have bothered bringing the dirty plates with him. He didn't need an excuse for leaving the cabin. Jenny was sound asleep.

He tossed another log on the fire, then stooped to check the ground between her and the flames. Just as he thought, the woman was a total greenhorn. All she needed was for one of the logs to fall out of the rocked area and she would be roasted where she lay.

It took him only a moment to clear the dried grass and wood chips from around her. He picked up the plates and went on down the small hill. Moonlight danced across the rippling water and Cade found himself following the stream's winding path. He wished Jenny were awake to share the rare beauty with him.

After a while, he stopped and looked up at the distant hills. Who was he kidding? Even if Jenny was awake, she'd not waste her time walking with him. She had her fortune to make—a fortune that would buy her freedom from him.

He stooped down and dipped the plates in the water. As he bent over the stream a twig snapped in the cold, crisp mountain air, setting Cade's nerves to tingling.

Someone was watching him. He was sure of it. Cade forced himself to remain calm as he appeared to be casually washing the plates in the stream while all the time he was searching the bushes to catch a glimpse of the intruder. Finished, he stood and made his way back along the path to the cabin. He was almost to the clearing when he smelled the wet wool burning. He dropped the plates and ran.

Jenny lay curled up beside the fire as he had left her. Only now she had company. One of the burning logs lay on the edge of her blanket. She was fortunate. Without the warmth of the fire to sustain its flame, the pine log merely smoldered and hissed against the damp wool.

Cade wanted to scream his rage, but it was more important to get Jenny safely behind the walls of the cabin. He kicked the log aside, then pulled Jenny from beneath the blanket.

CHAPTER 19

Jenny woke up with a start. She blinked her eyes in disbelief. Cade was running toward the cabin with her in his arms. "What do you think you're doing?" she screamed.

"Lie still until we get inside!"

Instinct told her to follow his directions, but what was that awful odor? It smelled like something was burning.

Cade slammed the door closed behind them. He crossed the room in a few quick strides, then dropped her onto the bed.

Jenny started to protest his high-handed treatment, but before she could form the words he turned away and left her lying there. She felt like a sack of weeviled flour he had just tossed out on the garbage heap.

He gave her no explanation but returned to the door and rammed the board into the wooden hook on the wall. Jenny's protest died in her throat when he retrieved his pistol from the shelf behind the table and blew out the lantern. She could see his dark silhouette framed against the room's only window. Jenny lay back on the canvas-covered ropes that made up her bed.

"What are you doing?" she whispered harshly.

Using the barrel of his gun, Cade eased open the slit in the oil paper. "I'm trying to save your fool life," he said as he checked out the clearing below.

"My life?" she breathed.

"Someone rolled a log from the fire onto your blanket. If I hadn't returned when I did, you would have been lit up like a damn Christmas candle."

The smell. It had been the damp wool. "Why would someone try to hurt me?" she asked.

"That's what I'd like to know, and come daylight, I intend to find out."

Jenny hugged her knees to her chest and shivered in the darkness. Who hated her enough to do this? She'd made no enemies that she knew of. She tried to remember the story of the old lady and her grandson. The papers had said the same thing about them. No one knew of any enemies. But they were dead just the same.

Minutes went by, then hours. Jenny found herself nodding off. She didn't know how Cade remained awake. He had been notching logs along with his men all day. He had to be tired. Jenny closed her eyes.

The next thing she knew, Cade was shaking her. "Wake up, Jenny."

Jenny snuggled deeper into the warm blanket. Cade must have covered her sometime during the night. "Go away," she mumbled.

"Oh, no you don't. It's your turn to watch."

"My turn?" she groaned. "No one said I'd be taking a turn."

"Did you think I could stay awake all night?"

Jenny opened one eye and stared up at him. "You were doing a good job of it the last time I looked."

He pulled the blanket off her. "Well, it's nearly four in the morning and I'm not doing as good a job. Now get up."

Jenny dropped first one leg, then the other over the edge

of the bed. Even getting up in stages didn't help. Cade jerked her into an upright position, but her head and shoulders refused to remain at attention.

"You're not much of a gentleman," she said.

Cade pulled her to her feet and started her across the room to the bench. "That's all right. You're enough of a gentleman for the both of us."

"Me?" she said, stopping dead in her tracks. "That's a terrible thing to say to a woman. I'm a lady. Only men are gentlemen."

He gave her a gentle push toward the bench. "You couldn't tell it from the way you've been acting. If your damn independence means so much, here's your chance to be treated like every other man. Now sit down. Here's my gun. Wake me if you hear anything."

He turned and left her standing with the pistol in her hands. Jenny blinked back a tear at his coldness. Had she truly been acting more like a man than a woman? It certainly hadn't been her intention. She had merely wanted to be free of all men. It wasn't the same, or was it?

Jenny nudged aside the torn flap of oil paper and checked the moon-washed clearing. It was deserted. She sat down and rested the gun in her lap.

Well, she'd finally gotten what she wanted. Up until now, Cade had always treated her as a woman, yet she had fought him all the way. Now, in his eyes, she was no different from any other man.

So why did she feel so miserable? It wasn't that she had been forced to take her turn at the watch. It was more than that. Cade had taught her how to be a woman—a woman not to be bullied and controlled, but loved and desired. And somewhere along the way, she had grown to appreciate it.

She looked over to Cade. He was sound asleep. Had she thrown everything away before she even realized what she had found?

As the rest of the night slowly crept by, Jenny vowed

she would make him see his mistakes—and hers. She had always judged men against the domineering standards of her father and now she could see that she was wrong. All men were not alike.

Jenny took another look out the window. The gray light of day trimmed the distant hills. Morning would be here before long. Then Cade would waken and she would be forced to live with the coldness that had taken over his heart. But what could she do? He would never believe her if she told him she was willing to change.

Jenny rose from her chair and unlocked the door. She only hoped it was not too late to show him. Being as quiet as she could, Jenny carried the empty stew pot down to the creek.

She had watched Bear make the stew for weeks. With the dried meat Bear left behind, it shouldn't be too difficult to round up a few of the wild plants and roots Bear used to add to the pot. Cade would be so pleased with her efforts to help.

Using a handful of gravel like she'd seen Bear do, Jenny scrubbed the pot. Once it was cleaned and rinsed, she filled it with water and carried it to the cold campfire.

The sight of the charred log lying by Bear's blanket sent chills racing up Jenny's spine. Cade was right. There was no way the log could have rolled off the fire and over the ring of stones to fall onto her blanket. Someone had meant to harm her. But why? What had she ever done to anyone? Cade said he'd find out and she trusted him. In the meantime, she would do her part.

Taking a small stick from the wood pile, Jenny poked it into the gray ashes. Luckily a few coals had survived the cold night air and she blanketed them with wood chips and dry grass, then she sat back and waited for the fire to catch. This was going to be easier than she thought.

Patiently, she waited. Where was her fire? Jenny took the stick and stirred up the coals. Nothing. Nothing but smoke.

Instead of the grass igniting the fire, it seemed to have smothered it.

What was she going to do for hot water now? She didn't have any matches. But Cade did. She looked up at the cabin. Hadn't she seen him pull one out of his pocket only yesterday? Well, there was only one way to find out. She'd have to search his pockets.

Jenny crept into the dark room. The snores coming from the bed told her Cade was still asleep. Even so, she hesitated. The plan seemed so easy when she was kneeling by the fire. She had forgotten the fact that he was sleeping in the britches with the pockets she needed to search. Jenny reached out her hand. Perhaps if she was real careful, she could slip her hand inside and get the matches without waking him.

Gently she eased her hand into his pocket. She had just reached what she thought was the matches when Cade shifted on the bed and Jenny was forced to move with him. Drats! With her hand bent at this impossible angle, how was she ever to retrieve them now? She studied him a moment. If she was to crawl up on the bed, at least she could get her hand free. There. Now if she could get her leg on the other side of him, she might be able to get the matches as well.

With her hand on the bed to one side of his head, she threw her leg over him. It took her only a moment to brace herself just so. There, now to get the matches. She slipped her hand deeper into Cade's pocket.

With a groan, Cade rolled over on his side, taking Jenny with him. She couldn't move—couldn't breathe. He had her against the cabin wall, her hand pinned beneath him.

"There's a lot simpler ways of doing this," he said gruffly.

Jenny was sure her heart stopped beating. Desperately she tried to push him away. "How long have you been awake?"

"Long enough . . . to find out . . . I have a lustful

wife who is determined to have me,'' he said between placing kisses along the side of her neck.

Jenny twisted against him. ''Let go of me, you—you—''

''Yes?'' he breathed against the arch of her throat.

''Don't you understand?'' she asked through gritted teeth. ''I don't want you. I'm after the matches in your pocket.''

Cade lifted his head. ''Matches? You were fishing in my pocket for matches?''

Jenny pounded his chest with her free hand. ''Yes, you imbecile. Now get off my hand.''

Cade grinned down at her. ''I rather like it where it is.''

''Well, I don't,'' she informed him.

''Don't lie to me, Jenny. Your heart's beating fast enough to pass a train going down a mountain.''

''I don't have time for this nonsense,'' she said, twisting to free herself. ''I have water to heat, then breakfast to cook. How am I expected to do that if you won't let me up?''

Cade swung his leg over her. ''We heard about your cooking.''

''Bear told you?''

She looked ready to cry and Cade gave her a swift kiss.

''News like that travels fast, sweet thing. But don't worry about it. Millie sent up some of her special fried rolls for our breakfast and Albert should be here about noon with our lunch. So you see, you don't have to do a thing but make me happy. And with what you've learned, you can do that very well.''

With his body pressed intimately against hers, Jenny knew what would please him. It was what only hours ago she had told herself she wanted. Jenny closed her eyes for a brief moment. ''You're saying that I should not be concerned about my failures in all the other wifely duties but concentrate my efforts on pleasing you in bed, am I right?''

Cade thought about telling her how well she had managed his household and what a great little hostess she had turned out to be, but he knew she wouldn't appreciate his opinion. If there was one thing Cade had learned about his wife, it was that when she got a bee in her bonnet about something, she didn't stop until she did something about it. The only way to deter her was to take her mind off it.

"Why worry about who does the cooking? I pay Millie to do that. Remember, you have more than enough to do working your claim. Besides," he said as he kissed his way up the side of her neck, "a woman with your natural talents for pleasing a man should be happy her husband is willing to settle for that."

While Cade's warm breath sent tiny shivers skittering up Jenny's spine, his words doused her emotionally with cold water. Just because she had once tried to seduce him, Cade now wanted a wife only to warm his bed—one who was expected to be at his constant beck and call. That was not what he said was expected out of his other mail-order brides and he'd soon learn he'd not get it from the one he married.

"Let me up, Cade Morgan?"

He arched a brow. "Why should I?"

She shoved her face close to his. "Because if you don't let me up, I'm going to wet my britches."

Cade rolled on his back and pulled her hand from his pocket. "Good Lord, Jenny, why didn't you say so sooner?"

Jenny scrambled over him and headed for the door. It wasn't until she reached it that she turned and answered, "Because I didn't think of it."

She could hear his roar behind her as she headed for the stream and her pan.

The days passed smoothly. Jenny spent her days panning for gold and her poke was growing fat with her efforts. Albert continued to bring the food for their meals. After a few failures on both their parts, Albert taught her how to make a tolerable pot of coffee on the campfire.

Jenny was pleased with her efforts, but the fact that she'd not mastered a simple pot of stew still nagged at her. She sent a note to Millie asking her for a list of the ingredients Bear might have used, but the answer was as confusing as cooking itself.

Roots, herbs, leaves. Jenny's shoulders slumped in disappointment. How was she to know what was what? She glanced up from the note. She could ask Cade to collect the things she would need. It would give him something to do besides harassing her. Ever since the first night he was either looking for clues as to who had tried to harm her or watching her every move. He was about to drive her crazy.

Her only choice was to ask Millie to send the stew and not tell Cade about it. She hated to trick her husband, but he deserved it. Before she left him, he was going to know just what it was that he had lost.

Jenny squeezed her eyes shut. Why couldn't she just admit that when she left, Cade wouldn't be losing a thing? Well, no more lies. Especially to herself. Cade was married to a woman who had taken his money, lied to him, and sold his precious whiskey.

But then marriage hadn't been her idea. It was his. He said it was to be her punishment. Jenny smiled for the first time in days. After all she had done, staying with him might be her only chance for revenge.

She wrote the note to Millie.

The stew arrived bright and early the next morning. Cade was off on one of his mysterious jaunts. For one that was so concerned about someone trying to harm her, he sure left her on her own a lot. But that was just fine with her, she told herself. It made it all the easier to carry out her plan.

As soon as Albert left, Jenny poured the stew into the old pot Bear used and hung it over the campfire, then went to the creek to pan until lunch. Let that Cade Morgan tell her that she was only good for one thing after he tasted the stew.

* * *

"I just came from town. They caught the killer," Bear said as he crawled up on the rock with Cade. "Would you believe it. It was Elmer all this time."

Cade moved over to make room for the miner. "A liar and a thief, but a murderer? No, I find that hard to believe."

"Seems his last name was Smith."

"W. E. Smith?" he asked.

"That's the one. They found the papers where he had filed on the claims. Imagine him trying to take that wagon down Runaway Hill with all that gold in the back."

"What surprises me is how someone that dumb could have pulled off what he did."

Both sat in thought as they watched Albert come and go at the campsite below.

"What's she up to now?" Cade mumbled to himself when he saw Jenny pour the food from one pan to the next.

"Looks like she doesn't like your pots, Cade."

Cade frowned. "She's liked them well enough up until now. She's up to something. I can feel it."

Bear leaned back against one of the rocks on the narrow ledge. "At least she's alive."

"Only because I couldn't sleep that night. But at least we've seen the last of the killings."

"I almost forgot. Your hunch was right. Each one of the miners murdered had hinted at a big find shortly before their bodies were discovered."

Cade watched a rattler curl up on one of the rock ledges below. "And the old woman and the boy?"

"The woman kept to herself, but the boy was always walking the creek beds looking for a spot of color. I told you what the assayer said. The boy brought in a nugget just like Jenny's. You suppose he got it out of this creek?"

"It doesn't make sense." Cade tossed a small pebble at a stand of scrub oak below. "Didn't you tell me once that you had tried your luck here years ago?"

"It's been over ten years."

"Did you find anything?"

"If I remember right, there was some gold to be had. Even Jenny has proved that. She's been working hard."

"That was the idea. I wanted her to find out that panning for gold isn't worth the work. Maybe then she'll give up and come home to be a real wife." Cade turned and looked at Bear. "You don't suppose she's finding a lot, do you?"

"She's panned a good bit of color, but I doubt there will ever be enough to kill someone for."

"Lord help us if she's stumbled onto something. I'd never get her away from that stream."

Cade stood, sending a shower of gravel off the edge. "I think it's time my wife took a break from all her work. I'll offer to take her into town. You check out her workings while we're gone."

Carl bit down on his lip to keep from shouting when one of the small stones hit his ear. He didn't have time to be out here lying on his belly watching Morgan's wife pan for his gold. If he missed many more days of work, he'd lose his job. The railroad wouldn't believe his excuses much longer. If he could get rid of Morgan and Bear for a few minutes, he'd be able to slip his little surprise into the food Jenny had set to cooking on the fire.

An evil grin curved his thin lips. The old man had guaranteed him pleasurable results. Whoever swallowed the poison would be writhing in pain—a pain so fierce the victim died with a scream frozen on their face. It was probably better that the poisoning was left to him. Elmer would not have appreciated witnessing the event.

Carl looked around the small niche that kept him hidden. Where was that fool Elmer anyway? He hadn't seen him in over a week. If he didn't show up soon, he needn't whine about how small his share of the take was to be. Not that

Carl would have given a share to Elmer anyway, but Elmer didn't know that.

"Damn!" he cursed to himself.

Morgan and Bear were coming down the rock. Carl slid farther back into his small quarters. What were they up to now? he wondered.

"We should be gone for two hours, so that should give you plenty of time," he heard Morgan say.

"I'll start working my way up the stream. What do you want me to do if I find anything?"

Carl held his breath waiting for Morgan's answer.

"Come get me," Cade said.

No! Carl wanted to shout at the top of his lungs, but they would be on him in minutes if he did. Even with his rifle, he knew he needed the time to take careful aim. He wouldn't have that chance up against two men. Carl dropped his head in his hands.

"The gold's mine," he kept mumbling over and over again to himself. "It's not fair. The gold is mine."

He didn't know how long he lay there, but when he raised his head Morgan and his wife were gone and Bear was wading upstream with a gold pan in his hand. Every few feet, the miner bent to dip the pan into the gravel. Carl sat up and watched Bear swirl the pan, check its contents, then dump it back into the water.

Carl smiled to himself when Bear walked farther upstream—away from Jenny's workings. As long as he continued in that direction, Carl's find was safe. Carl had checked that portion of the stream for himself. The rich deposit did not extend beyond the ledge.

Even so, he couldn't risk them finding it. He had done too much for the gold to let Morgan step in and take it away now. A few more feet and Bear would be out of sight of the camp. He could slip in then and deliver his little bottle of pain.

Carefully he made his way among the trees to the pot

bubbling away on the fire. Bear was out of sight and it took just a moment to pour the crystalline granules into the hot stew. The colorless powder didn't appear to dissolve, but lay on the bubbling surface taunting him. He grabbed up a big wooden spoon from the rock beside the fire and stirred the contents. He had just dipped out a spoonful to check his success when he heard Bear running along the stream. Carl dropped the spoon back onto the rock and ran.

Carl made it back to his hiding place with only moments to spare. He grabbed up his rifle and waited. He wished he knew what Bear had found to have come hurrying back to camp. He wasn't long in learning the answer. Bear dived for the bushes just as a wagon came around the curve.

Morgan and Jenny? Why had they returned so quickly? Carl hugged his rifle to him and slid closer.

"It won't take me a minute to get my gold dust and we can be gone," Jenny tossed over her shoulder as she climbed down from the wagon.

"I can't believe you forgot it," Cade growled down at her. "You haven't let it out of your sight all the time I've been here."

Jenny placed her hands on her hips and glared up at him. "I told you I thought I had it with me. Is it my fault I left it behind? If you hadn't rushed me so this would never have happened."

Bear's attention was drawn away from the quarreling couple by a movement at the fire. He smiled. It was only a raccoon with a healthy appetite chewing at some food left on Jenny's wooden spoon. What Cade said about Elmer not having the sense to pull off the thefts nagged at him. Next he'd be jumping at his own shadow and there was no reason for it.

He shifted his position beneath the bushes. Jenny was sure taking a long time to get her gold, Bear thought. Even Cade was beginning to look worried. She must be coming though for the raccoon suddenly dropped the spoon and raised up on his hind legs. The coon stood perfectly still for a moment, then as Bear watched the furry animal fell over in a fit of convulsions. Its tortured cries brought Jenny from the cabin.

Bear didn't care that he was giving his position away. He came scrambling out of the bushes. "It was eating Millie's stew off that spoon," Bear said as he and Cade bent over the dying animal.

Cade moved so Jenny couldn't see the struggling animal. "Poison?" he asked.

"Looks like some of the stuff the miners used up near King Mine to get rid of the rats."

Carl couldn't hear what they were saying, but it didn't take much to see that they had discovered what he had done. Bad luck seemed to dog his every step. Finding the gold had been the only good thing to happen to him and the meddling of that stubborn black-headed bitch down there was taking it all away. A lifetime of pent-up anger boiled to the surface and Carl eased the rifle up to his shoulder. After taking careful aim, he fired.

Jenny's brown eyes widened at the lancing pain in her shoulder. "C-Cade," she gasped as she fell to the ground.

Jenny woke up on the bed in the cabin. Cade was bending over her. The black scowl on his face was sour enough to curdle milk.

"Lie still," he growled when she tried to move. "You've been shot. Luckily the bullet went through your shoulder. Millie has seen to it so there shouldn't be any chance of infection. She's used to these things, but in the meantime I don't want your wound to start bleeding again."

The pain forced her to comply more than his words. "Why would someone want to shoot me?" she asked.

The confusion and fear evident on her face tempered his answer. "I warned you your damned independence would bring you nothing but trouble," he teased.

"Am I going to die?" Jenny asked, ignoring his attempt to make her smile.

Ice splintered Cade's blue eyes. "Hardly, but whoever did this will."

Jenny almost felt sorry for the one who had shot her. Cade was not a forgiving man. She knew now he'd hunt the man down with his last ounce of strength if need be. "Could it have been an accident?" she offered.

"Hardly, unless you would consider poisoning our supper an accident also."

"It's my gold, isn't it?"

Jenny struggled to get up, but Cade held her down.

"Someone wants my gold," she shouted up at him. "I won't let anyone take my gold."

"Calm down, Jenny, or you'll have no more need for the gold." He pulled the blanket up and tucked it under her chin. "I have to go now," he said. "Millie will stay to help, but Bear has picked up the killer's trail and we need to get on it before the scoundrel gets away."

Jenny wanted Cade to stay, but knew she was being selfish. Cade had to stop whoever had done this. She placed her finger on his lips. "Don't be long," she said.

Her words stayed with him as he and Bear followed the trail. Was Jenny finally beginning to accept him? He'd never forget the pain that gripped his heart when he saw her fall beside him. He thought he'd lost her forever. The thought only spurred him on.

It was late afternoon when Cade and Bear struck out on a side path to a small spring. The tracking was a long tedious chore. They had been in the saddle for hours and their mounts needed a short rest. Cade dismounted and started toward the water when he spotted the distinctive hoofprint of the horse they had been following. He knelt to examine the print. It was at least an hour old.

"He's backtracked on us, Bear," he said as he swung

back into the saddle. "My guess is he's headed back to the cabin."

"That would be mine too," Bear answered.

They rode in silence, each lost in their own thoughts. They had to reach Jenny and Millie before the killer did. They were two miles out when they spotted the smoke. Without a word they touched their spurs to their mounts.

The cabin was nothing more than a smoldering shell by the time they reached it. Seeing Millie lying in Albert's arms sent a cold chill up Cade's spine.

"Jenny?" he asked as he dismounted.

Albert dabbed at the blood on the side of Millie's face. "Millie says he took her. They rode west."

Cade knelt beside them. "Did you see who it was, Millie?"

"It was Carl Turner," Albert answered. "He's the station-master in Gold Shoe."

"Turner? But why?"

Millie opened her eyes. "It was Jenny's gold. He said the claim was his."

"And I'd be willing to lay odds that Elmer was his partner."

Bear was used to the mask of coldness Cade wore for others, but the anger and despair he saw there frightened him. "Carl used to own the old Lame Donkey Mine on the other side of Gold Shoe," he offered. "He might have taken her there, Cade."

Cade looked at their horses. They'd never make it to the mine. "Will you be all right, Millie, if we take the wagon? I'll send it back with Bear as soon as I can get a new mount in town."

She looked up into Albert's face and smiled. "You go on ahead, Cade. I'll be just fine here with Albert."

Seeing the love in her face only made Cade feel his loss all the more.

Carl Turner was a dead man.

* * *

Carl knelt over Jenny, the ax in his hand. "With you gone, the gold will be mine again."

Gravel bit into Jenny's back. She ran her hand along the stone floor. She listened but only the distant sound of water dripping broke the silence. They had to be in one of the many deserted mine tunnels that spotted the area. There was no use hoping someone would find her. If she was going to get out of this mess, it was going to be up to her.

"You plan on killing me, is that it?"

The flickering light of the candle played across the cruel grin that twisted the man's face. He touched the ax to her breast. "Not if you treat me nice."

"Cade will kill you for this."

"He has to find me first and until he does, you're mine."

She knew she should try to concentrate on anything but the vile bloodstained ax he trailed down the front of her cotton shirt, but it was impossible to ignore. This man was the murderer of the little boy and his grandmother.

The ax stopped at the juncture between her legs. "Take them off," Carl snapped.

Jenny swallowed hard against the bile that rose in her throat, nearly choking her. Too much had happened too fast.

She reached down to unbutton her britches. The movement induced a white-hot pain that pierced her shoulder.

At her hesitation, Carl leaned over until his face was next to hers. "I could cut them off," he threatened, ramming the cold blade between her legs.

Jenny could hold it back no longer. She vomited.

"You bitch!" he squealed, wiping his face with the back of his hand. Still clutching the ax, he scrambled to his feet.

"You're going to pay for that," he threatened. "As soon as I wash off, I'll be back and you better be undressed when I do."

Jenny breathed a sigh of relief at her reprieve, but it was cut short when Carl bent to pick up the candle. Hysteria closed in on her. He was going to leave her here with no light. No, a part of her screamed. She thought she had overcome her childish fears, but now she knew she couldn't face the nightmares of the dark again. Panic lent her the strength to pick up the rock and stumble after him.

Carl didn't hear her until it was too late. He turned just as she slammed the stone into the side of his head.

Cade found her there, standing over Carl with the ax in her hand. "Jenny?"

She turned and gave him a lopsided grin. "It's about time you showed up," she said. "A woman doesn't like having to do everything herself."

Cade took the ax from her hand and gathered her in his arms. "You don't need to worry about that. I'm not going to allow you to risk your life further. Your gold-panning days are over."

"But my place . . ."

"I'll buy you your place."

Jenny searched his face. Gone was the anger. It had been replaced with resignation. Here was a man who was willing to compromise.

"Can I have *any* place I want?"

Cade's brows shot together in a frown. "Greedy, are we? Because if you are, I'll tell you right now, I'll not get you a place too big for you to handle."

Jenny smiled shyly up at him. "I've had my eye on this one place for quite some time, but I don't know if it's for sale."

A muscle twitched along his tight jawline. "Name it," he demanded.

"Trinity Ranch."

His eyes met hers. Jenny held her breath. A myriad of emotions seemed to be warring within their smoky blue depths.

"That particular ranch comes with me," he finally said in a tone of voice that was meant to brook no argument.

Her gaze never left his. "I was counting on it."

"You'd give up your independence?"

"No, but I'd share it with you."

Careful of her shoulder, Cade gathered her in his arms. "I guess some things *are* meant to be shared," he whispered.

SPECIAL PREVIEW!

If you enjoyed *Swept Away*,
you won't want to miss . . .

SCOUNDREL
by Pamela Litton

Book Three in the enthralling
"Brides of the West" series.

*Here's an exclusive excerpt
from this exciting new romance—
available from Jove Books
in January 1994 . . .*

Please God, let him love me.

Lucy Drummond opened her eyes and stepped from the train onto a long, wooden platform. The powerful locomotive vibrated the boards beneath her feet, allowing her the lie of steady knees. Forgetting not to squint, she peered into the distance. Something appeared in the gray uncertainty of the train's vaporous breaths and her own near-sightedness. Something vague and dark. Her future.

The man dressed in black stepped off a loading dock next to the train depot and crossed the road separating the two buildings. His stride was long and purposeful, yet unhurried. Without her spectacles, Lucy couldn't distinguish his features, but he moved as if he owned the street. No one else waited on the platform and no other men approached her.

The man walking toward her must be David McQuaid, the man she had traveled half a continent to meet, the man she planned to marry. Love had nothing to do with this match, but one could hope, even pray. Maybe she was a dreamer, just as Aunt Rose claimed, but dreams were all she had left and a prayer all she had to give.

Steam spewed from the engine, clouding her view, masking her long, deep sigh. All the speeches she had rehearsed flew out of her head. What did one say to a stranger one had arranged to marry? Nice to meet you. When's the wedding?

She had suggested a get-acquainted period in her last letter. The idea appealed to her more and more as the man in black strode through the wispy curtain of steam and drew closer to her strained inspection.

Something about him disturbed her. Nothing tangible, nothing she could put into words. Simply an uneasiness, an odd sense of . . . foreboding? No. A sensation she had never experienced, and couldn't name, a confusion of emotions that waited in the back of her mind, alien and adrift, just as she waited at this lonely train station high in the Black Range of New Mexico.

The man climbed the stairs at the end of the depot's platform; his boots clipped out each unhurried step. She saw that he was tall and his hair was dark beneath the western-style hat just as David McQuaid had described himself, but somehow she had never pictured him dressed in a black frock coat and brocade vest, a black leather gunbelt strapped to his hips.

The strange uneasiness grew stronger with each step he took. Lucy reached for the wire frames usually resting on her nose and, instead, tapped the soft skin between her brows. She dropped her hand self-consciously and focused on the dark-clad man, willing him to match the respectable husband she had conjured from his letters back in Boston.

Perhaps he wore his dress clothes and . . . Her gaze dropped to a gold watch fob swinging gently against the satiny cloth of his vest, then lower to his gunbelt and its row of leather loops filled with brass cartridges. Lucy shifted her weight and stole a glance at the waiting train. Her gaze swept the empty depot, then veered back to the man in black.

With his measured, steady pace, he advanced toward her, his gaze direct from beneath the wide brim of his hat, his hands relaxed by his sides. He looked like one of those pistol duelists on a cover of *Beadle's Half-Dime Library*—particularly, the issue about Tombstone.

Ridiculous! She was allowing her imagination to run away with her good sense. Mr. David McQuaid was a very sweet, exceptionally sincere man. Only such a man could write the earnest letters he had sent to her; only such a man would, she hoped, agree to help her. Once his features were clear, her silly imaginings would be forgotten.

She trained this optimistic view as well as her myopic vision on the man. Slowly his face came into focus and her hard-fought reassurances crumbled. His mouth had a hard line to it, almost grim, despite the fullness of the lower lip. A broad, sharp angled jaw matched the stern resolution of his mouth. Her gaze rested on the slight cleft indenting his chin and she wondered at nature's caprice in giving a boyish charm to so forbidding a presence. She looked for more clues to this man who had courted her so eloquently with pen and ink, but his eyes remained a mystery, shadowed by the flat-crowned hat he wore low on his forehead.

Lucy watched for a smile, longed for a mere hint of the humor so apparent in David's letters to appear on that tight-lipped mouth. Judging from his unwelcoming expression, removing her spectacles hadn't helped in making a good first impression after all.

Lucy struggled with her growing confusion. This dark stranger couldn't be the author of those warm, friendly letters to her and if he was, he appeared very displeased with what he saw—her. Distressed with either conclusion, Lucy gripped the copy of *Ivanhoe* she carried and pressed the leather-bound volume against her unsettled stomach.

"I see that's *Ivanhoe* you've got there," the man said. "You must be Miss Lucille Drummond."

Disappointment crept into Lucy's throat in a pitiful lump

that might prove dangerous. Tears would be disastrous. She held no doubts now that the man was David McQuaid. She had written to him not long ago agreeing to his suggestion that she carry *Ivanhoe*, a favorite they both shared.

The weariness of the long journey settled over her shoulders like a wet wool blanket. His gesture had fit so wonderfully into her romantic notions, her certainty that the man who had written those letters, who had admired a story of knightly chivalry would agree to send for her mother.

"Miss Drummond?" The deep-voiced question held the sharpness of a command.

Squaring her shoulders, Lucy prepared to meet the man who had enticed her with his obviously misleading letters to traipse across the country on a fool's errand. She cleared her throat. "Yes, I'm Lucy Drummond."

She turned to say more, but found her thoughts scattered by the intent blue eyes fixed on her. She didn't need her spectacles to see the calm disinterest expressed in blue eyes that possessed a worn, hardened look as if they had seen too much, like hands that had worked too hard. Her disappointment grew to a quiet panic.

"I'm Sam McQuaid, Miss Drummond." He touched the brim of his hat. "We have something to discuss and—"

Lucy dropped her bag. "*Sam* McQuaid . . . not David?" She couldn't disguise the relief in her voice. Her future didn't depend on this dark-visaged man. David had sent his brother to meet her. She paused, her relief short-lived.

But why?

She clutched her book hard against her pounding heart, holding on to her hopes just as tightly. "What's happened to David?"

Sam tipped back his hat, his coat parting slightly to reveal a dull tin star pinned to his vest, and lifted his gaze past her shoulder. "Nothing a good horsewhipping wouldn't cure," he muttered.

"I'm afraid I don't understand." She ventured a look at

the five-point star that read: TOWN MARSHAL, STAR-LIGHT, N.M. TERR.

''I can't say I do either, Miss Drummond, but he left you a letter.'' Reaching into his coat, Sam pulled a white envelope from an inside pocket and presented it to her. ''This should explain the situation.''

> *Dear Lucy,*
>
> *I suppose by now you realize our marriage is not to be. I have wed another, a woman I thought lost to me forever. There is little else to add, except I regret I had no time to cable you before your departure from Boston. My brother, Sam McQuaid, will see to your needs while in Starlight and assist you in returning to your home.*
>
> *With sincere regrets,*
David McQuaid

Sam caught the soft sound of rustling paper and cast a glance toward Lucy. Her head was bowed, the straw boater she wore guarding her face from his view. A nosegay of faded paper violets decorating the hat quivered slightly, whether with the breeze or with reaction, he couldn't be certain. Quick, jerky movements dispatched the note to its envelope. She fumbled to loosen the strings of her reticule while she held the book clamped to her side. Obviously, Miss Drummond was stalling for time. He would give her what he could.

Stuffing his brother's letter away in her bag, the Boston woman jerked the reticule's cords, then lifted her gaze to him. Sam saw trouble. Gold and green and gray trouble. Eyes like hers caught a man's attention, made him want hers. In a boom town full of half-wild cowboys and lonesome miners that meant trouble. Now she was his trouble.

With a sharp sigh that didn't come close to venting his

disgust with his younger brother, Sam jerked his thumb toward the ticket window behind them. "Morning train east leaves at 9:00 in the morning, Miss Drummond. I'll purchase your tickets now, then I'll take you to the hotel."

Lucy cocked her chin a notch higher. "Don't bother, Marshal." She swallowed hard before she spoke again, but she was no unwanted package to be dumped in the return mail. "I . . . I don't require your assistance," she finished. The words felt good slipping off her tongue. She had never expected a lie to taste so sweet.

"My brother brought you out here, Miss Drummond," he said. "While you're in my town, you're my responsibility." His eyes flicked over her once more, his mouth pulling as flat as his tone. Presenting his back to her, he walked toward the ticket window.

Lucy took a step, raising a hand. "Marshal . . ." Her arm dropped to her side. Protesting was useless. What a tangle! Lucy twisted around, unable to witness the consequence of her foolish trust in well-written promises and her own blind optimism.

"Here's your tickets, Miss Drummond."

Lucy's eyes flew open and her spine stiffened. "I can't—"—*go back.* This man wasn't interested in her problems. No one was. Furiously thinking of something else to say, she turned and faced the marshal once more. "I can't accept—"

He took her free hand and pressed the tickets into her palm. "We've discussed that, Miss Drummond."

Lucy fought to escape the firm grip of his large, warm hand, an unexpected loss of breath stealing away her voice.

His grip tightened and he captured her attention with the compelling intensity of gun-metal eyes aimed straight at her. "Don't make this situation more difficult than it already is."

Releasing her hand, he bent and caught up her bag, then

started for the corner of the depot. "Come along, Miss Drummond. I have rounds to make."

Disappointment dragging at one foot and frustration shackling the other, Lucy forced herself to obey the impatient wave of the marshal's arm. She started for the corner of the depot where he waited.

Crossing the platform, her heels hammering the weathered wood, Lucy tried to summon proper feelings of gratitude, but found only resentment and bleak expectations. She rested those on the man dressed in black, his tall form a dark silhouette set against the approaching night. She hated accepting his help almost as much as she hated returning to Boston.

Don't do either.

The thought startled her. She paused at the edge of the platform, walking around the idea in her mind, examining it, searching out possible flaws. She recognized the obvious hurdles—no money, no job, no friends or family. Yet, the notion remained solid, clear and gleaming, far brighter than her prospects in Boston, where the same problems awaited her, except for the lack of family. She refused to be an added burden to her aunt and uncle. She couldn't go back, only forward.

"Watch your step, Miss Drummond."

Lucy frowned at the marshal's deep-voiced intrusion into her plans, then realized he couldn't know her thoughts. Still, his dark presence couldn't be ignored or dismissed, nor could his unintentioned advice. Her book of romantic notions lay heavy in the crook of her arm. She couldn't make another mistake in judgment.

Marshal McQuaid stood on the road directly in front of her, his eyes level with hers, his hand raised to assist her down the steps. Lucy hesitated, the decision she must make her only concern.

"A moment, Marshal." She looked past his impatient grimace to the busy thoroughfare behind him. Her eyes narrowed, bringing the nearest buildings lining the wide, rutted road into focus, while the more distant shops and businesses gradually dimmed into tiny splashes of light and evening shadows.

Starlight. Forward led to the rough, raw settlement of Starlight, New Mexico.

An excitement built in Lucy, an excitement fueled by all the stories she had ever read about the West, all the possibilities waiting to be discovered. Perhaps, her journey here hadn't been a mistake after all.

Without further comment or knowing exactly where she was to go, Lucy set off down the road, confident she would find her way.